Dirty White Collars

A Novel

By

Diane Collins

Ernest Esquer, I could not have finished this without you. I really don't know anyone else who would have done what you did. I didn't understand the meaning of true giving of ones self until I met you. I appreciate you- I love you and I thank-you from the bottom of my heart for being there when I needed someone most.

April Rivers-Bland, I know what it is to have a sister. You have always been a kind-hearted, generous, older sister to me. No matter what we go through - We are still standing. You are invaluable and I appreciate you.

Dawn Gilliam, When I started working in the film industry, I could not get into the union world. You were the first to step up and help me. I appreciate you and your loyalty to the sisterhood.

Marcella Dawson, You keep me spiritually grounded. Thank you for reminding me that, 'There is a God who sits high and sees low.'

Michelle Perry, My baby cousin, thank you for your words of encouragement and pushing me to finish.

PLEASE NOTE: This entire novel, story, content, characters, events, names and places are all entirely fictional and created by me.

Chapter 1

"I'd like a cash advance, please!" Naomi Caldwell demanded in her usual indignant manner, as she tossed a Black Visa Express card on the counter in the merchant teller's direction. The young woman was walking on Christian Louboutin, sporting black Chanel, leather gloves, four-carat studs and a Birkin. The two non-descript gentlemen guarding her, stood like Buckingham Palace Guards, draped in black Armani caps and dark shades. They carefully scrutinized the posh surroundings of the Beverly Hills bank, as well as the elite clientele strolling about handling their transactions. A few of the patrons took casual notice of the stunning woman's presence.

The mousy teller scrutinized the credit card for such a long time that Naomi became instantly agitated. "Naomi Caldwell," the teller read slowly and verbatim from the card. The affluent woman removed her Prada sunglasses revealing a pair of striking, seductive green eyes. The wealthy patron halted her gaze at the teller's name badge, which marked the beginning of her rather loud, melodramatic antics.

"Abbey Joseph is your name one could safely assume, correct?"

"Yes." The teller touched her name badge and proudly flaunted a wide medal bracket smile.

"Well, now that we've established who each of us is, can we get the ball rolling expeditiously please?" Mrs. Caldwell cut the frumpy teller a sharp look. "For God's sake swamp turtles move faster than this!"

Mrs. Caldwell's remarks caused Miss Joseph's pleasant expression to turn to blatant annoyance. The teller, now uneasy, fidgeted aimlessly trying to ignore her comments and gather her thoughts.

"I'll start on your transaction right away ma'am, " she said timidly.

"I certainly hope so since we did not come prepared to spend the night," she blurted out impatiently. The petulant woman removed one glove and clicked her long red nails on the counter. "And don't ma'am me."

The teller continued with controlled composure as she sluggishly unlocked her drawer, removed a cash withdrawal slip and handed it to her customer.

"Oh, and by the way AB-BEY, I'd appreciate large bills if they are accessible," Naomi demanded. "I know that they are because I phoned in the order ahead of time, as I usually do, to avoid just these types of obstacles." As Abbey watched Mrs. Caldwell fill out the form, her expression contorted as if she smelled foul meat. Clearly, she was aggravated by her rude customer's tone and impatience. The wealthy woman looked at Abbey, "Your Branch Manager, Mark Henderson, is familiar with our accounts and prearranges all my transactions. Mr. Henderson assured me he would be here if I arrived at precisely 2 p.m." Mrs. Caldwell glanced at her diamond face Rolex, "Well I'll be damned; it's precisely 2 p.m."

The patrons at the merchant's window who were waiting to be helped also glanced at their watches. A few impatiently shifted from side to side and tried to be inconspicuous as they mumbled amongst themselves.

"Well, I think it is safe to assume, from the look of his empty desk, that Mr. Henderson is not available," Mrs. Caldwell voiced patronizingly. The insecure teller nibbled at her bottom lip and asked primly, "So, what will it be today?"

"One seventy-five." Mrs. Caldwell snapped as she abruptly pushed the slip in the bank clerk's direction. The matronly, muddy-brown complexioned teller squinted through her bifocals, struggling to read the slip. Pursing her lips, she gently positioned her glasses farther up on the bridge of her nose. The glasses appeared heavy enough to fracture her face. Suddenly, a burst of cockiness surfaced in her voice. "It would seem that someone of your caliber would know that we do not honor cash advances for a mere dollar and seventy-five cents at this window. You have to go to the regular teller's window for that. Sorry." The triumphant teller crossed her arms with pompous gratification. A smirk of joy played around the edges of her lips at having delivered this information to the Beverly Hills snob standing in front of her.

The haughty spirited woman's expression cracked with the intensity of an egg slammed on concrete. She glanced at her bodyguards, they glimpsed at each other. Mrs. Caldwell leaned over the counter, face-to-face, nose-to-nose of the dim-witted teller and said, "It isn't difficult to figure out that your poor eye sight is only one of the many maladies you suffer. Clearly, you are severely deficient in other areas as well."

One of the bank's security guards edged closer to the vault to establish a direct eye line on the commotion. Naomi, now seething, stood back and attempted to regroup. Not entirely composed, she stepped back to the counter and articulated slowly and distinctly,

"I want one hundred and seventy-five thousand," the teller's smug energy flat-lined.

"Dollars?" she asked in a barely audible voice.

"No, damn it, Monopoly money!!! Are you kidding me?" she scoffed, as she pounded her gloved fist on the counter. As the flustered teller blew her straggly bangs out of her eyes, she also shook her head in an attempt to flip her long, oily, hair off the nape of her neck. The jarring motion caused her bifocals to fall off of her nose and slam onto the marble floor. When she put them back on, the thick lens had completely shattered but remained in tack inside the flimsy frames. Abbey panicked, squinting and patting aimlessly at air,   "Why is it suddenly so dark in here?" She questioned as she knocked a few items off her workstation and rammed into the back of her chair.

"Oh my God," Naomi simply shook her head in disbelief, as if almost defeated by the tellers haphazardness.

"Excuse me, I have to make a quick call for a work order to fix the lights in here." Abbey informed Mrs. Caldwell. As she dialed the phone, Naomi released an ear-piercing screech that reverberated throughout the bank, "The lens is broken, you imbecile." Patrons gasped, Abbey flinched and dropped the phone. "I am so sorry, Mrs. Caldwell, I'm new here. In fact, this is my first day at the window and the largest request I've had so far. It caught me by surprise and I'm nervous, that's all. I'm just really nervous." she pleaded humbly with a quivering voice.

"I don't need a dissertation, I – AM – IN – A – HURRY!!! Do you have enough money here to honor my request, or not?"

"Money… I mean we have money, of course. Yes, yes ma'am. We do have that, that's one thing I do know for sure, quite sure of that." The broken spirited teller produced a phony cordial smile and timidly handed the card back to the intimidating woman who snatched it from her.

"Would you please, if you don't mind, slide it through the terminal sitting there to your right?" She pointed to the terminal straining to see it out of the one eye with the good lens.

"Just slide it, please."

The woman sighed as she tossed her raven locks out of her eyes. Impatiently, she swiped it through the terminal.

"I certainly do mind. Why do I need you here if I must do all of the work myself?"

Abbey ignored the impolite customer's remarks and completed what she needed to on the cash advance slip for the withdrawal.

"Now, all I need to see is your driver's license. Her hands shook as she pointed a finger in reprimand.

"What!!!!!! Since when do I need ID at the merchant's window?" Now, incensed, Mrs. Caldwell searched her bag for her identification then hissed, "I am a long-standing customer. Are you serious? This is an insult that has gone far enough. I want the assistant manager, this instant!" She threw her driver's license at the teller, a hair away from striking her in the face.

The merchant teller's line was much longer now.

The unskilled teller ignored her request and desperately tried to complete the transaction on her own. Abbey really strained to see through the largest piece of glass in each frame as she slowly pecked information into the computer, one key at a time. Minutes passed.

"Now, all I have to do is wait for your account information to pop up and that will be it," she stated reassuringly. Miss Joseph rested her chin in the palm of her hand and hummed as she stared at the screen.

Mrs. Caldwell pounded her fist on the counter again this time so hard that the loud sound reverberated throughout the vault.

"Get me the assistant manager, now!!!!!" It startled Abbey so that she fell off her stool. Her hopeless eyes and bewildered expression mirrored the insecurity that only a new, inexperienced employee would exhibit. Abbey felt around the floor blindly for her glasses, then scrambled to get up. She instantaneously locked her drawer and sprinted off to find the assistant manager.

Mrs. Annabelle Nielsen was a homely, pint-sized, hefty, Caucasian woman with unruly, salt and pepper hair. She had just returned to her desk. After listening to her protégés' brief explanation and a quick once over of the transaction, Annabelle snatched the identification and the bank slip and flew over to the station where the woman stood infuriated. Without checking anything, the accommodating bank manager promptly signed her officer's approval on the cash advance slip and offered an endearing smile as she pleaded, "I am so terribly sorry about the inconvenience, Mrs. Caldwell. Please, your patience would be so greatly appreciated. This is Miss Joseph's first day and she is just nervous." she emphasized emphatically. "She isn't familiar with all of our accounts yet much less, with some of our distinguished clientele such as yourself."

"Then she should not be allowed to work at the damn window until she is properly trained." Mrs. Caldwell retorted.

"The order you phoned in yesterday is ready. All that is left to do is sign a currency transaction report."

The assistant manager spoke reassuringly as she handed her the form with one hand and one of the bank's pens with the other. Mrs. Caldwell sneered at the manager, insulted by the gesture, Naomi left both her hands dangling in mid-air as removed a vintage, 18-karat, diamond encrusted Mont Blanc from her handbag. She ripped her signature across the paper and began tapping her foot, still waiting.

"In the future, when the bank manager is away and you have phoned in your order, please don't hesitate to request an authorization from me." Mrs. Nielsen paused suspiciously, somewhat confused.

"That's strange. You and your husband always make withdrawals directly from your money market account. Why are you suddenly taking out a cash advance?"

"Are you quite sure you want to aggravate me even further by questioning me about what me and my husband do with OUR money right now?" Naomi screeched.

"No, now is definitely not a good time for questions. Next time, just please send the teller directly to me okay?"

"You weren't there Annabelle."

"I was in the back doing.........."

"I DON"T CARE!" Mrs. Caldwell interrupted. "If you were at your desk, as you should have been, I wouldn't be going through this right now, would I?" At that moment the nervous teller approached the counter.

"We really do not make a practice of keeping our VIP investors waiting, Miss Joseph," the manager scolded. "It is imperative that you remember this for future reference." A nod was all the confused apprentice could muster as a response.

"Well, I am absolutely positive that Big Daddy will not be pleased to hear about this ordeal. Why, Mr. Caldwell may insist that we move all of our money to one of your competitors. How would I be able to stop him? He so terribly hates it when his little love bug has to be stressed or inconvenienced."

"Hopefully, Big Daddy won't have to find out that his little love bug was inconvenienced," Mrs. Nielsen implored. She then turned and took notice of Abbey still by her side, "Where is the money, for God sake, girl? Go get it right now," she commanded.

She soared to the back vault as if she had suddenly sprouted wings. In disbelief, Mrs. Nielsen put one hand on her hip and wiped the tiny beads of sweat off her forehead with the other. Her mind raced of thoughts on how to rectify this situation with her long-standing, multi-million dollar client before she departs. Losing an account of this magnitude could mean a serious pay cut, a demotion, no Christmas bonus, perhaps all of the above, or worse, getting fired. She contemplated about what could be taking Abbey so long.

As customers entered the branch, they instantly checked out the hullabaloo that had most of the patrons mesmerized.

. Then, against her better judgment, Mrs. Nielson took a stab at altering Mrs. Caldwell's mood. She cleared her throat and spoke pleasantly, "Oh, Mrs. Caldwell, that is a stunning black suit you are wear....." Before Mrs. Nielsen could complete her thought, Mrs. Caldwell raised one hand, "Oh no. Don't!"

Mrs. Nielsen knew instantly her intuition had been right on target about this being a desperate strategy. Now, in addition to being frustrated, she was also embarrassed. She didn't know whether to try and persuade Mrs. Caldwell that she really did admire the suit, which could lodge her foot even deeper into her mouth, or just shut up and cut her losses. Mrs. Nielsen looked away and at the same time tried to take a furtive look at Naomi out the corner of her eye keeping her head straight. Then, her worst nightmare happened. Her elite patron asked brashly, "Mrs. Nielsen, why the hell are you trying to sneak and stare at me? Are you some kind of weirdo or something?"

The dejected supervisor's proud twenty-five years of professional bank experience had projected the same unpolished impression that a dilapidated outhouse would on the cover of an Architectural Digest.

At that moment, Miss Joseph jetted back, stumbling over

herself with two zippered moneybags. The manager snatched them and immediately handed them to Mrs. Caldwell.

"Do I need to count this?" Mrs. Caldwell asked rhetorically, as she secured the bags in her Prada briefcase and handed it to one of the bodyguards. She stepped away from the counter, hesitated, and then came back. "Miss Abbey Joseph," she hissed distastefully, "due to your inept performance today," she stared in utter disgust, "I predict you won't be working here when I come back." She eyed Annabelle, "If I come back!!!" The teller's jaw dropped as she volleyed looks from her mayhem to her manager, like watching a tennis match.

"And your prediction would be absolutely correct," Annabelle concurred as she dabbed, the sheen of sweat on her face. Abbey gulped and cupped her hand over her mouth, shocked.

The pretentious woman rolled her eyes heavenward in disgust at them both. She slipped on her glove and sunglasses, then positioned herself between the guards. The patrons stood motionless, watching, as they paraded out the front door and into the rear of the Maybach Landaulet parked in front of the bank. A uniformed chauffeur, dressed like the guards, closed the doors simultaneously. Once the chauffeur was secured in the car, Mrs. Caldwell ordered sternly, "Back to The Red Rose, Raymond."

The chauffeur weaved into the congested late morning traffic and within seconds faded into the mass of cars.

Chapter 2

At the main headquarters of The Red Rose Corporation in Los Angeles, Torsten Forte sat, absorbed in a 'marks' case study in his private suite. The German beauty was perched on a high-back art deco stool, with one hand strategically positioned on his hip and the other dangling limply in mid-air. Diamond rings embellished both of his floating pinkies.

He was 6'4, a former model, and had been quite famous on the European circuit. Although his birth name was Torsten, his older brother nicknamed him Toi (pronounced Toy) when he was nine years old because Toi stole all of his toys. The name just stuck. Toi was strikingly handsome, muscular, dark hair, swarthy skin and island water blue eyes. All that packaged with a well-defined bone structure were the reasons European designers sought after him.

He worked in a crisp white lab coat and some semblance of what he considered professional attire underneath, like dress slacks and a shirt. On rare occasions a tie.

Toi's crossed slender leg, fluttered in constant motion as he intently studied a multitude of photographs and live video footage on the flat screen of the same woman. He mixed and matched color palettes of make-up and hair swatches, one last time before he performed his magic. Everything had to be set up to perfection before he demonstrated why his European-trained expertise had earned him the big money.' Toi was one of the highest paid and most sought after special effects artists in the television and film industry.

When Holiday, one of Malone's friends and trusted business partners, rushed into the studio, Toi leaped to attention. "Oh no, please dahling, I know you are not going to try this with me today. I told you I would call you when I am ready to start your procedure,"

He voiced sternly, snapped his fingers, and pointed to the door. "You know damn well, I am not the one. Go find someone else to play and bond with." He studied for twenty minutes longer then summoned Holiday to return by intercom. When she arrived he yanked her inside, slammed the door and locked it.

Toi's studio was located in a desolate area of the vast estate, classy as a Beverly Hills salon and as immaculate as a hospital operating room. All of the furniture was the finest quality and sparse. His eclectic style included a custom sage green leather couch and chair, antique coffee table from the 1930's, art nouveau end tables and Turkish rugs.

He whisked Holiday into his chair and covered her with a large plastic smock, a bald cap to protect her hair, and applied vaseline to her facial hair. He drew a line along her hairline with a tattoo pencil. Toi applied mixed alginate liberally over Holiday's face up to the pencil hairline and underneath her chin to create the 'positive mold.' He dipped some plaster bandages into hot water, and then applied them on the alginate to reinforce and support it. When the bandages were dry and hard, the casting was complete. Toi slowly eased it off her face.

Malone and Toi's paths had crossed during an award benefit honoring Toi for, 'Most Original Artistic Contributions in Special Effects Makeup in Hollywood.' Malone had attended as an invited guest of a set designer who was also a mutual friend of Toi's. Malone was mesmerized by Toi's artistry. What had astonished him most was Toi's avant-garde style. The audience viewed clips on his vast amount of work during the ceremony. Malone was intrigued by Toi creations of rare textures, rich quality, brilliant colors, and indescribable and original designs. A prosthetic bust Toi had created was what sparked a clever vision in Malone's head of how he could expand his organization to yet another dimension. Toi is a master of disguise. His schedule had grown rapidly into full-time employment in addition to his career at the studios. Toi agreed to accept the position because he received twenty thousand dollars for each makeover and an additional five thousand if he had to travel. That had been five years ago.

Toi removed a case from his duffel bag. He cautiously peeled a small, paper-thin piece of form fitting, skin colored, flexible polyurethane from the case with a pair of tweezers. The form resembled human skin fingerprints. He applied the small pieces of the foam onto each of Holidays fingertips with a thin, watery substance, which he brushed on from a tiny bottle. He blew on her fingers for a few seconds and then smoothed the rough edges with a nail buffer until the pliable substance appeared to have vanished on her fingertips. Once finished, he sprayed a solution on each finger, until they were thickly coated. After it dried, he wiped them off with a sterile, white cloth, and examined her fingers one by one with a jeweler's eyepiece and remarked, "After these finger prints set, whatever you're doing out there, they will never show up as your own."

"Hopefully, things will never get to a point where I have to be fingerprinted," Holiday responded as she examined each of her fingers. "I thought you were crazy when you started this a couple of years ago. Whatever made you decide to start doing this little number in the first place?"

"Mr. Carson wanted me to start it as an extra precautionary measure for all of the staff. No one will be able to detect that you have them on during a general fingerprinting." After he had inspected his handiwork, he whipped off her smock and threw it inside a silver basket. Admiring himself in the mirror as he washed his hands, he saw Holiday's hand had moved to touch the chair as she stood up. Toi screeched, "Holiday, oh dahling please, you can not touch a single thing for a solid fifteen minutes until they dry completely." She almost fell, but caught herself with her arms, obeying his piercing orders. He stated softly, "Okay Miss Holiday, you are dismissed for now." She remained next to him as he continued to work.

"Men don't dismiss me, Toi. I dismiss them," Holiday joshed as she brushed off her clothes with the backs of her hands.

Toi understood Holiday and sincerely enjoyed her company so he decided to humor her. He indulged her a bit more than everyone else since she was one of his bosses. It was difficult for Toi not to get involved in their lives and their conversations. The more he stayed detached and appeared aloof, the more curious the workers became.

"Well, you know dahling, there are no parts of that statement I disagree with, honey, because that is exactly how I run my program now and forever. Men know I am not the one they would want to dismiss. My qualifications are long," he looked her in the eye and winked, "if you know what I mean- Hello."

"You are too funny," she blushed.

"This type of quality isn't processed in a factory nor is it packaged and placed on a conveyer belt. This is a gift. All men are not gifted and I know you know what I mean," he gut bellied a laugh loudly. As Holiday agreed she raised her arm to slap hands in a high five and Toi slapped it down. "Didn't I tell you – not – to - touch anything," he scolded. Holiday, still tickled by his comment, eagerly plopped down in the chair to continue their tête-à-tête. He grabbed her arm, stopping her in mid-air from sitting back down. It was apparent by her delighted expression that she enjoyed his company and truly yearned for more of the excitement that exuded from every pore of his body. He seldom joked around, and when he did, it was brief. Toi's hips swayed gracefully as he chaperoned her to the door. Holiday pleaded, moaned, and bargained to stay, like a spoiled preschooler, to no avail. As he gently shoved her out in the hall, Holiday turned to speak and he slammed the door in her face. Her nose touched the door as she heard it lock from the other side.

"Now I know, you know damn well, I have tons of work to do honey. Don't act like you don't understand. You have an appointment today and need to be outta here in the next couple of hours. – Hello! So, I will call you when I'm done," he exclaimed from the other side of the door. He shook his head, smiled tenderly, and spoke softly underneath his breath as he made his way to his workstation. "Whew! That Holiday just loves to play."

Toi continued the process of making a positive mold. He layered mixed plaster on the inside of the alginate and repeated the procedure until the plaster was 1/4 inch thick. He then placed plaster soaked burlap inside to reinforce the first layer and put on a final thin layer of plaster to smooth out the surface. After the plaster had set, Toi pulled the alginate off the mold, threw it away and applied oil and wax-based clay to the positive mold. Toi sat down and sculpted the clay with metal and wooden tools until the face in clay was textured and properly formed, perfectly identical to the 'mark', the woman in the photos and on the videos. He added flashing, thin strips of clay to create an overflow area, around the sculpture, leaving a fourth inch gap between the sculptures and flashing clays. He sprayed the clay with a thin veneer of acrylic lacquer to seal it.

Then he started the 'negative mold.' With a brush he built the plaster. Same as the positive, Toi applied the plaster a ¼ inch surface and detail coat, several layers of plaster soaked burlap for reinforcement, and a layer of plaster to even out and smooth the exterior, until it resembled an upside down bowl with a flat spot on top. After the 'negative mold' heated, cured and cooled, he painstakingly separated the 'positive mold' from the 'negative mold' by removing the clay with solvent and adding a mold release to both the 'positive' and 'negative mold.' Toi airbrushed a thin layer of vinyl plastic onto the outside of the 'positive mold' and inside of the 'negative mold,' then applied a layer of silicone adhesive to the vinyl plastic. Lastly, he poured mixed liquid silicone gel into the 'negative mold,' placed the 'positive mold' into the silicone and tightly strapped it until it cured at room temperature for an hour.

After it cured, Toi opened the mold, removed the prosthetic and summoned Holiday over the intercom. A second later, there was a knock at the door.

"Did you ring?" Holiday glided past him to resume her

position in the chair.

"I rang indeed. That was quick honey. Were you waiting in the hallway all that time?"

"Nope, just happened to be passing by. Toi, I don't know if I have ever told you this, but I love that cleft in your chin."

"Oh honey, this is a dick rest." Holiday's face reddened at his remark. He continued in frustrated firmness, "Now turn around and shut up. I am running behind schedule because it took me forever to sculpt that mold to look like Cole. Then once I finally did get it right, I couldn't get the air bubbles out of that damn thing or get those edges to lay right. I haven't had that much trouble since I was in school for that shit. You both have to be ready to leave in the next hour, so please, dahling."

"Well, did you get it right?"

"Flawless." Silence prevailed.

Many of the crewmembers thought Toi was kidding or just being melodramatic and paid no attention when he tried to enforce his simple rules. Silence was of the utmost because it was imperative for his concentration. Finally, when Toi had had enough, he bailed out on a half completed job; because the employee he worked on did not respect Toi's request. The loss of a one million dollar job, that had taken months to set up and his subsequent resignation, demonstrated how serious he was about his rules. Following four grueling hours of renegotiations with Malone, Toi had agreed to resume his duties. The moment Toi returned, he had felt sparks generated by their compliance regarding his 'kidding and drama.'

Toi had emphatically proven that he was not one to be toyed with.

He mixed and applied a light coat of glue to the silicone mold and then securely attached it to Holiday's natural face. Once he secured the mold, he flipped a switch on the side of his table and the wall opened, exposing a colossal inventory of hair and beauty supplies of every description. There were holding sprays, lotions, perfumes, lace front wigs, hairpieces, and hair for weaving in every color, style, and texture, along with enough Ben Nye theatrical make-up to perform a makeover on every woman living on the west coast.

As he attached a lace front wig, Holiday immersed herself in the hours of footage on her iPad of how the 'mark' she was about to impersonate walked and talked. She inhaled all the subject's mannerisms and idiosyncrasies. Holiday also practiced writing and rewriting Madeline Taylor's signature until she forged it perfectly. As Toi applied her make up and styled her hair, she practiced duplicating the women's rhythmic vocal tone and speech pattern by playing and constantly rewinding tapes of her speaking voice.

Toi worked rapidly, careful not to compromise his pursuit of perfection. He turned the plush leather swivel chair around so Holiday could view the finished product in the mirror. She gazed at the photographs he was working from to compare them to the way she looked. As many times as Holiday had undergone this procedure, she was in awe of how her own face disappeared and transformed into an identical replica of someone else's in an eight by ten photo. It was eerie. Lastly, he pulled open a drawer in his worktable revealing a rather large plastic case with various sections containing contact lenes in every color ever made. He dropped a dot of contact solution into each of her eyes and then applied a light brown pair to match the color of the woman's eyes in the photograph. After blinking a few times she commented, "Toi, I've watched you do this a million times on me and the crew and I still don't understand how the end result turns out like this. You certainly are a special effects master, but how in the world did you learn to style hair like this?"

"Oh Holiday honey, hair was my bread and butter for years. I was a renowned Beverly Hills stylist. Lots and lots of stars and superstars clamored for my glamour, dahling," he boasted. "That's how I transitioned into the film industry so easily when I finished school for glamour, make-up and special effects. I told you, honey, I'm a gift."

"Remarkable work, as usual," she said as she clamped a hand on his shoulder.

"Really? Thank you so much," Toi replied humbly, but proudly. Still concentrating, he turned her around slowly, in full rotation, five or six times more to examine every intricate detail of her face, makeup, and every strand of hair. He helped her out of the chair.

"You're done, now off to wardrobe." She stood up and stretched, then looked in the mirror one last time. He glanced at his watch. "Oh wait, gotta put in your teeth."

"Now wouldn't that be a give away," Holiday said as Toi inserted them in her mouth.

"I'm so late for my flight. As you well know, I have three makeovers in New York in the morning, three in Chicago the day after tomorrow, and five to prep back here for next week. So, see you then, dahling."

Holiday left. Toi sashayed to his dressing area in his usual swan-like grace, to begin his cleaning and closing ritual. Within moments, everything in the shop was sterilized and back in its proper place. He showered, primped, changed clothes, grabbed his vintage Louis Vuitton duffle, and was out the door.

Gone.

Chapter 3

Miles away from the bank, Raymond let down the tinted, soundproof, window as he removed his mask. He had brown eyes, bronzed skin, freckles, and red hair that shone like tail lights on wet asphalt-way too red.

"How did things go in there, ma'am?" Raymond inquired politely.

"Honestly Raymond, why so formal? You've only been working with us damn near the whole seven years we've been in business. I told you to call me D." Raymond continued driving and offered no response.

Suddenly, December began laughing so hard, tears formed in her eyes and dribbled down her cheeks. Soon the whole car was laughing. Brick, the bodyguard sitting to her right quizzed, "What the heck are we laughing about, D?"

"Come on, Brick, you saw her carry on like a fool in there. A stunning debut as a teller, she played it like a straight pro. If I didn't know any better, I would have really thought she was an absolute idiot. She hasn't worked in the field, but maybe once or twice in the last three years. It was interesting to watch her play."

Both bodyguards removed their prosthetic disguises and revealed Jordon Keith and Chang Jones. Jordon looked like a cadaver, ghostly, translucent clear skin, large teeth, and kinky, dark brown hair. He had inherited the nickname Brick because of his wide, hard body resembled a brick wall. Chang was Chinese and African-American, soft-spoken, straight black hair, slanted eyes, swarthy skin, and at six feet three, he had racked up tons of belts and trophies in the art of self-defense.

Whenever staff was on duty in the field, disguises had to be worn.

December gazed out the window. A sudden crease formed in her brows due to anxiety and was quickly replaced by a smile of satisfaction that eased across her face.

"I sure would like to know how the hell we got such a great research team. The caper was perfection, it went as planned. The bank manager wasn't there, Nielsen didn't check if the order had been phoned in, which it had been, and she questioned the cash advance because of the credit card, but ignored it because she was so worried about losing the account. She knew this couple only gets cash advances off of their investment accounts. Our research team found most of their accounts required two signatures and they couldn't get a match on Mr. Caldwell's. That's why we took a chance with her credit card and played it the way we did. Whew, for a minute I thought it was going to get sticky."

"Why do you even bother putting someone on the inside at all?" Brick asked.

"We only use plants when absolutely necessary because believe me, it's a lot of work. Birthing a worker is arduous, you have to create credentials, background checks, driver's licenses, social security numbers, college degrees and on and on that have to be set up, so they can be verified. The interviews, and then getting them hired is the most grueling part. All that for one day maybe two at most. On this case, one day of work and Abbey gets fired. Technology is so advanced now that it only takes a matter of seconds for things to go wrong. Usually, by the time we get a warning something isn't right, it's too late to leave the bank because they have contacted security. If we have someone planted and our well designed plans starts to unravel for any reason, they signal us to leave. That extra step or shall I say ninety steps is what keeps the heat at bay."

"Well, you two steered that manager away from suspicion the second it popped in her head."

Even if Michelle hadn't been sick we wouldn't have sent her on that kind of play, Way too risky. December mimicked Farren's jittery tender voice and motions. 'Money...we serve... I mean we have, money. Yes, yes ma'am we do have that. Money, I mean, I'm at least sure of that, quite sure." Brick chimed in also amused. "She was amazing in there."

"I couldn't agree more. That role wasn't too far out of character for her though because she is a riot. That was a commendable acting job. So, in answer to your question, Raymond, it was outstanding." December smiled contentedly as she sat back and adjusted herself comfortably in the seat. Chang popped the cork on a bottle of champagne and distributed it to everyone. Raymond refused. "No thank you, Mr. Chang, I'm driving."

December leaned towards Raymond, "Please hurry up and get me back to the office, so I can get this prosthetic off my face and this wig off my head. It's extremely uncomfortable and hot as hell under here after a while."

"It is hot as hell for real," Chang and Brick agreed in unison.

"Burning alive," Raymond chimed.

She placed several drops of solution in her eyes, popped out the green contacts and placed them into a lenes case. Brick followed suit with his contacts. He looked in her eyes and gushed, "Ooh, those gray eyes-- even better. I know you hear it from all the guys, but, D, you've got some incredible eyes. I speak for all of us when I say we wish we knew what you really looked like. We only see you when we work, and you're always faced up. How come you don't take yours off like we do? Tell us what the D stands for."

December took out her appointment book from one of the compartments in the back seat, leafed through the pages, and glanced at her watch. Brick knew what her response meant and that's what he did.

"Mrs. Taylor has to be at Crombie and Lynch in the next hour. It's imperative that she be on time. I have to be at the Rose before she leaves." Raymond acknowledged December with a glance. "Right away ma'am." He pushed the button for the privacy window and picked up speed.

The Maybach turned off the main thoroughfare onto a two-lane dirt road and passed several huge estates that sat on opposite sides of the private drive.

The Red Rose organization encompassed three sites, Los Angeles, New York, and Chicago. The Los Angeles office was the main headquarters and it was, by far, the largest and most lucrative branch of the organization. The head of the organization chose Los Angeles for the sunshine, New York for the energy and Chicago for the culture.

When the Maybach arrived in front of the fortress, one of the three uniformed security guards immediately left the booth, unlocked the small door connected to the main gate, and approached the car for inspection. The windows rolled down in unison. After the guard thoroughly checked the contents, including the trunk, he signaled back to the booth. The guard inside tapped in a sequence of numbers and electronically opened the enormous, white wrought iron gates.

Both sides of the road all the way to the top of the compound were lined with fifteen-foot high light poles. There was plush green grass, a forest of beautifully landscaped fruit trees, precisely trimmed shrubbery, and red roses of every variety within the fifteen-acre estate. The backdrop was a breathtaking view of spectacular snow-capped mountains combined with floral and pine fragrances.

The car continued upward on the graveled road until it reached a cemented circular driveway lined with hundreds of large, lush, red rose trees. The palatial, hilltop estate was an exact replica of the White House, but with more of an artsy, high-tech flair.

As the car halted, security descended the staircase to open the doors. Everyone exited the car. Brick, Chang and Raymond immediately went inside the estate carrying their prosthetics. A guard drove the Maybach down the path out of sight. Minutes later, the same security man returned in a Bugatti Veyron. Holiday McCormick, stunningly dressed, appeared at the top of the stairs with her personal assistant, Cole Alton, fully clad in ivy league Tommy Hilfiger, short cropped hair, great posture, and thick black rimmed glasses.

When Cole wasn't masked his name was Caesar McCoy, African-American, articulate, studious, and shy. Mrs. Taylor's sidekick swiftly replaced security in the drivers seat.

December, carrying the briefcase, passed Holiday on the white marbled staircase, they stopped to acknowledge one another.

Chapter 4

"Good Morning Gentlemen, this is your Captain speaking. I have received a change in your itineraries so I'll recap our plan of action. You'll now be staying in New York overnight. We will be departing from New York at 8:30 am tomorrow morning and returning to Los Angeles. Should these plans change, Mr. Carson or Mr. Young, please notify me immediately, Thank you." John Alexander signed off of the plane's intercom.

John Alexander was the pilot Malone Carson and Grey Young hired to fly the posh, custom designed *Hawker 4000* Malone had purchased three years earlier following their joint decision to terminate the use of commercial airlines. John had been in the air force for years and retired from major commercial airlines after twenty years. He only flew now for Malone. They frequently traveled throughout the U.S. and abroad and found that the amount of time they spent in airport terminals could be better utilized in the privacy of their own airliner. Discretion was paramount to achieving their goals, so avoiding commercial flights was in their best interest. The organization had expanded rapidly over the past five years. There were always plans to be made, schedules to confirm, payroll to sign off, endless meetings, and a host of pending emergencies, which always required immediate attention.

"This is a quick in and out thing Grey. I don't have time to be looking for your ass man." Malone spoke matter-of -fact. "We need to go to the office, take care of the payroll, re-check all the assignments and what staff members are executing them for the week. We have a lot of situations coming up in the next couple of weeks and I need to make sure Toi is one hundred percent." Malone never looked up from his New York Times. His eyes were nearly covered by his fedora as he crunched on sliced apples, cubes of cheese and smoked a cigarette. "Hey man, we haven't played golf in a while. Let's get a game going when we get back to LA."

Malone was ruggedly handsome, at six foot two, slim, muscular and a far cry from the mid-western executive, cookie-cutter type. He had strong, distinguished facial features, jaws like a pit bull, faded butterscotch complexion and penetrating, round, brown eyes. His coarse, tightly curled, ruddy hair looked and felt like a dense, plush carpet. For every word he uttered, there were corresponding hand gestures and facial expressions underscoring his animated moves. Unbeknownst to him, he was comical, conversational and charismatic beyond his 35 years. His personal style consisted of Ozwald Boateng, Hugo Boss or Savile Row. The mastermind behind the Red Rose had a signature laugh that sounded like a hyena's cackling. He was known to most by the name Blue.

Grey was sleep on the recliner with a fedora also covering his face. He lifted his hat, looked at Malone's and mumbled, "No problem. In and out of New York - golf in LA when we get back." He placed the hat back over his face and resumed his nap.

"You know man, I'm startin' to worry that your appetite for your," Malone hesitated for a moment then said pointedly, "Companion is becoming insatiable man. It's starting to interfere with the business. You can't disappear and show up three days later marinated in that shit."

"Don't threaten me man, you are my partner not my damn boss," Grey said softly.

"Partner?" Malone chortled, "Hey man, we didn't sign no lifetime contract, this is a day to day rental agreement. You got your thirty day notice." Grey sat up and shot him a steely gaze as if he were going to refute his comment, but instead replied,

"No problem man, it's all good."

"Then it's all good man, no problem," Malone cackled.

Comparing Malone to Grey was like trying to find the similarities between a go-cart and a formula one-race car.

Grey Young was 6'1 and a substantial bit thinner than one would ever dream of seeing in a playgirl centerfold. He was peerlessly handsome like a classic Bentley. His rich, dark, complexion was like the car's flawless paint job. Grey's creamy, soft skin was like the buttery leather upholstery. Irresistible, blackish brown, almond shaped eyes. His silky eyebrows were exquisite like the wood grain dashboard. His thick eyelashes and dark, curly hair, was masculine and subtle like sleek profile body style of a convertible. As handsome as they were neither had any ego connected to their looks.

Uniquely different. Both irresistible.

Chapter 5

December gave Holiday head to toe once over and exclaimed, "That's a sharp suit. A little on the conservative for you, but make no mistake, guuurl you are rockin' it. Can you breath? Will you be able to sit down? I mean, it looks painted on you? That suit is tighter than the clothes you wear which I didn't think was possible." The two hugged and laughed.

"From the pictures and footage I've seen of this Madeline woman, I hope I have her down pat. Everything the woman wears is painted on her and she has the figure to perfectly make it work too. Her voice is a little challenging." Holiday added.

"Well, so do you. Oh girl, and the face is fabulous. If I didn't know better, I'd think you were Mrs. Madeline Taylor herself. We're gonna have to give that Toi a raise."

"Well Benton, look who's talking. You seriously look gorgeous in that Chanel."

"The bank managers at the bank seemed to have liked it too."

"Thank you. Now, you know me, Holiday, what's my motto?"

Holiday said slowly, "I know." The two of them leaned on each other and said, playfully in unison, "If you can't find it on Rodeo Drive, then let it slide."

"I have had the hardest time staying consistent with the tone of this 'marks' voice. She has the strangest voice."

"Talk about strange. I can't believe the 'mark,' I just played. That woman, Naomi, really has these full blown tantrums, about one thing or another, every time she goes to the bank. I had to study a long time to get her down. Now, she is a real live bitch."

"Think of the fit she is gonna have once she gets the credit card statement and sees the unauthorized activity on it from today."

"Just a reminder," December switched gears to a serious note, "plans have changed as you well know."

"I heard they had, but I don't know why."

"This is the last play on the Taylor's. We received an updated print out yesterday from our correspondents who are tracking them. They will be returning from Europe this coming Monday instead of the following Monday as originally scheduled. I can't believe that it took us six damn months to set up this caper and they are returning so quickly. Apparently, Mr. Taylor's gambling problems have escalated and Madeline is insisting they return home so she can seek professional help for him," December expounded.

"We were originally supposed to work the Taylor's yesterday, which went as planned, today, and once more on Monday right?" Holiday checked.

"Right?"

"Well, at least we are working it two days before we have to shut it down. Think of how many times our research team has worked on capers for months and months and they got shut down all together at the last minute due to changed plans."

"Really, remember the time the correspondent lost track of that client in Vegas. Thought he was in his room and out of commission for two days. He didn't know the 'mark' had left out a side door in his suite until he turned up at his bank in L.A. at the same time our staff was in route there."

"Oooh, our plant saved our ass on that one." Holiday said as she glanced at her Cartier, "Girl I gotta get out of here before we're late.

As Holiday took her position on the passenger's side of the car and the tinted windows went up.

"To the Crombie and Lynch building Miss McCormick?"

"Right away please. Thank you Cole." Holiday answered replicating the 'marks' voice.

Chapter 6

After a pleasant drive to Hollywood on the Los Angeles 101 Freeway, Vanessa Saffore exited on Gower, made a right turn and headed down the street until she arrived at Roscoe's House of Chicken and Waffles, near Sunset Boulevard. She was there to have breakfast with Prudence Michelle. Roscoe's is a Hollywood landmark, as well known as the Hollywood sign that rest in the hills about a mile or so away. The popular eatery is renowned for its fried chicken, waffles, grits and biscuits, along with all the traditional southern breakfast delicacies.

As usual, when Vanessa arrived, there was a lengthy line of people waiting patiently for their names to be called. Vanessa noticed Prudence sitting in the center of the bench in front of the restaurant. To her left were two very feminine, well-dressed, drag queens. On the other side was a tall gorgeous basketball type and next to him was a young couple in need of a hotel room. The rest of the long line of nondescript patrons was immersed in conversation.

Vanessa left people intrigued by her presence. Gorgeous was an understatement. Her color matched a perfect slice of toast, She was down-to-earth, statuesque and svelte. She wore her shoulder length, brownish- blonde, wavy hair stylishly unkempt. Her expressive hazel eyes were the keys to her soul. Her style fluctuated between mid-western and east coast fabulous and her intriguing androgynous demeanor only added depth to her sexiness.

Vanessa and Prudence were called to the hostess station.

"How many in your party?" The hostess asked.

"That should be pretty obvious." Prudence quipped. The hostess glanced at her and restrained her smile. They were seated and given menus. Prudence sighed impatiently, looked at her watch, and said to Vanessa, "Thirty minutes late. You have no respect for people's time." Ignoring her, Vanessa peered around the quaint restaurant to see if she could find anyone she knew or spot any celebrities. Roscoe's attracted many of them. The waitress came to the head of the table.

"Have you ever seen Patrick Dempsey in here?" Vanessa asked as she scoped the restaurant. The gum- smacking waitress answered, "Star struck? You are certainly in the right town if you are an aspiring groupie. MAY- I –TAKE- YOUR -ORDER –PLEASE!"

"I'll have one of everything on the menu." Prudence antagonized playfully.

"Jokes? You are certainly in the right town if you are an aspiring comedian," The waitress snapped.

"Ohhh, she's quick. I like her." Vanessa smiled. The waitress restrained her smile.

"Hold on, we are going to order." Prudence kept her face in the menu deliberately to provoke her. The waitress shuffled from side to side as she waited.

"Ladies, I have tons of customers, will it be sometime today?" They looked at each other, then the menu and placed their orders. The waitress grabbed the menus and left.

"Prue, why do you love to give waitresses a hard time."

"It's only a hard time when they have no sense of humor."

Prudence Michelle was a secure and confident woman. Anything she participated in had to appeal to her sense of passion, love, and strong convictions. She was a Christian and basically an ole fashioned girl. She wore classic Chanel No. 5 and mostly tailored clothing to   wane attention away from her perfect 36,24,36, hourglass figure. What others saw as voluptuous she viewed as voluminous. She had oval brown eyes, a flawless, deep brown complexion, nails, short and clear, fly short hair cuts and full lips. The only place she wore color.

"So, what time do you have to be at work?"

"I have to be there tomorrow at 5:00 o'clock to find out what's happening and whose involved in this new case. I hear it's pretty complicated but I am sure it's the same, high profile, white-collar crime stuff. Nothing I can't handle and I'm positive no big surprises," Vanessa rejoined.

"I don't know why you still take those cases so lightly after the last horrible ordeal you went through. Plus, it must be something big for them to call you back early from your vacation with Venice. You hardly get to spend any time with your son."

"Oh Prue, don't be so dramatic. So, I got roughed up a little on that last case. It's part of the territory, and they called me back because they're understaffed."

"I'd hardly call three weeks in the hospital with a fractured rib and a bruised jaw roughed up a little."

"Roughed up a <u>lot</u> means you get killed. I got roughed up a little," Vanessa brushed her off.

"After that last episode, it would seem as though you would want to find another job other than being a Special Agent. They don't pay you enough money to risk your life. No job is worth that."

"Are you a cream puff or do you just make them." Vanessa said flippantly. "It's not a job, it is my career- my life's work. It's the thrill, the challenge, and the conquest makes it fun. That's why I've chosen this profession, the idea of not knowing what's in store." Vanessa smirked wickedly, "And of course, the most rewarding perk in my line of work stems from the fact that there's nothing as gratifying as making a man submit. I love what I do. Besides, if I wanted to know what I was getting into each and every day, I would go punch a clock from eight to five, like you."

"Now, wait a damn minute girl!" Prudence snapped back defensively. "Back up. I went to school and graduated just like you.

So don't even trip. I studied extensively in Italy and all over Europe. I make a comfortable living as a chef, my dear. Don't put my career down. It's as gratifying and important to me as yours is to you. At least I won't get killed doing it."

"I was playing damn," Vanessa smirked. "It's amazing how you'll pick one little thing out of a billion and suddenly decide to get sensitive." Prudence's defense softened as quickly as it had hardened.

"Not all over Europe, you've never been to Paris."

"What?'

"You have never been to Paris."

"Not yet. Your point."

"I was just saying," Vanessa reminded her.

"Anyway, you know my feelings about a career and money. It isn't important if your heart is empty," Prudence exhaled and continued wearily. "Okay, Madame *hardhead* something you'll have to learn on your own. Who do you go home to when you can't handle a day at work?"

"There will never be a case that I can't handle. Trust that. Besides, what could possibly happen any worse than the things I've already been through? Madam cook." Vanessa teased. Prudence's rolled her eyes upward,

"Madam Chef, please. There is a difference," she protested.

Vanessa and Prudence were both only children raised by single mothers on the south side of Chicago. Dodie, Vanessa's mother, and

Stephanie, Prudence mother had been best friends since childhood. They both attended Southern Illinois University when they both found themselves pregnant at the end of their senior year. That discovery was made a month before their graduation and was what cemented their lifelong bond. Dodie married Robert, Vanessa's father. Prudence's dad dropped out of school when he received the pregnancy news and was never seen again.

Immediately after graduation, Stephanie, Dodie, and her new husband Robert moved into a duplex on the south side of Chicago. Stephanie was on one side and Robert and Dodie on the other. A month after Robert and Dodie had settled into marital bliss, Robert went out of town on a weekend fishing trip with an unknown friend and never returned. A year later he phoned Dodie to let her know that he was all right, inquired whether he had had a son or a daughter and informed her that he had filed for divorce. That conversation was the last communication they ever had. Dodie and Stephanie decided to raise Vanessa and Prudence as sisters, even after Dodie re-married Frank Lewis when Vanessa was ten years old.

Vanessa had to speak loudly to be heard above the constant restaurant chatter, smacking, clanking dishes and ringing of cell phones. She said disgustedly, "You don't understand."

"I do understand one thing for sure. You are obsessed. Your

personal life is shallow and your career is now becoming who you are rather than what you_do," Prudence asserted with a worried inflection in her voice.

"Rather than what_I do?" Vanessa mimicked.

"I didn't stutter. You don't even bother to pursue any of the interests you used to find so fulfilling like your painting, playing golf, reading novels – none of that. Your life has become one-dimensional."

"I love my work. Besides, everyone can't be Oprah or Tyler. Vanessa and Prudence froze and looked at each other with utmost sincerity. "She really should have consulted with me on that move." Vanessa voiced seriously.

"What the hell am I supposed to do with myself everyday from 3 to 4 o'clock p.m.?" Prudence wined.

"Let's hope she brings the talk show back on her own network. Oprah, Gale and now Tyler." She mulled. "I ought to be part of that crew," Vanessa declared as if she could easily make that happen.

"Just paint them on your wall the same way you did when you decided you wanted Patrick's companionship. Excuse me, can you bring us some water please?" Prudence turned to beckon the waitress as she flew by.

"Got jokes huh? I'm proud of what I do and proud of myself for doing it so well," Vanessa uttered sincerely. "There's nothing more rewarding than finding your niche in life, a career filled with passion Prue. Most people never find anything they really love to do, much less get paid for doing it."

Refusing to be interrupted Vanessa continued, heartfelt, "I've worked so damn hard, sacrificed seven grueling years of my life to get where I am. Law school was the closest I've ever been to death. Then two years of law enforcement experience, twenty weeks of training in the academy, and all of this was back to back. I won't even mention how I sacrificed my relationship with my son. Everyone has to go through the basics Prue. It's the personal touches that got me promoted so quickly," Vanessa boasted.

"What's so personal and promoting about your touches?" Sighed Prudence with an air of indifference.

"First and foremost, I've got my convictions. I don't allow my personal feelings to stand in the way of making rational decisions. I'm honest and corrupt proof. My job isn't designed for me to stand in judgment of others. It's to bust the rebels who break the system's rules, period. There's only one rule and that is, there are no exceptions to the rule," Vanessa bragged.

"Gee. I'm sorry I asked. Girl, please don't break your arm."

"Break my arm? Break my arm how?"

"Patting yourself on the back. You won't be able to work." Prudence grinned. Vanessa rolled her eyes.

"Now, I can almost buy all that other stuff, but corrupt-proof. Everybody has a price." Prudence taunted and winked.

"I don't and never will."

"Everybody over twenty-one knows about never, " Prudence teased her.

"Girl please, you must be losing your mind. Do you think I would ever consider taking a payoff? No amount of money or anything that could come up is worth risking what I've worked so hard to establish with the bureau. I am well respected in a job that's really about the good ole boy's club. I don't need money that bad to be a sell out."

"A price doesn't have to necessarily be in the form of cash you know. And who are you trying to convince, me or you?" Damn where is our order, I'm starving."

Prudence leaned out of the booth trying to catch a glimpse of the kitchen.

"Then you tell me what else **is** there?" Vanessa implored as she refused to be brushed off.

"What difference does it make since you would never do it? Why bother exploring the possibilities? Look, Vanessa, I'm saying you will never achieve true balance in your life until you understand tolerance. One day, you are going to have something happen in your life that's going to make you eat all these words and finally teach you there are exceptions to every rule. Plus, I just will never understand why someone from your background would want to be an FBI agent anyway. Now can we drop this subject and agree to disagree, little sister?"

"That suits me fine." Vanessa said as she squeezed lemon juice into her water.

"Well, on another note, does Grey and your cousin Malone know what you do for a living?"

"Hell no! Under no circumstances, I mean it Prue, do not tell them what I do. I'll tell them myself after I see what they're up to these days. For now, as far as they're concerned I work as a freelance writer."

"Oh, come on. Not one in your family told either of them you are an FBI agent?"

"Let's hope not. It's odd that as much as Blue was around that you haven't met him by now. You were in Europe chasing food during my Grey interludes."

"Girl please, don't insult their intelligence with your freelance writer bullshit. At least tell them something believable, let me think." Prudence paused for a second scheming. "I know, tell them you're a ho." They erupted in peels of laughter oblivious to others around them as though they were back in their cozy childhood bedroom sharing an inside joke.

"When the young waitress returned with their orders Prudence touched her arm and whispered, "Oh girl, I was messin' with you."

"Oh, I know," she popped a bubble.

All conversation was lost as Vanessa and Prudence gobbled down syrupy waffles, savored scrambled eggs oozing with cheese, sopped golden brown gravy, chomped on crispy fried chicken, scoffed up buttery grits and chased it with fresh squeezed orange juice. Then laid back.

"Well look, I'd better get home so I can start getting ready for my date tonight. I'll see you later on tonight." Prudence burped and released the top button on her pant.

"Prue, I can't wait to see Grey again," Vanessa purred euphorically.

"I know Vanessa, believe me I know," she empathized tenderly.

They tossed a coin for the bill. Prudence lost, paid and left the waitress a larger than twenty percent tip. Both fell into stride and waddled out of the door from eating so much.

Chapter 7

The secretary in the front office, on the third floor, of Crombie, Lynch and Kaplan investment firm spoke pleasantly on the phone, "Mr. Stevens, Mrs. Madeline Taylor and her Assistant Cole Alton are here to see you." She smiled warmly. "Mrs. Taylor and Mr. Alton you can go right in, he's expecting both of you."

As they entered the investment broker's lavish office, Mrs. Taylor immediately sat down, crossed her legs seductively, and positioned herself in front of the large, mahogany desk at their long-time investment firm. Cole sat tentatively on the couch behind his boss.

"Hello Mr. Stevens. How are you feeling today?"

Paul Stevens was a distinguished, middle-aged, black gentleman with coarse salt and pepper hair. Impeccably dressed with a sizable gut. Stevens was the fresh face in the Crombie and Lynch family. He had risen quickly in the ranks and was well respected among his colleagues. He had arrived with stellar credentials, a summa cum laude from Harvard with an undergrad degree in finance and a JD in law from Stanford. He had passed the bar on his first attempt and had fifteen years of experience and great references. Within his first couple of weeks at the prestigious firm he had received nothing but rave reviews from his supervisors and colleagues and was offered a promotion. He had signed on more new investors and reinvested more money during his one month of employment than most of his colleagues had in three years.

"I'm fine. How are you today, Mrs. Taylor? I would swear to it that you are prettier today than you were yesterday, if it is at all possible to improve on perfection," she gushed. She smiled as she lifted her dark eyebrows and responded in a soft, playful voice.

"Oh, you are asking for it, and one day you're gonna catch me at the right moment and you're gonna get it." She reacted coyly.

Burying her face in the palm of her hands she remained fixed for several moments. Mr. Stevens deliberately avoided eye contact as he studied the couple's file on his computer. When she lifted her head, eyes at half mask and teary her mood had flipped drastically. Cole jumped to her aid by handing her a handkerchief. Gingerly patting her eyes, she edged closer to his desk and spoke faintly.

"May I talk to you in confidence?" Without waiting for his response she vented. "What I have been going through lately is simply devastating. I would only wish this on my worst enemy. You must know what I'm talking about. It's such a well- publicized situation," she declared grief stricken with tears cascading down her face.

"If your circumstances have afforded you to look this great, perhaps your situation is more motivating than you may have imagined," the broker expressed gallantly as a tension-breaker/compliment. Even though she felt agitated by his lightheartedness, she didn't comment because she knew it was just a heartfelt attempt to keep her mood buoyant.

"You really are too kind and always manage to find a way to lift my spirits. Flattery does go a long way, even under the worst of circumstances," she strained a mirthless laugh. He extended his hand to her compassionately; she complied and held it tightly. "Howard again, huh? He gambled away everything you withdrew yesterday?" She didn't respond, she knew he knew. Everyone knew. Her husband was a public figure, an international tycoon.

A co-worker with a stack of papers and an air of urgency barged into his office. Paul waved him off that *now was not a good time.* The worker u-turned and left. Cole slammed the door behind him. A sudden surge of tears flooded Mrs. Taylor's eyes. As the tears fell they formed blackish, brownish streams down her face from the mixture of eyeliner and heavy mascara. She wiped her face gently. Cole hastily whispered something in his employer's ear and promptly returned to his seat. As she extracted her makeup out of her Chanel 'Diamond Forever' bag she started retouching her makeup back to flawlessness. Even through the pain, her vanity demanded that no traces of this weak moment stain her perfectly made-up face.

"Yes, yes, his gambling binges are much worse, if that's at all possible. He stops for about six months, sometimes a year. After he stops for any length of time and starts back, he's much worse than he was before."

"That's the nature of addiction," Stevens offered in his most consoling tone. "I'm sure he'll eventually get a handle on it. He's a spiritual man."

Madeline paused to catch her breath. "Between you and me, our family is trying to get him to join.... I'm so upset I can't think of the name right now."

"Gamblers Anonymous."

"Yes, Gamblers Anonymous. Thank you Cole. It probably won't do any good for Howard. This is the hundredth damn time he's been in treatment. I am so frustrated."

"Is there anything I can do?"

"No, Thank you. He sent me to pick up more money to clean up his debts from last night's binge."

"You know, Mrs. Taylor, I'm really beginning to worry. You were here to pick up two hundred thousand dollars yesterday," he warned cautiously. "Now another two hundred and fifty thousand today. At this rate, no investment, no matter how large, can sustain itself," Mr. Stevens warned.

"My husband is an exorbitantly wealthy man, as you well know Mr. Stevens and that is the least of our problems right now. I'm really more concerned because lately he never comes home anymore. I'm beginning to wonder what other habits his insatiable appetite is cultivating after hours in addition to gambling. Did you hear what he said when he came to your office last month?" she inquired.

"Well, the staff told me he swore that would be the last time." She dabbed her eyes as more tears formed.

"It's a sad situation. Oh my God, it's so sad. Oh, now I am going to have to fix my make up again."

"Are you and Cole going to be okay getting to the car?" Mr. Stevens inquired.

"Aren't we always," she brushed him off. "Thanks so much for your concern."

"My first thought was to take the money out of one of your joint off shore accounts, but I decided to withdraw the money out of one of your joint CMA accounts. Are you sure you wouldn't prefer a cashier's check?"
Madeline smiled at him affectionately gently rubbing the back of her hand on his cheek

"Oh dear, sweet, Mr. Stevens, bookies don't honor anything but cash."
He blushed.

"I don't know what in the world I could be thinking. I'll phone the Bank of the Coast and have cash sent up right away." Ten minutes later, two security officers appeared with a case. One of the men stated to Mrs. Taylor and Cole, "We're here to escort you to your car."

"I thought you were here to bring me the money. Oh, it isn't necessary to usher us down stairs. Thank you so much though. Just to the elevator will be enough. Cole and I will be fine on our own, like always," she maintained kindly. The security men removed the cash from their case and gave it to Cole who packed it in their own case.

"Well then, all that's left is to sign the CTR and I'll drop it off at the bank for you," Mr. Stevens offered. After she signed the form he stood up to shake hands with her and Cole as they got up to leave.

"Mrs. Taylor, once again, it's been a pleasure doing business with you."

"Oh, nonsense, the pleasure has most assuredly been mine, you'll never know how much," she smiled sweetly. A tinge of lust flickered in Paul's eyes as he followed her, Cole, and the two bank officers down the hallway. Catching a whiff of her Clive Christian perfume he watched her firm, round behind switching all the way to the elevator. Stevens felt a surge of sensual pleasure. He could only imagine what it would feel like if he could squeeze one cheek of her luscious ass.

As Stevens passed the secretary in route back to his office he caught her eye.

"Dillon is waiting in your office Sir with the files you ordered she smiled warmly. "Oh, by the way Mr. Stevens, I heard you turned in your resignation and tomorrow will be your last day. I guess I'll say good bye now because today is my last day."

"This was supposed to be my last day but I won't be able to wrap things up until tomorrow. Good luck to you." He said with a pleasant smile and never broke his gait.

When Mrs. Taylor and Cole reached the first floor, they rapidly pranced out of the building and into the Bugatti Veyron.

Chapter 8

THE TRIO

DECEMBER BENTON

December, was gifted with a rare combination of street smarts and business savvy that was unparalleled. She could manage any type of business.

She was a Swedish born, Christmas baby with translucent white skin and straight, dark, hair and eyebrows that gave her a bi-racial, Swedish –Italian flavor. The penetrating, exotic cat eyes lent even more uncertainty to her origin. At 5' 7, she was slender, and when she dressed for business she wore sophisticated, timeless attire. Other than that, it was all jeans, boot cut, straight leg, low rise, ripped, apple bottom, all styles, all the time.

Malone and December's friendship began at a nightclub on the south side of Chicago.

Robbie Baldwin had been December's new love interest for maybe three days when they returned to his apartment after a dinner - movie date. It was in total disarray, like it had been burglarized but the door was locked. It was December's first visit to her handsome, tall and new prospect's apartment. And him being good looking and high in stature was all she knew about him. According to Robbie, thieves had purloined all his worldly possessions along with a priceless, family heirloom. The irreplaceable piece of memorabilia was a one- of -a kind, authentic punching bag that had been owned by Joe Louis. Not only had Joe Lewis autographed the bag, everyone who the Brown Bomber had known during his reign as the heavy weight champion including famous boxers, movie stars and well-known politicians had also signed and dated the bag. Joe Louis had always considered the bag his lucky charm and trained on it rigorously unless he was out-of town. Joe's widow had gifted it to Robbie's grandfather after the champ passed away as a gesture of appreciation for all his years of dedicated service to Louis as his personal assistant. Robbie's grandfather had then passed it down to his son, Robbie's father, who had in turn given it to Robbie. He felt lucky to be the beneficiary and planned on giving it to his son when the right time presented itself. This robbery had permanently halted the passing of the heirloom from one generation to another.

His story and grungy apartment had December confused He drove a new, mint condition, Mercedes Benz and his apartment looked like a crack den. She was positive this would be their last date.

Robbie's emotions teetered from seething to heartfelt tears. December had decided to phone the police as a goodbye gesture of kindness. When the officers arrived, they took a report, dusted for prints, and checked for forcible entry, all to no avail. Still, he whined and complained until December finally suggested they go out to a club and have a drink in hopes of calming his nerves. They went to the Last Word lounge, a little hot spot on the south side of Chicago. It was one of those joints where everybody showed up at some point on Saturday night. When they arrived, there were a few of Robbie's old friends there whom he hadn't seen in a while. Many shots later, Robbie began telling his friends, December and any one at the bar who would listen about his heirloom. "I can't begin to tell you the lucrative offers I have turned down over the years. From museums, art enthusiasts and world-renowned collectors, all who wanted to buy Joe Louis's punching bag." One of his buddies responded, "That's odd man because as long as we have known yo' ass we ain't never seen no damn punching bag. We have only heard about this alleged bag over and over again from you." Another buddy remarked, "that's right man, I been coming to your apartment for years and I have never seen that shit either." They laughed at him.

"Man, shut the fuck up!!! He slurred. When I get my big ass check from my insurance company Ima see what you have to say then. That bag is gonna be worth it's weight in gold."

December decided she had had enough. the drunken liar. "Hey

Robbie, it's time for me to go home."

"Okay, I'll call you tomorrow," he slurred.

"There will be no tomorrows for us," she whispered so his friends couldn't hear.

When December got up to leave the loud, packed, club he followed her demanding a reason for her sudden change of heart. After two failed attempts at letting the worrisome man off easy, December had had enough. She finally blurted out, "I don't want to deal with a boozer."

Loser is what the Hennessey told him he heard. The intoxicated, wannabe boxer repeated what he thought he heard her say. "You don't want to deal with no loser." In front of large crowd waiting to enter the club Robbie motioned to deposit his meanest right hook on December's left jaw. She dodged the punch and she kicked him in the groin so hard that his legs buckled from underneath him. The crowd roared with laughter as December made her way to the parking lot. Robbie was dazed but managed to get to his feet. He ran after December, as he motioned to snatch her arm, Malone appeared out of no where, grabbed Robbie's arm, yanked it behind his back and tossed him with the same ease he could a five year old. Now irate, the staggering, slurring Robbie got loud, belligerent, and cocky. As he got up he grabbed his crotch and shook it at Malone as he hissed, "suck my, di..," were the last words that crossed his lips before Malone cold-cocked him.

Without a second thought, Malone and December stepped over Robbie's unconscious body and went back into the club. Their body language resembled two people who had known each other for years. They danced, toasted with Champagne, shot Tequila, sipped Absolute, blurted out peals of unadulterated laughter and danced until daylight hastened their departure.

Robbie was like a repented sin, forever forgotten.

That had been eight years ago.

HOLIDAY McCORMICK

Holiday, could con anybody out of anything and was an exceptional money manager.

She was an avant-garde, femme fatale who marched to the beat of the drummer inside her head. She was drama. Dramatic makeup, classic mink stoles, fur boas, vibrant colors and hats galore. She was loud, bossy, blunt, and honest. Buttermilk complexion, platinum buzzed hair and four-inch heels were Holiday's deal. Designer clothes were her passion. No hidden agenda. Holiday was the down –to- earth gangster. She and Malone shared a love for red roses and making money.

Malone and Holiday's friendship began on the Las Vegas strip.

Malone orchestrated a formal introduction to Holiday, through a mutual friend after a private a star-studded fashion show in Las Vegas. Malone was captivated by her flawless, old fashion Hollywood glamour. The introduction never happened. Holiday had sent messages to Malone by a friend that said, 'Got shit to do.'

Malone went to Plan B: Malone had taken notice of Holiday on the Las Vegas blackjack circuit. He searched for her playing cards. She played Blackjack, cheated and was amazing at it. He sat at her table and couldn't tap into her game.

Casino security had escorted Holiday into their office when her winnings climaxed at $142,000.00 even though they had nothing on her. They had her play with their pros. She won every hand and they couldn't track her cheating. They requested her to leave anyway so she wouldn't break the house.

The next casino she wasn't so lucky. She had pissed off $170.000 and was up by $30,000 when the cage caught her mouth moving while counting and hauled her to security.

Malone interceded and after endless hours of deliberation, worked out a deal that if Holiday would make restitution of $150,000 of the $170,000 and forget she knew Las Vegas existed, they would let her go. Malone fronted her debt. It was that gesture which had sparked an instant camaraderie. Holiday and Malone left Las Vegas hand in hand in Malone's white, 1969 convertible Cadillac, Holiday had looked at him and said,

"Huh, I hope they don't think they hurt my feeling, I've been kicked out of better places than this." Malone cackled uproariously.

This had been seven years ago.

FARREN LOCKHART

Farren, had a BA in Liberal Studies from Cornell and MBA from Harvard. She was brilliant at organizing new businesses.

Her creamy, coco brown complexion had a natural glow that easily avowed twenty-two, but never thirty. She was a slender, curvy, overall beauty with deep dimples and a perfect smile. She was a wholesome, girl. Her unkempt hair extended past the middle of her back and huge sad brown eyes. Much like Malone, was soft spoken yet commanding and coquettish.

Farren had fulfilled her desire to primp during her corporate career in New York. Now she dressed solely for comfort.

Malone and Farren's friendship began at a back-yard cookout.

Farren was giving an outdoor party to impress her friends, colleagues, and her boss. Malone had escorted Tanya, his younger brother's wife, and Farren's best friend to the function because Victor, Malone's brother had been incarcerated again. Farren, at that time, was the senior manager of the west coast fraud investigation division for a major bank. Her employer relocated her to LA from New York. She had just purchased a townhome. Malone and Tanya had arrived several hours early so that Tanya could help Farren out.

She had introduced Farren to Malone in hopes of a love connection. Tanya thought that the two of them together would equal sensational.

Farren's specialty was preparing food on the grill with her family's secret sauce that she drenched her meat and chicken in, making it finger –licking good. Anyone who tasted it urged her to market it including Malone. A couple of her friends were there to DJ and tend bar. Tanya, Farren and Malone laughed, talked and drank Perrier-Jouet Champagne from Malone's private stock. Not quite drunk, but way tipsy, Farren and Tanya scorched at least a thousand dollars worth of meat and poultry until it was inedible. Farren, through her tears, confessed she had no more money.

Malone had graciously replaced and upgraded the meat, poultry, and added a fine selection of quality seafood to the menu with a quick call to a friend. He also called a well-known chef to prepare the whole cook out. The barbecue was more successful than Farren could have ever imagined. The party Farren had given that Friday was suppose to go from 5pm until. It lasted, in full swing, until Sunday morning, all subsidized by Malone's generous financing.

For the next six months Malone and Farren were inseparable. They fell in love and formed such a strong bond of friendship that sex sometimes felt incestuous to both of them. Once they decided to make a commitment to one another in business, they both agreed that it was in their best interest not to mix the two. Farren was the only one of the Trio whom Malone had ever been romantically involved.

That had been eight years ago

Chapter 9

The exterior of the Los Angeles home that Vanessa co-owned with Prudence was devoidof color. The absence of flowers and the year round hay colored grass couldn't be blamed on the coolness of September. The dismal, unkempt appearance provided an aura of desolation, and further gave the distinct impression that the house was empty. However, the interior was a complete contradiction. The sophisticated art deco motif, and the richly coordinated colors of white, tangerine, and royal blue flowed smoothly throughout the multi-leveled home, creating a mood of tranquility and harmony.

Despite Vanessa Saffore's relentless effort to diminish the twelve-year old torch she carried for Grey Young with each passing day, the feelings she still harbored for him seemed to grow stronger. She was finally convinced that their romance would never happen but still hoped that it would. She waltzed around the bedroom of her secluded house nestled in the mountainside, preparing for his imminent arrival. She hummed and danced around like a tickled-pink five-year-old who had found out that Christmas was coming early this year. The only thing she could do to calm herself was what had always worked in the past concentrate on her workout. Vanessa giggled as she walked over to the sunken mini gym that was sectioned off from her bedroom. She was fanatical about keeping her 5'5, 110 pound lean frame in peak condition. As she worked out with free weights, ran on the treadmill and climbed the stair master her mind drifted into another thought provoking trance about Grey.

The moment she learned of Grey's arrival, it had taken a concerted effort to keep from simply laughing out loud during the course of the day. She reflected back on how he had never bored her because like her, Grey was energetic, rebellious, and prone to try anything once. The only thought that consumed her now, as much as she hated to admit it to herself, was reconciliation. '*This time things will be different,*' she crossed her fingers.

As much as she wanted to believe it, the crinkles in her forehead and sadness in her eyes conveyed a sense of disbelief as she attempted to avoid the onset of the migraine heading in her direction at full steam. She took something for it. Plagued by the uncertainty, she slowly massaged her forehead and temples, expertly moving her fingers back and forth to relieve the strain. Vanessa's life had changed drastically during the time she and Grey had been apart. She had a career that provided security and stability, elements that were as remote to Grey's realm of understanding as flying south for the winter is to a goldfish.

Vanessa and Venice's bedrooms were next to each other and comprised of the second level of the house overlooking the living room. Her double size, walk-in closet was filled to capacity with designer clothes, shoes and handbags. On the back wall of her closet was a life-size, three dimensional, hand-painted mural of the actor Patrick Dempsey, which looked so real it was uncanny. Anyone who walked in the closet for the first time was taken aback. At first glance, Patrick actually appeared to be standing there. Vanessa's habitual interaction was a hot topic of concerns amongst her close friends and family. At first, after a while and some deliberation, they thought straightjackets and little cups of pills. As time passed, everyone had shrugged it off and opted to place it in the category of 'most eccentric quirks.' As a matter of fact, frequent visitors found themselves surprisingly engaged with the Dempsey's persona.

Vanessa pondered what outfit would make a statement, if she could only figure out what statement she wanted to make. Normally she wasn't indecisive. But this occasion couldn't be categorized as normal, which was obvious by the way she ransacked her closet. She again recalled the incidents of her sordid past with Grey and the events leading to their break up. For a brief moment, Vanessa wondered why she even missed him at all. Dispensing with that thought, Vanessa wondered what Grey would say and how she would respond when they met again. Having played out the entire scenario in her mind, she kept starting over again, completely changing the conversation each time.

"What's up, buttercup?" Vanessa was startled by Prue's usual, uninvited and loud entrance into her bedroom closet. She jumped like a mouse had run across her feet. Prudence immediately began her usual routine of hanging up and organizing Vanessa's clothes. Vanessa's dressing area was piled high with discarded clothes covering an orange silk loveseat and the floor surrounding it.

"Damn, Prue, why do you storm in here like you've lost your mind? You almost scared Patrick and me to death. You don't know what we could have been doing in here. You should knock first. I don't like it and neither does he."

"Well, I know for a fact that the two of you only make out at night because I've heard you on several occasions." Vanessa was amused by her comment. "Plus, I wouldn't have to come in here at all if you'd hang up your own clothes sometimes," Prudence snapped.

"Nobody ever asked your ass to clean up after me. In fact, I really wish you would stop. It is fucking annoying as hell and totally unappreciated. You drive me to distraction with this bull shit," Vanessa said dryly.

"If I thought you really meant that I would never come back. As long as this room looks like it should be on a segment of Hoarder's, I'll be all up in here." Prudence didn't flinch.

As an afterthought, Prudence turned to look at Vanessa and said, "You know, you might strongly consider taking that filthy mouth of yours and dumping it in the same place the city unloads its garbage."

After her grueling workout Vanessa tossed off her sweat suit, climbed in her steamy heart-shaped Jacuzzi to relax and sooth her aching muscles. Her thoughts drifted back to the first time she and Grey had broken up. It had proven that bruising easily and healing quickly didn't mean the pain had completely gone away. She slid deeper into the luxurious bubbles.

Malone had introduced Grey to Vanessa at Dodie's house, when she was twenty- two years old and about to start law school. It was during a one-night layover. Malone and Grey were scheduled to catch a flight to Las Vegas to see a show and a championship fight. From that moment Grey and Vanessa were like bees and honey. Grey couldn't tear himself away from Vanessa long enough to make his flight. In the days that followed Vanessa didn't keep any of her appointments and floated around like she was incased in a bubble that Grey had blown. A grubble. They swept each other off their feet. For the next seven months, Vanessa absorbed every sweet nothing he whispered in her ear. That's why she was positive she'd heard him correctly when he said "he had to go out of town on business and promised her that he'd be gone for a few days. He swore that the thought of being away from her any longer than that would be more than his heart could bear. Grey returned two years later.

Vanessa stepped out of the Jacuzzi and sighed, "Oh Prue, wait till you see Grey. He's gorgeous." Vanessa boasted "He had me floating in a grubble for months when I first met him. One kiss and a smile and I hope it doesn't happen again."

"More gorgeous than Patrick?" Prudence teased. "And what the hell is a grubble?"

"No one can be more gorgeous. I should only hope, for Grey's sake, I don't run into Patrick before I see him. It would be curtains." Prudence stopped what she was doing to look at Vanessa and asked seriously, "What would you do if you actually saw him? You'd make a fool out of yourself wouldn't you? You couldn't just like try to follow him or kidnap right?"

"Don't be ridiculous Prue. I work for the FBI. You know I know better."

"So, what would you do? Seriously. I mean really, If you saw him sitting alone in a restaurant eating what would you do? I sometimes wonder how serious and deep this obsession goes with you. You do know this isn't not normal right?" Prudence pointed to the mural of Patrick.

'That's a good question. I'll have to give that some serious thought and get back to you on it. Oh, and a grubble is a bubble you float in because of a certain person. Grey equals a grubble. If I met

Patrick I'd be in a pubble."

"Hummm, more Vanesssaisms? Nice. I'm sitting on the edge of my seat to meet Grey and your cousin, Malone. I've known you all my life and I have never, seen you this hyped over any man. And for the record, I've seen you with quite a few fellas." Prudence hugged Vanessa as she joked.

"H-e-e-e-y, watch it now!" Vanessa responded with dry humor.

Chapter 10

Grey drank the last corner of Cuvee Dom Perignon from a crystal flute, sniffed another couple of lines of cocaine then stared out of the window.

"Man, really? Let's keep in one hundred. Don't you think you've done enough blow for one day?"

"Blue, how about we talk about your bad habits for a change of pace man. You know, the ones you have that you think don't exist. Like smoking man, you are infecting everyone around you with all that damn second hand smoke."

" Hey man, I only smoke in the privacy of my own domain. So, if there is anyone who doesn't like it they don't have to be here. On the other hand man, you aren't a youngster any more. I have known men a lot younger than you that have snorted that shit, to the degree that you do, and it stopped their heart."

"Well, it's my heart I'm doing it to and not yours." Grey trumped. Malone continued reading his book.

Grey's mind raced. He was happy about Vanessa's sudden change of heart. He tried to reason why after eight years of being adamant about never seeing him again she had suddenly conceded.

Grey was always a bit jealous of Malone and Vanessa's relationship and their whole family dynamics. Malone and Grey's thirty-year friendship took root on the south side of Chicago. Vanessa and Malone were related through a common law marriage. Dodie's first cousin, Cheryl Newton, and Malone's uncle Terrance Carson, had lived together for ten years, until Terrance died of cancer. Vanessa's stepfather Frank had taken Malone under his wing after Terrance's death. Terrance and Cheryl had stepped in to help Malone, Victor and their mother as much as they could financially when Malone's father, Kenneth (Terrance's brother), abandoned them. Malone was fifteen. Without warning, Kenneth Carson one day decided the responsibility of marriage and raising kids was too much for him. So, he left. When Malone had been released from prison on a three-sentence term he stayed with Dodie, Frank and Vanessa until he left for college.

"I just hope you don't OD on this motha fucka man and I have to take your ass to the hospital. Then, have to answer to the authorities why the hell I was up in the sky with you while you were taking drugs and didn't make you stop." Malone chided.

"Make me. Blue, you can't make me do a damn thing. Why the fuck do you care anyway?" Grey said as he inhaled another line and chased it with brandy. His nose ran and his eyes were stretched open wide as felt the drain from the cocaine.

"Why? Are you serious man? You are my brother and my best friend. Why would you think I don't care? Grey, I'm not co-signing for this bullshit and if something does happen to you, I'm dropping your ass on the side of the road somewhere and Ima keep on going. I got too much going on for you to bring that kind of spotlight on me."

"What are you talking about now?"

"Shit, if you get busted buying that shit or have to go to the hospital how am I gonna explain an overdosed or a dead body to the cops."

"Well, if I'm dead, then it really won't matter will it." Plus, you are confusing care with control."

"What?" Malone snapped.

"You don't give a damn about me. You just wish you had enough control over me to make me do what you want. "
Malone shook his head in disgust, looked at him pathetically and continued reading his book.

Grey was a mama's boy. His mother, Arlene, had never made him do a thing and nothing was just what he did until Malone came along. She kept his precious room intact because he always came home when he had no funds, no way to get any, over-exhaustion from drug usage, or eviction from a woman's house. She wanted him home and if he had stayed for an eternity it would have suited her. Arlene washed his laundry, laid out his clothes, prepared all of his meals, made his bed, and cleaned his room. She broke her back to serve any girl Grey brought home to live with them.

Whatever made Grey happy made Arlene happier.

Chapter 11

Dusk had settled when Prudence finally left Vanessa's room. "Just remember, don't go building up your hopes," Vanessa warned. When Prudence reached her room she hollered back, "Why not? Hey, if you can build hope about a man painted in your closet mine doesn't seem farfetched at all."

Vanessa grabbed her glass of juice and walked up two stairs to Prudence's room on the third level.

Prudence's strikingly decorated bedroom resembled a miniature penthouse that had been caught in a massive snowstorm, everything was white. The fireplace enhanced the coziness of the sitting area of the loft. A small, guest bedroom sat adjacent to the sitting area.

Vanessa plopped down on the king-size, brass bed. She snuggled under the large Eiderdown comforter, gathered the pillows, and beat them into a position that she could comfortably nestle her head.

"I'm a realist Prue. You, on the other hand, are an eternal

optimist."

"Oh, here we go." Prudence scratched her head. "I believe in staying open-minded and positive. You never know when true love will come. I'll find it though, one day, and when I do, I'll be receptive to it. You are in a constant war with yourself all the time cause you fear it. You try to hide that you want it. Everyone wants love and no one wants to work for it. Love is not free."

"The word 'love' triggered thoughts of Grey and how his lifestyle must have changed.' He surely had to be on the legitimate side of the tracks by now. Grey's line of work caused their turbulent break-up before and might possibly be the reason they could never reunite. Vanessa shut her eyes to dispel any of the thoughts that ushered in her insecurities. Besides, she thought, *'Why in the world would he have contacted me if he hadn't modified his career choice and gotten in deeper? Not even he could be that dumb.'* Vanessa carefully nibbled on the tips of her long fingernails trying not to mess up her French manicure. Her body tensed as she made a fist and nervously popped all the knuckles on her slender fingers. She thought, *'he sure waited a long time to call. Eight years is ample time to have made a transformation.*

Returning from her thoughts she replied, "How poetic. My life doesn't have to revolve around a man Prue. I don't need one to validate me."

"No woman with any sense does Vanessa. By the way you're acting you sure couldn't prove it by me. Stop lying to yourself, girl, you're covering your feelings. A meaningful relationship shouldn't consume your life it should only enhance it. It's one of the many facets that gives you balance. The power you give to negative energy is what causes you to feel like a victim and being victimized is where you opt to place all your failed love affairs. Every relationship isn't meant to last forever. There are no winners and losers, it is simply about compatible or incompatible." Prudence cheerfully prepared for her date as Vanessa hung on her every word.

"You're ridiculously overbearing half the time. The other half, you spend adding new layers to your facade. You cover up to shield how fragile your feelings really are. Vanessa, your competitive hard ass edge is only apparent when it comes to men and work. I must admit you make concessions for your friends, family and especially your son Venice."

"I don't trust people the way you do," Vanessa attested.

"Trust people, you are the most cynical person I have ever known." Vanessa ignored her.

"Men are the first to remind us that this is a man's world. If this is their world and they can't make it in their own world, then too bad. I don't feel sorry for not one of 'em. What satisfies their sexual wants and needs from moment to moment is all they know. This sex thing in society is far too overrated and much too out of control. Everything revolves around getting laid and paid. Where is the love and integrity?"

"What about women who know this is happening and allow it? Why do you only blame men for digging all the dirt that happens in a relationship? There are a lot of women that shovel it, too." Their voices escalated.

Vanessa began pacing. She would argue to have the last word with the same kind of resolve an athlete exhibits when competing for the gold. Prudence flowed on to humor Vanessa for the sake of argument, but certainly not to influence her chiseled- in- stone opinions.

"When men cheat, Vanessa, who the hell do you think they're cheating with?"

"It could be any number of things. Basically, anything that has a hole," huffed Vanessa.

"See, now, you're being ignorant. So it's not wrong when women consent to relationships with married men?"

"They probably don't tell them. Plus it's the responsibility of the person who's married not to do wrong."

"That's a cop out. So what you're telling me is that you believe there are no married women who cheat? Vanessa, you're being downright prejudice. You're doing the exact same thing you dislike men for doing."

"I'm entitled, I'm finishing what they started."

"You know, with all we've gone through as Black people, I don't know how you tune your mouth to make a statement like that.

You hate being stereotyped, yet you do it. There's good and bad in both men and women, and in all nationalities. Everyone should be treated and judged on his or her own merit," her voice had risen.

"Most men don't deserve to be treated with respect." Prudence stopped dressing. The two of them stood face to face in the middle of the room consumed in a shouting match like two kindergarten kids on the playground waiting for the other to throw the first punch. Prudence peeled herself away and stomped into the bathroom.

"I hate it when you walk away from me like that."

"Here's a news flash, ears were designed for permitting a person to do two things at once, walk and hear." While applying her makeup Prudence turned away from the mirror to make eye contact with Vanessa.

"You must have dealt with some real losers in your day, because you really have a low opinion of men."

"I only know males. No. I am not talking about just men that I have dated. I am talking about the ones I see around me. Husbands and boyfriends of my friends, co-workers, and women I went to college with, politicians and movie stars. Men will cheat.

"What about Grey?"

"He's the best out of the worst. Surely, is a product of his environment. What makes a man is his character Prue and that's innate. The ability to stand up for something, draw the line, be responsible for himself and his family that is what makes a man. The size of his dick makes him a male. Most of what we do is a learned behavior. Grey had no role models."

"Do you love Grey, or is it a challenge to get him to conform like you do with the men you deal with socially and the cases on your job?"

"That has nothing to do with gender. It's just that I rarely get assigned to cases involving female I don't understand the logic of your analogy, but I love Grey."

Prudence completed the final touches of her makeup and added accessories to compliment her casual white gabardine pantsuit.

"Well, how do I look?" Prudence twirled in a three sixty.

"Girlfriend, you look marvelous. Who is this guy anyway?

"I met him at an art auction last week. He's really charming. He's been calling and calling, so I finally agreed to go out with him. He's an attorney."

"A public pretender?"

"For your information he owns his own law firm."

"I'm so impressed. What's his area of expertise?"

"Criminal law."

"Does he have any money?"

Agitated, Prudence answered, "How the hell would I know. Plus, gold digging is your area of expertise."

"Now, why do I have to be all that? If I rather go out on a date with a man who drives a Porsche over a man pushing a grocery cart, I'm a gold digger?"

"If that's all you want then that's what you are."

"Look, I'm not gonna date a no-class, ignorant man, whether he's rich or poor." Vanessa emphasized. "So what about these men who date us, and all they want to do is get a nut? I guess that makes them sex diggers huh?" As much as Prudence hated to laugh she did.

"I don't know why I let you talk me into moving out here with you. I should have kept my ass in Chicago, cause girl, you are nuts and bolts."

"Don't act like you are here by special request. If you could have found a decent job as a cook, you know you wouldn't be here now."

"A Chef if you don't mind. And that's true. Look, I have to finish getting ready."

"What time is Mr. Charm supposed to be here?"

"Seven o'clock."

"It's seven thirty!"

"He's the one who insisted I go out with him, I know he'll be here," she said reassuring herself.

"That is a crime. He worries the shit outta you to go out, then he's late as hell and doesn't have the decency or common courtesy to call and say a damn thing. Now that's class. When he comes, I wouldn't go out with that inconsiderate ass hole," Vanessa lectured.

Prudence stared at Vanessa hoping this man wasn't going to add another notch to Vanessa's '*I told you so belt*' by not showing up.

Vanessa's eyes shifted into space as if she had, again, taken flight into her thoughts.

Chapter 12

Grey couldn't wait until they landed.

Malone began packing his book, *GQ, Times, Forbes* and *Architectural Digest* scattered everywhere in the opulent cabin of companies' private airliner. When he finished, he picked up the *New York Times* to read the closings on Wall Street. Malone spoke barely above a whisper as he always did until he became irritated. Then his voice would rise to a normal pitch.

"Hey Grey, check this out, man. Remember that stock I bought six months ago?

Man first it dropped, then, no return for a long time. Now, it split." He peered over his paper at Grey, " Hey, man, did you hear what I said?"

After ten years of marriage, Grey's stepfather, Martin, resented the open door policy Arlene held for Grey. He didn't pay rent or help fix up the house Arlene and her mother owned. No matter how much money Grey made, finances were always an uphill struggle for Martin, Arlene, and his grandmother. They earned a meager living in a janitorial business. Arlene had informed Martin that he would leave before Grey did.

"Hey man did you hear what I said," Malone repeated.

"Man, get off me with that bullshit. I don't know why you try to put me down on your investments all the time. I can't fathom handing no white man my money, so he can take it and make him some more money off my money."

"You're making money, too."

"Thanks for your concern man, but I make enough money, okay? From where I sit, it doesn't look like I'm ever going to run out, okay?"

"Man, get real, that's all you do is run out. We've been playing at one game or another for what, some twenty years now. I know if the pattern of our lives hasn't taught you anything else, you should know better than that. No matter how much money you have, it can run out."

"Look Blue, we ain't never made money this long before."

"Yeah man, but you know how this shit goes, we've been down before. You should invest some of that money, so if the Feds ever put the spotlight on this operation, you'll have something to support your back. The most important thing you continually fail to realize is that this organization wasn't built to make money for your personal gain."

"I've never seen you once participate or donate anything to any of the causes we sponsor."

Grey's voice displayed a slight hint of agitation,

"Look Blue, that's your shit man. I don't force you to be involved with what I do."

"Out of curiosity, what do you do?"

"I do what I have to do and I have to do what's right for me. And you, of all people, should be able to understand that, and, if not," he shrugged his shoulders with outstretched palms and let out a sigh, "Oh well."

Malone squinted as he looked at Grey in the usual, *'why the hell do I deal with him at all'* expression, which he always did after they had finished one of their futile debates. As Malone continued to watch him, he shook his head, not the kind of gesture that symbolizes *'no.'* but the shake that meant disgust and disappointment.

Grey's hands trembled like he had been stranded in a blizzard, as he snorted another line of cocaine. The deep furrows in his forehead were drenched in sweat. In his usual tactless arrogance he responded, "Why don't you focus your little, misguided worries where they would be better utilized, like with that addle-brained Vincent. Ride him about keeping that clothing store and office in better order when the Trio can't be there. You also need to check out some of the bullshit your girls have been doing lately."

Struggling to maintain his composure, Malone took a deep breath before he spoke. He grit his teeth together so hard it made the round, alligator-like muscles in his solid, stern jaws more pronounced.

"Look man, number one, it was initially your job to keep up with the Camouflage and Blossoms offices. You gave yourself the authority, against my behest, to delegate your duties to Vincent, which I let slide. Not to mention you wouldn't have had to do that if you handled your own responsibilities. Case and point, you stay marinated in that damn cocaine and can no longer control your obsessions. Since you can't do it in moderation any more you need to stop. Now you want me to kick Vincent out of the organization because you feel he's not doing your job properly. That's not going to happen."

"I don't need a critique from you on how much I should or shouldn't get high," Grey said defensively.

"You're right, you're past the point of needing a critique from me. What you really need is a professional drug counselor. You have gone to the extreme with that shit, man."

"Cause you don't use drugs doesn't give you the right to judge people who do."

"You don't use drugs either you abuse them."

"Because I do an occasional blow doesn't mean I'm a drug addict Blue! I can quit whenever I want, not when you want."

"I know how the story goes man, I hear it all the time. Man, you've been doing drugs for fifteen years but you ain't hooked right? Man, get the hell outta here with that bullshit."

"Forget it, Blue, I'll fire Vincent my damn self." Grey spoke as if he had the authority to make final decisions.

Chapter 13

When Vanessa emerged from her fleeting thoughts Prudence was still talking.

"You know, Vanessa, you might need some therapy for your issues with men."

"You know, I resent your holier than thou attitude about what I might need. You act like your life has been filled with kind and considerate men. Honestly, I wonder how you can keep on defending them the way they have crapped all over you."

Prudence ignored Vanessa's outburst and spoke in an undisturbed tone, "With your attitude, I can understand why the real love of your life is painted on the wall of your closet. Who for real would be bothered with you?"

"Bitch please." Vanessa laughed. Prudence continued haughtily.

"Well, the men I've been in relationships with treated me with the utmost respect, besides, can you truly love anyone you don't respect or trust."

"Girl, you know, now that I think about it, you're absolutely right. I shouldn't let my messed-up experiences cloud the fact that there are some good men out there and you have definitely had some. I'm wrong, I apologize."

Prudence looked at Vanessa. She didn't believe what she heard, but decided to go along for the ride.

"Well, I'm glad you finally admit I'm right." Prudence humored.

"Hey, when you're right, you're right," Vanessa offered. "You have had some wonderful men.

I get so down on men that I forget about the good ones. Under no circumstances should one be able to forget the authentic gentleman who left you stranded at the Hilton when we were in New York. I had to come from Jersey to pick your ass up in the middle of the fuckin' night. Why?" Vanessa continued. "Because that crack head impersonating a knight in shining armor stole your damn purse and left while you so generously went to the bar to get his coat. There was no damn coat. You didn't have any money to pay for the room. No train fare, cab fare, nothing."

Prudence was smug.

"That was a dismal evening. He was a low life, probably born in a garbage dumpster. Yes, he left me stuck with the tab and I still say you can't judge the masses by comparing them to that trash."

"Well let's see, " Vanessa plowed on, "What about that filled to the rim with manners son of a bitch who escorted you to your close friend's wedding and all night long blatantly hit on the chick singing in the band. Oh, and let's not forget the overwhelming amount of chivalry he demonstrated when the dirty slob left with the bitch.

Another night you got stranded."

Prudence snickered, "Well, at least he didn't steal my purse."

"How gallant of him." Vanessa walked toward the door then paused, "Shall I go on?"

"Huh, I think you've said enough, but hardly proven a point. As luck would have it the few bad dates I've gone on, you were the closest to me and the only one I could call who wouldn't throw it in my face." She chuckled. "I see things in gray and you see things in black and white and no matter what you say Vanessa, I still feel you can't crucify the whole population of people for the errors of a few low class bums."

"A few my ass. Please. You know there are a lot more low class bums. I'll give you a break. But I still say, the day I meet just one man who stays faithful to his woman and keeps his word, possesses the slightest semblance of integrity," Vanessa continued, "I'll allow him to restore my faith in the male gender and will treat him the way a man deserves to be treated. Until then, court is adjourned."

"I hardly think so." Prudence said as she glanced at the clock, rejected.

"Damn girl, look what time it is. He'll be here soon, and I still have things to do."

"I'm leaving now so you can finish getting ready for your date."

"Providing he shows up, for God's sake," Prudence said softly so Vanessa could not hear. A comment like that would trigger another two-hour conversation.

Prudence scratched her head as her eyes followed Vanessa out the door. She wondered how she continuously allowed herself to get cornered into these repetitive discussions. Prudence was glad she left. She wanted to enjoy some last minute primping alone thinking about the wonderful evening she knew was going to have with the now more than fashionably late, new, handsome, man she had met.

Chapter 14

"Good evening gentlemen, this is your pilot speaking. We will be landing in New York City in twenty minutes. The weather conditions are clear and the temperature is about 45 degrees. I received a message that your car will be waiting at the gate in front of terminal three, which is where we will be landing. Have a wonderful evening gentlemen.

Grey 's face revealed the scorn pumping through his veins.

"Yeah man," Malone said wryly, "that would be fine, except for one small detail you overlooked. Don't worry though, I'll keep reminding you. You do not have the authority to do THAT." Malone warned coolly.

There was nothing they did not <u>understand</u> about each other. Since the inception of the organization, Malone had refused to disclose anything to Grey about his charitable ventures. A decision based on Grey's increasing desire for drugs. Through it all, their loyalty to each other was the only thing that never waivered. They were brothers with a history that had been built on a solid foundation. Frank taught Malone at an early age that showing anger to your opponents gave them an unfair advantage. Malone always remained true to the theory that if the opposition knew where he was vulnerable, it would kill his chances of winning. Frank use to say, *'If you remain in this business you're guaranteed to get busted sooner or later. Losing your cool insures you get busted sooner.'*

"Since when do I need your fucking permission to do something?"

"Since when have you ever not needed it?"

"Blue, you know I trust you with my life, man, but you know better than to bother me about my personal decisions or money."

"Look Grey, I picked you up and put you down on my, I repeat, MY program. Anytime you don't like my program, guess what, you can't change a damn thing. You know, man, you weren't drafted into this. I invited you."

"So, what's that supposed to mean?"

"You can leave at any time and resume your well-deserved eternal position on your prestigious throne at your mama's ghetto palace." Grey stood up. His eyes were squinted and pupils dilated. He yelled at Malone so loudly the veins in his forehead rose and his voice reverberated throughout the plane. He licked his lips repeatedly and wiped the corners of his mouth.

"Fuck you Malone, kiss me and my mother's black asses man! I've taken as many chances as you have. You never agree with anything I say or anything I do." Malone replied calmly.

"If I agreed with you, then we would both be wrong. The chances you take are on my work. I put this thing in motion while you were still in the joint on that one-year bit. Remember, my business was already established, running properly, and layin' golden eggs two years before you hatched in the nest." The exchange of words was so loud it was heard in the cockpit, John chimed in, "Excuse me Mr. Carson and Mr. Young, is everything okay back there?"

Malone walked to the phone next to the bar, pushed in one of the many buttons and answered in a pleasant voice,

"Everything is fine Mr. Alexander, everything's cool man. Emotions are running a bit hot and heavy over some business discrepancies that's all. Thanks for your concern though, man."

Malone hung up the phone and launched back into the conversation. "Look man," Malone decided to try not to hurt Grey's feelings. "I extend the courtesy of allowing you to make suggestions. I really do have a sincere regard for your feelings and the utmost respect for your opinion; some of your advice has influenced my decisions. However, I didn't bring you on board under the presumption that we were, or ever were going to be, partners. Vincent is doing fine. I wish that you would quit standing on me about him. I need to hire a referee for you two, cause quite frankly, I'm sick a' baby sittin' your asses. He stays with the organization, and that's my final decision. So let's pull the plug on this bullshit conversation."

"Huh, your decision. Oh, now we can only talk when you feel it's necessary? Ain't that a bitch."

"Man come on, I'm sick of wrestling with you about this Vincent shit, that's all. We're in our prime with this thing man. There's more than enough money in it for everybody. Come on Grey. I really wish you would stop fine-tuning every little thing Vincent messes up. I'll handle him man. If he's creating that much of a disturbance for you, Grey, take your position back, and I'll move him somewhere else. If not, you'll have to…"

Grey interrupted Malone, yelling, "Have to, since when do you tell me what the hell I have to do?" He smirked and sustained his tirade, "Well, since you have every thing under control, what do you need me for? Let me make this clear, I refuse to work with him anymore, and that's final! And you better respect my opinion in this particular situation."

Malone cringed, lit a cigarette, took a drag and exhaled a monstrous cloud of smoke fighting to maintain his composure. He took a deep breath as he mulled over what Grey had the gall to say. His face faded as though he had suddenly been stricken with a deadly virus. He spoke slowly and deliberately,

"This play is way outta bounds, man. Whatever gave you the impression that I," he emphasized, "NEEDED YOU? As far as your opinion goes, it matters, but only when I ask you for it." Grey turned around in his chair to make eye contact with Malone,

"OOOOh! So it's like that now, huh?" He spoke gruffly.

Malone erupted like a molten volcano spewing red lava, "NOW!" He paced and smoked.   Malone's voice boomed louder, hands and body steadily in motion. "The rules ain't changed, man, and don't expect them to any time in the near future or ever, for that matter. You know Grey, It's unfortunate that we must rewind this discussion one... more... time.   Grey's snake eyes penetrated Malone's every movement as Malone continued his discourse,

"Let's try this one more time, man. We volley ideas, you and I, to see which ones sync-up. Hopefully they all will. BUT, in the event they do not," He stopped to establish eye contact with Grey, pointed to himself and said, "I determine the final verdict. This is my business. You work for me."

Grey became more unraveled with every word Malone spoke. Grey screamed as if he were talking to someone sitting outside on the wing of the plane, "Man, you must think you're talking to one of your bitches!"

Malone inhaled a mass of smoke from his cigarette. His sarcastic voice hovered barely above a whisper as he scoffed through clenched teeth, "ONE, of my bitches. Huh! Well, now that's so unfair of you Grey," Malone's eyes narrowed to slits, "cause I've always treated and taken care of you like you were **MY-ONLY- BITCH!**"

Grey stiffened as if paralyzed by shock. Grey rarely saw the part of Malone that was like an inbred pit bull turning on its owner.

He sniffed a hit of cocaine, poured some Champagne, and followed Malone's every move. Simmering, Malone awaited Grey's rebuttal. Grey resumed observing the sights below. Malone's expression reeked with disgust as he continued to smoke and pace, leaving trails of smoke rings in every direction. After an extended wait, Malone, unresponsive let the conversation he had tried so desperately to avert, rest. Silence prevailed.

Grey's biological father, Walter never married Arlene. He had been instrumental in bringing up Grey, until he died from cirrhosis of the liver. In Grey's case, no influence would have been better than the alcoholic, consistently unemployed father that he had. Walter conned Arlene into believing he drank so heavily because she had no respect for him as a black man. In truth, he refused to work out of resentment he had towards Arlene who had convinced him to quit his lucrative career as a pimp after the boys were born. Charles, the eldest of the two boys, died from an overdose of heroin at the age of twenty-one. That prodded Arlene to be more protective of Grey.

John's voice punctuated the silence in the cabin, "The temperature in LA is about sixty five degrees cooler than it is back there and hopefully more tranquil. Present time is 12:30 a.m. Let's wrap it up and fasten those seat belts gentlemen."

Grey buckled up after he finished the last line of cocaine,

wiped off the mirror, and glanced into it to ensure that nothing remained on his mustache or in his nose. He placed the paraphernalia into a zippered compartment in his carry all. Malone slipped on his Bally loafers and neatly tucked all his papers and notes inside his Hermes briefcase, along with his custom gold pen and pencil set. The case was engraved with the initials P.A.W. (Present, Able, and Willing), which was the acronym Malone and the Trio had given to the corporation they started solely for charity work. P.A.W. was a completely separate entity from the Red Rose. None of the employees who worked for The Red Rose knew about the existence of P.A.W.

Malone walked to the closet to remove his topcoat and fedora. He put them on then buckled up in preparation for landing.

Not another word was uttered between them.

Chapter 15

Undercover Special Agent Vanessa Saffore arrived at the Wilshire Boulevard headquarters in Westwood promptly at 4:00 p.m. Her slew-footed stride was rhythmic to the little ditty she hummed to that was stuck in her head. She repeated the song up to the moment she paraded through the automatic glass doors of the Federal Bureau of Investigation in Westwood California.

Vanessa's Escada tailored suit was accentuated with matching accessories. At the end of a long dead-end hallway, she turned and entered the cubby-hole size room where the agents were sprawled around a small conference table stacked with mountains of files, paperwork, stale coffee, concrete donuts, and shriveled fruit. It was apparent by their wrinkled suits, uncombed hair, and bloodshot eyes that this assembly's session was in overtime. The intensity of the brainstorming sparked Vanessa's curiosity about the case instantly. Vanessa deduced that every card in the deck had already been played and still no one had the winning hand.

"So, what's up guys? Like I really need to ask," she said as she closed the door behind her.

"My, my, aren't we feeling chipper today Special Agent

Saffore. I am going to sit here and take a twenty minute break,"
one of the agents commented, leaning on the table, barely able to
keep his head up. The other agent acknowledged Vanessa by
casting a forced smile, then resumed his position of weariness.

Vanessa scanned the contents of some of the files, as the
agents remained slouched and haggard.

Then the youngest and newest Special Agent in the agency
ripped through the door flashing a high beam smile. He brushed
himself off in a feeble attempt to freshen his crumpled appearance.
He approached Vanessa, reached for her hand and she reciprocated
with a firm, enthusiastic response. "I am Special Agent Peter
Mason, and boy, it is a pleasure to finally meet you. Your
reputation precedes you."

"Really?" Vanessa was taken aback.

"Oh, absolutely, Agent Saffore."

"You have got to be kidding me, right?" She stared at her
hand still being shaken with vigor and politely eased it out of his
firm grip. She proceeded toward the front of the office. Peter
swirled his 5'8, oddly cute, medium frame body around the floor
and positioned himself directly in front of Vanessa. She flinched
and took a discrete step backwards. She glanced out of the corner of
her eye for a reaction from her nearly comatose coworkers. They
remained unresponsive. Vanessa stroked her forehead.

"Okay I give up. I'm stumped," she declared.

"About what?" Peter inquired.

"This unnecessary adulation." She stood back and glanced at him puzzled.

"Well to be honest," Peter boasted, "I was transferred to this office a few days ago. Although I haven't gotten an assignment yet, it's been exciting knowing what's in store. An extensive part of my training in the academy entailed studies of past resolved and unresolved cases, as I'm sure you well know. What you probably don't know is that several of the successful cases we used as an example in training were yours." Vanessa uttered, "Hmm, that is a fact I didn't know." She forced a slight grin and felt a spark of curiosity as Peter expounded, "Out of all the cases we studied, in my opinion, you've done the most phenomenal work. There were quite a few others who also deserved recognition, but yours were a cut above." He remained directly in front of Vanessa, almost toe to toe, attempting to establish eye contact as she continued reading the case files.

"The thing that sets you aside from the others for me was that, unlike most, you executed the best judgment. You have had some extremely difficult under cover cases especially for a woman. In fact, you were the only woman who was assigned predominately male cases."

"So now you are playing the woman card?"

"I mean, not at all, but I think that women," Peter explained, "must find it some what more difficult than men to separate their emotions from their work. Especially if the case drags out and they get more involved in the suspect's personal lives, wouldn't you agree?"

"I can't honestly say. I've never noticed that with any of the agents I have worked with," Vanessa countered.

"Well, I'm sorry, but it's true. Women do have problems in that area more so than men. Once a female establishes a connection their conscience bothers them more when it's time to make the bust and even more after it's done. Men don't feel anything."

"That is precisely my point. I do agree that men don't feel anything, on the other hand, how the hell can you come within a football field of arriving at these conclusions when you haven't been on one case. These are all assumptions. My guess is this is something you misread, or misinterpreted." Vanessa motioned to walk away and as an afterthought rebutted. "Agent Peter, you are here to solve cases, not to examine the emotional psyche of your female counterparts."

Peter's deflated body movement conveyed disappointment. He motioned for Vanessa to follow him over to the other side of the room. She reluctantly followed. He sprinkled her face with a spit shower as he whispered, "Would you please request that I be on your squad for the case you have coming up?"

Vanessa frowned at him as though he had feces stuck between his teeth as she reached for a Kleenex to wipe her face. Peter's face reddened in embarrassment. In a pleasant, but strained voice she acknowledged,

"What a wonderful compliment Agent Mason. Thank you so much. Only one problem though, I don't work with newly assigned agents. I only do priority investigations of white collar crimes." He made an abrupt exit and everyone applauded. Vanessa turned toward Robert Johnson and asked,

"Hey Johnson, would you like to tell me what that was about?" she asked smiling as if she were a tiny bit flattered,

"Hah, he is our neophyte, leave him alone. He's a good kid, young, eager, willing to learn, and hungry. You remember how it was when you first started, don't you? Or do you? I know old age has a way of clouding long term memory," Robert belted with mirth.

Special Agent Robert Johnson was handsome, had masculine features, bittersweet chocolate skin, and a salt and pepper mustache that matched his receding hair. His stature was tall and his physique thick and strong.

"Ha! Ha! Ha! I could take fewer showers with him around," Vanessa joked.

"You're his hero. Imagine that?" Johnson guffawed.

"Must be a real shortage of heroes out there," Lawrence Wilcox added dryly.

Special Agent Lawrence Wilcox looked like a real right wing, conservative, skinhead, republican - but he wasn't. He looked that way because he was an ex- military man. He wore a precision crew cut, a couple of tattoos, had a desert dry sense of humor and was a staunch liberal.

As they all chuckled, Supervisory Special Agent Donald Dayton made his way through the open door with the finesse of a bull in a china shop. He rolled in two boxes of files. At 6' 1, his body parts protruded out where they should have caved in. He was clean cut with a rugged edge. He clapped his hands.

"Come on guys. Let's get this shit in motion. Lotta work," he pounded on the podium, "Lotta work we have to go over. Is everything in order Agent Johnson?"

"Yes sir."

"Well, let's get this moving then."

Donald peered through his reading glasses as he examined the files he brought in the room with him.

"So awfully impolite of me," he paused. "How are you Vanessa? Hope my rudeness doesn't ruin your day."

"There is nothing on the face of the earth that could ruin my day today. Lets make this quick, 'cause I have plans, wonderful plans tonight." She pulled up a chair and took a seat between Lawrence and Robert.

"It's still early," Donald mumbled, then changed his tone. "Glad to have you back. Sincerely sorry, I had to interrupt your vacation. The department is short of staff right now. Special Agent Washington couldn't have picked a better time to have triplets. He and his wife thought they were having twins. Seems as though three of our other agents had emergencies, all at the same time.

"We have enough men to carry our load but we'll have fewer agents in a squad." Donald continued.

"I know you Donald, you could have easily brought in agents from other offices, you wanted me on this case." Vanessa didn't look up as she flipped through the case files.

"OK, so you're right. You may resume your vacation as soon as this case is resolved. I'll see to it that you get an extra week."

The combination of honesty and a rarely understood sense of humor is what cemented Vanessa and Donald's exceptional work relationship.

"Anyway, Vanessa this case has been kicking the departments asses every way but loose. The other squad couldn't crack it so the powers that be decided to send it to our unit. We have a bunch of crafty sons of bitches here. Some piece of work."

He took a seat on a tall, high-backed stool behind the podium and directed his attention toward Vanessa. He peered over his glasses.

"This is the deal in a nutshell. These guys have taken fraud to a new dimension. They're taking money from everywhere and moving it to places we can't pinpoint. It's not in the Cayman Islands, Aruba, or any of the usual hideouts. They haven't left one damn paper trail in the four years we've been investigating them, and, stranger than that, we have never been able to match anything on them not even so much as a fingerprint. They've got inside connections on every credit card known to man, gold and platinum Visas, MasterCard's, American Express and even info on cash management accounts. We think they have direct access to every states DMV records. They have also attained information on bank accounts and all related information including social security numbers, mother's maiden names, DOB's, and birthplaces to coordinate with the driver's license numbers. We believe they receive complete up-to-date print outs of information on a daily basis and again, we have no proof." Vanessa listened intently.

"Do we have any clues, where or how they might be accessing this information?" Vanessa inquired.

"Not even the slightest," Donald continued. "We know they rob banks and nothing for under $100,000.00 and sometimes capping out at up to $500,000.00 on better days. We've arrested three people in a four-year period whom we suspect were affiliated with this ring. They didn't talk. They were intelligent, professional, and experts in understanding of the law. They had exceptional attorneys, relinquished no information, and exhibited no fear."

"Are the ones you arrested still in jail?" Vanessa probed.

"They all made bail and disappeared."

"Trust me, once I start bringing things to a head, there will be someone who won't want to do the time, and they'll turn in state's evidence. Anyway, if nobody is talking, how do you know these particular people worked for the same organization?"

"Well, we really don't know for sure. We're assuming this by the quality of work that was confiscated when they got arrested. The quality is unmistakable."

Donald responded.

"So, listen Dayton let me get this straight. There are really no facts that an organization exists. For all we know, all these people could be coincidentally buying the work at the same place," Vanessa asserted.

"Anything is a possibility at this point. They are either skillful at making credit cards and driver's licenses to perfection, or the cards came straight from the bank card center and the DMV. They could have someone on the inside doing it. We've had businesses examine the work and they couldn't identify whether it was or wasn't their own. We've pulled this guy Carson and his partner in before on bullshit, hoping we could find something, not a damn thing. We have a gut feeling he's the head of this outfit, but the department has never been able to make a damn thing stick. We didn't even have enough evidence to hold him twenty-four hours, much less a conviction. We couldn't hit him with charges for money owed on late library books. They were as clean as white clothes in bleach water. The only thing I know for sure is he's giving me severe migraine sort of pain but in my ass. He's made our agency look like a bunch of amateurs.

"If we don't solve this case soon The Director of National Intelligence is going to step in on this." Donald added. He threw up his hands in disgust.

"Look Vanessa, we must have financial records. We need to substantiate where this Carson operates from, the location or locations. If there is one place or more than one place, where the hell is it or where the hell are they? Shit, even if he operates from the back seat of a car, where is it parked? How many people does he employ, if any, because the people we think are affiliated with him managed to evaporate on us. As much as I would like to blame the lack of allotted man-hours on our failure to solve this case, I can't. He's got way too much going on to pin him down. We had and lost a direct inside lead on someone we thought might be connected to this organization. This particular incident took place recently here in L.A., but the same scenarios have occurred from coast to coast. This case was reported to us. Apparently, this guy, Paul Stevens, was working for Crombie and Lynch. He was an excellent employee, credentials in place, a remarkable resume, and he recruited three new multi-million dollar clients to the company in less than a month. He was a verified graduate of an Ivy League college. The company didn't find out until after his suspicious resignation that all the withdrawals he conducted were fraudulent. After a month on the job, mind you, and a week after he departed, they discovered that he might be an alleged accomplice to the disappearance of five hundred thousand dollars from a couple named Taylor. That happened a few days ago and another 250,000 dollars was stolen from a couple named Watson. This all happened in the short time Stevens was with the company."

"He handed them that kind of money and they walked out of the building?" Vanessa inquired.

"It happened on three separate occasions.   Here's the conundrum, He gave large sums of money to two different couples who looked exactly like the people who owned the accounts. All the staff in the office attested to the fact that they looked identical to their clients.   The employees see these people all the time, and a lot of them have known the Watson's and the Taylor's personally for a number of years."

"Wait a minute. Hold on. Are they wearing some kind of mask to look like the people they are robbing is that what you are saying?"

"Not just look like them, walk, talk, sit, sign their names, dress, everything. So much so, that the real clients would have been suspects if they had not been able to produce concrete evidence on their whereabouts doing the time of robberies. It's a good thing they had real evidence, because if the clients did have to go to court there would be no way they could have proved that wasn't them on the surveillance tapes.   They did notice that Mrs. Watson's loud-mouthed, obnoxious husband ordered more money than he ever had before, which was odd considering he's a borderline miser. This one revelation developed during Agent Johnson's questioning. Then of course it was, '*Oh boy, how could we have possibly missed that?*' After further investigation, we found the <u>real</u> couple vacationing in the Caribbean during the time of the withdrawal. The

Taylor's scam was handled identically, except that they had been in Europe. Transactions like these have been reported in investment firms and banks here in L.A., Chicago, and New York. They are connected and we have to prove it. An exceptionally qualified new hire doles out hundreds of thousands of dollars to clients who look like the owners of billion dollar portfolios, while the real owners are out of the country. Without notice, the new hire disappears along with his elite group of impersonators. Leaving no evidence, we've dusted for fingerprints in all the institutions that were victimized and we can't get a read on these strange prints. There are no clues, no particles of hair, no nothing. Even if we could locate this Stevens guy who gave them the money it wouldn't matter because he followed company procedures. We have no proof that he was involved and all his credentials checked out. In Mr. Steven's case, he was the new guy on the block acting at the behest of his experienced, co-workers who assured him `that the people who got robbed' were exceptional customers and informed him to fully accommodate their needs. Everything was done within company guidelines and policies meaning, 'give them anything they could possibly want and no questions asked'. Mr. Stevens stayed within the guidelines to avoid stepping on toes, so I guess it would be fair to say he left the company in good standing. Can't really figure out the details, but one thing is for sure; the money is gone, Stevens is gone and the culprit's are gone," Donald stated matter-of- fact.

"Do you think Mr. Stevens may have been in on it with any of the employees who are still at the company?" Vanessa quizzed.

"We don't know. We think it is strange that an employee of his caliber would go thru weeks of rigorous protocol to get hired, work for one month, and then disappear off the face of the planet. Giving up lucrative pay and a bright future in a jobless market doesn't add up," Agent Robert concluded.

"I can't begin to tell you how many times we've had surveillance on these people and for months federal and state agents have made attempts to bug Carson's house, but there were no phones. We've gotten warrants, raided several locations that we thought he was operating from, and the joke was on us. I can't stress enough, Vanessa, that it is absolutely imperative that you get photographs of financial records, documentation, something to verify what he's doing with all this money that oddly disappears and never resurfaces in the system. In fact, all we do know is what Carson is not doing," said Donald.

"Oh well, now, that should solve the large majority of my problems. What is he not doing with it?" repeated Vanessa.

"No drugs, gambling, prostitution, weapons or living large." Donald said.

"How do you know that?" Michael chimed in.

"Because we've had countless investigations by the U.S. Drug Enforcement Agency, the state and local police, the Internal Revenue Service, the U.S. attorney, and various local district attorneys. He's only been arrested twice and that was when he was in his 20's. Someone at the top who he's had in his pocket all these years had either cleared him or he's unusually skillful.   I swear this guy must have a guardian angel. You must find out who's in his pocket. He must have half the police department on his payroll.   He might even be employing bigger people than that, like Senators or Governors," explained Donald.

"Which would explain why he's almost invisible. Not being seen is the number one component of developing longevity as a successful career criminal.   So, the only reason you think this Carson is head man –in- charge is a gut feeling only?" Vanessa asked.

"Please don't remind me," Donald buried his head in his hands and in a continuously motion, raked through the sprigs of hair on his head.   "No, not only a gut, he spends a lot of time here in New York and Chicago.   When he was arrested it was for fraudulent credit cards this same type of perfection and a beef he allegedly took for someone else.   He's never had a legal job.   Shit, I don't know. Check his taxes, TRW, or if he's negligent in his child support payments. Look at everything.   Oh, hold on, don't unbuckle your seatbelt yet. This is only a pause in the ride. When they say, '*save the best for last,'* this last shit I'm about to tell you is what made that expression graduate from another cliché to a classic ole' adage." Dayton found his own disbelief in the information amusing.   He removed his glasses, rolled up his sleeves and delivered the remains of his report with chuckles that sounded like drum rolls.

"In every community we've tracked Carson, every person we've questioned about him, they all shared in the opinion that he possessed the makings of a patron saint. A ridiculously overwhelming number of people gave nothing but the utmost rave reviews about him. The compliments he received were vast coming from helpless old ladies to little girls jumping rope. All the neighborhood kids volunteered that he promotes education and abstinence from drugs. Donald raked the sprigs back in place and rearranged his files.

"Well, that's all I have. Here are their photos and the boxes on the floor is everything we have gathered so far." He jumped off the stool and rushed over to hand Vanessa the outsized stack of files. She sprang to her feet and took his place on the high stool. "They're all yours, have a look at it kid, I gotta go. Review everything, but please don't call me unless it's absolutely necessary. I really don't want to see this case again until it's ready to be filed in our case - closed and resolved vault," He said, as he headed towards the door.

"Well, if that's what you want, that's exactly what I will deliver. You can count on it," Vanessa promised him.

"You're gonna get your wish on this one, too, and work with minimum backup. If things get too heated, I can pull in Peter and someone from other offices.

The two detectives collected their belongings to leave. Vanessa looked at the photos and studied the list of people who were allegedly affiliated with Carson.

Robert peered over Vanessa's shoulder. Right away he began to forward her any pertinent information he could recall.

"The women he allegedly worked with have some unique names. I've checked to see if either of them have past records under those names or aliases---drew a total blank on all three.

"Is December her legal name?" asked Vanessa.

"From birth."

"You mean to tell me this is her birth name?"

"December Benton, Lawrence peered over her other shoulder.

Vanessa leafed through the pictures and carefully analyzed each of them. Robert called off the names of each person on the eight by ten photographs as Vanessa turned them over, one by one, along with their rap sheets. "Now that's December Benton and Holiday McCormick, Vincent Holt and Thomas Winfield." He handed Vanessa another picture and said, "Wow this Farren Lockhart, a real cutie pie, huh?"

"Oh, much more than cute Johnson, adorable even," Vanessa commented. She continued to flip through photos while discussing the alleged nature of each person's involvement. "You have told me everyone's name, except for the main two guys. Is it a secret or are you saving the best for last?" she said lightheartedly. As she finished her sentence she flipped over the last two photos, her facial expression flat lined and her heart did the same. It was noticeable to both men how the photos swept her expression blank and in a blink of an eye, the color in her face drained. The pencil she was nibbling on fell on the floor.

"These are the two men we allegedly think are pulling the strings. This is Malone Carson, and that's his alleged business partner, Grey Young," Robert said. Both agents stepped aside and waited for a response from Vanessa, but none was forthcoming.

"So, what do you think about these guys?" Special Agent Robert asked. Vanessa couldn't speak. She couldn't lift or lower her head away from the photos. Neither Agent purposely reacted to her radical change in behavior. She couldn't make the slightest eye contact with either of them. She felt paralyzed. She muffled, "I'm speechless. Please leave. I need some time alone," she begged.

Special Agents Robert and Lawrence gave her a quick once over and then glanced at each other. After communicating silently with each other they followed her request and left. In slow motion, Vanessa sank to the floor and curled into a fetal position. As she fell, she knocked over the podium and all the file folders scattered around her. Vanessa was so overwhelmed by the irony; she wasn't cognizant of her surroundings anymore.

Vanessa's eyes shut, stomach queasy, sighs of despair and so traumatized she blacked out on a sea of files.

Chapter 16

When Vanessa came out of the shower she stood on her tiptoes in the center of her room and stared out the window, spellbound by the movements of a small spider busily weaving its web. She was so despondent since she had left the agency that she didn't notice the things that normally inspired her like the vibrant beauty of a full moon suspended in a cloudless, dark blue, night sky, or the myriad of stars that looked strategically placed. She didn't feel the periodic, gentle gusts of air from the cool, September evening breeze.

When the spider no longer intrigued her, she nervously clicked her nails and wiped the corners of her mouth. A depressing void overwhelmed her to the point that it had become impossible for her to recapture the exhilarating feeling she had reveled in just four hours ago.

Distraught about the assignment, Vanessa wasn't able to get a handle on her emotions. Dressing her naked, dripping wet body was an effort. She was sprawled on the edge of the bed with her heels resting on the frame and her head lodged into a pillow. Instantly, she was fixated by the words written on the top of a puzzle box sitting on the floor. Vanessa summoned the strength to pick it up to read. *'Taj Mahal, level: advanced. One thousand seventy-seven pieces,'* were all scattered on the floor. Vanessa's life felt like that puzzle, hard decisions, thoughts adrift and shattered into bits.

Prudence had worked on the puzzle for a couple of days. Three pieces were connected. Prudence had insisted on setting up the puzzle in Vanessa's room hoping that she would help her complete it. Prudence felt that puzzles were exercises in patience. Vanessa pondered; how *working puzzles relaxed Prudence to the same degree they frustrated her. She wondered how two people could see the same thing and formulate totally different points of view. No matter how much they frustrated Prudence, she received gratification from starting them and seeing it through to completion. That is the attitude Vanessa felt she was going to have to adapt on this case. She, on the other hand, felt it was a huge waste of time and effort to work so long at putting something together only to take it apart again. She stared at the picture on the box for so long that her eyes went out of focus, She pondered about the things in life that are temporary, including life itself. Nothing should be done with the intention of lasting forever that's what creates disappointment.'*

When the doorbell rang it jarred her body and disrupted her self-induced trance. Every dormant jitter and mixed emotion in her body were setting off shocks like live electrical wires. Vanessa pondered her interludes with Grey. He single handedly restored her faith in romance, blushing, explosions in the heart, and making love. Until him, those were things that existed only in movies and romance novels. Being with him was the first time she had giggled and the last time she had wished a date would never end.

Feeling listless, she made her way to the front door, without asking or looking through the peephole; she flung the door open, "Prue?" Her face dropped.

"Okay then, don't even to pretend you're happy to see me." Prudence saw instantly that Vanessa was deeply upset about something and didn't want to be bothered.

"I couldn't find my key, and I have to pee, bad." Prudence, pranced, hopped, and squeezed her legs together all the way to the restroom. "I think I left them here." Seconds later, Prudence hopped out of the bathroom walking in baby steps, trying not to trip over her pants and underwear cradled around her ankles. "Why are you in your robe?"

"Got back late, runnin' behind," Vanessa said just to be saying something. "Why are your pants now wrapped around your ankles?"

"Cause, girl, I didn't quite make it all the way, and this mess is wet. As bad as I had to go, I'm surprised I got any of it in the toilet. Where are your boyfriends? Did they come yet?"

Vanessa shrugged her shoulders as she headed back to her room, "How was the date last night." Vanessa inquired as an after thought.

"Not worth mentioning," Prudence responded. She took a second look at Vanessa and asked, "Girl, do you feel okay? You look kinda flushed. Has the excitement of Grey's arrival *finally* taken its toll?" From the stairs, Vanessa gave a deflated nod. Twenty minutes later, the upbeat ditty on the doorbell chimed again. Vanessa ignored it. Prudence galloped down the stairs, two at a time to the front door. "Well, well as I live and breathe. Do come in. We have been expecting you two for the longest." Malone stepped forward, removed his fedora, and handed her a huge, fragrant, pastel colored floral arrangement.

"Oh, Vanessa will love these," Prudence said with exuberance.

"These aren't for no damn Vanessa, these are for you, baby." Malone grabbed and hugged her.

"I don't think I have ever seen any of these types of flowers before. They are exceptionally gorgeous," Prudence complimented.

"Why of course you haven't. I had a business associate of mine fly these in from Blossoms, an exclusive flower shop in Chicago especially for you two. Your reputation precedes you. My name is Malone, Malone Carson. How have you been my cousin's sister and best friend all these years and this is the first time we've met?"

"Conflicting schedules." Prudence said admiring the flowers. Prudence looked into Malone's eyes. Her schoolgirl blush was all he needed to confirm that she appreciated the gesture. Malone ran to his car and came back with another arrangement of flowers.

"Now baby, these are for my cousin." He handed them to her. Without an introduction, Grey slid by both of them and took a seat on the couch.

"Prudence is your name right?" asked Grey looking like a frozen, pop-eyed cadaver, gritting his teeth.

"Right," Malone responded and pointed to Grey. "That, over there, is Grey, Grey Young, that's my brother." Prudence strained to ogle Malone inconspicuously. She couldn't keep her eyes off of him. Malone grabbed her hand and led her over to the couch to sit with him and Grey,

"Baby, you can stare at me if you want to, 'cause I want to stare at you, too." He cackled. Prudence's face turned tomato red from embarrassment. She jumped up and said, "Oh, that's right, you all haven't seen Vanessa, yet!"

"No." Malone answered. "And Grey's so damn wired, I don't even think he's cognizant we've arrived."

"Look Malone, don't start that shit, 'cause we got an audience man. So, where is Vanessa?" Grey asked enthusiastically.

"She's upstairs.   I'll get her," Prudence responded enthusiastically.

"Don't run all the way up their baby. Call her ass down here," Malone teased and cackled.

Vanessa stood in the closet in her pastel pink jeans, matching form fitting top and suede loafers. She laid her head against Patrick and said in frustration, "I sure the hell wish it was someone else downstairs, some new shit, instead of going backwards to this mess. So, Patrick, is this some serious bullshit I've got goin' here or what?" She stepped away, pivoted around in a circle and asked, "So how do I look? I knew you were going to say that, you always think I look fantastic." She blew him a kiss, took a deep breath and forced her mind to switch gears. Now was the time that she had to remember and remain focused on the reasons she had chosen this career.

When Vanessa finally made it into the F.B.I., Venice was so proud of her. He felt like his daughter was graduating instead of his mother. She, too, felt the role reversal because she had desperately wanted to make Venice proud of her, especially since his deadbeat father couldn't kick his habit. The first night Venice was brought home from the hospital Howard demonstrated his inability to cope with fatherhood. He complained his sleep was disrupted because of a hungry newborn. Venice's father, Attorney Howard Hudson made the decision to divorce after only eighteen months.

Prudence made her way upstairs to get Vanessa, half way up, Vanessa appeared.

"You regrouped and refreshed pretty fast." When they walked back to the living room, Vanessa and Grey's eyes locked and they remained in a trance until Malone ran interference.

"Hello, hello." He snapped his fingers.   Prudence was amused. Vanessa stood motionless, and she said softly, "Well, well, eight years, and we finally meet again." She nervously picked at her nails and held her head down. Malone heard her comment and flashed a bright smile in Grey's direction.

"Damn man, that seems unreal, eight years gone in a flash! Seems like eight months." Malone briskly walked over to hug Vanessa and gave her the arrangement of rare flowers.

Grey and Vanessa exchanged smiles. They felt as uncomfortable around each other as an elephant would feel doing a ballet in pink slippers and a tutu.

"Hey baby, how are you?" Grey removed a handkerchief from the inside of his jacket and wiped the sweat from his forehead as he got up from the couch.

"You look gorgeous," He said in an attempt to melt the ice.

"You look good too, Grey. You are high as a Georgia pine and growing a few colored hairs that match your name, but good."

"What does that mean, high as a Georgia pine?" Prudence asked.

"It means he looks like he's in a cocaine stupor." Malone answered.

Finally Grey made his way to hug Vanessa, she was stiff and unresponsive. Prudence and Malone sneaked away and settled comfortably in the kitchen. Malone kicked off his shoes, perched himself on a stool, and leaned across the counter and rested his head on his propped up hand. Malone watched Prudence's every move.

The two of them made eye contact and Malone said, "I'm not part of the boy's club. I don't try to sneak off away from my woman or any of that stuff. I like finding the right one and being with her."

"Well, I'm gonna marry you then 'cause you're the kind of man I've dreamt of having for years," she joked.

Prudence casted a lasting impression on Malone because of the natural charm that oozed from her pores. Her alluring, firm behind, petite waist, healthy chest, bowed legs and mid-western candor was a death trap for a man like him.

The kitchen smelled of fresh roasted percolated coffee. The counter was covered with Prudence's gourmet edibles. Malone's face beamed as she served him berries with fresh whipping cream, espresso and a warm roast beef sandwich on a crusty bread. Malone savored every bite as he watched Prudence whip up a homemade lemon meringue pie. Prudence was in her element. The two of them blended as well as the fluffy meringue she scooped out of the mixer. They couldn't get enough of each other.

Malone was euphoric.

Grey gently pulled Vanessa into his arms with a passionate and firm hug that appeared to be a long awaited release of desire. When she pulled back he stroked her hair and the ice thawed. She absorbed his display of affection returning every ounce of the gesture with equal intensity. A distinguishable glow of happiness seeped on her face.

Their emotions and heavy breathing were flowing in sync. They moved close to one another to hug tighter. She stroked the top of his head and the faintest smile appeared on her face. She clutched his face with both hands and pulled his mouth to hers. They began slowly, and within seconds, were engulfed in a passionate display of affection. Vanessa looked into his eyes and whispered,

"I still love you Grey, and I don't care how much I try to deny it or stop, I can't do it. I just love you. Guess I always will. He grabbed her up in his arms and squeezed her tightly, reciprocating, "I have never loved anyone else. You're the only woman I have ever truly loved. I know we'll be able to work through our differences this time. Everything is going to work out for us this time." Grey reassured her.

He reached into the lapel of his jacket and pulled out a gift-wrapped box. Vanessa opened it revealing a large pair of two-inch hoop earrings. "Are these real diamonds all the way around?" Grey laughed, "Inside and out. You know how I roll."

"Thank you Grey, I love them, they are exquisite." She grabbed his hand and laid it inside the palm of hers, rubbing it softly. He attempted to situate himself in a comfortable position but was just to hyped he couldn't get comfortable.

"Baby, where is the restroom?" Vanessa pointed to the restroom and watched him until he closed the door. Grey was probably going in there to get higher Vanessa deduced.

She reached under the coffee table and pulled out her cigarettes and a lighter. After a drag, she reclined on the couch. She kept her eye on the bathroom door waiting for her guest to return. She mused about how her case had gotten easier. A devilish contentment lurked on her face as she contemplated, *'this went a lot smoother then I had planned. I'll cut to the chase and get Grey to show me everything and introduce me to everybody. Instead of rationalizing how everything should fit, the challenge for me will be to recognize those things that don't fit and get into some acceptance. My only real dilemma is what am I going to do about my heart.'*

She couldn't concentrate on devising a plan because of the loud cackling and rollicking in the kitchen, that interrupted her train of thought. The fact that they were getting along so well, lent clarity to Vanessa that it might be better if Prudence knew nothing about her new assignment for now.

Vanessa started to have mixed emotions about whether she should have taken this case.

Chapter 17

The onset of daylight and brisk morning air ushered in the bustling sounds of printers and fax machines cranking out data, ringing cell phones, and exchanges of conversation. The sixty-members of the Los Angeles crew were all on deck for a rare mandatory meeting at the Los Angeles headquarters.

The five bedrooms, two offices, and maid's quarters on the massive first floor had been converted to private offices. At the rear of the building next to the no-frills breakfast nook was what the employees referred to as *"the stainless steel kitchen."* A mouth, watering aroma of *everything breakfast* lingered from the kitchen and permeated the manor. Chef Renee viewed the eccentric beauty of her kitchen much in the same fashion in which she viewed herself. She considered her thin frame, natural silver hair and gently aging, walnut-colored complexion as her transformation into a classic beauty. To onlookers, it was over the hill, she felt it was living life on the easy side. When mandatory meetings were scheduled, Chef Renee's presence was compulsory as well.

The Trio, Holiday, December and Farren sat in a large glass, private office on one of the lower levels of estate, it was off limits to the staff. The large almond shaped Plexiglas desk in the center of the office was stacked high with, books, papers, file folders, and junk that rendered the unit disorderly. The women attentively jotted down pertinent information and opened stacks of mail from their inside sources. Perforated printouts continuously emerged from the fax machines and printers that were connected to an up-to-date mainframe computer.   Unwanted printouts were immediately disposed of in one of three monstrous paper shredders.   Holiday rolled her eyes in disgust at Farren.

"Oh girl how could you. That monstrosity you are wearing is nauseating. Can't you ever wear anything besides those God–awful, hideous ass sweat suits, and as ugly as it is, you have the nerve to have shoes to match. I'd rather put on a tin beak and pick shit with the birds than wear that shit, Holiday said conceitedly."

"Here you go. Now you know girl this diva can break super bad when she wants to, so why does it bother you, Holiday?" December mediated.

Farren never looked up from the printer, "You are truly wasting your time explaining anything to Holiday, December. How in the world would you expect someone with a full face of makeup, who looks like they have been sculpted to understand someone wearing a leisure ensemble? It's questionable if you are getting any oxygen at all in those tight unflattering cheap jeans." Farren rebutted.

" A pant that fits and flatters a woman." Holiday corrected her.

"And a plaid coat with three inch high heels all before 7:30 a.m. You go girl."

"Burberry and Fendi. Not just any coat. I know you don't know designers. They aren't at the 99 cents store where you must have gotten those sweat pants."

"Whatever Holiday. I can out dress most woman on the planet, when I feel like it. And that means you too."

Farren looked at December and they both smirked. Holiday looked at December and said,

"Oh no girl, I know you did not, with those tired burgundy jeans that make you look like a truck driver. And Farren, if you ever make the effort to comb out that tangled ass horsetail and succeed, it would be history made at the Rose. Why is it all you bitches with long hair think you can wear it any kind of way and it looks cute. That shit looks unkempt."

"If you want to get into a debate about hair, shouldn't you at least have some?"

When Holiday walked away, December and Farren shared a wink at each other. The three resumed their positions silently at the printers. Holiday continued,

"And don't play with me either, winking behind my damn back like that, shit. You know it really wouldn't hurt if either of you took a little more pride in your appearances. Apply some make up. At least look clean."

Malone and Grey drove to headquarters using back roads. Malone's office was a modest two-story guesthouse on a secluded area of the property. When they arrived, Malone headed upstairs to his office and Grey went to check on things in the front office. When Grey arrived Vincent and the Trio were working. Vincent caught a glimpse of Grey out of his peripheral and zealously walked over to shake his hand. The Trio also greeted Grey, but exerted far less excitement.

"Hey, hey, so, what's happening on the east coast, my man?" Vincent inquired.

Vincent Holt was light brown, 5'10, and slender. He had keen features, brown hair and eyes.   His look overall was forgettable. He was a Harvard law school graduate and a man who could stifle you with his intelligence or baffle you with his bullshit. Grey knew Malone really would have preferred Vincent as his business partner, but since he started with Malone he was confident Malone would always remain loyal to him.

When the Trio heard Malone's voice summoning Vincent over the intercom, they shut off the main computer terminal and took off to Malone's hideaway office with the excitement of kids en route to a candy store. Malone gave and received heartfelt hugs and kisses to all three girls when they arrived.

Malone pulled Vincent close to speak in his ear in an inaudible voice; he firmly patted him on the back.

"That's how we do it, man. Good work on that Taylor situation, Crombie and Lynch damn good work, man. I don't know anyone who could have pulled off Paul Stevens any better than you. From now on, it's nothing but working in the field for you. I know you don't like holding down Camouflage and Blossoms when Holiday and December can't be there, I'm turning that over to Michael. You are now our front runner."

"Is that good with you?"

"Outstanding. Thank you."

They shook hands again and Vincent left his office.

Chef Renee announced on the intercom, "Guess what ladies and gents the time has finally arrived for Chef Renee's long awaited breakfast fiesta." The staff stampeded through the building from every direction. "Take your time folks it's breakfast not the last supper." Renee said as she greeted everyone at the door and then served them all. They poured into the seats and picked from her breakfast entrees, lobster eggs benedict, ham and spinach quiche, Belgian waffles, caramelized banana French toast, and fresh fruit. "Please enjoy your breakfast," The chef said pleasantly. The crew inhaled the food like navy men at sea.

Malone, Grey, and the Trio didn't dine with the crew. Chef Renee fixed their plates; Farren retrieved them from the dumb waiter and took them to the office. Grey sat his normal distance away from the group. Holiday then joined December and Farren as they gathered around Malone's desk. Instantly, they bombarded him with questions and updated him with information. They discussed, deliberated daily business, laughed and ribbed each other like kids at recess. When Grey entered, the tone changed like the principal had entered. The Trio took their seats around the huge, old oak desk submerged with paperwork.

Frequent practice had enabled him to become a master at showing his contempt like that of a four year old. On rare occasions, he enhanced his child-like act by pouting.

"Well wonderful ones, brief me on what's been going on with all the work I set up before I left," Malone inquired as he picked at his food and made pictures in the plate with his fork.

December rushed to swallow the hot food.

"We incurred an ever so slight problem on the Taylor case. We were only able to work one play because we received notice from research they were coming back early. They came back this past Monday instead of next Monday as scheduled."

"So you had two situations, Taylor and Caldwell?"

"Not exactly," December spoke between little bites. "Vincent retrieved enough information on a mark named Watson while he was there. We made up a profile, faced up a team and sent them in to get another two hundred and fifty thousand, which is all we could do on such short notice."

Malone checked off items listed on his steno pad confirming the current status in each category. "So the Taylor's was 500, Caldwell was 175 and Watson 250, for a total of 925. Not bad for a three days work. Great job ladies."

"And what about payroll?"

"Out and on time. I sent out the loan payments, balanced and closed the books for this month," Farren gulped down her juice. You'll also be happy to hear that we've finally finished paying off three of the largest loans for the housing projects. And received approval to build another trade school or university.

Malone sat back in his chair and beamed humbly. He played, twirled, mixed, stacked and shuffled the uneaten food on his plate until it looked pulverized. He sat up straight and said,

"Now, let's go over the new changes in payroll that I've deliberated about long and hard."

"Long and hard, interesting," December mocked him. Everyone laughed. Malone cackled the longest.

"I have finally worked it out tentatively of course. We'll review them. I want to get solid feedback from all of you and providing all our responses are positive, we can implement the new plans for the crew ASAP. I want you Grey, to inform the employees of their new benefits and how it's going to be implemented when we are finished. First off, there's some not-so-bad news and some great news. The not-so-bad news is as follows: All the bank jobs and investment company rates done by the crew, will have to be reduced from $15,000.00 dollars per play to $14,000.00. For our informants and research department we'll be reducing from $10,000.00 to $9,000.00. Now, here's the moment you've all been waiting for, the great news. As we all know, a couple of our people have experienced some pretty tedious and lengthy legal problems in the past. I've had to intervene by sending my mouthpiece out or a random lawyer to get them out of whatever situation they were in by using money from the organization or my own personal funds. Sometimes I get repaid, but in most cases I don't. People don't have enough money to cover all these high ass legal expenses. If they do have money saved, those lawyers will take every dime of it. For that reason, I've elected to reduce salaries by as little as possible. In turn, we will set up a fund to cover the entire cost of our employees legal expenses, bail, attorney fees and taking care of their families and all household expenses until they are released." Malone glanced at all four of their expressions for positive reactions, suggestions, or feedback.

The Trio burst into hearty, down in the gut laughter. Barely able to catch her breath Holiday said, "You can't be serious about this, right?"

"And why would you think I wouldn't be serious or have a reason not to be taken seriously?" Malone quizzed.

Holiday continued, "You deliberated on it long and hard Malone?

Now this must be a joke, right?

"A joke, what's funny about it?" Malone was curious.

"Taking on those kind of expenses can do us in." December calculated numbers.

"We don't have a lot of employees who get busted for one thing. What has it been, maybe two in eight years, and none since we started facing up. I've told you again and again that we should feel more than willing and certainly responsible to provide benefits Holiday. We as people have to love, and look out for each other. That is why our planet and all the systems in it are in total chaos. There is no love. It's all about me, me, me, me, me." Malone said humbly.

After the Trio sat back and digested his words, December said, "Malone what we are doing is not our life's work if we were a legal corporation, I could see it."

"Everybody knows that was Farren's original idea. Good work," Holiday complimented.

"Was it really necessary for you to clarify that?" Farren protested.

December changed course, "I set up the construction workers to meet with you at 9:00 am day after tomorrow."

"I did all the reordering for the boutique in New York, and if I must say so myself, we have some outstanding winter stock. We purchased a fabulous line of furs, both mid and floor length."

"Fur?" Malone's eyebrows shot up. "I don't want PETA on

our backs." Holiday chimed in, "I'll handle that should it happen. I also delegated an extra allowance from the budget to pay a buyer I know to go to Paris and select pieces for fall since we couldn't get away this time. We also added the most original and innovative new line of clothing and accessories I have ever seen called 'one of a kind.' I am selling the line for a new designer on consignment. That being said, the budget for the boutique is overall quite a bit more substantial this month, but the receipts show that there has been a consistent surge in the business, and the inventory is out of the door as quickly as December and I can stock it," Holiday informed Malone.

"Who would have thought it? That's damn good news." Malone smiled pleasantly adding,

"One day all we might have is legitimate businesses to substantiate our income."

"That wouldn't be the worst that could happen to us. I would love for all of us to transition into legitimate businesses. That's what we should be starting now instead of a plan for lawyers. When you start treating crime as a way of life, that's what gets you in trouble. We've got a little paper, businesses, P.A.W. is set, and your talking about how we should be treating people right and looking out for each other. How long do you want to keep stealing from innocent people?" December stared at Malone. "Frankly, I'm ready to get out." December voiced. Malone stared at December.

"I hope I never have to wonder what life would be like

without you acting as my nerve racking, unauthorized conscience. You are right though."

"Maybe we should consider opening a chain of those boutiques." Holiday offered as a suggestion. She continued, "By the way, the new sign you ordered was finally installed. Now *Camouflage* is in lights. The black and white neon colors turned out to be very subtle and elegant like I predicted. Did you have a chance to see it?"

Malone rocked about in the swivel chair as he tapped his gold pen nervously on the desk.

"Yes, It really gave the front of the store a face lift and made the boys in the office feel more secure since for some reason they always felt the cops thought it was a place to launder money. They don't feel like the boutique is a front for the office anymore since it has taken on a life of it's own." Malone got up and paced.

"One last note. The three of you start planning for our annual party for the staff. Since it is going to be at the beach this year, we need to do it before it gets too cold. Also, the line of furs has to go back. No fur. December, I'll strongly consider your concerns before making a final decision. My closing remarks ladies, I have finally responded to your long requested proposal Farren and, on a serious note, it's brilliant, or at least it was until December hit me with this new shit. As much as I hate to admit it, you were right, it should have been in place years ago. Luckily, no one has faced any serious troubles that we couldn't handle or deal with up to this point. So Grey, go inform the staff of our now alleged vision. We may find that staff won't like it due to the salary cut. "

The Trio closed their note pads and gathered their other belongings. Farren and Holiday exchanged a devilish grin. Farren's serene voice said, "My, my, age does bring about a change."

"Hopefully," Malone responded to her sarcasm.

With all the gestures Grey could muster to show his lack of interest, he nonchalantly picked at his nails and asked in a cocky tone of voice, "Is that spot on 82nd and Broadway or 83rd?"

His comment rubbed Malone the wrong way and in one brisk motion, an explosion vibrated the silence from the slam he planted on the desk with his hand,

"That's it. No more. I can't believe you ask these stupid ass questions. And what's more ironic is that you expect an answer. This, my friend, is the last stupid question you'll ever be allowed to ask in a business meeting. It's over Grey you got that? This discussion is over. Now, would you like to do us the honors and wait downstairs with the rest of the staff until the grown ups finish this meeting?"

Unconcerned by his remarks, Grey calmly said, "Relax man, its okay. I'll stay here, if you don't mind, 'cause I need to know, and have as much right to be here as everyone else in this meeting."

"Let me rephrase what I said." Distinctly and slowly Malone repeated, "Wait downstairs until this meeting is over. That wasn't a question; it was an order," Malone commanded.

"Then let me rephrase what I said. You either, one, apparently don't know that I don't take orders or, two, didn't hear what I said." Grey mocked the distinct and slow voice Malone used.

"Now, let me repeat this for the last time and please, listen closely, cause repetition isn't my strong suit. No, I am not leaving until the meeting is over. Blue, look, I do what I have to do and I have to do what's right for me. And you, of all people, should be able to understand that, and if not," he shrugged his shoulders with outstretched palms and let out a sigh, "Oh well."

Farren, Holiday, and December gasped as their eyes locked on Malone. "Oh here they go again," Holiday, remarked.

Malone walked around to the front of the desk where Grey leaned back in his chair with an arrogant smirk displayed proudly on his face. Malone comfortably anchored himself against the desk, which positioned him directly in front of Grey. Malone dropped his head down as if he was looking at the floor. The Trio scooted themselves to the front of their chairs and turned all the way around, engrossed about how this bout would be resolved. Malone's face was creased as heavily as a pitted prune when he asked, "And what would be the reason that you feel you need to stay. You have the nerve to ask where the store is when it was your black ass that was assigned to oversee it in the first damn place?" Grey looked around the room as if he were searching for the person Malone might be talking to. The women remained transfixed in their seats.

"So check this out. My suggestion to you, Grey would be to get up and get the fuck out and I mean now, before this situation takes a turn for real ugly. I have had it. It's over. Done. From now on, the only part of this organization that you'll be a part of is when I have an assignment for you, and if you keep pushing, it'll be cleaning toilets. Other than that, you've got nothing coming. So, you need not even go downstairs."

Grey casually sat up and watched the reactions of Holiday, Farren and December with his normal, arrogant disposition intact. The coldness in Grey's eye's transformed into a vicious stare. His face muscles tightened as his anger escalated. He briefly looked at each of the Trio, then, stared at Malone, and spoke softly so they wouldn't hear,

"You can't kick me out, you might want to think about kicking me out. You all think you can disrespect me like this and I'm not going to do a damn thing about it, well, think again. Fuck this Blue, I'm gonna make you all regret this day and the day you met me. You all are laughing now, but trust me I am going to have the last laugh on all this bullshit."

"Well man, that was about the best goodbye speech I've ever heard. Nobody in here gives a damn. Now, come on, what's it gonna be? Time is running out. Get out of this meeting." Malone demanded.

That was the first time the Trio had ever witnessed humiliation in Grey. He appeared to be disoriented and shocked as he witnessed

Malone transform into something unrecognizable. As much as they sincerely wanted to conjure up some semblance of emotion, they had shut down like electricity does during a power outage. From where the Trio sat, they were quite sure Grey's eyes were slightly tearing and appeared glassy in the distance. They sat comatose at the turn of events. A second later, they watched his mustache absorb water from his tearing eyes and running nose. As they looked closer, it was clear they were seeing symptoms related to his overindulgence in cocaine rather than any heartfelt emotion.

This being Grey's only source of income, he didn't know whether or not to save face, or turn the other cheek in disgrace.

Chapter 18

Vanessa had received authorization from within the agency for consensual monitoring. She drove to headquarters to meet with agent Edward Fairfield from the tech squad.

Lawrence had found a location where Vanessa could drop off the information she obtained as needed to him and Robert. They would in turn deliver the new found information back to the field office. After he finished his duties, he joined Vanessa at headquarters to inform her of the new location and assist her with the remainder of their assignment.

They waited for the late Special Agent Fairfield at Westwood Headquarters to come unlock the door to the huge, technical room. Once he finally arrived he escorted them inside. Stainless steel shelves covered all four walls from floor to ceiling, and were heavily stocked with newly state of the art equipment. There were digital cameras of every size and description. The voice-activated recorders were as small as a thimble, and others, the size of a jukebox. There were monitors, cameras, memory cards, microphones, jewelry, earpieces and belts. Any type of high tech top-secret equipment that was conceivable was there.

Vanessa and Lawrence sat at the table trying to gage who was most tired by who yawned most frequently. Carefully, the tech agent surveyed the intricate details and the overall appearance of the broaches, belt buckles, and other jewelry that lay inside a huge blue lined carrying case. Each of the jewels were designed to encase micro surveillance cameras and microphones.

"Vanessa, I know you want cameras. Are you going to want a transmitter or a recorder or both?" asked Thomas.

"They have dirty white collars Edward, not terrorist concealing weapons of mass destruction. The cameras and recorders are enough for now. I'll see how it goes though. If I need it later, we'll deal with it then." Vanessa responded defensively.

"I, for one, can't think of a damn thing I'd rather be doing at 7:30 in the morning," said Robert.

"You two couldn't have picked a more decent time than this?" Vanessa chimed.

"Don't act like this routine is a new addition to the usual one. If making this early is too much of a strain on you, perhaps you'll have to cut down on that wild nightlife of yours. What do you think you're supposed to do, haul all this shit out in the middle of the afternoon?" Thomas answered pompously.

After Vanessa selectively chose a wide variety of jewelry that housed everything from cameras to recorders and a couple of belts that she thought would match most of her wardrobe, she proceeded to be fitted for the body wiring Edward had prepared, so it would be ready if she needed it during the investigation. She and Edward recapped instructions until she was clear on every facet of the surveillance equipment. After several stressful hits and misses, she at last understood all of the functions. She reached for his hand as a gesture of closure on the session. Edward reciprocated. They shook hands.

"Thank you for your help and patience. This equipment is a lot more technical than some of the other I've used in the past. I can't keep up with the innovation. By the time you learn it, it changes." Vanessa said with a smile.

"Yeah, but the clarity and reception is flawless. Plus, it doesn't loose a generation until about the third copy," responded Edward.

"It clicked after only five takes," she winked.

"A record. I wish I could say that about the rest of these people. A lot of these old school agents I have worked with don't have the desire to grasp the basic steps of modern technology."

Vanessa got up and walked casually over to the locker to gather her belongings and observed how Lawrence had kept himself busy writing down step–by–step instruction schedules on a *things to remember* memo pad.

"For you, my dear," Lawrence said.

"You're much too sweet," Vanessa responded dryly.

"Vanessa, there is one last thing to remember about the broach's and buckles. When you activate the motionless camera, the sound responds automatically. You don't have to worry about installation or removal of any film. You have an alternate camera when the card is completed. You get three hours max on filming and because of its microscopic size, it must be unloaded in the lab, but you already know that. Give your co-case agent the camera when it's completed. We'll process it and give the camera right back to you within a day. Any problems, questions or remarks?"

"Look, this filming is one part of the job I don't like and you know that." Edward put one finger to his lips signaling her to hush.

"Grievances are not my area. If you don't like it you shouldn't have accepted the position of case agent on this assignment," he scolded.

"No, what I shouldn't haven't done is excepted you as a partner. I'm just hoping like hell I can do something as simple as aiming the damn thing straight, okay?" Vanessa whined.

Special Agent Lawrence and Edward laughed.

"That's the easiest part of all. A perfect idiot can aim straight," Lawrence jested.

"Well, if aiming is so damn easy, why after years of daily practice do men constantly pee all over the toilet and the floor?" She laughed - they stopped. Slightly repulsed by her lack of taste, yet certainly not surprised.

They gathered their belongings and left together.

Chapter 19

Malone's body had gone from a leisure rocking motion to a rapid shaking over his entire body. He awaited Grey's decision to exit in silence or be forced out and find alternative means of financial support once and for all.

Obviously, Malone and the Trio came to a unanimous decision, since nobody suggested a vote. The Trio never took sides against Malone whether they agreed with him or not.

Grey slid back in the chair and gave everybody the long, lingering, look of 'how could you do this to me?' Slowly, Grey got up and walked across the room. After he opened the door to leave, he turned around to look at them, only to find them eyeballing him with strained frowns. Malone's eyes and stony face remained directly fixated on Grey's vacuous, coked out face. Grey turned his back thoroughly disgusted. Malone dropped his eyes to the floor. Grey recognized that distinguishably soft, but deep, raspy tone in Malone's voice, which occurred when his steely patience had finally worn out. Grey wasn't afraid but respected him enough not to push him. He decided to leave without another word or any further eye contact with Malone.

Malone stared at the door, then back at the floor. He stood up and brushed himself off en route to his desk to continue the unfinished business.

"Sorry for the interruption. Shall we continue ladies?" He said soberly as if nothing had happened.

"You two are too funny. You go through all this and our black sheep brother will be back in the morning," Holiday said.

"Not in the morning, day after tomorrow morning. You know I can't get rid of him. He is invaluable to us. Who would deal with the staff if he left? I go off on him so much because he pisses me off. He stays so damn high on that damn shit all the time now and frankly I just don't know what to do." Malone spoke calmly.

"Not a damn thing you can do, he is a grown man. He will get high when he wants to and he won't stop until he wants to." December said to Malone.

"Really," said Farren. "I don't feel safe around him Malone. I have never heard Grey say anything like that. What did he mean when he said we'd regret this day?" Holiday interrupted, "Girl please, you should know by now it's those drugs talking, not Grey. He ain't gonna do a damn thing. He always says shit like that and he'll be back the next day like nothing ever happened."

Malone smiled reassuringly, "Boy, you all have some eagle ears. I have to watch what the hell I say around you three."

"Canine ears Malone. Eagles have great sight," said

December, and they all joined her in a light chuckle.

"Puleeese Malone, you're sayin' that shit, because you are the only person I have ever seen in my entire life who can sit right in the center of a group of people all bunched together, I mean, on top of each other like new born puppies, in a room so quiet that you could literally hear a feather fall, and the only person who can hear what your ass is saying clearly is the one you're directing your conversation to." Farren continued. "The entire group could be staring directly in your mouth and wouldn't understand one damn word."

Holiday stood up and cleared her voice as if she were going to give a speech.

Malone laid back in his chair, rested his elbows on the arms and propped his head on his clutched hands. He grinned with affection as he watched the Trio's playful antics."

"It's a skill he acquired because Malone hates it, and I mean with a fiery, red passion, to be fronted off. Wanna go for his buttons? Yell at him in a public place", December voiced.

"Malone taught himself to speak in a low tone because he never wanted the person he's talking to feel like they are being fronted off either." Farren added. When they finished their assessments, Malone turned to Farren somewhat preoccupied and said, " If you don't mind, please inform the staff that the meeting is cancelled."

"I don't mind conducting the meeting just this once,"

Holiday and Farren said at the same time.

"No interaction with the staff. Inform them of the new policies over the conference phone and tell them that a new memo will be issued as to what date we will reschedule, to discuss the new polices and procedures with them. Make sure Vincent gets his bonus for the Crombie and Lynch situation and commend him for taking the lead on the Watson's also." Holiday put her hands on her hips looked at Malone and said, "And?"

"And what?"

"Why don't we get a damn bonus and a pat on the back for a job well done? It wasn't easy being Mrs. Taylor if for no other reason than walking around in that tight ass-shit," Holiday said in a playful tone. Malone grinned, "Sorry Holiday, I guess I take it for granted that you know how invaluable you are. You were a great Mrs. Taylor, but you know tight-ass shit ain't out of character for you baby. December, Naomi Caldwell doesn't do the justice to herself that you did." He took a deep breath, "Farren, I'd like to sincerely thank you for stepping in for Michelle at the last minute. I heard your Abbey was so good it took the manager off of her square. It was already in motion, we wouldn't have been able to reset it. If you hadn't stepped in, all that work would have been null and void. I appreciate it cause I know how you hate playing in the field. Ladies, you all do a stellar job and you know you aren't getting any damn bonus because you are way to overpaid as it is." He went into an adjoining room. As he closed the door, Holiday yelled, "Why the hell does Vincent get one then?" Malone yelled back, "Because I said so.

"The boss isn't always right but he is always the boss."

Grey stood outside the office door eavesdropping. Frantically, he rubbed the palms of his hands together and nervously traipsed in circles wiped his drenched face. He motioned to knock, then hesitated. He drifted down the hall, then back to the door. Finally, he went to the main building. The staff had dispersed to different areas of the manor. Grey caught up with a few staff on the veranda smoking. Holiday's voice summoned the staff to the conference room. Grey noticed anxiety in some of their faces. Meetings were held so seldom that staff always assumed something was wrong. When the employees went to the conference room, Grey left.

The employees gathered around the conference table with a speakerphone in the center.

"This meeting is now in session. Anyone opposed? Say I." Holiday lead. There was silence.

"All in favor say, 'I', Holiday continued. A chant of *I* 's rippled across the room and the meeting was in session. Farren took the speaker and briefed everyone, "A memo will be distributed with a new date to discuss these polices and procedures at length," Farren ended. The staff left feeling relieved

Chapter 20

Vanessa arrived at the Stanton's Moreno Valley Development Company construction site in Riverside County, sixty miles east of Los Angeles at 10:00 a.m. Neither the power of the strong winds nor the sun's potent rays could blow or burn away the powdered matter that permeated the air. The dust cast a distinctive haze over the site making it barely visible. The gated property was humongous and stockpiled with unlimited material.

Malone, the general and regular foremen, a contractor, and the site supervisor were huddled around a podium engaged in a heated screaming match over a set of blueprints they were studying. Tempers flared, hands slammed and blueprints were shoved in faces during the conversation. Malone abruptly threw up both hands and the group was silent. Malone lit a cigarette and calmed himself down. As the meeting wound down, so did the hostile tone of the conversation. Malone pleasantly gave the group a once over and asked patronizingly, "Gentlemen, explain to me why in the world would I purchase this one hundred fifteen-acre parcel, like the ones in Chicago, Jersey and Detroit, design them exactly the same and then suddenly change the design when I get to L.A.?" He asked as a rhetorical question. "These should have the same two hundred fourteen tracks and be built identical. I made it perfectly clear to Stanton at our meeting that I wanted exact replicas because of the overwhelming success we have had with these in other cities. I mean all you have to do is check the models."

The men stared at the blueprints, bewildered. The anguished general foreman removed his hard hat, wiped his forehead, and said hesitantly, "Well, that's not the message we received from Stanton. These prints do not match with the plans you're talking about Malone. Sorry, that's the way it is." The foreman blew him off.

"Well gentlemen, here's another fact to add to your sorry, that's the way it is agenda. We'll have to do a put and call on this operation until further notice."

"Put and call." The foreman quizzed.

"Put it in check until we call Stanton and see what the hell is going on around here." Malone directed with authority.

Malone was leaving when general foreman Roger Spruce said in a no nonsense tone, "No. It's admirable how you think you're running things around here. I've indulged you long enough. That is over. I do not take orders from you. Imagine the problem we would have if every unskilled *wanna be boss* started giving orders? I know you're havin' trouble figuring out the blueprints.

We take orders exclusively from Stanton, these are the blueprints he sent to complete the rest of the project and this is what my men will be using. Now, I hope you understand that." Roger announced smugly. Roger strolled in Malone's direction and was aghast when he saw the transition in Malone's face. It was rage. Malone snatched the Foreman by his collar leaving the pompous little man just enough room for him to barely breath. The foreman trembled, "When Stanton hears about this you will be fired. This strong- arm shit isn't going to make me discuss this with you."

"Nice touch. Make sure you do tell him. This is over. You have a choice, have those men stop working, or have them watch you get your ass kicked." Malone spoke through clenched teeth and stared through squinted eyes as he violently shook him by his collar.

"Is there any part of what I said or what I'm going to do that you might not understand?" Malone answered as he reared back to follow through on his promise he let Roger jerk away.

"Boy, I sure as hell had you pegged all wrong my brotha, damn. I was just kidding with you." he said insulted by Malone's inability to take a joke.

"Well, damn man, if you were kidding, then my bad." Malone cackled and shook his hand.

"Work will be shut down until further notice," Roger obliged. The hundreds of hardhat, tool belt wearing, construction workers, instantly halted their work after the shrilled announcement from the megaphone reverberated across the site. Malone walked in the direction of the cars with the crumpled blueprints, cellular phone, carrot juice, and a large bottle of extra strength headache medicine.

A motorcycle passed Malone as it roared through the construction yard with the fury of a herd of untamed horses and came to a screeching halt next to Malone's jeep. The rider removed his helmet.

"Hey Malone."

"Jethro."

"Stanton had me rush these blueprints over because the ones the foreman has is not the right ones to complete the job on this site. None of you brainiacs figured that out?" the tatted biker wisecracked.

"Can you imagine that? Not the foggiest notion," Malone laughed.

"Well, it would have been okay anyway, because although the foreman's copy is wrong, the workers had the correct copy, but I'm sure you knew that too." He jabbed sarcasm.

Malone's eyebrows shot up in surprise, "Is that a fact?"

"Come on man, give me a break," The messenger nodded, as he reached for the signed confirmation from Malone. Back on his bike and prepared to leave, he said emphatically, "You are the man."

Vanessa remained hidden behind the parked work trucks in an effort to observe, determine and note any questionable actions from a distance. The homes were simple and elegant two-story tracks. Affixed to the homes were large signs with 'Tours' written on them. which detailed, hours, days and week schedules for the tours of the model homes. A few people congregated for the tour and a line was also forming at the sign-up booth.

Before Vanessa approached Malone to determine his ulterior motive in this full-blown venture, she took a stab at drawing her own conclusions. None came to mind. She activated the button on her belt buckle as she walked behind Malone and aggressively knocked on his hard hat. She frightened him as he jerked around. His caught off guard expression was quickly replaced by an unwelcomed one.

"Surprise!!!!" Vanessa greeted him.

He turned his back and refused to acknowledge her. "I bet you are surprised to see me?"

" How, did you know I was here?" he remarked sharply.

"Grey told me. I'm sure he didn't think you would mind and frankly neither did I. He knows you are my favorite cousin. I just wanted to come and hang with you. We haven't talked since you've been back. I just took a chance. I'm sorry, I'll leave."

Malone toned softened. "Baby, you know I don't ever mind seeing and hanging out with you. You do not have to leave, don't be silly. You just caught me off guard."

"Before we went away to college, Remember all we did was hangout in the basement, talked, listened to records, and smoked weed."

He winked and flashed that innocent boyish smile he used on her when he lived with her family. That was the smile that granted him instant forgiveness no matter what his offensive deed. Malone put one arm around her shoulder,

"I apologize, 'cause I really do like hanging out with you. It's been years since we've hung. Remember we use to go see two and three movies in one day. Sitting in the ice cream parlor for hours listening to the jute box." Malone reflected back and was now relaxed.

"What about the skating parties I use to come to in your basement when you moved in the projects. They were fun. We use to slow dance on skates to Smokey Robinson." They both laughed.

Vanessa desperately wanted to question him about his vested interest in the massive endeavor, but she knew questioning him about anything would automatically put him on the defensive. Vanessa devised a quickie plan: 1. She would just smile. 2. She would compliment the houses. 3. She would keep staring around the site in the direction of the completed homes. Vanessa worked the plan then repeated her three movements. Malone took note of her actions as he continued to reminisce. In true form the host in Malone prevailed.

"Vanessa, baby how rude of me. Would you like for me to show you around."

"Of course." Vanessa accepted.

Malone held her hand and they began walking.

"This specific venture alone is going to house sixteen thousand underprivileged families when it's completed. One thousand units per track, four tracks, are four thousand homes with three to four people in each family at the most."

Now, when you count this many tracks in fifty different cities so far that's two hundred thousand homes and eight hundred thousand people." He nodded, smiled and spoke humbly, but in a proud manner.

"That's how we do it."

"How you do what?"

"Do you finance this on your own? Why do you do all this?"

At that moment, a couple in their thirties walked up to Malone and smothered him in hugs.

"Oh my God, thank you so much," the woman sobbed.

"We couldn't have done this without you," said the man and shook Malone's hand. Both of them pulled him over to the back yard of one of the nearly completed homes. Vanessa followed. Two children were in the back yard frolicking in the grass.

"They have never seen grass before Mr. Carson," the woman said showing joy through her tears. At that moment, the youngest child ran over, grabbed one of Malone's legs, looked up at him and said,

"Tank you for our house." The second child stopped and yelled,

"Daddy, you said we could have a puppy."

"I got suckered into that," the man said as he picked up his son and reached to shake Malone's hand. The woman locked her arms around his neck and couldn't stop crying. Malone held her until she let go.

"Thank you." The woman wiped her eyes as her husband' lead her and the children in the back door of their home. Malone and Vanessa continued walking.

Vanessa was wordless but not without tears.

"That's why I do all this."

"I know this is none of my business and I'm not trying to pry, but how did you, get involved with something like this?" She paused, "Especially to this magnitude?"

Malone detected her sincerity and answered, "Let me tell you a story. Check this out. You know what I wanted to be when I was growing up?" Vanessa looked at him intently and said wryly,

"A bank robber?"

"Ha, ha very not funny. I wanted to be a doctor and only for the money and self-gratification, mind you, not for the need to help others. Then one day out of nowhere daddy abandoned us. I was 14 and he left us drowning in a sea of gambling debts. So, me mama and Victor had to move from Hyde Park to the projects. That's when I discovered people were poor. Well, I knew it before that, but I never knew that many people were that poor and living in such indigent conditions. I didn't know rats had the capacity to grow as big as a full - grown Chihuahua. The whole change in life and lifestyle screwed me up and changed my outlook on life forever. I really didn't care either until we were forced to move to the ghetto. It ripped my heart into shreds. I couldn't comprehend that shit. That was a defining life moment. I knew I would dedicate my life to helping people and the community. I wanted to become a pillar in the black community. I changed my major to Political Science and English and was heading to the political arena. I wanted to be an alderman, governor, or senator. My focus was to be an advocate and initiate new programs entirely for underprivileged people. The seniors who lived in my building were once productive, working- class citizens. When they retired, they had no savings. Some still carried mortgages on their homes and were forced to give them up and move to the projects because they couldn't afford their homes on a fixed income. I watched elderly people literally eat dog food and most often didn't eat at all. I really wanted to help them. I wanted to save the world." Malone's voice faltered.

"I hate seeing people starving and homeless. In a country as rich as America, every person should be entitled to have a damn good public education, food, shelter, and clothing," a tear meandered down his face.

It was the first time Vanessa had ever witnessed a display of passion and emotion from a man to this extent. She saw how dedicated Malone was to his convictions by the solutions he provided. She could actually see in Malone's eyes the angst he felt for mankind. Vanessa was entranced.

"So, I graduated from high school on the honor roll my last three semesters and had been accepted to the University of Chicago on a Political science and English scholarship. I was mama's last hope of having a son who might turn his life into a bright, shining star. My younger brother, as you well know had walked up to the line of crime in grammar school an after daddy left, he crossed it. Here's something you didn't know. There was this chick named Kim."

"Yeah. That girl you went to jail for right? I never got the whole story on that."

"Well here's what happened. Vanessa, she was the most gorgeous woman I had ever seen. Kim was charcoal black, long, thick dark hair and the most gorgeous brown eyes I had ever seen. She had thick lips, perfect white teeth, a pug nose and an angelic smile that lit up her face." Malone paused and reflected on Kim.

"Oh, how I loved her. She had two babies by two different daddies and another one on the way and on welfare of course. The baby on the way was by another man she hadn't been dealing with that long. I think two months and she was two months pregnant. This fool's name was Daddy Low. Kim called him daddy. I used to bring her flowers, candy, diapers, groceries, helped her fix up her apartment and gave her all the money I hustled. I bought the kids milk, I took them to McDonalds, did her laundry, cooked, took them to the museum, the whole nine yards. I couldn't prove it, but I really believe she gave Daddy Low all the money I gave her.

Needless to say, I never got any sex. I got off just being with her though. She gave every man in the neighborhood some pussy but me. The men never gave her anything, but babies and a hard way to go. During rare moments when we were alone," emotion lumped in his throat, "I got a chance to know her. She really wasn't the whore her reputation made her out to be. She didn't know how to do it any other way. It wasn't like she had multiple choices. Nobody raised in the projects had a clue about how to make a change. That's what project living does, it conditions you to fail, it's generational learnt behavior. They didn't even know it could be done any other way. Anyway, Kim was the funniest, most down to earth, honest woman I have ever met. Boy could she make me laugh make a whole room laugh. She could have been a comedian. Sometimes we stayed up all night at her house and we'd dance, drink wine and eat popcorn. She sang to me all the time. Whew, she could blow. I asked her why she didn't want me. She said I needed a college girl, my age, no babies and a career. She loved me but wanted more for me, plus she thought she was too old for me and that I needed someone my own age. I loved her unconditionally Vanessa and I don't know why. I know it's hard to understand."

"Oh, I understand!!!!! She exclaimed. When you get that call, you got no say at all. She just wanted you to go farther, do better and didn't want to stand in your way. Now that is love."

"Nobody ever took the time to know the real Kim beneath her actions. I wished for many years I had been in a position to offer her and the kids a better life, just get them out of the projects. I told her I wanted to marry her when I got out of college if she promised no more babies and to have sex with me at least on our wedding night."

They arrived at a concession stand on the site. After their orders were ready, they sat at one a table. As Malone ate his sandwich, he continued, Vanessa listened with the intensity of a child being read a good night story.

"So dig this shit, here is the conundrum. One night I go to the liquor store with this dude named Billy. Who's there? Both with loaded pistols and robbing the liquor store, none other than Kim and this pond scum, Daddy Low. Before they can make an attempt at pulling off the heist, sirens are flashing, and the joint is surrounded with gun-drawn cops. I grab the 38 special from Kim; the police rush in, and boom, I'm arrested, carted off to jail on a state beef for first-degree robbery, for the one I love. So, do I care? Hell no. I would have died for her in a second. It's my first arrest with no priors, but I get tried as an adult, because I'm nineteen."

"Hold on, hold on. If you were so smart how come you graduated from high school at nineteen?"

"I have one of those birthdays that fall in the wrong place." He took a couple of distinct breathes, "So, I served a three-year bit in Joliet prison. I never saw or heard from Kim again, know why?"

"Why?" Vanessa responded spellbound. He put his head between both his hands.

"She got killed. She was going with some new crazy ass

niggah. This new one preferred beating on women as opposed to having them help in robbing liquor stores. He went too far one day, and killed her. The state took her kids. I told my mother to get her kids and keep 'em for me until I got out, and I'd raise them."

"What'd she say?"

"You don't see no damn kids do you?" Malone got up and threw the trash away. Vanessa tagged along carrying a soft drink. He grabbed her hand and continued to guide her through the site.

"I get out of jail, needless to say all my scholarships had been retracted I still go to Princeton and the next four years of my life are hell trying to hustle that money every semester. I graduate, Magna Cum Laude with a bachelors, in a double major, political science and liberal arts.

For the next two years straight, I go everywhere looking for a job, including outta state. No one would hire me in any political office, government job, city, state or federal or anywhere else for that matter with an armed robbery on my record. Then the realization hit. I'll never have the big career in politics or make decent money because of a rule that states your criminal past is a matter of public record even after time is served. There I was, at Dodie and Franks, unemployed, broke, depressed, still hurtin' about Kim, and now, mad and rebellious as hell at the system for taking away my political calling to save the world. I decided to make my own rules." Vanessa didn't know what to say. One minute she was spinning in a whirlwind of presumptions, and now thrust into an eruption of truth.

"I hope like hell, all those people I saw in line earlier decided to sign up," he beamed humbly. There was no way Vanessa could misconstrue the authenticity of Malone's kindness.

Malone looked at her and said, "There is only one prerequisite to get into our housing. One requirement needed. You must have a certificate from an accredited, trade school with no less than a three-year program or a four-year degree also from an accredited college or university and we have those. My motto - if I can help a few people in this world before I leave, then I'll die a fulfilled man. If I can help a lot of people in the world before I leave, then I'll die a happy and fulfilled man."

For fear that her voice might crack, she shrugged her shoulders and turned off her recorder. "Oh, by the way, I'll see you at the end of the week. Me and Grey have a surprise for you and Prudence."

It had taken the greater part of three hours to complete the tour of the construction site. There wasn't one single item that was left unchecked. As they reached the front gate, Vanessa concluded that even though she had looked at Malone, looked at his lifestyle, looked at what he was wearing, looked him over, and looked at his friends, this was the first time she had ever seen this Malone. He had the same exterior, but the interior was new and mature. She couldn't help but feel proud of the fact that at least he was a man who stood for something. At this point, she struggled with the idea of whether it was better to stand for something, be it right or wrong, or stand for nothing.

Chapter 21

The sky dissolved into a sea of white lights as the approaching city faded into view.

Malone, Grey, Prudence and Vanessa were pleasantly awakened by the sound of John Alexander's raspy voice over the intercom,

"Time to rise and fly, ladies and gentlemen, we'll be landing in the romantic city of Paris in thirty minutes. The temperature is about 40 degrees. Present time, 9:00 p.m. on Friday. Fasten those seatbelts please." They all disregarded the request and took off in different directions to spruce themselves up. When they finished, Prudence sat snuggled between Malone's legs, and he affectionately embraced her. Prudence's body quivered. She was flabbergasted by her own willingness to join in on the spontaneous moonlight excursion that began twelve hours ago.

"Oh baby, this is so exciting, I think I'm going to faint. I have never been on a private plane," she said as she pranced around Malone.

"Neither have I. This is pretty amazing Blue and Grey."

Vanessa flashed a smile.

Malone looked at Prudence with a passion he couldn't conceal and contentment in his face that he couldn't hide, all of which confirmed that his search for the right woman was over. He dialed out on the plane's phone.

"Guyleguy, my man, how are you? A party of four including myself... we'll be there in about an hour. I wanted to know if picking up those items I ordered was a problem? No, I'm on a turn around, so I'll be leaving late tomorrow morning. Okay then, man, great, so it's all set? Fantastic. I'll see you in a few and looking forward to it. Hey man, thank you."

The Hawker taxied down the runway of Orly International until it came to a complete halt. The foursome exited, whisked through customs then transitioned into a Mercedes limo within seconds.

The shearling and cashmere overcoats the four of them wore tempered the shivery winds that greeted them as they walked hand in hand down the brightly lit Avenue des Champs Elysees. They browsed the windows of a few shops while heading in the direction of the Follies Bergere. The boulevard was lined with several outdoor cafes designed to lure unsuspecting tourists from all over the world into a Parisian lifestyle.

"Look at that, a McDonalds in Paris." Prudence pointed out. There were voices chattering in French, a bouquet of scents from the

Parisian street food vendors, mixed with Gauloises cigarettes, and the lively fashions worn by urban Parisian teenagers.

"You know the Musee d' Dorsay isn't far from here." Grey mentioned in exceptionally good and sober spirits.

That was the first time Malone had witnessed a clear, valid thought emerge from Grey's polluted head since their business trip to New York. Vanessa asked Grey as he leaned on her back hugging her playfully, "And what might the Muse d' Dorsay be?"
Malone explained, "It is a museum of modern art not far from the Jardin des Tullieris, a huge, beautiful garden set in the middle of Paris. Although not as packed with the grand masters like the Louvre, it seems more accessible and interesting. They have a very fine collection of contemporary modern artists such as Picasso and Liechtenstein. However, if you two would like to see it, we'll have to do it when they open, and that will probably be on a return trip. Don't any of you find anything to do tonight because I've made plans for this evening if that's okay with everyone." Malone informed the three of them.

"Well, I don't know about anyone else but it's great with me." Prudence said with the kind of excitement you feel while riding a roller coaster. Vanessa remarked, "Hey, I love surprises I don't get 'em that often." She nudged Grey as she spoke. He laughed and turned to Malone.

"You know, I'm always down for a good surprise myself man. Whatever you have planned is fine with me."

"Good, 'cause here we are," Malone replied as he approached one of Paris's finest establishments, *Le Banquet Royal,* a five star restaurant, which sits on the bank of the Seine. Vanessa stepped from behind Malone and Prudence and reached to open the closed door. Even after her discovery of its being locked, no one made the slightest gesture to walk away. Vanessa and Prudence were puzzled as they looked at Malone. Vanessa used her hands as binoculars to gaze through the window in the door of the pitch-black restaurant. She cleared her voice and exclaimed, "Hey guys, in case nobody's noticed," she looked back and forth from Grey to Malone and continued, "I don't know, but I'm here to tell you, this place is closed."

At that moment, the front door opened from inside and a man in a tailored black suit beckoned them to enter as the crystal chandelier and the clusters of candles dispersed throughout the dining room came on and casted just enough light to create a romantic ambiance in the vacant restaurant. Malone stepped in the front to lead the way. Vanessa and Prudence were astonished as they followed him in a single file. Grey was the caboose. Malone looked back at Vanessa, laughed and said, "Things aren't always what they appear to be cuz, you know?" Vanessa nodded pleasantly, and smiled.

"Malone the only thing that's predictable about you is that you are unpredictable. You are an enigma."

Vanessa paused for a moment of futile silent prayer in hopes that

Malone would be as receptive as she was to receiving those words when the time came for her to be the barer.

"WOW!!!!!" Vanessa and Prudence repeated as they turned in circles taking in everything. "I have never seen anything like this in my life." Prudence said captivated.

"This is absolutely amazing." Vanessa agreed mesmerized.

They took notice of the gleaming copper bar that accented the small liquor salon on the side of the restaurant. The marble shelves contained thousands of bottles of fine aged wines and exotic liqueurs. Breathtaking floral arrangements provided a vivid explosion of color, which blended perfectly with the faint, creamy yellow and white silk-lined walls adorned with famous lithographs. The four of them sat comfortably close. Exquisite, white, damask linen tablecloths and napkin ensembles adorned the small intimate table. The four place settings consisted of heavy filigree silver and long stemmed Baccarat Crystal. The satiny, hard wood floors were lined with Aubusson tapestry rugs. Grey pointed to one of the elegant works of art on the wall and commented, "Now, see that piece over there, that's a Liechtenstein. Oh, and further down is one by Paul Klee." Vanessa and Prudence carefully studied each of the pieces and Prudence uttered, "I've never seen art, or a city, or a restaurant, or a man as beautiful as this."

Malone blushed. Prudence continued, "This isn't a city, it's original art. It doesn't have personality it has character."

"Everything here seems as if it were designed by hand. It looks antique and rare. You don't see a lot of things that match. I don't get the feeling anything here is mass produced," observed Vanessa.

The four gazed out the picture windows in their surroundings. From every position they took in a breathtaking view of the Eiffel Tower on the left bank. Old lights cast a faint brightness on the river that bordered it. The dated, but quaint gas lamps illuminated the crisp, brilliant view of the Bridge of Notre Dame to the north of the tower.

Chef Guyleguy appeared, wearing stiff chef whites and a toque, along with the wine sommelier, who had greeted them at the door. Behind them a quartet entered and began to serenade them with soft music in the background. The sommelier, in a heavily accented English, informed Malone and his guest, "I am Emile, your sommelier for the evening and I have taken the liberty of choosing the appropriate Champagne and various wines for your dinner and dessert." The waiter, Pierre, distributed menus as the sommelier poured chilled, Cristal Brut 1990 Methuselah into each of the glasses. Chef Guyleguy began, "Good evening Mesdames and Messieurs. I will be your personal chef for the evening. My name is Guyleguy, and this is my assistant for the evening Pierre." The three of them took a half bow and the Chef continued, "The pleasure of having you here is all mine." Pierre placed the appetizers on the table. Chef Guyleguy whispered, "Hors d'oeuvres will be our first course for the evening. We did a *terrine de gras.*"

Prudence quickly responded, "And what exactly might that be?" She gave him a wink.

"It is a rich, buttery duck liver," He smiled kindly.

"I love liver of any kind. My favorite. I already know I'll want seconds," she declared.

The four of them browsed the menus. Prudence closed hers first then announced, "Well folks, I'll follow suit on what every one else wants to order. Oh, and by the way, is there a certain reason these menus don't have prices?" Malone said, "Mine is the only one that has prices listed."

"Is that a custom here?" Vanessa questioned.

"Certainly not," Malone responded, "But, for the purpose of this very special occasion, I officially grant myself the authority to create the customs for tonight."

"Why do you even need a price list?" Grey questioned. "We're paying for everything for these two sensational women no matter what it cost, so it really doesn't matter, does it?"

"No, it really doesn't." Malone laid down his menu.

Pierre returned to freshen the glasses. He added whipped butter and fresh warm crusty baguettes with that hot out of the oven aroma to the table. Everyone at the table salivated. Vanessa said, "As far as what everyone else wants to order, I'll see them on that and second the motion." Grey closed his menu, looked at Malone and said, "Hey man, why don't you do the honors?"

"I have already done them. I prearranged for the Chef to run with the ball tonight. I told them to give you menus in case there was something special you might have wanted. Now we'll all be surprised." Prudence blushed and smiled as she rubbed the top of his leg, "I don't think a girl's heart can handle another surprise tonight."

"Now that's something I'll second again. You guys, this is a wonderful experience and quite extravagant for a little spur-of-the-moment get away." Vanessa proclaimed.

Chef Guyleguy approached the table followed by Pierre who was pushing the dinner cart. The chef stood to one side to narrate the details of the second course, "We did a *"Sole a la Minute"* in a lemon, herb, and butter sauce with lightly sautéed baby vegetables." Emile poured a fine Sauternes.

Prudence's eyes lit up, "This is a great choice. I couldn't have done a better job myself," said Malone. Everyone stopped socializing to savor their meals. When they finished everyone sat back to relax. Pierre entered, cleared the dishes and prepped for the next setting. Once done, Guyleguy explained the meal as Pierre served.

"Here we have a luscious platter of silky beef carpaccio with capers, parsley and truffle oil."

"What is that?"

"It is the freshest, most succulent, thinly-sliced raw beef garnished with capers," He explained to Prudence.

Prudence and Vanessa's faces formed frowns as if the meat

smelled. Neither of them made a move for it. They watched the men devour almost every morsel of the beef. After Prudence and Vanessa noted how satisfied the men appeared after eating it, they mustered up the courage to taste the tiniest piece.

"This is the first time I've ever tasted carpaccio. It is delicious." Prudence was surprised. "I don't like rare meat so how could raw meat be this amazing is beyond me. It is better than I could have ever imagined."

Vanessa excused herself, "I have to go to the restroom, I'll be right back." Malone and Grey stood to help her with her chair.

"I don't believe this," She said looking at both of them.

The moment she walked in the restroom she plopped on the sink with her legs dangling. Moments later she jumped down. Her body movements were antsy as she rinsed her hands and wiped her forehead with cool water. She walked in one of the stalls and stood there. She examined her nails then walked back to stare in the mirror.

"I don't know what to do. I'm liking this shit too much." She paced. "Patrick, do you have any suggestions on what I should do to stay focused on the fact that, I am working on a case here," She exclaimed looking around. She tilted her head to one side in an effort to hear him better. Lifted her ear higher, waiting for a response. "What! Oh really, if you were me you would do what? What, you would just relax and go with huh? I might as well you say. What other choice do I have?" She freshened up her lipstick.

"Well, I guess if you put it like that, I really don't have a choice. What? You said it's not like I can flag a cab and go home. Point taken, I certainly don't want to make anyone suspicious by acting strange. Why do I ask you for advice because I never follow it. What? Okay, okay, I'm only gonna do this because you want me too. Of course I don't mind doing this one favor for you. Yes, I promise I'm going to relax and go with it." She took a deep breath,

"Okay gotta go, talk to you later."

When she returned to the table both men stood again to assist her with her chair.

"You were in there for a little while, is everything okay baby?" Grey asked concerned.

"Everything is just fine." Vanessa appeared more relaxed.

Pierre trailed Guyleguy to the table to serve the final course, which included a variety of beautifully prepared desserts, fine cheeses and sweet crackers seated on a stunning antique, dessert cart. First they served a lemon ice to cleanse the palate.

"It's the most delicious thing I've tasted in some time," Vanessa remarked.

Malone and Grey studied the dessert choices. He looked at Grey and said, "Man these things look like they should be framed not eaten, don't you think?"

"Let's hope they taste as good as they look," Grey responded.

"It's hard to pick. Vanessa interrupted Prudence, "Each one looks as scrumptious as the next."

Guyleguy pointed to each dessert as he detailed what they were,

"We did a Dainty gateau Opera, a gooey chocolate ganache cake, assorted miniature fruit tartlets, and crème brulee. Enjoy." The sommelier poured a late harvest Riesling.

"Man, it fascinates me how the beauty of the desserts and the antique cart they sit on both require highly skilled craftsmanship," Malone commented.

Grey joined in, "They are so different, but equally as artistic." Vanessa and Prudence were taken aback by their appreciation of the beauty in a simple cart.

"Well, has anyone made a decision on a choice of dessert yet?" Vanessa inquired.

"Or better yet, maybe we should live a little and eat the antique cart instead," Prudence piped in. A round of laughter broke out.

Malone stroked her face affectionately. Pierre added fresh-roasted coffee, Martell Condon Bleu, brandy snifters and Pernod-Ricard Perrier-Jouet champagne that Malone had flown in for the occasion. Malone tapped his flute lightly with a knife, and after the chimes faded he announced, "Indecision over a final decision for dessert has forced me to make the call. I say, let's eat it all." He paused then added, "With the exception of the cart," He glanced at

Prudence and blew her air kisses. They didn't come up for air - they ate it all.

After dinner they retired to the VIP section. The sofas were plush and the music was exquisite. Malone, once again, tapped his glass and stood, "Ladies and gentlemen, a toast."

The three of them raised their glasses in accordance with Malone. He focused on Prudence, "To new beginnings and a relationship that finally won't end. Happy two month anniversary baby." Prudence's heart fluttered as she melted down in her seat. Malone resumed this time focusing on Vanessa, "To reuniting and renewing family ties, love and loyalty that nothing can destroy." Vanessa bit her bottom lip and drank to his toast.

"My best friend, my worse enemy, my brother. What can I say? We go back all the way. Through it all man, we are here to stay." Malone swallowed, shocked by Grey's sincerity as he continued. "A lot of relationships couldn't ride the tide the way we do man, they couldn't hold on. They can say what they want about us, but the fact remains man, we are still standing."

Grey stood up and added, "Here's to having it all. I love you man." The two embraced in a warm, sincere brotherly hug. Grey kissed Vanessa passionately and then sat back down.

Prudence reflected on the way the day had unfolded from its surprising start to an end that would forever hold first place in her memories. Even though she and Malone had been dating for two months, they had become closer with each successive day. The love she now shared with Malone was now in direct conflict with her life-long friendship with Vanessa. She now pondered why Vanessa wasn't being honest about her occupation and now had her party to the deception with her own cousin and the man she swore was the one love of her life. She couldn't attach any rationale to why it was being kept such a big secret. All she knew was it was causing her to lie to Malone. '*Well*' she thought, '*I'll dismiss it for now.*' But she didn't know how many more *for now's* she could stand.

"This is the most delicious champagne I have ever tasted. I have never had bubbles tickle my nose like this before. What I have been drinking, it tastes like water compared to this. Who does this? You planned a turn-around trip all the way to Paris for me to have dinner for the evening. Thank you so much Grey," Vanessa said.

"Here's to a fine dining experience." Prudence said as she held up her glass. Now I know what it feels like to be treated like a queen. I just hate to see it end so soon," Prudence said with sadness.

"Fuck it then, we'll stay for the weekend." Malone announced. Prudence and Vanessa screamed. Grey smiled. For the rest of the evening they remained engrossed in conversation like four friends who had been together for years. They nibbled caviar, sipped cognac, reminisced, kissed, laughed and slow danced the night away.

The next morning, Malone and Grey hired a driver and the four of them went on a scenic tour of Paris. The chauffer played the raconteur as he rattled off anecdotes about the city and the Parisians.

"Paris is the capital of and the largest city in France. This is Place Vendome, a prestigious square located in the first arrondissement of Paris." Vanessa and Prudence's eyes remained glued on the sites.

"This is the famous Café Les Deux Magots, it is an institution here in Paris. It's a huge tourist trap and no trip to here is complete without sitting and relaxing in there." He continued driving, "Now this is 'The Arc De Triomphe'. This building and 'The Cathedrale Notre-Dame de Paris' have the best views of the city and the skyline if you climb to the top." He pointed out the interesting sites like, the Metro train station and the Arch de Triumph.

"This is 'Porte de Clignan court one of the best flea markets in France." After touring all the famous tourist sites, the driver stopped in front of the Eiffel Tower so Vanessa and Prudence could snap photos of the four of them posing in front of it. Malone and Grey purchased lithographs and a wonderful assortment of re-strike prints by famous local artists and funded a shopping spree for Vanessa and Prudence that would fulfill the desires of any woman's heart. After scoping the city in its entirety, they went back to the hotel. They lounged, laughed, had massages, facials, body scrubs, pedicures, manicures, mud baths, aroma therapy and ordered room service in the five star penthouse until their departure Sunday morning at 6:00 am.

They were in rapture.

Chapter 22

Thomas Winfield and Toi Forte arrived in Haight Ashbury, San Francisco, at 6:30 a.m. on a brisk, clear Monday morning. They were flown in on the Red Rose company jet. They arrived wearing cashmere overcoats, dark glasses and carried a few pieces Vuitton luggage and a trunk. Thomas had on an expensive suit and Toi, black leather pants and a V-neck T-shirt. Raymond was there in a Mercedes limo waiting for them by the exit gate. Thomas was caucasian, mid- thirties, medium build and very average looking.

Haight Ashbury known as "The Haight," evoked images of the long gone 60's; hippie culture, afro sit ins, protests against the Vietnam war, The Beatles, The Temptations, flower power, burning incense, dropping acid, tie-dye clothing, bell bottoms and love beads. "The Haight," today is one of San Francisco's commercial courts with exclusive boutiques, Internet cafes, high-end vintage clothing shops, second-hand stores, smoke shops and eastern influenced outlets. The Haight Ashbury back in the mid 1960's was perhaps the most famous intersection in the world. Young people came from all over the world in search of love and peace. The Haight has a long and colorful history. Beautiful Victorian homes surrounded the areas, stores and shops, murals. It also boasts on concrete, yoga classes, vegetarians and detox retreats.

Thomas and Toi checked into a hotel near Golden Gate Park. It's populated with panhandlers, drugs, sex and tourists. A diverse group of people from ages 16 thru 45 lived there.

Toi immediately began to set-up and prepare Thomas for his 12:00 noon appointment with Charleston Heinz, an, eccentric, billionaire who was both star-struck and passionate about filmmaking. His chosen route was by financing his own independent film. After careful scrutiny of five finalists for the position, Leaford Jackson was the one who Heinz had elected to produce his film. As Toi's leg fluttered in constant motion, he began to work on applying Thomas's face. He said matter-of-fact, "I will be leaving immediately after I am finished, dahling."

"What!! Oh, Toi, come on man, you've got to be fucking kidding me. You mean you aren't waiting for me to finish the play so we can fly back together? If something goes wrong I need someone here to help me," Thomas responded perturbed.

Toi took a step back, poised with both pinkies spread wide as he stared at Thomas. Toi's twisted expression exemplified how pathetic he felt Thomas sounded. He sighed, then reiterated. He spoke slowly and distinctly, "HELP YOU!!! Oh dahling, I'm gonna help you alright. Help you put this prosthetic on your face and that is as far as my job description will carry me. I am going to say this one more time. **I WILL,** be leaving as soon as I am finished. I don't know what you are doing out there and I don't want to know. If something goes wrong, do not waste one of your cell phone minutes calling me boo-boo. Call someone who gives a damn. If you needed a backup plan, your organization should have assigned one of your staff to come up here with you."

Thomas didn't bother to respond. Toi worked feverishly to complete his work as he reviewed the information compiled in the Leaford Jackson's profile. Thomas repeatedly, listened, and emulated the marks voice while forging his signature on an iPad. Toi inspected his work thoroughly from the various photos until the disguise was perfect.

Toi had been specific with Malone when negotiating terms after his offer of employment. He had seven demands. First, he wanted all of his instructions to come directly from Malone. Second, the only employees in the organization he wanted contact with were the employees he had to work on. Third, he wanted the employees informed that he wasn't there to socialize or make new friendships. Fourth, he wanted secluded studios in the New York, Chicago and Los Angeles. Fifth, he wanted an unlimited budget for supplies and decorating options for his studios. Sixth, he wanted the clients instructed that they were not, under any circumstances, to discuss the nature of their business. Toi didn't know what line of work they were in and never inquired. He resolved that the less he knew the better off he would be.

Seventh, and most importantly, he wanted no paper trail connected to his name. Cash only. Malone knew right away that Toi wasn't going to accept "no" on any of his terms. Certainly the high demand for Toi's work more than secured him financially. It had given birth to a new millionaire.

After Toi finished Thomas's makeup, hair, and slipped in his teeth he put his materials back into the trunk. Opening the door he said sweetly, "Now sugar, you be careful out there honey."

Toi exited the hotel and then the city.

Charleston Heinz's opulent office was located in the Upper Haight, an affluent area. When Thomas arrived in the reception area a young, sexy, bleach blonde secretary with gigantic boobs, announced him right away over the intercom.

"Mr. Leaford Jackson is here to see you." When she released the call she told Leaford, "Mr. Heinz will see you in a few minutes. We weren't expecting you till tomorrow," she said in a breathy high-pitched tone of voice.

When Leaford entered the office, Heinz stood up from behind a massive, antique, mahogany desk to greet him. Charleston tracked Leaford's every move through a director's viewfinder.

"So nice to see you again Leaford. I wasn't expecting you until tomorrow afternoon," Charleston remarked. Leaford motioned to shake hands, but Charleston ignored his gesture.

"Yes sir, I know. I thought, why wait for tomorrow to do what I can get a jump on today."

"Charleston."

"Excuse me sir?"

"Charleston, not sir."

"Copy that." Leaford replied.

Charleston smiled brightly and responded. "Film talk right? I love it."

Charleston Heinz was tall, gaunt, grizzled, with shiny tresses of shoulder length hair, olive flesh and a well-toned body. He dressed like an ole cliché 'Mel Brooks' image of a Hollywood Director. He wore a black beret, dark sunglasses, riding pants, high boots, a partially unbuttoned white shirt, and spoke through a mega phone. He conducted the meeting stooping and moving in various contorted positions while looking at Leaford through his viewfinder. The quirky, eccentric man puffed a cigar and coughed from the smoke as he spoke. He was easily seventy years old, but didn't look a day over fifty.

Leaford swiveled around in the chair following his movements. Leaford was spellbound and pleasantly amused by Heinz's stamina and eccentric appearance that he had to restrain himself from laughing out loud.

"I could read the excitement in your voice over the phone. You don't mind that I came early, do you? We have a lot of pre-production work to get in motion if we expect to meet your deadline."

"No, I like your thinking. No, No, I love your thinking. Have something to eat and a glass of wine," Charleston offered cordially as he shook his hand and escorted him over to the bar. It was set up with an array of gourmet deli foods, crackers, fruit, chilled Champagne, wine and hard alcohol. A built-in, cooling, humidifying system encased every visible wall in the office, housing a massive private wine collection.

Charles picked up on his stunned expression and assumed he was impressed by his wine collection. "It all came from my private vineyards I own here and abroad."

"Excuse me?" Leaford responded.

"I see you are enamored by my extraordinary collection, yes, no? They all taste exceptional. It all came from my own vineyards," Charleston repeated proudly.

"I must have a glass then," Leaford requested. He picked out a Cabernet Sauvignon, fixed a plate of food and then headed to his seat.

"I'm so excited about making this film with you and glad you accepted my offer. In my opinion, the producer is the one who can make or break a film. I know you will make this a Charleston Heinz film one to remember," He exclaimed with vigor.

"I can guarantee you this will certainly be one you will never forget," Leaford assured him.

"A Charleston Heinz Film. Don't you love the way the sound of that resonates in the ear?" He flashed a Hollywood smile then completed his thought, "This is something I have wanted to do since I was a boy," He declared with passion.

Leaford went over to the bar and poured another glass of wine. He handed it to Charleston and lifted his, "Hey Charleston, a toast. We're bringing in a hit, my friend." Charleston nodded with satisfaction.

"You have all the elements for a great movie. A magnificent script, a great director and a talented ensemble cast. Now you tell me, how can you lose with that combination? This is what Oscars are made for, I am ecstatic you hired me."

"Out of all the people I interviewed you were the most qualified and my intuition says the most trustworthy," Charleston revealed with authority. He reached in his desk drawer and removed an envelope that he handed to Leaford. "This is the check for 15 million dollars. I made it out for cash. I know, I know, it's low budget, but if this goes well there is plenty more where that came from my friend," Charleston stated with confidence.

"I will open a production account as soon as I return to LA. I have already picked an office and a crew. Things are in full swing. When will you be coming to LA?" Leaford inquired. "This Friday,"

"Well, I'll see you then," Leaford said as he abruptly got up to leave. He reached to open the door when Charleston beckoned, "Wait, come back and be seated, please.

Nerves ripped through Leaford's body at a rate of zero to one thousand within a second. He reluctantly went back to his seat, praying that this summons wasn't because a red flag had been sighted. Charleston's expression was serious as he waited for Leaford to be seated. Charleston stared at him in silence. Leaford now heard his stomach, as it turned over in growling flip-flops. Charleston put on his glasses and gathered some photographs from the top drawer of his desk. Leaford instantly noticed his red rimmed eyes as tears formed in the corners as Charleston's viewed the photos. He handed them to Leaford one-by-one.

"These are photographs of my daughter and her two children. My granddaughter, Tyler was seventeen and my grandson Tailor, was twenty-one when they were both killed in a car accident. Both of them had passion to be filmmakers far beyond their years. Tailor had directed three brilliant, independent, little films that Tyler had written and I funded. My daughter, Keaton was driving when someone blindsided them on the passenger's side. She could never accept the fact that it wasn't her fault. She was never the same.

After the accident, she mentally checked out then two years later died of anorexia." Charleston's weeping caused his eyes to redden and swell instantly.

"Man, I am so sorry to hear that. Were you married at the time?"

"Yes. She divorced me, moved over seas, and I haven't seen her since. I lost my entire family, except for my son. I have a problem accepting the fact that he is gay and a female impersonator. So, we haven't exactly paved a path of harmony for ourselves since he decided to come out." Charleston paused struggling to continue, "I'm trying desperately to accept it because he is all the family I have left. He is my only heir and I do love him very much. I had gotten to the point where I was beginning to come to terms with him being gay. Then, when he started dressing up like a woman, that was a little more than I could handle."

"When did all this happen, recently?"

"Ten years ago. I promised my grandchildren, when they were in the hospital before they died, that I would someday fulfill their dreams to make movies. Films have also been my passion since I was a child, but I never had time to pursue it. I am going to build a film studio in their honor." He sat back in his chair and swiveled toward the windows. "When I first met you, you were the son I wished I had had." Charleston walked around the desk and placed a hand on Leaford's shoulder.

"If this goes off as planned I want you to be in the forefront helping me to build and staff the studio. Would you like that?" Charleston inquired. Leaford cried on the inside. His emotions choked him to the point of almost being rendered speechless. He muttered, "Wow, I can't believe that you would put that much trust into someone you barely know," Leaford responded humbly.

"What do you mean? Are you being modest? I have had you checked from stem to stern and we spent ample time together in L.A. I know a man of integrity when I see one." Leaford didn't know how much time they had spent together. That must have been an oversight in his report.

"Sure I'd be honored to help you, providing this goes as planned and yes the money will be used properly." They shook hands.

"I want you to meet my son. He has a part in this also. Now, do I have your word on this? Charleston asked. Leaford hesitated.

"I can see clearly you are surprised by my offer. Don't be, you're a good man." Leaford made direct eye contact and responded,

"Yes, you have my word." Charleston walked Leaford to the door and added,

"I am a God fearing man. I believe when a door is closed God will open a window. You are my window."

"Thank you Sir." They shook hands.

The second Thomas reached the hotel room he peeled off the prosthetics and packed it away so he could return it to headquarters to be incinerated. He looked at the check and walked in circles around his room like a caged lion. It took all of thirty minutes for him to hone what he would say and to calm his jitters. When he finally got the nerve he made the call to the emergency answering center. No answer. He left a message. "I have completed my assignment and I need to talk to someone right away." He hung up and continued to circle as he waited. All of the employees knew *'the person in charge'* was to be consulted when situations like this arose. Holiday called back promptly.

"Returning your call," announced the unknown voice to Thomas at the other end of the phone.

"I can't do this one."

"You can't do what one?"

"Turn the check over to the organization." Thomas's voiced firmly. "I'm going to tear it up."

"Let me call the *person in charge*," She responded.

Thomas held on. Holiday phoned Malone from the LA headquarters on another line to explain the situation. Holiday listened intently to Malone's instructions then returned to the phone promptly repeating to Thomas what Malone had said to her verbatim.

"So, why are you doing this? And is this your final decision?' Holiday asked calmly.

"This was the first time I ever had to put a face to the work. I looked at *that* man in his eyes and I can't steal from him. So, yes, that is my final decision."

"Hold on."

Thomas could faintly hear Holiday relaying his message to someone as if she were a translator. When she came back to the phone she spoke curtly. "Is that solely the reason or did something else happen out there?' Thomas avoided answering Holiday's question, she waited for a response.

"Well if that's it, that is not reason enough for you to keep property that doesn't belong to you. It takes a great deal of time, effort and money to orchestrate these scenarios. This is a business. Anything that is confiscated because of a plan set in motion by this organization becomes the possession of the organization once it is seized. So, this will be your last".... Thomas interrupted.

"I gave him my word. I told him that I could be trusted. That's the real truth. This is the first time I have accepted this type of assignment and thought I could do it, but I can't. I know the rules. I was leaving as soon as I made the score. I was forced to engage. He called me back to talk. If I had left at that moment, it would have raised his suspicions. He would have known something was wrong. If you can't understand that, I'm out and I can live with that." Thomas's voice trembled as a couple of tears streamed down his cheek.

"You do realize that he was talking to Leaford and not to you directly?" Thomas offered no response to her comment.

"Hold on please." There was a pause.

When Holiday returned to the phone this time her tone had softened.

"Destroy the check. Bring it to headquarters with the files and prosthetics to incinerate. I'm sending a limo right away and the jet will be waiting for you in an hour." Thomas stared at the phone then put it back to his ear.

"If you gave your word, we understand." Click came from the other end.

Chapter 23

Malone pulled into the driveway in front of Prudence and Vanessa's house. He tapped the numbers on his cell, "Hey baby, I'm here." Prudence was out in a flash. As she locked the door, Malone opened the car door for her.

"What is this surprise?" She asked bubbly.

"You'll see. Baby, you look amazing, "He said undressing her with his eyes.

"Thank you," Prudence blushed. "You look good enough to eat too."

"To eat." Girl you better watch it."

Malone turned down one of the desolate streets, parked, and turned off the engine. He slid next to Prudence and slipped his tongue deep in her mouth. She returned his passion until it reached a feverish pitch. He unbuttoned her blouse, licked between her breasts and sucked her neck. She stroked his erection through his unzipped pant. Suddenly, noise from some kids skateboarding past their car broke their intensity.

"I'm glad we heard them before they saw us." Prudence said looking around as she buttoned her blouse.

"Well, on that note, we better get going," Malone, cackled as he zipped up his pant and scooted to the driver's side. Malone grabbed her and pulled her next to him. He-man handled her and she liked it. He turned on the CD and Sade serenaded them as they breezed through the mountainous paths.

"I have never introduced you to my three best friends and business partners, my extended family. I want you to meet them today. I love them unconditionally baby. I would lay down my life for either one or all three of them. They would do the same for me too. I told them all about you and they wanted to meet you with a quickness."

"I would love to meet your business associates."

" I have mentioned they are women, right?"

"Wrong." She answered unfazed.

Malone was uneasy about introducing his new woman to the Trio. He couldn't imagine what her reaction would be when she saw the three gorgeous women he kept company with all of the time. Prudence was the first woman Malone dated who would meet them.

"There is one thing I think you should know. I met Farren eight years ago and she is the only one I have ever..." Prudence cut him off.

"Is what you're going to tell me something that will present a problem for us now or in the future?"

"No."

"Then let's leave the past where it should be." Her response took him off guard, in a good way. He pulled into the garage at the back of his house and escorted her through the yard.

"Who lives in these three cute little houses?"

"Holiday, December and Farren," Malone said as he held her hand and led her inside.

The Trio immediately stopped what they were doing and walked over to welcome her. Holiday pulled a gift from behind her back and handed it to her. Prudence didn't flinch. She hugged them one by one like she was greeting her sisters she hadn't seen in a while.

"You make yourself at home." Holiday insisted.

"We couldn't wait to meet you, honey. Malone never stops talking about you. Open your gift," Farren prodded.

Prudence carefully opened the package, trying not to rip the paper. "Girl please just tear the shit off." December smacked her lips. Prudence was flabbergasted at the contents.

"An iPad, I can't believe it. I've wanted one of these for the longest. That was so thoughtful. Thank you so much." As

Prudence kissed each of them it was obvious she was looking behind them to see if they were also carrying a present.

"Are there two more or is this one little gift from the three of you?" She asked with a serious tone in her voice. The Trio snapped looks at her like *'they knew this bitch couldn't be that ungrateful.'* Prudence took in all of their reactions before she bellowed a laugh. "Kidding." They really thought she was serious.

"She got you good. I told you she was great, didn't I?" Malone boasted,

"Shut up Blue, don't front. She got your ass, too. You thought she was serious just like we did." December checked Malone, amused.

"Okay, okay, I did say to myself, I know she has more class than to be hustling gifts." They all laughed. As the snickering faded Farren said to Prudence, "Malone told us you're a chef. You can use it to store your recipes and download new ones and the Apps store has tons of cooking icons I bet." I am elated by your thoughtfulness. I love it. I feel bad I don't have anything for you."

"Me too, I love surprises." Holiday, said straight-faced.

"We were hoping you brought a homemade cake or something since you are a cook supposedly."

"A chef. I just found out I was meeting you all on the way here."

"Shit, I thought you all would be finished cooking by now, I'm starving." Malone said as he pranced around the kitchen and scoped the dishes they were preparing.

"None of us are any good at cooking. We wanted to do something special for you," Farren smiled. Everyone jumped as the smoke detector suddenly honked, honked because the oven burped a big cloud of black smoke.

"We should have ordered some great food, put it in containers and act like we cooked it," December said as she fanned smoke while removing a charred roaster from the oven with a pile of burnt ash inside.

"What were you trying to cook?" Prudence asked as she snooped around the kitchen.

"Our favorite dishes. A golden brown, roasted chicken," Holiday said as if she could taste it. "Burnt," Prudence said.

"Creamy, country style mashed potatoes with brown gravy," Farren added as she licked her lips. "Country from this box?"

"Tender baby green peas with pearl onions and home made dinner rolls," December's mouth watered as she spoke. "Rolls in the can!!!" Prudence threw them in the trash.

"Oh, lets not forget a mouth-watering dessert." Malone completed their dinner wish list. "Like fresh apple pie with either vanilla ice cream or homemade whipped cream."

"All that!!!! Maybe I can come up with a gift after all. Depends on what's in the kitchen. I might have to go to the store."

Prudence took off Farren's apron and tied it around her waist. Then waved the four of them out of the kitchen. As Prudence rummaged through the cabinets, "Holiday said, "You don't have to do all that. Everything you need is right inside the refrigerator."

"I doubt that. I need flour, cooking oil, and."

"The frig," Holiday interrupted and repeated. Although the kitchen was an average size it had state of the arts appliances. Prudence opened the door and everything she needed to prepare what they had requested was there.

"A setup." Prudence was amused. "You got me good." They had a good chuckle on Prudence. Malone huddled around the counter to keep Prudence company as she prepared their favorite meal. Watching her Malone suddenly became sexually aroused by the way Prudence interacted with his family. He wanted to take her right there on the kitchen floor.

"Hey baby, can you come with me for a quick second, I want to show you something in my room."

"Oh hell nah. We know what's up with that shit Blue. It ain't happening,"

December jested. "She came to be with us and we want her undivided attention," Farren added and Holiday laughed as she turned on some oldies and blended martinis. Prudence rolled out dough for crust and rolls and sliced apples for pies after she placed the roasting chickens in the oven. Farren set the table and December whipped the fresh cream with a hand mixer to help Farren out. Two hours later dinner was served. Conversation and laughter never ceased during the course of the meal, "I have never had roasted chicken this delicious," Holiday remarked as she smacked her lips and licked her fingers.

"These mashed potatoes are so light and fluffy and the gravy taste like a butter sauce," Farren said as she piled them high on her plate.

"Well, damn can anybody else taste them, or is your greedy ass gonna eat 'em all." December grunted.

"Why don't you have a pea and onions sandwich with your warm rolls and stop worrying about what's on my plate," Farren and December joked. Prudence returned to the table with a replenished bowl of mashed potatoes. She fixed Malone's plate, then hers and sat next to him. Prudence watched the four of them savor the meal.

"I have never tasted simple food this delicious. I have dined in restaurants all over the world and I have never tasted a roasted chicken this succulent and delicious. This is the best country meal I have ever tasted baby, Malone said lustfully.

"That's true. These flaky dinner rolls will make you hurt yourself. Malone we need to invest in a restaurant for her if we decide she's a keeper." December commented as she unzipped her jeans because she had eaten too much.

"So, what are your intentions with our brother?" Farren pried. Prudence's cheeks redden in embarrassment.

"I don't really know how to answer that just yet."

"That figures."

"So, are you the slightest bit jealous that Malone has three pretty women so intertwined in his life? We are permanent fixtures. No matter how close you get to him, whether you like us or not - we stay. You would go before either one of us." Farren stated.

"That's the truth," Holiday said as she admired herself in a hand mirror touching up her make-up. Malone observed to see how Prudence would handle them antagonizing her. She was not rattled in the least.

Malone loved December, Holiday and Farren. On rare occasions, they were his daughters other times his mothers, at all times his sisters and best friends. This happened after years of rejection and hearing no, getting kicked in the shins and on rare occasions slapped by December and Holiday. It had taken time to heal his ego and finally convince himself that it was either family all the way or nothing at all. He had learned to trust and view them as business partners once his desire for them had been crushed. He loved them each and every day and more and more with each passing day. He knew it would take a certain type of woman to fit into this lifestyle. Their presence were like birds that would always remember to take their grounded, featherless friend in flight with them.

"All finished? Girls please, pretty? That's a stretch, neither of you can cook a lick and all three of you suck at acting. Look at me, do I look worried to you? " They roared and cackled. Prudence smiled.

"We had her going for a second I could tell," Farren directed her comment to Holiday and December as she clenched her teeth from the pain of trying to brush the knots out of her tangled locks.

Prudence cleared the dinner dishes for dessert. She sliced hot apple pie, dolloped whip cream or scooped vanilla ice cream and served pie alamode. She enjoyed watching them dine. What surprised Prudence most about her first encounter with Holiday, December and Farren was their great sense of humor and how playful they were. It was interesting to see how they captivated and entertained Malone. He enjoyed their company. The four of them reminded Prudence of a frisky puppy playing with three equally frolicsome kittens, chasing spools of yarn. Prudence understood they said those things in a kidding manner, but they were not kidding. It was clear, if she wanted Malone he came in a non-negotiable four pack.

"I don't have to ask if you are enjoying dessert. I can tell the way you are licking the plate Holiday. You girls eat like a team of pro football players. There is nothing as pleasing to a chef as it is to find a group with healthy appetites." The Trio whispered amongst themselves, grabbed their martinis glasses and rose. "At first we were a trio and now we are a quartet," they said in unison as they held up their glasses and toasted to Prudence.

Malone stood, "I'll drink to that." Tears formed in Prudence's eyes and her loving expression confirmed she accepted their invitation. Prudence was down.

Chapter 24

Vanessa and Grey took swift, long, cautious strides down the dimly lit almost pitch-black hallway of the main headquarters. Vanessa quickly took pictures, noting every barely visible detail along the way. Their journey ended at the entrance of a large vaulted, stainless steel door on the lowest level of the estate. As Grey punched in a five-digit security code, Vanessa took a mental note on every number and procedure to disarm the alarm system. Once she adjusted her eyes to the bright, fluorescent lights in the office, what she saw was astounding. Grey's love for showing off made him a perfect and congenial informant and tour guide and Vanessa responded like an enthusiastic tourist. She activated the antique broach on her belt buckle.

"Silly, wasn't I, to hope that your lifestyle might have changed by now," Vanessa commented, referring to his continued involvement with illegal activities and his only source of income. Grey was instantly agitated by her sarcasm.

"Yeah, you are silly to hope for that, especially since my lifestyle seems to work splendidly for everyone except you," Grey finally responded. "Now realistically, how does this sound? I change my whole life around because it doesn't suit you. What else would you suggest that I do to make the kind of money I make? Where would I get a job with my record? Law school perhaps? Think society will let me be a lawyer even if I had graduated from law school? Oh, don't answer. I already know for a fact that the bar would overlook my criminal record and let me practice, and do you know why?" Grey snarled.

"Why?" Vanessa responded meekly.

"Because you think my lifestyle should change? No. I got it, even better, how about I become a Special Agent for the F.B.I." Vanessa thought he found out. He then gazed at Vanessa the way a father looks at his six-year-old daughter and said, "Vanessa, I do what I have to do and I have to do what's right for me. And you, of all people, should be able to understand that, and if not," he shrugged his shoulders with outstretched palms and let out a sigh, "Oh well." He grabbed both her hands and kissed them.

"Baby, you don't have the slightest inkling, I mean really, how much it means for me to hear you say what you did. If you can be fair enough to stand by me and understand anything I do then, hey, far be it for me not to act accordingly. I'm sorry baby, a girl can't ask for any more support than that."

He chuckled at her remarks, kissed her on the lips, and hugged her affectionately around her waist with both arms as he guided her to the entrance of a room with *Wardrobe* written on the door.

"This is where all the clothing is stored. Holiday and December study the attire of all the marks on each of our cases, men and woman, and then purchase all the wardrobe."

"My goodness, these clothes cost a fortune. Every designer known to man must be in here." Vanessa said as she admired the outfits and checked labels.

"Well, our clientele are not nickel and dime you know. We don't touch anyone who earns less than fifty million a year."

"These shoes and handbags are utterly stunning. These price tags are way out of my league. What do you do with all these clothes? It must be at least a million dollars worth of stuff in here and it all looks brand new."

"They have only been worn once if that. Malone usually auctions them off at one of his charities," Grey said as he rummaged through the woman handbags and pulled out a white alligator Chanel.

"If you guess how much this bag cost I'll give you my red Porsche."

"The convertible. Stop lying." Vanessa examined it closely.

"That bag is rare. All the diamonds on it are real. It easily cost over a half million dollars." Grey was dumbfounded and visibly sore that he lost.

"Hey, hey. Oh yeah," Vanessa threw up a hand to high five

him and he blew her off. She danced victoriously as she followed him into the next room, marked *DL* on the door.

"Is this the down low room?"

"Close. Drivers License." Vanessa could tell he was still melancholy about the bet, and wanted her to say forget about the car. She glanced around the drafty room quickly and then clicked on each item one by one. The room was fully stocked with office supplies. It was spit-shine clean and as well organized as an army barracks on inspection day.

"That blue material in the middle of the wall sure is a tacky wall hanging," asserted Vanessa.

"That color is for the background on the California driver's licenses, the grayish color is for New York and the white I think is for Chicago." Adjacent to the backdrop was a high-powered digital camera anchored on a tripod. In the corner were four, high-powered color laser scanners and state-of-the art high-resolution copiers and a DMV license laminating machine.

"The laminating machine is used to encase any of the driver's licenses we make. Drivers licenses are getting harder to duplicate because of the holograms and the magnetic strips."

Vanessa continued to pan each item individually, picking up one thing after another until she had about examined the entire contents of the office. There was Teslin paper, ID laminator, fake holograms and drivers license templates. She backed up to gain a wide-angle view to pick up anything she possibly overlooked.

Hanging on to the entrance of another well-secured steel vault was a large plaque that read, *'Holding Tank'* on the door as they entered.

"All the necessary blanks for any transactions we make or take are stored here. Both blank and printed drivers licenses, social security cards, every credit card, security codes, endless account numbers, anything you can imagine," Grey boasted. A little further down the hall stacked against the wall were countless boxes of blank white cards. Every one of the sixty shelves on the ten foot high metal racks were heavily stocked with blank Master Cards and Visas from every institution that offered one. The green or gold business American Express and Discover cards were in a separate section. Ultra violet lights sat on each table positioned at the end of each rack.

"These lights are used to check if the hologram on the credit card is authentic before we purchase them," Grey continued.

"No kidding. That's really interesting. What in the world do you do with all those blank white cards?" Vanessa asked, intrigued.

"On rare occasions, when we fall short of supplies from our processing centers, we have to make the card from scratch. Or if you know someone who works in certain stores, you can encode the magnetic strip, and slide the card for purchases. That rarely happens anymore."

She sighed in disbelief, "I never in my wildest imagination thought you guys could develop a scam to this magnitude. How in the world do you manage to get all these different cards out of the processing centers?"

"How else? People on our payroll, yes, in our pocket, isn't that the American way?" Grey quipped. "We're set up to make our work undetectable. Over the years, we have developed inside connections in every credit card center and department of motor vehicle in every state, investment firms, and banks from coast to coast. All our inside people deliver an easy thousand cards a week. We do all card encoding and magnetic strips. Our inside employees, who work for the credit card companies and the banks, feed us all the account information, account numbers, limits, mother's maiden names, expiration dates directly into our computers. In the bank, we have access to all the client profiles and account numbers. Once we finish we can call our contacts at DMV and they make a duplicate drivers license for any mark we need."

Vanessa acted nonchalantly as she continued to browse and ask questions. Vanessa made sure to examine the contents of everything she saw and asked detailed questions to ensure that she had every verbal confession and photo she needed to incriminate him and Malone when the time presented itself.

"Why so many cards?" Vanessa inquired.

"A card is only used once for a large cash advance or merchandise. Then we get rid of it. We never do a re-hit on a card. Never. Too unprofessional, especially when you only deal with the huge sums of money being taken from these accounts. Malone and I sell driver licenses and credit cards to other people who don't have the inside connections. We do it at damn near the same price we bought them for," Grey chuckled.

"What do you mean?"

"Well," Grey sighed before he spoke, "We set up the cards and driver licenses for purchases or cash advances and sell them to people. We know the billing date of each card, and we don't put a hit on it until the owner of the card receives their bill. For example, if they get a bill on the 25th of the month, then we don't use the card until about the 27th of the month. On a thirty day cycle, you get billed about every twenty-one days, give or take, so that gives you a leeway of twenty one days to use the card before the client gets his bill. So, in answer to your question, the card is authentic because we have the billing information along with the mother's maiden name, social security number, address, and last purchase, anything needed to verify the card. We have it all and supply it to the buyers. Most people aren't privy to this information. They have to use the card and pray they don't get popped."

"How would someone get busted, say for instance, trying to make a cash advance?"

Grey thought for a moment and then said, "Well, one example would be a card from the street, a teller will swipe the card through the machine and it will say 'call the authorization center for approval.' At the center, they ask the teller to ask the customer his mother's maiden name, because there are a lot of hits on the card.

"What is a hit?"

"A hit is the same as activity."

"Wow, this is a real organized set-up you and Malone have going on. What is the difference in cost for original cards versus the ones on the street?" Vanessa probed.

"On the street, you might pay a flat rate, or buy it where you pay a third of the account's balance. The higher the balance is on the card, the higher the cost of the card.

So, for instance, if the balance is $27,000, you have to pay $9,000.00 for the card. At least that's the way it used to be. I really can't say for sure anymore because it's been so long since I've played on that level," Grey boasted. He continued with the pride of a biker showing off his vintage motorcycle.

"Yeah so, we've been buyin' in tremendously large bulk for some time now. The cards that come directly from the processing centers are costly as hell because they are authentic. They have the hologram, strip, and encoding. The hologram is the hardest thing on the card to duplicate, and in most cases, is what triggers problems for our workers. Our price is also based on the color of the card. Regular account cards, the green cards, are the lowest price; the gold is next and then of course platinum, which used to be the highest, but now they have been out-ranked by the Black cards. Our cost for the cards, except the black, can range from $500.00 up to $10,000.00, maybe more," he reported. He paced back and forth as he continued, "We always pay a flat rate, and the rate depends on how high the line of credit is on the card. Now, the black American Express and Black Visas are for the high rollers who are the truth. You have to be an invited guest on some of them. I think you have to charge and pay off $250,000 a year to have it. It's about prestige. I would imagine the real heavy hitters in sports and entertainment carry those.

"What's the most you can get in a single cash advance transaction on a personal investment account?" Vanessa quizzed.

"On large business accounts, up to eighty percent of their net worth, Masters and Visa, it depends on the credit limit and the amount of money the client is worth. The more money you are worth, the higher your balance, generally, the higher the cash advance limit. We get all that information from our sources, though."

"Oh my goodness, your sources." Vanessa sighed. "They must be vast."

"Vast would be an understatement." He said as he gently stroked her face. Holding it in his hands, he smiled at her and affectionately kissed her on the mouth. She responded with equal tenderness. He chuckled as he said, "Boy, I don't understand what's up with that cousin of yours. Why the hell would he refuse to bring you down here? I swear he's getting paranoid in his old age. He even had the nerve to demand, and I mean threaten me in a rage, not to bring you."

"So what would happen to you if he found out you brought me

here anyway?"

"He'd probably get mad at me like he does about everything. Then he'd get over it."

Vanessa responded, "Well Grey, maybe I shouldn't have come here if he doesn't want me here."

He frowned at her with a twisted mouth and snapped, "Forget your no-good ass cousin. He can't tell me what to do in a business we started together. It's his choice if he doesn't want to bring his cousin here, but he can't tell me not to bring my woman here."

"Damn baby, I didn't know that. So what do you do?" He looked at her reassuringly, "I wouldn't worry about it if I were you. Malone has taken his new policy of checking people out to the extreme. He even had his own mother checked out last year."

"Really?"

"No silly, it was a joke. But he has this ongoing suspicion that the F.B.I. is monitoring his every move. The way Malone's been acting, you'd think he thinks you work for the Feds or something, damn. He was freaked out when you showed up at the construction site."

"I told him you told me about it."

"Yea baby, but Malone doesn't like surprises like that."

He released a gut-busting laugh and Vanessa followed suit with her best impersonation of laughing out loud.

"Have you ever heard of anything so damn ridiculous in your life?"

They walked inside the room with the door marked PR. "This is the payroll room. It's no reflection of the large amount of information contained in it. We don't like putting employee information on the computer–too many hackers. The folders on the wall contains payroll numbers, assignments, starting dates, addresses, and an in-depth history of all our employees backgrounds," Grey said as he walked across the hall into the mailroom with Vanessa falling behind to click information.

"No MR on the door?"

"Do these metered mail machines looked like possessions of the U.S. post office?" He turned as Vanessa entered.

"Keep up. These are compliments of the United States Postal Service. This is where we meter and receive all of our credit reports from Experian, Equifax and Transunion, along with any and all other pertinent information we receive from check systems, banks, investment companies, you name it. We mail payroll and send out new assignments solely from this office. We only mail information to the other offices because we don't want to send that kind of information though emails, and Malone is paranoid about fax machines."

"Shall we finish the tour?"

"We use invisible ink to sign off on any information sent by mail so if confiscated, it will be harder to detect or trace."

It was obvious that the brunt of the workload was executed in the last and most congested office with a door plaque that read, '*Last Stop Shop.*' "This is where all the twins are conceived, driver's licenses and matching credit cards. We also cash large corporate and payroll checks," He stated, as his chest protruded even more.

"On the internet, you can purchase real company checks with water seals through certain web sites. You can download any company's logo off their web site and copy it to the checks used by the company. The codes at the bottom of the checks need to be printed with laminating ink in order to be accepted by check scan machine at the bank. You have to pass a background check in order to purchase laminating ink." They proceeded toward the office machines as Grey continued, "The embossing machines are used to print the name, account number, and expiration date on the front of the card."

"Embossing?" Vanessa asked innocently. Grey shook his head at her and continued, "Boy, you don't know a damn thing about this game, huh, baby? Embossing is the raised letters on the front of the card. Now, the encoder machines, on the other hand, are used to print the same account number and expiration date that's on the front of the card onto the magnetic strip on the reverse side of the credit card. The strip only reads numbers. The account number must match the numbers on the front of the card, along with the expiration date. The driver's license strip reads exactly all of the information printed on the front of the card."

The lengthy wooden table, folding chairs, and areas around the floor of the room were covered with clutter.

"Either color peel-off tape is placed in the tipping machine and used to highlight all the raised information on the front of the same color card.

"This is the master computer; it's hooked up to the ones at our other two offices. Numbers and information we get that is out sourced from our agencies are sent here. All the work is set up here and when it's completed, it's mailed to the other locations."

"Other locations?" She asked trying not to seem too interested.

"When the numbers come up in this computer, it's the last stop. They have been tested and verified as foolproof and now we have a play that can be put in motion., All we have to do, at that point, is make up the bankcards and id's. Whether it's a simple in and out bank job or a job that requires months of planning by our research and prosthetics team where we have to change their identity completely."

Vanessa's eyebrows rose while she scanned papers and examined various little things on the desk.

"Amazing. How many locations do you have? How does this prosthetic thing work?"

"Let's talk about that another day, I'm tired baby. Tour over for today."

Vanessa now understood why they had not been able to catch

these people in the act. They were all wearing prosthetics to look like their targets.

Suddenly, a blaring sound roared as the front door slammed. Bright lights illuminated the hallway. Over the intercom, Malone's frantic voice blurted throughout the entire estate, "Is anybody here? "Is anybody in here?"

Malone cocked his semiautomatic and made cautious, quick moves downstairs.

Vanessa and Grey's expression froze as their actions came to a halt. They looked frantically for somewhere to hide. The lights needed to be turned off. There was no time. Malone had reached the last flight of stairs and there was nowhere to hide. Footsteps grew louder and closer to the door. Vanessa and Grey stared at each other motionless trance until Malone charged through the door.

A gunshot was fired.

Chapter 25

The Chicago headquarters was adjacent to Blossom's Emerald City Floral Designs located on Rush Street on the north side, overlooking Lake Michigan. It was situated in an upscale metropolitan area near a high-traffic, four-way intersection at Clark and Diverse. The area was a mecca of diversity in education, careers, age, and economic status. It was an equally populated racially mixed community. North Michigan Avenue was replete with high-end retail department stores and was the Rodeo drive of Chicago.

Blossom's was a quaint, classy floral design studio with hand cut green mosaic tile floors and walls, the business Farren had dreamt of owning all of her life. Farren's passion for flowers came from her grandmother, who had a breath-taking flower garden in her back yard. She sold, cut and designed fresh flower arrangements all of her life to supplement the family's income. Blossom's was famous for it's stellar creations and exotic artistry. Malone had purchased it for Farren during their six-month interlude after the back yard bar-be-cue.

Farren had become a floral artist and friend to the elite. She and Prudence had flown to Chicago a couple of days prior to Farren's event. Farren had recommended Prudence to prepare the menu for the reception dinner after her client's chef bailed at the last minute. Farren came to oversee the large shipment of flowers being delivered from Ecuador and Hawaii. She and her staff had been hired to design the arrangements for a famous high profile Rapper's elaborate wedding at his forty-acre estate. As Farren opened the boxes housing the rare flowers she commented to her designers, "These Casa Blancas and Lily of the Valley are going to look stunning with the Peonies for the bride's bouquet. The Sterling Silver Roses are for the fifty bridesmaids bouquets. Can you get started on those, Melanie?"

"I can't wait. I have never worked on an event for anyone this famous or rich," Melanie said, overflowing with excitement.

"Well, he is pretty damn rich. His budget for flowers alone is five hundred thousand. He wants real silk ribbons for her diamond studded bouquet." Farren's deep dimples took a bow as she smiled and wrapped a rubber band around her wavy hair.

"Stefano I want you to work on the fifty Sterling Silver Rose boutonnieres for the groomsmen and the Lily of the Valley for the groom."

Farren poured coffee for the staff. After preparing hers to taste she toured her flower shop. Sipping coffee, she clipped leaves, adjusted a few flowers on some pre-ordered arrangements, unpacked some unique vases from Italy and looked around, relishing the surroundings of her studio. She returned to the workroom to unpack the flowers she received from Hawaii for the overhead centerpieces for the one hundred tables.

"There is going to be a thousand guests and one hundred people in the wedding party. So we are talking ten people per table, one hundred tables, a head table with the wedding party, and a sweetheart table for the bride and groom. Oh honey, I may have underbid myself on this job," she said to Rosanne.

"That will be the day, Miss finance major."

"That is true huh? Anyway Rosanne, I want you and Rodger to start getting these overhead centerpieces assembled. The prototype you are going to follow is in my office along with the lead crystal vases. It is an all white theme, so the Siberia Stargazers, Dendrobium orchids, Bells of Ireland, hanging Amaranthus, Misty Blue and Virginia roses are going to be mind-blowing."

At 10 p.m. after the flower shop closed and the day staff went home, Farren turned on the sound system and had food and drinks delivered.

"Well guys, overtime for everyone. It looks like we are spending our Friday night here and we are gonna have a ball." She danced from the front of the store to the back work area, put on a clean smock, and dove into working.

"It won't be the first time that's for sure. We always have a ball, at least I do when I do your special events ma'am," Melanie said full charged and eager to please.

"These flowers are absolutely breathtaking," Stefano said as he examined each flower in detail.

"Well the wedding is tomorrow.   My goal is the arrangements be so unusual, that the guest will remember them even when they can't recall what the bride had on," Farren announced passionately.

The Chicago office was basic, with state of the art office equipment.   Through a hidden door on the side of the office was another room, slightly larger, which was Toi's Studio,   The office computer was logged into L.A.'s main headquarters.   The primary purpose was to send out and receive approvals from headquarters. L.A. made up most of the work needed for Chicago.   On rare occasions, the work was done in Chicago or New York.   Under no circumstances was any information to be used from anywhere until there was an official seal on it authorized by Malone, or anyone of the Trio in Malone's absence.   Once the completed package was returned from L.A. it was distributed, then, one person Malone hand selected from his one hundred and fifteen member crew carried through the assignments.

Michael Nixon's endless business work hours were due to his overseeing both the Chicago and the New York offices.   Even though they were modest in size, there was always an inordinate amount of work to be completed and time lines were critical. He managed both locations in the Trio's absences and because Vincent never showed. Purchasing and signing checks were solely the Trio's department. He had no involvement with the organization in any other capacity. He commuted from Chicago to New York three to four times a week and sometimes more if necessary. Michael's position suited him completely; it was like being self-employed because he made his own hours. His dream of one day being his own boss still remained high on his priority list.

More importantly, the position allowed him the proper space to divide his time equal between his wife on the East Coast, and his mistress, on the West coast.

He loved them both equally and was ecstatic he didn't have to choose.

Chapter 26

The New York office was furnished with the same basic essentials as the Chicago office including a thimble-size workshop for Toi, which sat adjacent to the extremely busy Camouflage boutique. It was located on the upper east side of Manhattan, between Park Avenue and Fifth Avenue, east of Central Park. Malone had purchased it three years ago for Holiday and December because of their joint passion for fashion. The community was a mixture of old and new money. From generation to generation, the elite caliber of people had maintained the same high quality and standard of living. There were high- end boutiques, art galleries, day spas and delis. During one of Holiday and December's impromptu visits to Camouflage, Holiday found herself in a blind stare focused on the antics of Michael and Vincent. Both were hovered over a small antique desk. The tops of their heads appeared to be connected from a distance as they apparently finished studying the contents of their large, diverse, investment portfolios.

Michael Nixon was 32, gingerbread brown with an erect stride, wavy, premature silver hair that he wore with a little length added to it. He was tall, clean cut, lean, and always dressed to the nines. In no time at all they evolved into obsessive gamblers consumed with betting on stock options. Michael used to wear single-breasted suits, plain loafers, and an ordinary briefcase. He always looked nice. Now, he carried an Armani briefcase, wore tailored, designer suits and exotic skinned loafers. Conversely, Vincent's style remained lackluster, neat, and well groomed.

Holiday went adrift on how it had taken Malone a year of diligent and tedious training to teach Vincent how to invest in and play the stock market. It had taken Vincent twice as long to train Michael. Malone swore by his proven theory, *'That no matter how well you develop your skills no one can predict exact results, just like in horse racing –luck.'* There was nothing Malone could say because they made exceptionally large sums of money and lost very little due to Vincent's business acumen and acute sense of timing. He had far surpassed Malone being able to judge the movement of the market. Vincent now advised Malone on tips and options to expand his already enormous portfolio and made calls to Malone's broker on his behalf in December's absence.

Holiday decided she had eavesdropped enough and closed the shutters on her side of the mirror. She wanted to black out the frantic energy rising between Michael and Vincent. Holiday checked figures in her accounting books and inventory sheets when she remembered she should have contacted Dexter.

After no response to her third text, she called Dexter's cell four times in succession. Also, no answer. On the forth try Holiday slammed the phone so hard it nearly broke. This wasn't like Dexter Howard, Malone's stockbroker for the past ten years. Between his three brokers, Malone liked working with Dexter from Crombay and Lynch the best. He was the most astute and asked the least amount of questions. That alone made him a valuable asset. Dexter had always answered Malone's text messages immediately when he saw his 333 code. Dexter knew Malone's calls meant revenue. Malone and Vincent had made Dexter a wealthy man.

Malone had heavily invested in a wide range of stocks with various investment companies. He gambled heavily in the stock market as another avenue to earn money to fund P.A.W. (Present, Able, and Willing). P.A.W. was an acronym of the Corporation Malone used for his empire of charitable donations.

"Finally," Holiday answered the call on the first ring,

"This is Dexter."

Holiday hopped from behind the desk walked animatedly around *the* room as he reeled off the purchases.

"First, is tomorrow triple witching day, or not?" Holiday questioned.

"Freaky Friday it is, and it is going to be volatile. AMD is going to be coming out with earnings, and why they are doing this on a triple witch day I do not know," Dexter responded.

"Here we go," Holiday began.

"I'm listening."

"Speaking of chip makers, I want to pick up 150,000 shares of Intel at the open, and I want it in three different blocks of fifty. Bottom line, I want the stock, but I don't want to bend over for it, so start with a limited order at 20.20, 20.23, and 20.27. If we don't get it filled in the first five minutes, change that to a market order. Malone will have my head if we don't get the stock."

"That is not going to happen." Dexter interrupted; Holiday let out a quick sigh of relief and continued, "As soon we get filled, put in a stop limit order a point and a half above the buy execution price." Holiday heard him punching on the computer keys and muttering to himself for all of a couple of seconds. Then he spoke very matter-of-factly, "Done. I'm listening."

"I've got a few orders for you for Malone's taxable account. Put the trades in the largest of the three accounts, especially the one that is cash heavy. There should be something like five million in the money market funds."

"Five point nine to be exact," countered Dexter.

"That's the one." Holiday continued to walk around aimlessly.

"Okay now, I want you to go long seventy-five thousand Intel, broken up into three, fifty thousand share blocks. Put them in at

20.20, 20.23, and 20.26, fifty thousand per block, and let me know if the market moves away from those prices. Bottom line, I want the shares, but I don't want to bend over for them either."

"No problem," he responded. After a brief pause he said, "Done at 20.20, 20.23, and 20.26. I'm listening."

"I want you to sell 100,000 shares of Sun Micro at the market. That one's going no where fast and we need to take a loss to offset some of the gains we'll take on Intel."

"We're selling 100,000 Sun at the market, correct?" he confirmed. She could hear his fingers as they sailed across the keyboard of his computer.

"That is correct."

"Done at 3.34 for 76,000 shares and the rest at 3.28. I'm listening." Holiday thought for a moment and glanced at her watch. Ten more minutes of trading left, she thought. *'What about Malone's retirement account? Have any of his bonds been called or matured lately?'*

"The Kern County GO bonds were called yesterday, so you've got a good twenty million in cash. The spread between the minis and high grade corporate is so big, I would go with Ford Motor's ten-year bonds," he suggested.

"Okay, sounds like a plan. Put all the available cash in the account into Ford, and be sure to call me when his orders go off. Now, I need a couple of picks for a quick in and out."

"Here are three that have been in a trading range of a point and a half. First off, let's go with Radio House. They are buying back fifteen million shares."

"So," began Holiday, "what does that mean to me?"

"Companies usually buy back their own stock when they feel the stock is undervalued. The expectation of Wall Street is that the stock price will rise on the news of the buyback."

"I understand. Buy twenty thousand at the market then, and put the sell in at the top of their trading range."

"I think they are going to finally break out of the drought they have been in, so lets set the sell a bit higher."

"Okay Dexter, put the sell limit order in at whatever price you think it's going to hit."

"Done. It looks like Cisco Systems is gonna break out of their range to the down side, so lets sell short twenty thousand at nineteen even and put the buy in at seventeen and fifty cents, but don't put it in until the sell is through. If it starts moving fast, it might skip over the sell and go straight to the buy," Dexter suggested.

"Go ahead with it all. I also want you to sell half of Home Depot. We need to take a loss to offset some of our gains that we're gonna get tomorrow." She waited in silence for him to complete the pecking sound on the keyboard.

"Done, I'm listening."

"Wire all the proceeds from everything into P.A.W." She stopped walking, sat down, leaned back in the chair and said, "Give me a minute." Holiday rested her eyes and tapped her nails on the desk, obviously meditating. Minutes later, "I'm done. Be well Dexter."

She hung up the phone and never broke stride to the front door. Thorough inspections occurred on a regular basis. Holiday and December decided their services were well needed when Grey and Vincent couldn't delegate work assignments in the boutique. With December and Holiday at the helm, this was a topic that Malone wouldn't have to broach again. Malone decided Holiday and December had enough to do, so Malone hired Michael for inspections.

The business had taken on a new face. Quarterly sales were the highest they had ever been since Malone's purchase three years ago. The boutique wasn't high on Malone's list of priorities, but it served many purposes for Holiday and December. He revered their business ventures and used twenty percent of all revenue for P.A.W.

"The new line of clothing is elite, classy and expensive. It was my first time as a buyer and a life-changing experience for me. We are creating a boutique that is gonna make a name for itself." Holiday beamed to December.

December traveled abroad frequently to stock the store with rare, one of kind, beautiful merchandise. She hired an experienced seamstress to sew all of her and Holiday's original designs. When Holiday and December first moved to Camouflage they had quite a few robberies. Their strategy was to change the look of the store and they designed it to attract people who had money and class. The specialized, high-powered security system Holiday had installed guaranteed theft detection and would automatically lock the front entrance door to the street.   No exit was possible.   The person would be detained in entry until security arrived.

December noticed a new energy in Holiday as she watched her leaf through elaborate designs and blue prints. She studied sketches for a new line of designs and examined material swatches. Holiday was very particular and never rushed decisions. The pure joy in Holiday made her glow like high beam headlights.

"Holiday, our boutique doesn't need anymore remodeling, it's breathtaking. Our color choice of green is stunning and elegant. To have all the walls look like a three dimensional New York skyline was so original on your part," ventured December.

"I'm not in the mood for small talk." Holiday said as she raked through endless piles of work.

"You know we're due back in Los Angeles tonight. Malone said to come back. So, I scheduled our flight for midnight. How's that for you?" December posed.

"Not good at all for me. I'm staying for a couple more days," Holiday responded blissfully. "I have so much passion for this clothing store. Thirty years old and I finally found my niche."

"Thirty? I remember when Malone bought this place for us.

You told him you loved fashion and wearing great clothes, but you didn't want the responsibility of a store. Now look at you." December sighed.

"I remember. He told me he got it for us so we could have some security in case something happened to him. Thank goodness you said you wanted it. Malone always has so much insight," Holiday marveled at her surroundings.

"I want to transition out of our business and make this my full time career. It won't in any way interfere with my other obligations. I mean, this is what I love, and let's face it, that other gig isn't going to last forever." December stopped her in mid-sentence.

"Holiday, don't sweat it. It's as good as done. Now you know, Malone bought this place without a first thought and he will curse you out without a second thought if you don't have your ass on that plane." Holiday considered both scenarios then stood and said, "We have a flight to catch."

"Hey Holiday, I believe you have found your stitch," December said jokingly and laughed. They gathered their belongings, locked up everything and headed for the airport in a cab.

"Boy this day went fast. Can't believe it is 10:00 p.m. already."

"Holiday I was telling a joke, don't you get it? Instead of you found your niche I said your stitch," she repeated tickled.

"Boy you have no sense of humor at all." she voiced with disgust.

"I get it December, I get it, damn.

The two of them relaxed in the back of the cab. December rubbed her arm reassuringly and said deadpan, "And I do have a damn sense of humor when I hear something funny."

Chapter 27

Malone was sprawled on the floor like a bearskin rug, dazed. He talked to himself and answered as if he was talking to another person as he picked himself up and groped for his gun.

"Well I'll be damned. I almost shot my damn self in the foot." Brushing off his navy blue gabs he focused on finding his reason for barging into the room. His hands felt around the walls in search of the light switch.

"How the hell does a person fall into a room? I can understand how a body falls out of one." Once the lights were on, he spotted the culprit; he had tripped over some tattered pieces of carpeting. The same frayed matting he had sung a song about for months telling the Trio to *'replace before someone broke their neck.'*

"I should had it done myself." After he positioned his gun back in his body holster, he tiptoed around the room in search of an intruder. He couldn't understand why the camera system hadn't been activated. If an employee neglected that, it was a mistake and a serious one. It was probably that damn Grey, he thought. During

Malone's extensive search of the mansion, he discovered broken scattered glass outside the stucco-framed picture window. "SHIT!! Had the culprits fled through the opening?" The gunshot caused a sizeable break in the glass large enough for a kindergartener to walk through.

He tired to reassure himself that this one incident wouldn't be cause enough to terminate the headquarters and staff as he had done many times in the past for something far less.

The numerous makeshift offices he had set up in the past were to shut down quickly in the event of a raid or bust. *Shut downs* were written off as a natural occurrence and part of the way the game was played. Shut one down, open another in its place in an ambiguous location. This time was altogether different because Malone had covered every possible base before heavily investing in a location that he deemed foolproof, secure, and stable. After much deliberation, he had reached a final verdict defining stability as the missing link he needed to elevate his business from a nickel-and-dime pastime to a billion dollar enterprise.

Malone loved Grey in spite of himself and the feelings were mutual. He knew if given the opportunity, Grey would take any and all money he could get his hands on, which Malone sincerely understood because he behaved likewise. Taking money didn't constitute mistrust. Trust meant never snitch.

After a final once over, Malone placed an emergency call to

repair window. He double checked the alarm system and activated it on the way out. The amount of incriminating evidence stored in the Red Rose was reason that Malone and Grey continued to use pagers, through a company they had purchased and had rigged. They could be called twenty-four hours a day, seven days a week, and on whatever continent they might venture. No service on the cell was ever an option for them. A clicking time bomb sound echoed from the door as the automatic locks engaged. That was the last sound Vanessa heard before she found herself helplessly tobogganing, at intense speed, down a long, winding, pitch black tunnel, with Grey inches behind her. They landed in pratfalls, one behind the other, and landed on each other. A four-foot thick black cushion centered in the middle of a soundproof twelve-by-twelve dungeon with padded walls served as their landing pad. Vanessa sat up baffled about why Grey had to soft–shoe around Malone about her being in The Rose since Grey insisted it was their fifty-fifty venture. Grey touched her leg while feeling around for something that he could use to light the room. He found matches and lit a candle. There were no signs of doors or windows, only some panels.

"Okay baby, I know this wasn't in the plans but at long last it's me and you. Alone." Grey said in a sensual voice. He took a double take at her and asked, "Are you okay?"

"What would lead you to believe that I wouldn't be okay?"

"Nothing," He smiled, "I asked for lack of anything else to say.

I know you're a trooper." Grey pushed the button on a remote control in his hand, and several of the smaller panels slid open and released handles. He pulled the handles to open the panels of a storage area of the same size. Vanessa remained against the wall, numb, with a bewildered expression.

After Grey laid out blankets, turned on the miniature, portable cd player and approved the smell of the brandy, as he swirled it around in both snifters, He undressed until he was naked. It was clear Vanessa had no intention of following suit, he laid on the blanket and eased over to undress her. She couldn't do anything but welcome his gesture. After the intensity of her satisfaction peaked, he removed his face from between her soft legs, then slid her body down, and positioned himself so he could cover every area. Her excitement grew as his passion intensified. She shrieked in ecstasy before he entered her for a second time. He first took time to caress, in detail, every part of her body. He moved inside slowly, then in and out, with long gentle strokes that aroused her again. As the tension thickened, their toes and hands curled.

She responded with a motion to match his every movement.

"Hmmmm," She purred.

"I love you Vanessa, I love you baby, and I always have." He hugged her in a way she hadn't experienced since the very first time he had hugged her. Before she knew it, her heart took over and it suddenly dawned on her that she had taken her second and worst fall for the evening "I love you too, baby." The longer they kissed, the more intense their love grew until they both released an outpouring of joy.

When they awakened several hours later, Grey eased off of Vanessa and embraced her with both arms. Comfortable and silent, her overwhelmed and him content.

"Baby, now tell me about this trap door and room."

"Well, if you've never seen Malone slip, literally, he did," Grey was quite amused.

"How did this hidden room get here? Where the hell are we?"

"I think you underestimate us."

"We had all this built in case the building was ever raided while we're here. This is the Doomsday Bunker. We are ten feet underground in a sound proof room that is impossible to find, if you don't know where it's located. I broke the window to distract Malone so he wouldn't see us enter the tunnel."

"Grey, come on now, it doesn't take a rocket scientist to figure that out," she responded. "I'm surprised Malone didn't catch us in that room before we went down."

Grey sighed, "Well, here's to not getting caught." He smiled. Watching him smile and being sober was something she rarely witnessed. She couldn't resist running her fingers affectionately through his dark curls. "How did you like the glide on our in home slide?"

"It was like a free-fall water slide, with no water."

After their third and most intense love making session, dusk waned, and the flame on the candle took its final flicker abandoned them in darkness. The new ambiance brought a silent and still sobriety into the room. Vanessa had a flash of clarity. The darkness delayed her uninvited trip back to reality. Grey turned on his side, searching for a comfortable position so he could stare into Vanessa's eyes.

When her relationship with Grey reconvened for the second time, Vanessa was twenty-five. He was still and had remained the first and only love she had ever experienced that was explosive, lasting, and deep. With every new encounter after their split, she tried to duplicate Grey. Their relationship had been a meeting of minds, a connecting of souls, and more importantly, a deeply rooted friendship. During the one-year they lived together, they had never gone to bed without pausing to make love. They were always in sync. Their second break-up caused Vanessa to become so deeply woven into a web of pain so severe that it left her bed ridden. The only peace of mind she found during that period was when she slept, and that wasn't too often. Daylight had seemed to heightened the pain which made it more difficult to handle because she had to function. Thoughts about him consumed her head and trampled her broken heart every split second of the day.

Grey lit another candle, "Vanessa, you know I have never loved anyone else." He sat next to her, stroked her face then eased his tongue inside her mouth. The two exchanged a display of sincere affection. Grey suddenly forced himself away to avoid being lured into her spell.

"I have enough money coming that will take care of us and leave plenty left over to maybe start a little business of our own. Vanessa, trust me, I will never leave again. I am here until the wheels fall off."

"Never leave again," she repeated his words, "You, saying that is a significant change. You, settling down, a colossal change."

"I'm pulling out, and I mean for good this time. Besides, you get my dick hard, there's passion, love and I want to marry you." He handed her a Cartier ring box. She removed a five-carat, pear-shaped diamond mounted on a platinum band, similar to the one she had told him she wanted when they were window-shopping on Rodeo Drive eleven years ago, Vanessa gasped.

"You, me, and Venice can finally be a family. We could buy a spot on one of those islands and lay back. We'd raise Venice, make plenty of love, like ole' times, but this go around, it will be for life and you will be my wife."

She knew for the first time since she'd met him that he was finally telling the truth, and yet she still couldn't believe what she was hearing and, most of all, feeling. It had finally happened. The moment she had hoped, imagined, cried, and prayed for was finally happening. Her heart fluttered, tears and her tough veneer crashed at the same time.

"Look, all that's left to do is make our plans. I figured we'd make our move some time after the New Year. I'll pick up a couple of tickets for a weekend trip, I don't know, somewhere, anywhere you want to go, to have some time alone to plan our future. Don't mention this to anyone until we come back with something firmed up, I mean if the answer is yes." Grey insisted. "In my experience, silence is a measure used for buying time when someone doesn't want to give an answer." Grey was antsy.

Vanessa leaned her head against the wall and looked up at the ceiling.

"Yes I'll marry you, right now if you want to. Go ahead and set the time and date. Tell me where to go and I'll be there."

He placed the ring on her finger. She flipped, turned, and rotated her hand in every direction possible to view it from every angle. Vanessa's heart exploded with an at-last contentment that only happens when there is no second-guessing about something being right. Grey's body relaxed. They were both calm and tranquil.

"You said not to let people know until our plans are final, so I won't wear my ring until then either." She had experienced this vulnerability on so many occasions that it felt like *deja vu*. Round three, a knock out. She was seduced one more time by whatever it was he possessed and she loved it. They intertwined their bodies and laid in silence. Vanessa thought, '*Oh God, what am I gonna do now?*

Chapter 28
The Whiskey Shots and Tits

After, Grey dropped Vanessa off at home Special Agent Vanessa met Special Agent Robert at 'The Whiskey Shots and Tits,' a red neck whiskey bar on the outskirts of the city. When she arrived Robert was standing at the stage, making it rain, for a half naked pole dancers who pulled out all the stops to entertain him. He was having a good time. She sat at a table in a secluded area of the bar and waited until he finished. When the song ended he joined her in the booth. Special Agent Robert collected the tapes and cameras.

"I'll process this and get it back to you right away."

"No hurry."

"Why, what's going on out there?'

"I've located the main headquarters and lots of documents. I'm hoping I can get some leads from the information in the paperwork. Everything is difficult to pinpoint because they allegedly have a lot of people on their payroll. They are receiving profiles straight from inside sources."

"Wilcox has been going to the banks and lending companies that were robbed to interview the staff and review surveillance footage. He has been drawing nothing but blanks. On every case we have concrete evidence that targets were out of town during the time the heist was in progress. Vanessa, I tell you, on the footage the people in those institutions look identical to owners of the accounts. It's uncanny."

"Would it make sense if they were wearing masks?"

"It would, if it were just for the way they looked. But these people walked like them; talked, sat like them I have just never seen anything like it. It's baffling."

Vanessa slapped her hand on the table.

"I'm out. I'll call you in a couple of days."

Chapter 29

Grey and Vanessa, both wearing dark shades, left L.A. at 6:00 a.m. cruising in a convertible Rolls-Royce Phantom Drophead Coupe. They were bumping the Bose en route to *The Red Rose's* fifth annual staff extravaganza. The party was being held at a beachfront estate near the Malibu Colony. They coasted down the 10 Freeway westbound with the top dropped. Vanessa stared at Grey as he drove. He caught a glimpse of her and asked, "what?"

"Nothing," Vanessa responded as she activated the microphone on her necklace and took in the sights as they dropped onto Pacific Coast Highway in Malibu. The homes sat flush against the curbs of the street and were uniquely designed. The area exemplified money, pristine beaches, fabulous homes, and coastline-beachfront- backyards.

"What's on your mind?" Grey inquired.

"Your career in banking has lasted you a long time. For as long as you have been going into these institutions, have you ever tried to funnel the money you make into something legal? I mean for instance a golf shop or a school that teaches golf since you love it so much?"

"Well, to set the record straight, I don't actually go into the banks any more. I haven't robbed banks since I got busted in Michigan and had to serve a three-year stretch. No, would be a better answer. Not my style. I live one day at a time and to the fullest. I never thought about any of those things until I decided I wanted to settle down and marry you." She turned off the recorder.

"So even if we decided to get a business of our own, would you still do these types of things on the side?"

"If things went bad for us for some reason and if I could set up a profile, face up and go make money, yes I would," He answered sharply.

"Did you mean <u>make</u> money or <u>take</u> money? What does face up mean?"

"When anyone from our organization goes in the bank and they are wearing prosthetics mask, that makes them look exactly like the mark they are impersonating and virtually making them impossible to catch. Our staff are professional and educated people. We have a handful of people who can duplicate anybody."

"MASK????"

"Yes. That is why we have been untouchable, and surveillance cameras and other employees can never identify anyone. It is the perfect crime."

"So, who makes these masks?"

"A freelance special effects make up artist we know.   He isn't with our organization though and has no idea why he's making up these faces. Nor, does he want to know or care."

"What's his name? Will he be here tonight?"

"He's not my employee, his name isn't important and, no, he won't be there because this event is only for our employees. I just told you he knows nothing about what we do. And unless you know, how could you ever figure it out. I do know him well enough to know, that if he had even the slightly inkling what we were doing he would quit in a heartbeat."

"Look Vanessa, me and Malone are partners and have been for years. None of our staff has ever seen Malone with exception of maybe one or two people. He runs the executive side and I run the employees and I wouldn't have it any other way. It just works out."

"Yeah right. All you run is your mouth." Vanessa challenged him.

"Malone is your boss and you do what the hell he tells you to do."

"You are infuriated with me Vanessa. Why?" He ran his fingers through her hair, trying to sooth her. Vanessa took a minute to gather her emotions.

"I am incensed. You want to know why? I have hoped and prayed for years that you would get out of the crime world and we would get back together. Instead your activity has burgeoned."

"I told you, I am getting out and getting us a business."

"Getting us a business? So when you get in trouble we'll have something to put up for bail. I don't want to get married Grey. You will never stop until you are stopped."

"Please don't say you won't marry me. I told you I love you Vanessa, and I do. You just have to understand, I do what I have to do and I have to do what's right for me. And you of all people should be able to understand that. If not," He shrugged his shoulders with outstretched palms, "Oh well."

"I understand and accept that. Now, this is all I want from you."

"What is it baby? Anything. You name it."   Grey said sincerely.

"When I do what I have to do, I want you to be just as understanding."

"That's a fair exchange. It's a deal?"

He reached out to shake her hand and she complied. They continued down PCH past Pepperdine University and Geoffrey's Restaurant, one of Malibu's finest. Malone had rented the isolated mansion from a business associate and friend to hold the affair. As they turned down a secluded street onto the huge beachfront estate, valet parking attendants were already on hand to escort them out of their vehicle. As they entered the well-tailored coordinator of the event greeted them. She shook hands with Grey and introduced herself. "Good morning, I'm Carmen Sanders, you must be Mr. Young."

"Grey is fine."

"How are you both doing this morning?" Carmen sized them both up and continued, "All the employees of the Red Rose, from all three offices have RSVP'd, been assigned rooms, and are scheduled to begin arrival around 3:00 pm."

"The event will flow like spring water, streaming down a mountainside on a warm summer day. Your three supervisors, Holiday, December and Farren were here working until all hours of the night for the last week finalizing menus, music, staff and activities." Grey interrupted her with a tone of self- importance,

"Excuse you, but I am their supervisor."

"I won't make that mistake again," she said to appease him. At that moment, Holiday, December and Farren approached Grey and Vanessa who were standing in the foray. Farren stood slightly off to the side as they mingled "I'm going to do rounds." Carmen addressed them all and left. Grey did the introductions.

"This is Malone's cousin Vanessa. This is the Trio, Holiday, December, and Farren.

Vanessa promptly snapped photos of them from her belt buckle.

"Well, at last we meet." December said as she gave Vanessa a once over.

"I have heard so much about the three of you."

"Likewise. Well, through association we do know each other. I cringe to think what you may have heard."

"I can't believe that in all these years our paths have never crossed,"
Holiday commented. Farren watched in silence.

"I know huh. Well, I guess things happen in their own time. By the way, this place looks remarkable." Vanessa said admiring the decorations. "Will the three of you be attending the party this evening?"

"No." December answered right on the tail of her question.

"Besides, I don't want to be in the vicinity when Grey starts running his mouth."

"Well, you're doing the right thing then. Time for you to go." He smirked.

"On that note, I guess we better get out of here." Holiday agreed. Farren trailed them as they headed for the door.

Once they were gone Grey decided to do rounds also. Vanessa and Grey headed outside.

"It's a spectacular day." She commented then asked, "Do you rent this place out every year for the event?"

"No, this is the first time at this location. We host a different venue and theme every year. This is the first event we've hosted that will take place over the weekend."

"Does Malone ever come by just to see how things are going?"

Never."

As Vanessa and Grey strolled along the beach, holding hands. She admired the beauty of the estate and it's surroundings. Vanessa was astounded by the depth of Malone's generosity for his employees and impressed by how organized and classy it was. The newest models of jet skis, water skis, boogie and surfboards lined the beach along with a staff of professional lifeguards. A twenty four hour rotation of chefs and waiters, full open bar, grills that seemed half the length of a football field, fresh seafood of every kind, cases of prime rib and two huge aquariums filled with live main lobsters.

"I love the idea of walking out of your backdoor and having the ocean as your backyard." Vanessa confessed to Grey.

"Maybe we should think seriously about buying us a little spot on the beach since you like it so much." Vanessa took note if he was serious or not.

"I love you Vanessa. I know it doesn't always look like I do, but I always do." Grey waited for her to respond or react. When she did neither, he kissed her forehead then proceeded back to the house. She watched him walk away until he was out of sight.

As much as Vanessa loved Grey, she equally cursed herself for being unable to stop loving him and cherishing their memories. Free flowing money, lavish gifts, traveling, shopping, and spontaneity were hard to compete with as far as her finding another compatible mate. She thought back to the money she made as a paralegal and it couldn't compete with his cash flow. She had lapped up every moment of being pampered and entertained. Grey kept the fun times rolling. If the bedroom walls of her old apartment could talk, they would attest to the marathon conversations, lovemaking sessions and movie nights. One of their favorite pass times was playing golf. Grey was versatile and well – versed but inflexible about making decisions regarding a commitment in their relationship.

6:00 p.m. and the party was bustling.

Vanessa began working. She checked a copy of the guest list that she had taken out of the office. One hundred and fourteen employees had arrived. The only person who hadn't shown up was Vincent Holt. People were playing volleyball, bid whist, board games, eating and dancing. Some sat on the beach and roasted marshmallows around the bon fire, while others watched movies in the home theatre or bowled in the private bowling alley.

He scanned the beach looking for Vanessa, and then whisked her over to where Thomas was standing with a group of people socializing. Grey and Thomas shook hands. Grey was a grand host, Vanessa played hostess right along with him.

"Vanessa, this is Thomas Winfield, Michael Nixon and my old friend, Chen Lee. This is my lady, Vanessa," Grey boasted proudly. "Are you guys having a good time?"

"We're having a ball," Chen said as he moved to the music.

"It's a fabulous party." Thomas agreed.

"Excuse us please." Grey then lead Vanessa to another group of employees sitting next to the bar.

"Good evening ladies and gents, I wanted you to meet Vanessa. This is Shelly, Debra, Bernard, Leslie and Ernest."

"Please to meet you," Vanessa greeted each of them. Grey kissed Vanessa on the cheek as he abruptly darted back to his retreat. Debra noticed Vanessa standing alone and invited her to get a drink at the bar. Debra did some introductions of her own.

"Vanessa, this is Raymond. This is Jordon, but everybody calls him Brick and this is Chang Jones." Vanessa shot Debra a look of question regarding Chang.

"He is Chinese and Black," Debra informed her. "Everyone is curious about his ethnicity when they first meet him."

Vanessa mingled and snapped photos of everyone there until she had met the entire staff. She struck up conversations easily. As the night went on it got much easier. Vanessa wondered if the alcohol had been spiked with sodium pentothal the way the workers talked openly about everything. Some were funny and some not so funny. Vanessa recorded an array of guilty confessions as she sat at the bar. Debra sat next to her and ordered a beer.

"So, this was a nice turn out. Was it a far drive for you?" Vanessa asked.

"You bet it was. I came in from New York. A far drive for the plane," she laughed.

"Why did you come?"

"Why did we come? Look around it's fabulous and it's for us. Plus, It's the only time the twelve of us from the office in New York and the fifteen from the office in Chicago get to see the people in LA."

"How many offices are there?"

"Just three. Los Angeles, New York and Chicago." I'm sorry we didn't meet. I'm Debra, I work on the New York research team."

"I'm Vanessa, Grey's girlfriend."

"Honey, I heard about you. A lot of the women I work with are crazy about him and jealous of you," she said jokingly. "Hey we'll talk later," she said as she grabbed a beer and went to greet some of her co-workers.

By 2:30 a.m. Vanessa was unwinding in the ballroom enjoying the bright reflection the full moon had cast on the ocean and the warm evening breeze. She had completed her assignment and was eating lobster tails when Troy Miller approached her,

"Would you like to dance with me?" He requested politely.

"Maybe later, thank you though." As he walked away Caesar broached her, "I can understand completely why you wouldn't want to dance with him. How would you like to dance with me?' Vanessa spotted Grey walking toward her.

"You know if Grey wasn't on his way over here I think I'd have to take you up on that." Caesar smiled and then grabbed another dance partner.

"How are you enjoying yourself baby?" Grey mumbled in a barely audible voice.

"This party is FAB- U -LOUS baby."

"I have been to some pretty amazing parties in my day, if I must say so myself, but I have never seen anything of this magnitude. How come December, Holiday and Farren didn't stay?"

"The Trio never has any contact with any of the staff face to face just like Malone."

"I thought Malone was the only one who had no contact with the staff. I didn't know it was the Trio too. Interesting." Vanessa thought, '*what an idiot, no one in this entire organization can identify anyone but Grey. She wondered if the drugs had pickled his brain to the point that he wasn't aware of the repercussions this could have for him.*'

Vanessa kissed Grey on the cheek and he lit up like a schoolboy who had gotten a gold star for the day. When the band took a short break after finishing their set the DJ stepped in to keep the music flowing.

"Thank you for inviting me Grey. Now, how do you feel?"

"Well, I think I have, how can I say it, consumed enough for one night."

"Your eyes look like they are about to pop out of the sockets. I don't see how anyone could like that stuff if it makes you look like that." Vanessa smiled. He gritted his teeth and looked miserable.

"So, I heard the spouses and family segment will start by 12:00 noon tomorrow. I'll be leaving before then."

"Why? I thought you were staying for the weekend." Grey asked with sincere disappointment.

. Vanessa thought about staying but ruled it out because she knew Grey was going to be locked up in his coke den most of the time.

"I must have misunderstood you, I thought the party was only for one day. I have other plans for the rest of the weekend."

"What do you have to do?"

Vanessa thought of a quick answer. "I have to go to my mother's tomorrow. I have a ton of things I want to do with Venice the rest of the weekend."

"It's all good. You know I have to stay though."

"I know baby, I'll catch up with you later in the week. Oh, I forgot one thing. I drove with you. How the hell am I going to get home?"

"Walk." Grey teased as he threw her his car keys.

Chapter 30

The Whiskey Shots and Tits

On the way home Special Agent Saffore met Special Agent Robert at the same red neck whiskey bar on the outskirts of the city. When she arrived, he once again, was ogling the strippers. Robert didn't see her come in and she sneaked to the same table in a secluded area of the bar and ducked down to watch Robert's shenanigans. After he read her text he appeared to be looking around the bar for something that he couldn't find. Not finding it must have been a good thing because he smiled. For a second he was out of her site.

When Robert returned he was being escorted to the roped section of the bar that was allocated for lap dances by a security guard. As he sat in the chair and waited for his lap dance he busted some hip-hop dance moves that left Vanessa mesmerized. Then another song came on that must have been one of his favorite joints because he unhooked the rope and broke into a hip hop dance routine that looked like it had been choreographed. He hit moves that you only see professional dancers or serious street kids doing. Some of the partygoer's noticed him and clapped as he danced. Before long everybody in the bar was gathered around Robert. His moves were right up there with Usher and Brown. The bar chanted, " Go Robert, Go Robert, Go Robert….. " At the end of the song everybody in the Whiskey Shots and Tits gave Robert an standing ovation and clamored for more. Robert took a bow and then joined Vanessa in the booth. When everyone settled the owner sent the girl back out to dance and announced, "Let's get it raining up in here gentleman."

"Well, that's a first. You aren't even out of breath. You can dance your ass off."

"I know, that's why I did it so you could see me dance. All my life that's what I wanted to be. My father thought dancing was for women and gay men. So, that was that."

" This little bar is your spot?"

Robert collected all the tapes, film and photographs she had taken Rose's annual staff party.

"Yep. So, how's it going?"

"Tonight was pretty major. What I got tonight is about a third of the information we'll need to bring them down. Whoever is the master mind behind this is one smart motha fucka."

"Bet there is a lot more going on that we never anticipated."

"If you make it in this career, eventually, you will get one of those cases that um, um," Vanessa couldn't find the words so Robert completed her, "Cases that exceed the law. They always involve masses of people who are gonna get fucked when the deal goes down and they didn't even know they are involved in anything. My pet names for them are, 'gray matters.'

" Wow!!!! "

As they headed out the bar Vanessa remarked as an afterthought, "Hey wait a minute, you said you set all that up because you wanted me to finally see you dance. I texted you that I was going to be late and then I sneaked inside. How did you know I was here? "

"I'm Special Agent Robert Johnson, F.B.I."

Chapter 31

The vacant hallways in the <u>Education for Life College</u> reverberated from the lingering ethos of the final bell, which meant being late was now official. Being tardy three times resulted in suspension and a fourth was instant expulsion. A few student stragglers rummaged through their lockers like shoppers at a flea market. Several others stormed through the huge, oak, double doors of the early modern designed structure and sprinted in different directions to their classes.

The building's exterior subtle aesthetics took front and center in the cul-de-sac and was surrounded by various vintage office buildings that complimented its rare beauty. The College was located in the inner city of Long Beach, California. An education allowed Malone to give people a gift that could never be taken away. He remained steadfast in his conviction that a superior education should be a human right, not a delicacy made privy for the rich. Recruiting and sometimes relocating the finest quality teachers in the world to work in his schools had cost him a tremendous amount of money. Even with the budget he received from innumerable scholarships, loans, private donations, constant fundraisers, the student's tuition was based on family income. He spent more money funding and maintaining the Universities and trade schools he founded than he did on all his other charitable ventures combined. All of the educational facilities were located in big cities in underprivileged areas. Malone kept the Universities and Trade schools student body at a minimum, which allowed for more personal attention. The Universities and how they were designed to provide an opportunity to receive a college education equivalent to that of an Ivy League school for those unable to afford it. Malone felt this was the key element to the overwhelming success rate of students who had graduated and gone on to attain lucrative careers. The success rate made all of his efforts worthwhile.

Vanessa cruised the hallway of the Education For Life College following up on a lead. She tried to remain as inconspicuous as possible for a grown woman wearing a cream-colored yellow suit and lurking down an empty corridor. She was selective about the photographs she took because she wanted to make sure she got information that would be pertinent to an indictment. She studied every wall from floor to ceiling and was intrigued by the array of past and present photographs of the staff, board members, administration, and alumni that were accompanied by literature describing their indelible contributions. Collectively Malone and the Trio created a broad, well balanced, four-year accredited neighborhood college. She found no evidence pointing to Malone or any information on the founder.

The 6'5, three-hundred-pound Mr. Security guard appeared out of nowhere and hovered over Vanessa.

"Sorry ma'am," he said in a dictatorial tone, " this isn't a museum. If you aren't a student, staff member or otherwise authorized to be here, then I'm sorry to say loitering is prohibited anywhere in the school or on the grounds." His attitude was far from that of a security guard, it projected the delusion of being a chief of police.

"I have an appointment to meet the Founder, Dean, President, I don't know his title, the head of this institution. If you don't mind, would you provide me with that information? I need his name and official title or just steer me in the right direction where he or she can be found and I'll be on my way." Vanessa felt he overstepped his boundaries when he grabbed her arm with a little more force than she deemed necessary, especially since she hadn't resisted his request. For a fleeting moment, she felt the urge to flash her badge and jolt his memory back to the duties listed in his job description. She couldn't find it in her heart to ruin the elation he was feeling from his self-appointed authority.

"It appears to me that you would know this information if you had an official scheduled appointment," he reprimanded. As he briskly escorted her to the door, she scrutinized the refinement around her and was astonished to think that Malone's name would be mentioned in the same breath of such a renowned establishment, much less that he could be the Founder. It gave her a sense of warmth to know Grey may be somehow affiliated too since most of his and Malone's endeavors were collaborative efforts. This was proof positive that she had been wrong in thinking Grey was incorrigible.   Malone's principles and sense of morality had exceeded far beyond what her expectations could ever imagine. Every facet of the building projected tireless energy and unbounded sacrifice in order to create an environment strictly for aiding others. She had read endless articles in the last couple of years and heard numerous reports on the news and talk shows, and had seen a documentary on these Universities.   If she had remembered correctly, there were also some orphanages and retirement homes that had been developed by this same anonymous Founder. The qualifications for attendance were inflexible and basic, a burning desire to get an education that was unattainable due to lack of resources.   Half-hearted effort or disorderly conduct was instant grounds for dismissal. The vacancy was replaced within twenty-four hours by someone else who was waiting for a golden opportunity. The strict, no second chance policy was enforced to quickly weed out the riff raff and make room for the ones who came to work. The waiting list was full and had remained that way since the doors opened six years earlier. She waited until Mr. Security got into some other business before sneaking back inside. Three steps inside and there was that familiar voice, this time with a little more bass for emphasis.

"Excuse me Miss, you seem to think the regulations don't apply to you. I hope I don't have to call the police. Are you aware you could be locked up for loitering on private property?"

"I understand. Thank you." Vanessa left the building with no further interruptions planned. When she saw he was out of sight, she ducked back inside again.

.

Working for the F.B.I. was what had finally desensitized Vanessa to shock absorbing intolerance, or so she thought. If Malone was or had been the silent director or founder of this school as stated by her informant, she wouldn't believe it until she witnessed it for herself. Even then, the shock would be a struggle for her to digest.

Her expedition allotted ample time to stop and scrutinize every intricate detail listed on her checklist. Vanessa had also been given the name of Rothschild by her source as the woman who could answer all her questions regarding the university's 'legitimacy, accreditation and where the money was coming from to fund the programs. Hopefully, interviewing a student or two would bring in some solid clarity. Finding out the degree of Malone's involvement was going to be a challenge.

It wasn't until Vanessa reached the last classroom on the

second floor that she decided to glance through the window in the door and cooking utensils immediately caught her eye. They were identical to the ones Prudence worshiped in their kitchen. Her peripheral vision provided only a glimpse of the instructor's white wrap chef's apron and hat. The instructor remained stationary at the other end of the class. Vanessa couldn't make out the faint voice. She took note of the expensive appliances, kitchen décor, and cookware that she had only seen in high-end cooking supply stores and magazines. On one wall alone were hundreds of vintage cookbooks ranging from Betty Crocker up to Modernist Cuisine. She thought how much Prudence would love this set up. All this triggered her curiosity to see who was teaching the class. She didn't want to disrupt the class by opening the door and looking inside. She pressed her face against the glass to see. When that didn't work, she waited. Then finally, the chef made her way to the opposite end of the classroom right in Vanessa's direct line of view. The unexpected face was startling. Her eyes widened and her hands sprung to cover her mouth.

"Prue?" she screeched with a piercing sound and ducked down. The plot had officially thickened. Malone had graduated from alleged to confirmed involvement. Vanessa was planted in the opened doorway, bobbing, winking and batting her eyelashes, fishing for eye contact. When it became clear that Prudence didn't notice her crazy gestures Vanessa stopped. Riveted by her newfound discovery, she continued listening and found herself captivated by Prudence's professionalism and knowledge on the art of making croissants. Then came the arrival of Mr. Security.

"Okay Miss, I'm going to take you to the office this time so you can clear up whatever business you have here and be gone once and for all."

"Thank you so much. That's all I needed in the first place was to find the office," she humored him.

On the way to the office with the guard Vanessa thought about how she initially felt that Malone and Prudence's lifestyle and sense of values would bond them for life. Prudence was surely unaware that her involvement in this training program could establish her as an accomplice. Prudence had obviously seen no stop signs when she decided to commit herself to Malone so quickly for what Vanessa gathered would be the long haul. Vanessa could see they had an unspoken understanding the first night Malone met Prudence. Vanessa knew them both well enough to know nothing could stop either of them now. Everything was moving fast forward. Offering advice to Prudence now would fall on deaf ears. She was in love.

Vanessa took a moment to collect her self before she journeyed into the main office. By seeing Prudence, she knew Malone was involved. Her biggest question had been answered but still needed proof.

"You can speak to anyone in here. I'm going to wait for you

to finish," announced Mr. Security guard.

"Don't tell me, let me guess why. You want to escort me to the front door when I'm finished?"

"Not only do I want to lead you to the door, I want this to be your last trip.   Look lady, I've been very patient, I should have had you arrested and questioned by now.   Don't push me because you are really starting to infuriate me," He said in a threatening tone, as he buffed up his chest trying to intimidate her.

"Well, I don't want to do anything to get you furious with me. So when I finish, I'm outta here," Vanessa promised in a meek voice attempting to appear shaken.

"For good," insisted Mr. Security.

Mrs. Yolanda Rothschild was in her early seventies, at least, well dressed and a staff member.   She was quite receptive to handling Vanessa's unresolved concerns and pertinent questions concerning the school.   The most glowing factor to Vanessa was the high energy level and sincere dedication the staff had to their work. After she and Mrs. Rothchild finished her checklist, Vanessa zeroed in on a few more people in the office who were more than willing to answer any questions as well.

"So, how long has this school been here?"

"Six years," the stately woman was prim and proper.   "The entire time we have been here, we have remained consistent in implementing and staying focused on what our initial goals were when we opened the trade school."

"And what are the goals?"

"To always strive for and remain true to the pursuit of continued self growth and inner truth. Always search for better ways to upgrade, improve, and seek the highest level of quality education," She rattled off as if she were saying the Pledge of Allegiance. Her attitude revealed a combination of satisfaction and pride in her work.

"Who is and where might the owner or founder of this magnificent school be?" Vanessa asked the office group as a whole.

"His name is Mr. Stanton, and he's rarely here. Is this for a magazine or newspaper article?"

Vanessa smirked, "Yes, the Valley Newspaper. Would you like to see some id?"

"No, we get reporters on a daily basis from somewhere."

"So, Mr. Stanton, right, of course. Thanks, thanks for nothing." The moment the words rolled off her tongue she wished she could have snatched them back. "I apologize, I didn't mean that the way it came out." Vanessa retracted. "I thought someone by the name of Malone Carson ran this school." '*A Mr. Stanton wouldn't account for Prue being here*' Vanessa thought. The regal woman smiled pleasantly as if she paid no attention to her remark.

"All I can tell you is we have a total of five of these schools all in different cities and they are all privately funded. The young people who attend these schools come from all ethnic groups, are underprivileged and sometimes are impoverished. If it were not for these programs thousands of young adults could never afford an education. We pride ourselves on having the best staff of teachers and curriculum. Most of the trades are two-year programs and we help our students find employment. That is what you should write in your article," She smiled accommodatingly.

"Hummm!!! Well, thank you so much for all your patience and information,"

Vanessa's disposition had mellowed. As she casually walked down the hallway mulling over what she had just been told, she glanced into another one of the glass cases housing a large number of photographs. Directly in the center of the board of directors was the Chairman of the Board, Malone Carson.

She didn't have to turn around, she could feel Mr. Security guard's presence and his eyes following her every movement until she exited the building.

Chapter **32**

"We will be landing in Las Vegas in fifteen minutes. It is 40 degrees and the time is 3:30 p.m." J signed off of the intercom.

Malone was more than fashionably late to his annual meeting with Clive Stanton, an extreme stickler about punctuality.

"You really deviated from protocol with this tardiness. This is just plain, out right late," Holiday, said disgustedly.

"Oh, the best was yet to come. Malone still has to deal with the huffing and puffing Stanton display he does to show his aggravation," Farren reminded him.

"Which Stanton will continue to exhibit because of our tardiness until he receives apologies from all of us. Then, he'll have to ponder whether he'll forgive us or not. I told you to hurry up Blue. Damn." December rolled her eyes at Malone as she fussed.

"You have talked about this since we left LA, can we drop it please."

The Stanton Inc. fifteen-story office building was unrivalled in beauty. Stanton's private penthouse was ostentatious from the solid gold imported toilets to the original 18th century Gothic art collection. The entrepreneur had a sealed gallon jug filled with various sizes of uncut diamonds sitting on his desk that he had found years ago during a mining expedition. His office was a vulgar display of wealth and he was a rudely wealthy man. As the four of them approached the massive brass doors, Malone whispered to Holiday, "Ring the bell baby. I can't believe the damn traffic in Vegas. I forgot it was going to be busy down here because Christmas is upon us. I hate being late when I have a meeting with this mother fucka. Shit! I'd rather take one for the team in an electric chair." Stanton buzzed the door. Malone walked in with the Trio behind him.

"My main man," Malone walked in with a swift stride, bearing a broad smile and offering a genuine bear hug. "Man, you know you're my main man. I humbly apologize for my unconscionable display of tardiness. I also apologize for December, Holiday and Farren. This however is all my fault. " He said humbly.

Stanton was large in stature and soft spoken to the point of being barely audible. He was sophisticated, bald, old fashioned and wore two chunky diamond picky rings. Malone and Stanton had been business partners for six years. Stanton was thirty years Malone's senior. After some deliberation concerning Malone's plea, Stanton embraced the Trio briefly with sincere warmth.

Everyone followed Stanton to the round conference table made out of Italian marble that matched the floors. It was piled with leather folders. He served French pastries, gourmet coffee, and no small talk. Immediately after positions were assumed, Stanton said, "Update me on the progress of the tracks under construction." He scanned his choices and pointed to Holiday. She opened her notebook to that section.

"We have fifty tracts under construction, consisting of two-hundred homes on each track equaling a total of 10,000 homes. Five of the tracks are already framed. ETC (estimated time of completion) is six months. The each home to build is $30,000 total. Price is $300,000,000. The selling price for each home will be based on the income of buyer. On Monday, $150,000,000 was wired into your Swiss bank account with a balance of $150,000,000 due after the completion of the project. Here is a detailed summary, a receipt of deposit, a notarized IOU for the balance, and a copy of the contract signed by you and Malone with the stipulations and rules for your backing of the project." Holiday itemized. She handed him a duplicate file. Stanton reviewed it quickly through his gold-leafed reading glasses. Peering over them, he said in his usual no-nonsense tone, "Update for the tract plans in Detroit?"

After a brief overview, he chose Farren. She flipped the pages to that section in her notebook.

"We have decided on the east side of Detroit, but have not nailed a specific date. We are having blue prints drawn for a new design on homes conducive to the demands, climate, and unstable economy of the city. We have priced materials and pulled comps on vacant land, but haven't found anything yet to work within the parameters of our general, but pretty much final plans. We researched and discovered a strong need for a school to boost the morale and create a venue to encourage interest in hobbies and trades that may uplift the sagging community. We have incorporated this into our permanent plans. A crew has been hired to scout land and resources to accommodate our joint venture. Midsummer is the earliest we will have everything finalized." Farren handed him a duplicate copy of the file. Stanton scanned it and nodded in a gesture of consent. Everyone had met his requirements wholeheartedly. Stanton represented the true definition of what it meant to *pay the cost to be the boss*. After he had scrutinized the contents of the file he spoke, "I'd like to have a brief overview of the current StatCar's portfolio and holdings."

Stanton was Malone's self-appointed Godfather. They had built a bond of trust over the years that was indestructible. The name StatCar was a combination of Stanton and Carson. They were one of the many companies that were under the umbrella of Stanton Enterprises. Malone and the Trio's entire charitable organization were under the corporation of StatCar or P.A.W. Malone had laundered and filtered the money into Stanton's legitimate enterprises since its inception. Stanton's billions were inherited from generations of oil money dating back as far as his great, great grandfather. His family's wealth continued to soar and never faltered because of his family's astute business acumen. Malone stood up, cleared his throat, and stalled as if he were trying to organize his thoughts.

"Our future goal is to aim for a program that builds more universities, trade schools, and housing projects in underprivileged areas nationwide. To implement non-profit funding programs so the programs we have started can sustain themselves. Projection time and goal: four cities a year until the forty chosen cities are completed. The cities we selected are based on how little access there is to employment, education and housing. We check average yearly incomes because these are the most costly ventures and take an astronomical amount of time to plan. I personally feel education, housing, food and employment are essential and should be a right for all human beings. So, as soon as our set of plans are solid, it will be added to the planning stages roster. Our purpose is to one day be able to provide every person the chance to get a fair shake at equal opportunity. "My dream is to go global for the needs of others. Well, that's all I have," Malone said and took his seat. He reflected back on the experiences that lead him to this great moment.

The last sentence Malone had served was much longer because he refused to incriminate Grey as his accomplice after he had been arrested for credit card fraud.   While Malone was doing time, Grey went back to live at his mother's pathetic dwelling because he had squandered all of his money.   When Malone needed money or help getting a lawyer, Grey had no answers.   He remained at Arlene's until Malone was released and had time to conjure a hustle for them to make more money.   No matter what, Malone always went back to retrieve Grey.   After Malone was released, he vowed to bury that easy come, easy go street mentality.   He began saving money once it was clearly understood Grey was not an option.   Malone started to invest money in legal ventures so all of his holdings wouldn't be confiscated if he ever got in trouble again. He employed one of the finest criminal attorneys that money could retain and most importantly made a conscience decision that if he was going to keep taking chances with his freedom, it would be for a much greater cause than flashing hundred dollar bills, expensive meals, luxury cars, and fraudulent deals.   He was going back to his original plan of dedicating his life to others.

Stanton rose and performed the ritual that had earned him the crown for being the renowned king of few words.   As he spoke, he made piercing eye contact with Malone.

"December, do you have anything to add?"

"No, all my points of view and all my concerns have been addressed," she responded.

"As long as your focus remains steadfast and genuine to the

principles you've outlined, my participation will remain as passionate and strong as yours. I will help you implement and fund a global network. Whether a mistake is intentional or unintentional is irrelevant to me because the results are still the same. Should you stray from these principles for any reason, my participation will end." Stanton gathered his belongings and departed his office. His *right to the point* closing statements flabbergasted the four of them. The wealthy businessman's policies remained inflexible. Stanton answered to no one.

Malone's voice quivered after Stanton's exit.

"Our dreams came true tonight. I can't believe he is on board."

Right on schedule, the color in Malone's face began to resurface. Malone didn't have a problem showing emotion and humility, which is why the Trio loved Malone so much. The most debatable, yet unsolved topic of discussion for his three best friends was how a man like Malone who was so astute, perceptive in business, strong and secure didn't try to cover up how deeply he sank in grief when he saw deprived people. He summoned the girls with a hand gesture.

"Well girls, dinner is on your man."

The four of them explored Vegas like it was their first time there. Malone first took them to a five star restaurant. Then they took in a concert and a live comedy show. Finally, and lastly went to the casinos to gamble. Holiday hit the blackjack tables and won big money so fast, the house instantly took notice. Malone had to take her out before she got kicked out again. On their way back to the hotel at the end of the night, Malone positioned himself between the Trio and hugged them one by one and told them each of them,

"I love the three of you so much. When I count my blessings, I count each of you twice." The three of them smiled.

"You are the most sensitive man I have ever known," Holiday replied lovingly.

"That's why I love you so much," Farren and December said in harmony.

The four of them held hands as they walked back to the hotel.

Chapter 33

Nature had announced the arrival of winter in New York. The layers of golden, bronze sunsets, continuous cool breezes and fall fashion divas were all gone. An ensemble of patterned clouds shed dark shadows on the horizon and served as the city's backdrop. The buildings were covered with thick, dingy snow, chiseled into the shape of the city as winter reared its unwelcomed head. New Yorkers were now wearing parkas and down.

Twenty eager volunteer workers congregated in the staff's office preparing to carry out the orders of the day. They were selected to complete the stress-oriented assignments dense with uncompromising deadlines. The holiday shopping ritual was the same every Christmas.

Special assignments were offered but not a requirement for the staff. The monetary compensation was paid in cash because jobs posed more of a risk of being questioned due to the holiday season due to the enormity of the purchases.

Michael, by his own request, instructed the staff to refer to him as Mr. Nixon. He distributed pamphlets to each of the workers and said, "The information contained in the handouts are the dos and don'ts of what should be done in the field. What you should do if you think you are being watched and what you should do if apprehended." After Michael had provided adequate time for everyone to read and absorb the information he addressed the Special Agents. "Are there any questions? " One of the female employees signaled to get Michael's attention and asked with the intention of belittling him. "Would it matter if we did have any questions, Mr. Nixon? You wouldn't be able to supply any answers. You have never worked on the front line. You are an office worker."

He disregarded her spiteful subtext as he answered her questions in the professional manner the rulebooks required, "I only work in the office true, but I am well versed on the policies and procedures that are to be executed while on duty in the field."

If the upper management, for any reason, got wind of actions exchanged by employees in anything other than a professional manner it was instant grounds for termination. That was a strict no fraternization and no confrontation policy. Both were prohibited.

One of the men inquired, "So Mr. Nixon, for this play. Are we getting a flat salary like last year?"

"Yes you are."

" I have a question," another worker raised his hand.

"Fire away," Michael replied.

"How much cash are we actually getting for the job?"

" $8.000 flat rate for each of you. That's a little more than last year because the orders are a little larger. The flat rate is contingent on the orders being filled properly. If the order isn't fulfilled exactly as stated on your orders forms the amount of your pay will be adjusted accordingly. So, get it right. Everybody wants to get paid all his or her money. Right after the play, you will be assisted in delivering the merchandise to the address highlighted in the instructions. Once you are finished, return here and you will be compensated."

Michael adjusted his imported silk tie that enhanced the beauty of his tailored, winter white suit, matching overcoat, ostrich leather gloves and boots.

"Now is everybody clear? Are there any more questions or concerns." No more hands were raised and the employees took off like a heard of cattle.

"Hold on, hold on. Slow down, I'm not finished." Michael insisted.

"One more thing. Please be careful out there. Even though you are making large purchases, be as inconspicuous as possible. Remember there are cameras everywhere now. Blend. No splashes of colors or flashy clothing. Do nothing to draw extra attention to yourselves. Our specialists are here today in makeup, hair and wardrobe because the assignments are pretty extensive this year. Even though we aren't facing up, there is heavy make up involved. Remember everyone will be shopping at either a high end grocery, toy or clothing store. Check in with me before you exit the building," Michael instructed.

The workforce gathered their belongings and scurried to begin the assembly line process.   Once they were done and passed Michael's inspection they were given their assignment packets that contained their master card or visa and driver's license.

"Well, on that note, let's get to the business of making Christmas merry."

Chapter 34

Toi agreed to meet Chen Lee at a posh hotel in Universal City in the San Fernando Valley to prepare her for a Christmas shopping assignment that was added to the roster at the last minute.

Toi's leg fluttered in constant motion as he tried to apply the mask he had prepared three day's prior in his studio for her face. Chen wiggled and squirmed as Toi worked.

Finally Toi halted his service on her. He stood back, put one hand on his hip and the other dangled limply as he stood over Chen and stared her down with no display of emotion. He remained posted in her face until Chen felt uneasy.

"If you don't hurry up Toi, you gonna make me late," she said indignantly and smacked her lips.

"Late! Oh Dahling, I'm going to do one better than late. If you don't sit your little ass down and be still honey you will be walking outta here the same way you came in. Oh, honey I am not bluffing either." Chen could see he meant business. She turned around and didn't budge another inch.

"I apologize Toi," she said humbly, sat up to attention and

studied the 'mark' on her iPad.   Not a word was spoken throughout Toi 's procedure.

The chic, upscale toy store was swamped with impatient, last minute holiday Christmas shoppers who swarmed the store like an army of ants, bustling about everywhere.   After Sandra Chow checked the list twice, she proceeded to the cash register, pushing a wide load overstuffed shopping cart. A procession of fifteen more carts trailed her being pushed by helpers hired for the holidays. After the cashier totaled the order at $135,021.76, Miss Chow, handed her gold master card to the cashier. The clerk looked at it briefly and immediately requested her driver's license. Sandra promptly handed the cashier a driver's license, which matched the same information that appeared on the credit card. After the cashier had both pieces of id in her possession, she gazed at Sandra suspiciously and said, "Excuse me, I'll have to get an authorization on anything over 100,000.00 dollars."

"Why, is there a problem?" Sandra inquired.

The cashier walked directly in the back without acknowledging her question. Sandra adjusted her poker face, but began to take notice of the exits surrounding her. After a few minutes, goose bumps slightly appeared on her arms and her upper lip started quivering. It took all the energy she could muster to keep her knees from buckling underneath her as the cashier returned sandwiched between two security guards. The nervous Chow then noticed four other security guards rushing from the back of the store. They dispersed to cover all the possible escape routes that were mapped out in her mind. The goose bumps were now quite visible and the hair on the nape of her neck was standing at full attention. This was the first time in five years in this line of work that she had ever encountered anything of this nature. She focused on the number one rule of the organization, never panic. Chow felt anxious but steadfast to remain calm. As the security guards drew closer, she tried to conceal her trembling hands. They surrounded her as the cashier confirmed,

"You are Sandra Chow?"

"That's what my id says, doesn't it?"

"Well then, we'll have to retain you," the security guards informed her.

"Look," a hint of panic surfaced in her voice, "I don't have time for this nonsense and unless you provide me with a viable reason for why you are detaining me, and I mean right now, then finish my purchase, give me back my id, and let me go about my business, or you'll have a lawsuit on your hands like you've never imagined possible."

As she motioned to leave, both of the security guards grabbed her applying mild pressure to her arms. She felt from their solid grips that her fate was now their decision. The tension inside her escalated as two store managers rapidly approached the register from opposite directions. Customers and employees swarmed around the calamitous situation in droves.

Chow stood there and watched the pandemonium and knew that the organization would have money and a lawyer in place before the jail door closed. In every case, *the person in charge* had always resolved the staff's legal problems. They minimized and often avoided incarceration because the organization never hired anyone with a prior record. Once an employee was arrested, they could no longer work for the organization in any capacity. The Christmas season would delay a hearing for bail, and the bust would disunite her employment, she thought. This most assuredly was not how she had envisioned bringing in the holidays. As she conceded to the fact that jail was where she would be bringing in Christmas, bright strobe lights flashed throughout the store, along with blaring alarms and jingling bells. The noise was so ear piercing that she could feel vibrations pounding inside her head as her heart pumped rapidly. The security guards forced her toward the end of the counter as she made an unsuccessful attempt at fleeing. Out of nowhere, hundreds of balloons, multicolored streamers, and colored rice was released from the ceiling. The sound of trumpets began tooting over the store's sound system and a man's enthusiastic voice announced over the intercom, "May I have your attention please? Sandra Chow is the ten thousandth person to make a purchase since the start of our Christmas gift giveaway sweepstakes. She is the winner of the grand prize and all her purchases up to $100,000.00 are free." The huge crowd that had gathered cheered and gave a heartfelt ovation. The adulation filled her with moments of feeling like a celebrity. On one hand, the gaiety jolted her desire to take a bow and throw kisses. On the other hand, despite of her relief, she wanted to take her free things and run out of the door. Sandra couldn't find it in her heart to refuse the cake, ice cream, and sugary watered down punch they served for the celebration though. Before long she found herself softening and enjoying the festivities. The Christmas spirit was apparent in the line of people who were wrapped round the store to congratulate her. A few tourists insisted on her autograph. It was difficult for Chow to share in the depth of the crowds' excitement for the free merchandise since it would have been free for her anyway. Nonetheless, she stood on a chair and toasted all the onlookers with her glass of punch.

"To all of you, have a Merry Christmas and a wonderful New Year!" she bellowed with joy. Sandra Chow exited the store and let out a colossal sigh of relief.

Chapter 35

It smelled liked Christmas. Roasted and fried turkeys, dressing, ham, yams, macaroni and cheese, were just a few of the traditional dishes on the menu. The last RSVP had been confirmed for the intimate dinner party of fifteen couples. Vanessa and Prudence assisted the set -up crew and added their personal and final touches to the quarters.

The caterers had set the long dining room table in accordance with the number of guests who had responded. In the past, Vanessa and Prudence's parties had always been informal, for singles or couples, and buffet style. They changed the entire format this year because Grey and Malone wanted to be included. After the decision to combine the event, Prudence insisted that the party showcase a more romantic theme. Impressing the guests was extremely important to Vanessa and Prudence because half of them attending were personal friends of Malone and Grey's. The party promised evening attire, a sit down dinner, and a female singer with a three-piece band and a DJ.

The ten-foot, white, flocked, Christmas tree in the entry hallway was as wide as it was tall. It was generously adorned with white lights, bulbs, and ornaments. Half of the small Italian lights flickered and the other half remained on at all times. When the house lights were off, the tree cast a dimly lit, romantic ambiance to the downstairs party area. Various shapes, sizes and colored lights added a festive touch to all the picture windows throughout the house and also illuminated the upper levels. The staircase railing, baby grand piano, and fireplace were garnished with various sized candy canes and huge red satin bows linked with long trails of embossed ribbon.

The bar and the area sectioned off for the entertainment was clad in silver tinsel. The house was fragrant with the distinctive scent of red currant candles. Malone loved the aroma.

"You know for the past two out of the three years we held this event we were thoroughly disgusted with our escorts," Vanessa reflected.

"Well' I'm excited because my friends keep telling me that they can't wait to meet my new mystery man whom I talk about incessantly." As they admired themselves in the mirror in Prudence's bathroom Prudence said, "Getting our hair designed at the Carl Montclair Salon in Beverly Hills was the best idea you have come up with in a long time. Our hair looks fabulous."

"Everything that could be done we did, didn't we? Mr. Montclair agreed to come to the house a couple of hours before the party starts to retouch our hair and makeup if needed he said."

"Look at this black evening ensemble. Have you ever seen anything so subtly sexy and elegant? It matches the tux I picked for Malone."

As Prudence gazed in the mirror, she reminisced about the excitement and anticipation she had felt when she went to her high school prom. That same thrill rushed through her veins all over again. Adrenaline pumped through her body like she had been announced the winner of a ten million dollar lottery. She imagined the four of them were going to have a ball.

"Now I understood how you felt when you told me Grey made you feel like a teenager all over again." Prudence beamed.

"Well, that perpetual grin and your radiant complexion makes it obvious you feel the same way about Malone."

"While you were getting your hair styled I shopped for a gift for him. It was difficult to purchase something for a man who has everything he wants. After toiling long and hard, I found the perfect present. I can't wait to give it to him at the party.

Just thinking about him makes me feel like I can walk on air. God has finally answered my prayers Vanessa. He is the kind of man I have dreamt of having all my life. He's romantic, thoughtful and sensitive and he loves me, I know he does."

"Hummm." Vanessa tilted her head to one side and stared in her friend's eyes.

"You are floating in a mubble."

Malone had been tied up with business for the past three days and Vanessa hadn't heard from Grey. He assured her he would try everything in his power to minimize the details of his cluttered work schedule early because he knew how much the evening meant.

Prudence was worried and nervous as she thought about Malone had disappeared at the onset of the holidays. This was behavior she didn't expect from him. She phoned the office and he wasn't there. The receptionist didn't know his whereabouts or time of return. His cell message chattered *mobile customer unavailable* and there was no answer on his home phone. Prudence left no messages on his voice mail. She would have to wait until he contacted her.

Vanessa strolled into Prudence's room in good spirits as she filed her nails and sang along to Christmas carols that played softly over the house's piped-in stereo system.

"Heard from my dear ole cousin yet?" Vanessa asked.

"Now Vanessa, you know I haven't heard from him, so why would you ask me that?

Prudence didn't mention her attempts to contact Malone.

"Well, don't worry. I haven't heard from Grey yet either."

Prudence responded defensively, "Who said I was worried? Besides, from what you tell me about Grey, you probably shouldn't expect too much anyway,"

"Well, you'll be disappointed to know that I am expecting more than not too much." Vanessa said with attitude as she left her room. Prudence's was unmoved and her expression was hollow as she watched Vanessa leave. Listlessly, Prudence used the remote control to open the circular blinds covering her bedroom windows. She placed her arm across her eyes to shield the glare of the sun as it illuminated her room. She focused on the colorless, faded by smog mountainous backdrop. Prudence checked to see if her cell was on. The ring from the house phone startled her. She wanted to sprint for it like hot coals burning under her feet. She played it cool. When the ringing stopped, her eyes remained on the phone. She tapped her foot, picked the lint off her pants, twirled her hair between her fingers, and examined her nails. Vanessa hadn't' called her to pick up the phone. Her heart pulsated faster the more anxious she became. She carefully bit her cuticles trying not to chip her manicure. Of course 'silly she thought, if it were Malone they would talk a while.' "It's probably Grey," she muttered to herself. When she glanced at the clock after what had seemed like an eternity, only ten minutes had elapsed.

Vanessa's temperament was melancholy when she strolled in Prudence's bedroom.

"I left my damn nail file in here, mind if I get it?" Prudence gestured okay.

"Who was on the phone?" Prudence grilled.

"My mother and your mother on three way." Vanessa responded.

"Again? You two talk a million times a day every day," Prudence smiled pleasantly.

"Wrong, a billion." Vanessa countered.

"What in the world do you two find to talk about?" Prudence inquired with her mind focused elsewhere.

"Everything, anything and nothing."

"How are our moms?" Prudence asked still distracted.

"Fine, I told them you said hello. They said they sent us a Christmas gifts."

"Did you mail our gifts to her?"

"Ages ago." Vanessa responded. "Did you mail our gifts to your mother?"

"Of course."

"I think that's so cute. When it comes right down to it, you're an ole fashion mama's girl," Prudence stated.

"You know that doesn't offend me. Ma and Venice are the loves of my life. There wouldn't be life for me without them. Besides, you should talk as much as you talk to Stephanie." Vanessa smiled tenderly.

"I know, the nerve of me. I talked to mama all night long." Prudence gathered her thoughts. "Dodie is special, I love her as much as I love my own mother and the same way you love mine."

"You know what I think by that statement you just made. I think Dodie is the only person on the face of the planet whose opinion and feelings you care about and respect, even more than your man, when you have one." Prudence baited. Vanessa's expression switched from pleasant to puzzled.

"Wait one damn minute now, what the hell is that supposed to mean?"

"You're acting like you don't know where I am going with this."

"Not acting Prue, I don't have a clue. What have I done now?"

"It's what you don't do," she was a little peeved.

"You're just upset because Malone hasn't called, and you need to vent some anger. Go ahead direct it at me," proposed Vanessa.

"This has nothing to do with Malone."

"Well, it hurts my feelings for you to think I don't care about your opinions." Vanessa waited for a response from Prudence. She gave none. Vanessa continued,

"Prue, are you trying to tell me that you think I don't care or have any regards for your feelings?"

"No, I'm not *trying* to tell you, that's precisely what I <u>am</u> telling you. When it comes to your job, that's your first priority no matter what's at stake for anyone else. You have tunnel vision," accused Prudence. Vanessa sat at attention, her mouth tightened and eyes widened.

"Where is this coming from?"

"When Grandfather died, you couldn't tear yourself away from your precious job, sorry, I mean your precious career to go home with me to the funeral."

"My God Prue, that was three years ago, and if I recall correctly, I asked you if you wanted me to go, and you said it was okay if I didn't go," Vanessa defended.

"That was only after you told me how important it was for you to take on that new case that had been assigned to you. Maybe I could have understood if you had already been tied up in something, but you accepted that case knowing how devastated my family and I were," disclosed Prudence.

"It looks like the problem here is not that I didn't go to the funeral. The problem is that you say one thing and mean another. What is this kindergarten bullshit about anyway?" Vanessa reprimanded.

"Look Vanessa, God forbid, but if something ever happened to Dodie or anyone in your family, I wouldn't ask you if you needed my help, I would be there. No exceptions, no questions asked. If I were the head chef at the Presidential Inauguration dinner and you needed me, I'd leave. Nothing takes precedence in my life over any devastation that would happen to you. You always say there wouldn't be life for you without Dodie and Venice. What about me and my mother, we are your family just as much as they are."

Vanessa sat back outdone. She held her head in her hand, crushed.

"I can't believe that you've felt this way all this time and never mentioned it."

"Well, believe it," Prudence held her position.

.   "Look Vanessa, obviously the misunderstanding is on my part. I thought we were all family. I thought you felt the same way about us that we do about your family." Prudence taunted bitterly because of hurt feelings.

Vanessa's voice descended I'm trying to understand this. If you wanted me to go to Pops funeral all you had to do was ask."

"Ask Vanessa, I was devastated. I shouldn't have had to ask. You should have been there. Do you think if something happened to Venice, God forbid, you'd have to ask? Prudence's voice cracked.

"Huh." Vanessa eased back on the bed diverting her attention to her hands; she rolled her thumbs rapidly around each other. "Now, I understand what you mean and I am so humbly sorry if I have been remiss in being there for you when you needed me. That will never happen again. Not in my actions or my words. Prue you are my only sister and I love you just as much as I do my mother and my son. I hope you understand that regardless of my actions. Will you forgive me."

"Forgiven. It never happened. Love is our actions," Prudence said with sincerity.

At that moment, the phone rang. Vanessa answered then switched it to speaker when she heard who it was.

"Hello Merry Christmas to you, too."

"Would you happen to know where Grey evaporated to?"

"I have no idea, I haven't seen him in a week," She attempted to conceal the disappointment in her voice.

"So where the hell have you been Malone?"

"Mind your damn business. May I speak to Prudence please?"

"What do you mean, mind my business?"

"Just what I said."

"You are so damn rude," Vanessa laughed and handed Prudence the phone.

Vanessa moved near the door during Prudence's conversation. Prudence gestured her to leave.

"Hello,"

"How are you?"

"Okay."

"Are you irked with me?" Malone asked sweetly.

"No, I'm not mad," she sighed.

"Baby I have a lot of things to do for the Holiday, I hope you understand.

"Yeah sure, I understand. So are you coming to the party?"

"I'm sorry I haven't called. Is everything okay?" Malone stalled.

"Are you coming to the party, yes or no?" Prudence persisted.

Malone was silent.

"So, you're not coming?" she was disappointed.

"Baby, that's why I haven't called, I didn't know how to break it to you," Malone spoke humbly.

"Well, now you've broken it to me, is there anything else? 'Cause I really have to go."

"Will you let me explain?" Malone pleaded.

Prudence nervously tapped her foot on the floor and rapped her fingers on the table. Her voice took a sharper tone as she ranted.

"Okay, explain if you must, but please extend me the courtesy of making it creative and believable. Oh, and while you're at it, maybe you'd like to offer a detailed explanation of why I haven't heard from you in the last four days."

"Three days," Malone corrected.

"Disappearing for the holidays, that is so tacky, Malone. Whenever men pull these stunts for the holidays, they either have another woman or a drug habit. You, to my knowledge, don't indulge in drugs," Prudence's voice cracked in frustration.

"Oh baby, you're jumping way out in left field now. If you would listen for one minute, you'd be able to spare yourself these ridiculous conclusions. Let me explain what's going on. I couldn't get anyone to cover for me. I tried like hell. I have given my word to these various organizations that every Christmas eve and Christmas day I donate my time. I do charity work, Prudence.   I started to cancel, but I just can't do that to these kids.   Besides, I already bought all the stuff and hired a crew of people to help me load and deliver it." Malone explained.

"If you knew you had these prior commitments, then why did you say you wanted to have a Christmas party with us in the first place?"

"My business partner Stanton said he would stand in for me. He cancelled at the last minute. I couldn't put this much work on the Trio. It's just too much for them to do by themselves."

"So what am I suppose to do now?"

"You want to come with me? My friends are cool. They can entertain themselves. You can let them in and as long as there is liquor, food and music they won't care if your are there or not." Prudence smiled. She didn't want to go, but she wanted him to ask. Her disposition perked up.

"No, I better stay here and oversee things."

"Have a good time with my friends 'cause now they're going to be your friends, too. Give them my apologies, look gorgeous, and represent. Prudence, I have loved you from the moment I laid eyes on you. I am so sorry I can't spend our first Christmas together. I'll make it up to you. I gave my word."

Her heart softened, "I understand. If you gave your word, you gotta go."

She hung up, laid back on the bed, closed her eyes, and counted to herself. When she reached fifty, she sat up. As Vanessa entered the room Prudence told her,

"Malone's not coming."

"Oh really, so why isn't he bringing his black ass over here? What kind of business could he possibly have that's more important than spending the biggest holiday of the year with his woman and his cousin?"

"Charity work," she replied in an understanding tone.

"And you believe that bullshit?".

"Yes, I do," Prudence, said without hesitation. "I trust him. Besides, I'm really not mad. Disappointed, but how can you be peeved with someone who does charity work on Christmas?" Prudence shook it off.

"So did he happen to mention where he was?"

"Nope. Although, I kinda got the impression he was home." Vanessa sprinted down the hall snatching off her loungewear all the way to her closet. "I sure wish I could be snowed in a secluded cabin with you for Christmas. Is that too much to ask? Everybody wants lavish gifts, spend tons of money and all I want for Christmas is you." Vaneesa said to Patrick as she pulled up her jeans, buttoned her shirt, and slid on some Cole Haan mules.

"Merry Christmas Patrick. I would bet the family farm you wish you had my life huh?. Chasing criminals on the Lord's birthday." She pulled Malone's case out of her private filing cabinet to get his address, which she had confiscated off of Prudence's computer one day after she left with him. Vanessa attached a broche and flew out the door.

Prudence saw her, ran to the stairs and yelled, "Hey Vanessa, where the hell are you going'?   What about the party!" By the time Prudence reached the stairs, Vanessa had disappeared like a rabbit in magician's hat.

Chapter 36

Dusk had already fallen when Vanessa arrived in the vicinity of Malone's house. The Valley Village California residential neighborhood was quaint and clean. Vanessa parked several blocks away, threw her purse in the trunk, and scouted the homes for addresses as she walked. When she turned the corner where she surmised the house should be she was stunned. Vanessa contorted in a pretzel-like position so she wouldn't be seen while getting a panoramic view of the immense activity underway in front of the house. The scene was the furthest thing from her imagination. She expected grandiose, but got modest. The dwelling was small and nondescript. The street was bustling. A caravan of six semi–trucks lined the block on both sides of the street. The cheerful band of people loading them obstructed her view as she attempted to identify the leader of the merriment.

Vanessa immediately activated her broach. After a quick overview, she didn't recognize any of these people working from the photographs or from the Red Rose staff party. Then in the center of the commotion, familiar faces.

"Holiday and December, this must be your favorite time of year," a man's raspy voice blurted out jokingly from the crowd. Holiday and December both looked in the direction of the voice but said nothing as the funny guy stepped forward.

"Oh, I see what's happenin'." You guys like to act stuck up. No, I take that back, you all aren't acting, you *are* stuck up. I know you all won't give a guy no rhythm."

At that moment, Farren emerged as the wise cracks continued. "Hey Farren, it would have been right on time if your mother would have jumped on the band wagon and named you Christmas. Then you three would have been the December, Christmas, Holiday." The crew applauded with an outpour of sidesplitting laughter. Farren, Holiday and December exchanged glances and couldn't help but to laugh.

They never lost step during their inspections of the cargo on the trucks. The workers hustled to finish, as they raced against time. A gargantuan number of gifts were being loaded with two wheelers and flat beds. There was everything from children's three wheelers to motorcycles and countless wrapped gifts. Everything from dolls and trucks that fit in the palm of your hand to life sized dolls you could take for a walk and trucks large enough to drive, and houses kids could walk in. As the pandemonium escalated, the Trio started directing the production. They were in clear view for Vanessa.

The smell of Christmas cookies wafted from the catering trucks. Holiday gleefully summoned everyone over with a megaphone to recap instructions, last-minute details, and sync schedules. Vanessa discreetly weaved in and out among the trucks making her way inside one that was loaded with two round, brown crates. Her suspicions about the contents in the crates formed at the same time the meeting adjourned. The drivers dispersed to their positions, leaving no time for Vanessa to get off or investigate the contents of the crates. The men pulled down the roller doors on the trucks and locked them shut. The blaring sound of accelerated engines was the only thing Vanessa heard and there was nothing she could see. The inside was pitch black. As the procession moved out, Vanessa got bounced and thrown around until the trucks reached their destination. When the door was hauled open, Vanessa was nowhere to be seen.

"Over here, we'll unload this one first," Farren yelled. The drivers responded on command. This scenario posed numerous questions, *'Where the hell were Grey and Malone,'* Vanessa wondered. Inside of the van Vanessa cringed as she applied pressure to pry open one of the containers. The contents contained thousands of porcelain dolls and dishes packed in heavy straw. It wasn't what she assumed.

"Thank God he's not smuggling drugs in addition to everything else he's got going on," she mumbled. She leaped off the truck, and camouflaged herself in the bushes directly underneath a building, and watched as workers scrambled to haul in presents, furniture, and Santa Claus suits wrapped in plastic.

After everyone was situated inside the Blue Sky orphanage, Vanessa climbed up a tree next to the building and made her way to a ledge four stories high. She inconspicuously peered through several windows; the rooms were dark and empty. As she crept around a little farther, she heard faint Christmas carols, and she tracked the music to its source. As it became more audible, it led to a vast, well-lit, picture window. She peered inside and was astonished. As she attempted to position herself more securely to establish a better view, she lost her balance and fell. She grabbed hold of a tree branch and every movement, the branch gave way a little more. She hung there, swaying. The last hard swing caused the branch to completely break. As she plunged toward the ground Vanessa somehow managed to break her fall as she latched hold to an even larger branch. Carefully, she pulled herself up and edged her way up the branch toward the tree trunk. She climbed back up, a jumped onto the ledge and planted herself more securely.

"Whooo, now Patrick you can't tell me you wouldn't have a ball hanging out with me." She glanced down to verify that the trucks were still parked in front of the building and to see if she had been spotted. She briefly scanned the grounds to see if she could locate the whereabouts of Malone and the rest of his laborers.

Vanessa looked in the window. In one of the huge barren rooms, there was a transformation in progress. The workers were building a playroom. In another part of the room, worn furniture was being removed and replaced with new, plush pieces that provided a warm charm. Some of the workers were dressed like Santa helpers and were scrubbing floors, tabletops, walls and anything else that appeared to need sanitizing in the kitchen. Holiday, December, and Farren, dressed like Santa girls stocked the refrigerator, deep freezer, the pantries and kitchen cabinets.

Vanessa moved further down the ledge. In another room, Santa, his helpers, and the toys that lay in abundance under the Christmas tree fascinated the children. There were two groups of children ranging in age from two to eleven. A small group of handicapped children were sectioned away from the other children. The children's bright smiles showed their happiness. The handicapped group tore and disintegrated the Christmas wrapping on the gifts with assistance of staff. Once they finished opening the toys, they were escorted to their rooms with their presents. Then the other group of children ripped the paper off of their gifts. Each present looked handcrafted by special order. The older girls grabbed the five life-sized, custom made dolls that were garbed in designer dresses, matching shoes, and handbags. The smaller kids amused themselves inside a walk-in dollhouse with a variety of small dolls. They acted out tea parties, sleepovers and having mommies and daddies.

The boys drove cars and trucks designed like real automobiles. The ignition started with a key and they were accessorized with horns, stereo systems, leather seats and sunroofs.

"Ho, Ho, Ho and a Merry Christmas," Santa belted in a hearty voice that echoed throughout the building. The children climbed onto his lap, hugged his legs, and jumped on his head. He looked after the special group with patience and constant attentiveness. The children laughed, played, and returned gestures of warm hugs. They played games, colored, tried on new clothes, and filled their bellies with warm, homemade cookies, cake and milk. Tasty goodies were artistically arranged around an edible gingerbread house. One of the children climbed on Santa's lap to visit and got a little overzealous by pulling off his beard.

"Malone!" Vanessa screeched and then ducked out of sight. Five moments later and feeling secure that she wasn't noticed, she moved closer toward the center of the window, instantly spellbound. Malone was Santa Claus. With the sleeve of her jacket she dried the tears that fell from her eyes without warning. No way could she have put these pieces together. At that moment, they made eye contact. Malone's eyes popped open as if he had seen a ghost. He marched over to the window, and yanked his beard down in disbelief.

"What the fuck are you doing sittin' on the ledge of this building? Have you lost your mind? Are you following me? For what? Did me missing the party make you so angry that it warranted you spying on me? This is totally out of bounds. Only someone with no class would do some shit like this." He spoke holding his beard.

"Hey wait a minute, I beg your pardon, I have class."

"You're right you do have class. It's just all low." Malone shouted.

"You know what happened? really."

He threw up both hands disgusted. "Not right now Vanessa." He slammed the window and locked it. Vanessa remained on the ledge struggling to hear and continued watching Malone and the helpers as they carried the sleepy children to their dormitories. After the last child was snuggled in, a wave of moaning occurred. A couple of the small children got out of bed, returned to the front and begged the staff to stay. A recurring incident Malone's crew experienced every year when it was time to leave. Farren, December, and Holiday tried to console them, rocking them and hoping they fell asleep. They stayed as long as they could, and were now behind schedule in getting to the next facility.

The orphanage's limited staff intervened, by taking the children. As Malone was leaving, one of the staff stopped him, "Mr. Carson, we are so understaffed that in most cases the kids don't receive enough attention or care because of state cut backs."

"How come I wasn't notified? I have been helping fund this facility for years."

"I don't know, maybe an oversight." Malone summoned Holiday.

"Tell Holiday everything you need and we'll take care of

everything with the State on Monday."

Vanessa watched one of the most emotional situations she ever witnessed on the job. One of the three-year-old girls went to Farren,, she picked her up and the girl begged, "Would you please tell Santa to take me whif him?" Tears streamed down her face.

"I wish he could honey, but he can't do that."

"Can you take me whif you, please?" She cried and laid her head on Farren.

Farren choked. The nurse walked over to get the little girl. The girl locked her arms around her. Finally the nurse got her arms apart and took her back to the room. The girl was still crying.

Vanessa's sleeve was moist from her tears.

Everyone removed their costumes and exited the building.

Malone approached Vanessa, "So you still have the nerve to be here. What is up with this bullshit?"

At that moment, Farren, December and Holiday joined them, forming a perfect huddle. From the information Vanessa had accumulated in her reports, her theory was solid. Malone was the boss and the three ladies were his real partners. Malone introduced the plans, and the girls implemented them, from inception to conclusion.

"Ladies, this is my bloodhound cousin, Vanessa."

"Your bloodhound is adorable. Does she have a name, or do you call her by her breed?" Holiday asked.

Vanessa laughed, "My name is still Vanessa. I am sure all of your memories can't be that bad. I feel like I know the three of you so well. "

"Oh yeah Malone, remember I told you she was at the annual party for the staff with her man Gre . If I remember correctly, you told us the same thing." December reflected back.

"No she didn't, she said she heard so much about us." Ferran corrected her, "I can speak for the three of us in saying that we are at an unfair advantage because we have never heard anything about you." She locked eyes with Vanessa.

"How odd," Holiday said dryly, "I usually never forget a face. Maybe the window ledge doesn't do you any justice. The last time we met you were grounded."

"Nice." Vanessa smiled at Holiday then turned to Malone. "You haven't told your three closest friends about your family?" Vanessa's feelings were hurt.

"She didn't say they had never heard about any of the members of my family. She said they never heard anything about you." Malone was curt as he affectionately pushed Vanessa aside.

"Malone had to miss the party. I know the preparation that went into planning it, Farren apologized.

Malone stepped closer to Vanessa, "You know I won't be able to make it. We have deadlines that have to be met.

"I thought you had another woman, so I came to see for myself."

"What's it to you if I have a harem of 'em or not?" Malone snapped.

"Prue is my best friend and my sister and I don't want her hurt," Vanessa threatened.

"So you're her bodyguard now? Grey is my best friend and my brother and I don't want him hurt either.   But have I ever antagonized you like this?" Malone refuted in a monotone voice.

"Call it whatever the hell makes your hair blow back. So you can't make it to the party tonight at all, huh?" Vanessa rolled her eyes.

"Baby, I'd be lucky if I get through with what I have to do in the next three days. I am really sorry. I gave my word that I would complete this project and this is an annual event for us. We have fifteen more facilities tonight."

"You didn't know you had these plans when you agreed to give this couples party with us?" Vanessa scolded.

"If you must know, I had someone to cover me, but he backed out at the last minute. Look, you've poked your nose in other people's business enough for one night. Now, go home." Malone and the Trio walked briskly toward the trucks. Vanessa followed on his heels, trying to keep up. Malone gave the high sign to move out as he jumped in the back of the lead truck and helped the Trio on.

Everyone moved out. Vanessa stood on the sidewalk and looked up at him,

"You posing as Santa Claus?" she shook her head in disbelief,

"I have a pretty vivid imagination. You have far exceeded anything beyond what I could have conjured up."

"I am not posing, I am Santa Claus." The caravan moved forward and she watched them leave. As an afterthought, Vanessa sprinted down the center of the street screaming,

"Hey Malone, Malone, I don't have a ride home."

The truck stopped. He motioned her to come on. Right as she made it to the door, it quickly pulled off. He peered back at her,

"Get back the same way you got here."

"I got here in the back of one of your trucks."

"Figure it out, you're resourceful."

She stopped running and walked fast, a little out of breath. She panted as she screamed, "Come on Malone, take me back."

He yelled, "Maybe this will teach you to mind your fuckin' business. " He laughed as he turned around.

"Don't play with me, Malone, I don't have my purse, no money or id on me." She screamed and flipped him the bird making her way onto to the sidewalk.

Chapter 37
The Whiskey Shots and Tits

She walked several blocks before she reached a main street where she finally picked up enough reception on her cell to call a cab. After she picked her car up from around Malone's, on the way home Vanessa met Special Agent Lawrence at the bar. When she arrived he was already seated. She slid in the booth across from him.

"So, what the hell do you want?" Vanessa snapped.

"I wanted to let you know that all those documents you took photos of at their headquarters, the files you got off their computers and the stuff you retrieved out of the trash paved a smooth paper trail right into the DMV, social security offices, master cards and visa centers. The documents were all encoded with the employees work ID numbers. Between the four places we have a lock on about twelve people who are in that organization's pocket. Those twelve are the ones who are sending them driver's license numbers, mother's maiden names, addresses, clean social security numbers, new printed credit cards and driver's license that are brand new and exact replicas of the 'marks.' That's why the owners of the accounts always have their cards and driver's license in their possessions. Great Work."

"So you called me all the way down here to Hicksville to tell me that bullshit? What's really going on?" Vanessa snapped.

"I just thought I'd give you the good news first. Agent Lawrence smiled "Now, here is the other news. It's been five weeks and you haven't turned in any thing else. Supervisor Dayton, Johnson and me want to know what's going on." Vanessa spoke little louder because the music started. "What's going on? You three wanna know what's going on do you? This shit is multi- layered and a lot larger than they thought. It's going to take more time than I anticipated. If the information were easy to get, the bureau would have busted them by now. Look, the agency has had them under surveillance for a couple of years and hadn't collected enough evidence to question anyone for as much as spitting on the sidewalk. Now, you want me to solve the case in a month. Here is the most important thing for you to remember, I am the case agent on this assignment, which means its is my responsibility and I make all the decisions. DO NOT call me any more. When I get some information, I'll call you. Got it!!!" Vanessa reprimanded indignantly as she stormed towards the door of the bar. Suddenly, she turned back around and headed back to the table.

"By the way Lawrence, have a Merry Christmas." "Same to you Vanessa." He grinned, then focused on the strippers dancing.

Chapter 38

The grandfather clock chimed seven times. The Christmas ditty from the doorbell cued personnel to assume their positions because party time was in session. The hired staffs were properly garbed in black and white tuxedos and in position to cater to the whims of the ten couples. Each of the three staff members, excluding the photographer, bartender and coat check person, had individually wrapped, long-stem red roses, gum, mints, homemade confectioneries, and a variety of hors d'oeuvres stacked on top of the festive red serving trays. Long stemmed glasses encircled the flowing fountain of multicolored Champagne. The personnel gracefully maneuvered around the room with trays balanced on the palm of one hand and a white towel neatly draped on the other arm as the guests began to trickle in slowly.

Prudence looked like the black satin, form fitted gown had been painted on her. The plunging V-neck in front of the dress stopped at the top of her navel and the plunging v-neck in the back rested a strand above the Creator's split. The four-inch red bottom shoes accentuated her dazzle. Vanessa featured a striking, understated black, Donna Karan gown. The wide black belt punctuated the pizzazz with an eight-carat, pear-shaped Swarovski crystal mounted in the center. Tiny black pearls were woven through her platinum upswept hairdo.

The couples who attended were close friends of Malone, Vanessa and Prudence. Vanessa decided she'd stick with them throughout the night in case they knew anything about Malone that would be of interest to the case. A personal Yuletide greeting was extended to every one who stepped under the mistletoe.

The guest valet parked in the front of Vanessa and Prudence's Hollywood Hills home. Malone's allies were sophisticated, handsome and established businessmen. Prudence recognized a few of them from various business magazines. Malone's friends were awed by Vanessa's various art collections. Some gravitated to the library and browsed the extraordinary collection of hardback novels, poetry, history and reference books written by black authors. Other guest were fascinated by the large library of black films that featured predominately black casts in the TV room. Two of the men toured the music room and leafed through the vast collection of albums and cd's. All featured black singers and musicians from classical jazz greats to rap. It had taken Vanessa years to collect the artifacts, sculptures and figurines. Originals and numbered prints of black artist covered the walls throughout the home.

'Where was Grey,' Vanessa wondered. Grey hadn't responded to either one of the five messages she had texted in succession. He had promised to be there no later than 8:30.p.m. By 11:30, the DJ jammed, the dancing slammed, the laughter roared, and the party soared. No Grey. Prudence socialized with everyone. Alcohol fueled a steady flow of loud conversation. Prudence halted the music, "I would like to make an announcement please. I want to extend an apology on behalf of me and Malone for his absence tonight." One of the gentlemen spoke, "Well, in my friend's defense, I know he must have a good reason. He knows we will make ourselves at home and party in his honor with or without him. This is great and thank you for inviting us."

"Oh, I liked your little speech that was so charming," one of Prudence's guest teased, then stumbled to the restroom. Prudence was shocked by everyone's calmness and signaled the DJ, "Crank up the volume," she resumed her hostess position.

As Vanessa watched the crowd from a ringside seat she noticed two girlfriends with three drinks headed her way. "I'm Kala and this is Terri and those are our husbands over there." She pointed to two men, one dancing with a woman and the other mingling.

"I know who you are," Vanessa responded warmly.

Kala was surprised, "How do you know who we are?" she slurred. Kala smiled and shook Terri's shoulder. Vanessa counted backwards from ten silently when she reached one Terri passed out from too much to drink.

"How?" Kala probed persistently.

"I'm one of the hostesses. I also talked to your husbands earlier. Plus some of the couples are our personal friends as well." Vanessa responded.

Vanessa finished her fifth glass of champagne as she spotted Grey squirming around in an attempt to sneak in with out being noticed. He greeted a few of his comrades and anointed Prudence with a holiday hug and kiss combo. Vanessa shot looks in Grey's direction. He felt the backlash and decided to seek refuge in the library. This was one of the same pieces of behavior that had added to the sum total of their stormy past. Vanessa sat next to him in the library.

"So, you've finally made it."

"Perceptive," he handed her the gift he carried. "Can you just open it please? I have been excited to give it to you for a week." Vanessa opened it. The 18-karat, white gold diamonded Cartier love bracelet.

"Wow! I've wanted one of these since I was in high school," she said with gratitude.

"I know you have. Look, I apologize for being late and I should have called."

"Thank you Grey. That was nice." Grey planted a series of pecks on her face.

"This comes with conditions," he said holding the bangle.

"Conditions???" Vanessa was instantly perturbed.

"Hold on. It's not that serious. I just want you to promise me that every time you look at it, you'll think of me." Grey requested as he screwed the bangle on her wrist.

"That's it?" Deal. Every time I catch a glimpse of it, it will bear a hint of its remembrance to you. "

Grey took Vanessa's hand and led her to the floor to dance. He held her closely as they stepped and moved to the upbeat rhythm of the music.

Vanessa restrained herself from talking during their slow dance. After it was over, Vanessa went to sit next to Grey and charged in with questions.

"Grey honey, what do you know about Malone's involvement with any of these universities, housing projects or charities I've heard about?" She activated her belt.

"There are tons of them. Charity is what he lives for to give them life."

"Are you involved in anyway?"

"Oh no! That's not me." He said as if it was distasteful.

"Charity begins at home and that's where it ends."

"Well, if you feel that way how come you have never helped Arlene? Don't you feel any compassion for her at all? The money you go through you could have paid cash for her a nice little house and got her out of the ghetto. As much as your grown ass has lived there, when you are on your ass that is the least you could have done."

"Vanessa you are really out of line. What I do for my mother is none of your damn business."

"That is precisely my point, you do nothing for her. A man who doesn't love and respect his mother or feel any obligation to look out for her certainty can't love any other women."

" I love my mother."

"Really? Vanessa said sarcastically. "Just finish what you were telling me because some things you just shouldn't have to explain to a grown man."

"That has been Malone, December, Holiday and Farren's life's work for the last five years. He started this business and those charities at the same time. They are dedicated to it twenty -four seven. None of the employees who work for his charities know anything about The Red Rose. None of the Red Rose employees know that Malone is a philanthropist or has anything to do with charity work, period. He doesn't mix the crews and runs those charities with razor edge precision. They are all legit and filtered through his godfather's legal multi-billion dollar corporation. Malone has set it up where they can never trace P.A.W. back to him. They have funded foundations across the nation and have recruited stellar businessmen to run them. They are all under the umbrella of P.A.W."

"What does that mean?"

"Present, Able and Willing"

"The have funded mostly educational programs, housing, hospitals, supported AIDS, drug rehabilitation, after school care, lunch programs, oh, it goes on and on and on into infinity. That is the thread of passion that binds him and the Trio. Anyway, enough of that, you get the point." Grey felt her finger between his two eyes.

"Well considering what you do is against the law and the amount of money you make doing it, I would think the very least you could do is give something to those in need rather than hoard everything you make for yourself,"

"I am giving it to someone who needs it, ME and YOU! Why would anyone step up into those institutions and risk their freedom to turn around and give it to people they don't know? Besides, I read all the time how people donate millions to charities and disaster relief funds and the money somehow never makes it to where it was allocated to go. Everybody is on the take. See that's why I do what I have to do and I have to do what's right for me." Vanessa lip-synced the words as he spewed them, "And you, of all people, should be able to understand that, and if not," he shrugged his shoulders with outstretched palms and let out a sigh, "Oh well."

She had justified that now his wrongdoing was at least done for the good of others along with Malone. He blasted that notion to smithereens. Magically, like a rabbit out of the hat, the real Grey stood up. It was still all about him. Vanessa admired her bangle as she sat back on the recliner. The bliss of having it lightened her mood from thinking about the mind-boggling situation she faced. The guest displayed no signs of going home any time soon. Prudence danced with Terri's husband Levi and Grey drank and socialized with a few of the men.

A sliver of faint yellow light that seeped through the living room window was the announcement that the party was now officially into day two.

As Vanessa watched the seriously inebriated partygoers, a single thought jarred her, '*designated drivers.*'

Chapter 39

'Tis the night after Christmas, partygoers were hung over all through the house...

The doorbell chimed four measures of a Christmas ditty."

Vanessa shouted over the bedroom intercom in a clouded voice,

"Prue, can you get the damn door, please? I'm on the phone."

Prudence ran downstairs and snatched the door open. Malone stood there looking like a cover of GQ. He was clad in a black, gabardine, double-breasted suit with suspenders, a mid-length cashmere overcoat, Cole Hann loafers, a black fedora, and a stark white shirt unbuttoned at the neck. Two dozen, long-stemmed, boxed red roses were under one arm and sitting on the ground on each side of him were exquisite floral arrangements in lead crystal vases. A colossal-size red box with a huge white satin bow and a twenty-pound box of Godiva chocolates in a Santa Claus shaped box accompanied the floral parade. Prudence's melted. She said in a voice still laced with disappointment, "Why are you here?"

He smiled and whispered, "Baby listen, I swear it ain't what you think." He handed her the gifts and then walked into the living room trailing Prudence. "You have people lying on the couch. There's a blow up bed in the dining room. I see the party was a success. The couples I invited are my business associates. Noah and Levi are huge moneymen. They handle a lot of our non-profit and fund raisers. Did they have a good time?"

"They had a ball. A limo picked them up about fifteen minutes ago. All your invites were picked up in limos. I thought I recognized them from several business magazines. I may have even seen Levi in Forbes. We have a few more people asleep in the guest room. Vanessa wouldn't let them go if they were drunk."

"Let's go in the waiting room." Malone suggested. She faced him and asked in a sexy, playful voice, "Ohhh, are all those presents for me?"

"Oh shit!" He opened the door and retrieved the other gifts he left outside. As he brought the vases in one by one, her smile stretched larger and wider.

"Those flowers are so beautiful, they must be from Blossoms."

Malone grabbed Prudence from behind and gave her the red box as she went to sit on the couch.

"Don't play coy with me. Open the box, you know you're dying to."

She frantically ripped the bow off the box. She didn't know how to react.

"Well baby, do you like it?" Prudence nodded,

"Yes." Her confusion left Malone mildly amused.

"I realize I haven't known you for that long. Listen, I swear falling out of a plane with no chute would have better than deciding on a gift for you," She had a perpetual grin.

Vanessa overheard their conversation from upstairs. She hid on the stairs to watch them gush over each other. As she went back in her room and closed the door she thought, *'Picked from the same tree those two.'*

Prudence's couldn't hold it in any longer, "What's this?" She unclipped a gold safety pin with a key dangling on it from a white silk pillow in a box. The gold key was inscribed, *'Only love.'*

"So, I give up. No one has ever given me a key. Is it a necklace?"

"You'll never guess."

"You're right, I never will."

"The key is to my heart." Malone said with excitement. Prudence was overwhelmed by his gesture.

"So as long as I have this key in my possession, I'll have the key to your heart?" She humored him. She closed the key in her fisted hand.

"I couldn't have said it better myself. And if you lose it, you'll still have it," Malone promised touching his heart.

"Can you take it back?"

"I'll never want to."

She was embarrassed. Prudence's voice faltered, "This is the best Christmas present I've ever had."

" You don't like it I can tell. Come on let's go for a walk."

"Wait, I have a present for you, too."

"Later, come on."

"No, I want you to open your present." He opened the gift-wrapped box.

"This is so beautiful baby. I love it." Prudence slipped the diamond- inscribed, white gold pinky ring on his finger.

" Do you know what the date 9-3 is?"

"Don't be ridiculous, of course I don't. Tell me, I'm not good with dates." Prudence was disappointed.

"That is the day we met, silly girl," he kissed her on the tip of her nose.

As they made their way around the circular driveway snuggled together, both noticed an enormous black box large enough to transport two horses and encased with mounds of black satin ribbon.

"What the hell is that?" they asked each other.

"Malone, who does that belongs to?" Prudence asked innocently.

"Hey baby, we started out on this little jaunt together. How the hell am I supposed to know? You're the one who lives here. You should know better than me," Malone retorted.

"Was it here when you came?"

"Nope." Malone rushed over to detach the card affixed on it.

After he read the envelope, he became angry, "Well, well, I'll be damned," he ranted.

"What does it say? Why are you so irritated all of a sudden? Why don't you calm your high-strung self down until we find out what's going on? It's probably for Vanessa. You realize I am not the only one who lives here right?"

"I already know what's going on, so don't even play that innocent bullshit with me." Prudence's face cracked and her body stiffened. Her stride was rigid and slow as she approached him.

"You can't be serious. Let me see what the card says."

"It's addressed to you."

When Prudence reached for the card, Malone snatched his hand back. She knew he was mad. When he started the pacing, she knew a thunderstorm could be brewing.

"Who would be sending you a box as large as a Lear jet with 'I love you the most' on the envelope, and you don't have a clue who it's from? And you had the nerve to question me about another woman." He lit a cigarette.. "I thought you weren't seeing anyone else, Prue?" Prudence, totally outdone, exclaimed,

"What!" Her jaw dropped.

"Oh, now you've suddenly gone deaf?" Malone taunted.

"Look, I told you I'm not seeing anyone. I haven't the slightest idea where this came from Malone. There must be some kind of mistake, not must be, there _is_ some mistake."

"Mistake my ass," his voice softened. He took a drag off his cigarette, "man and to think I trusted you. You're like all the rest. Give me my key back."

"Malone, for the last time, I don't know what's in that box or who sent it. Give me the damn card and I'll check it out."

"Well, why don't you open it, so we can both see what the person who loves you the most sent you."

"I don't want to open it. You think I should? I don't give a shit what's in the box." Prudence said not giving any credence to Malone's anger. She headed up the driveway toward the house. Malone ran to catch her and pulled her back.

"Oh no, you don't get off that damn easy. Open it!"

"No!"

"Now!"

"Okay." She walked over to the part of the box that had, 'PULL THIS STRING.' written on it. When she did, all four flaps on the box fell at once and made an explosive sound as they collapsed to the ground. She gasped. Her face turned red. "A black Mercedes 500. If this is from a secret admirer, he's a secret to me too. I wanna keep though."

She made a joke of it. Malone stared at the car.

"I am not amused," he said.

"Here's your card. Far be it from me to stand in the way of your little Christmas gift. Compared to this, my little key don't mean shit." He jumped in his car and spun around the driveway, leaving only skid marks and a cloud of dust. She ran after him screaming,

"Malone, I swear I don't know who this is from."

Prudence went into the house devastated. She frantically ripped the card open. The outside of the card had a glossy picture of Malone wearing a Santa Claus suit. The caption read, *'Well, do you know who loves you the most?'* She opened it, `Malone does.'` She hustled outside. Malone was standing at the door cackling. She jumped on his back. He carried her piggyback to her new car.

"You know, baby, you aren't so bright. You didn't make the connection between the key and the car."

"Thank you baby, I don't know what to say. I love it. Come on Malone," she asserted, and then questioned nervously, "Is it mine?"

"Of course it's yours, silly."

"No, I mean, is it in my name?"

"All you have to do is go to the dealer tomorrow and sign the final papers."

"Is it paid for, or do I have to assume a note? "

"At the time you sign the papers, they will give you the pink slip."

"Is it insured?"

"Of course." Malone assured her.

"Full coverage? For how long?"

"Paid in full for the next three years providing you don't want me to buy you a new one before then. One more question baby and I'm taking the car back." Malone warned.

Prudence said softly,

"Well, that won't happen unless it's over my dead body."

Malone walked around to the driver's side of the car, opened the door, and escorted her inside.

"Wait a second," she said, "I want to get something out of the house."

She returned carrying blankets and a large picnic basket.

"Damn baby, a picnic basket. What the hell are you gonna do with that today?" Malone wondered.

"I always said that if I ever got a Benz, I would always keep this in the trunk of my car." She put it in and slid in the driver's seat. Malone jumped on the passenger's side and away they went. Prudence came to a screeching halt and asked him affectionately, "Does this mean I still have the key to your heart since the key you gave me fits the ignition?"

"I'll answer that if you really need an answer," Malone smiled.

She took off. As she swiveled and swirled down the pitch-black two-lane road, Malone turned on some music.

"Pull over," Malone asked which she did. He pulled a slender box out of his inside pocket, handing it to her. Inside was a diamond-studded key on a long beautiful white gold chain.

"I knew you would ask me that shit, I knew it." Malone fastened the necklace and Prudence reached over and kissed him passionately. The kiss escalated to a hot, long and feverish pitch. She unbuttoned his shirt and slid her tongue slowly up and down his chest, stopping from time to time to lick each of his nipples. He pushed a button on the seat and reclined.

She unzipped his pants and for the first time, something she had been dying to do since she had laid eyes on him. She thought, '*as perfect as he is in every way, he has to have a little dick.*' He was stiff as a double shot of straight whiskey. She took it in her hand, gently rubbed it up and down and glided her fingers across the head of his penis.

"What the hell are you doing? You need a measuring tape?" He suddenly switched moods and asked, seriously,

"Am I okay for you?"

"You are perfect," she said reassuringly.

He blew out a sigh of relief. "That could be a deal breaker, if it ain't right. Well then, shit baby, please don't start anything you don't plan or want to finish."

"Wait." She fixed his clothes and roared back onto the road to find a private entrance in the mountains where she could park. The sun had been wrapped for about twenty minutes as she parked on a secluded mountaintop. She hopped out, laid out the blankets and the contents of the basket. She poured some wine.

"Are you getting out or what?"

"Baby, look at this view," Malone said as he got out.

Prudence enjoyed the scenery with him. Malone settled back and drank his wine.

"If you get hungry I have fried chicken and potato salad." She wanted to jump on him, but didn't want to seem frantic. In the last couple of weeks she had developed a strong sexual desire for him.

The last time he approached her she had said, *No. We should wait to get to know each other better.'* Better had come. A twitching sensation was throbbing through out her private parts. The anticipation of how he would feel inside of her made the throbbing heavier. All of a sudden he cackled."

"What?" she said. As much as she didn't want to join in she couldn't resist laughing along with him.

"What?" she repeated.

"I can tell you wish I would make it happen, right? Well, since I had to wait so long, I thought it only fair that you see how that shit feels. I don't want to give you the impression that I'm easy," he teased.

Prudence coerced him onto his back, and eased on top of him. He gently took control and rolled her over. He rubbed his hands through her hair, kissed her face, slid his tongue inside her ear and slowly nibbled her neck as he made his way down to her breasts. He flicked his tongue on her nipples and sucked them passionately. He worked his way down to her toes, leaving nothing unexplored. He nuzzled each toe, giving them equal amounts of attention. He moved his way slowly between her soft thighs and rested his mouth between her legs. He tasted her.

"You taste so good to me baby. You know that can be a deal breaker too." That tickled Prudence. He used his first three fingers on each hand to separate her tender labia so he could indulge himself in everything she had to offer. It was better than he had imagined.

"You smell so good." As he spoke, he became more stimulated. He rubbed her thighs with his head still deeply emerged between them. He pulled her even closer, lifting her from underneath. She moaned, louder and louder. Her legs pulled back further, straighter, and opened wider. Her face contorted with pleasure. He flicked his tongue back and forth, rapidly, softly, and in small strokes, across her clitoris, until he felt the tension in her body rise and reach its peak. During the height of her climax, he entered her. He placed his entire body securely over hers and held her tightly. She wrapped her legs around his back and held him firmly around his shoulders. As he moved in and out with the grace of an eagle in flight, his body remained stationary on her the entire time. He rubbed and massaged it with his body until she became hotter and wetter. With every stroke he went deeper until he reached that special spot. He kissed her passionately, and continuously ran his fingers through her hair.

"Oh baby," he continued to stroke. "Whooo it's hot in there. You're gonna make me cum. Hot – hot- hot."

"You feel good inside of me." she responded tenderly.

"I hope so baby. I think I'm gonna have to make this my regular stompin' ground." They stopped and cracked up.

"I loved you the moment I saw you Prue," He resumed his

graceful motion, and they both exchanged responding movements until Prudence released sounds of ecstasy for the second time. He remained stiff inside her and relaxed his body on top of hers, engulfing her in his strong muscular arms. Silence. More silence.

"But you didn't." He interrupted her,

"I want you to finish first, 'cause when I cum, it'll be curtains," he joked. Her heart throbbed. She had heard other women speak of multiple orgasms but this was a first for her.

"I have never done this, this many times in a row. It just feels right," she repeated because it was all she could say.

"You have no idea. Baby you have a hot tight spot. It feels like my dick is baking in a human oven."

"You talk so nasty." He pulled out. Prudence gave him a piece of chicken and laid next to him.

"It's funny how men of all ages think they know what pleases a woman when they haven't got a clue."

"I know baby," he smiled in agreement. "They jump up and down on you like they're on a trampoline right?"

"That is just what they do. Not you though. Malone I just want to say thank you for the beautiful car and the necklace. I have never been with anyone as generous and as kind as you. You have made me and this holiday so special."

She moved her head up and down, swiftly, thrusting him in and out of her mouth. He squirmed and moved around on the blanket, enjoying the sensation he was experiencing. She followed his movements. The two of them, absorbed in the moment, didn't even feel themselves moving off the blanket and closer towards the edge of the cliff. She gestured to get between his legs, so she could take him deeper. Suddenly, a blood-curdling scream was heard as Prudence fell off the side of the mountain. Malone screamed,

"Oh my God. Oh my God!" He frantically jumped up on his hands and knees to look over the cliff in the direction she fell. Prudence was instantly out of sight. Everything was pitch black. He was momentarily immobilized. "I can't believe what the fuck is goin' on here." He didn't know what to do. His heart throbbed. He didn't know if he should call 911 or look for her. Malone couldn't ever remember being this scared. He grabbed his cigarette lighter and frantically, climbed down the side of the mountain, for a couple of feet, then jumped the rest of the way settling into a tall brush area butt naked. He scouted the narrow path, which was only a few feet long and not even as wide -then a drop.

"Prudence," he shouted. Thinking his worse nightmare, *"suppose she went over.'* He looked over the edge it was black and bottomless. There was an enormous rock that slightly overlapped the small, confined area. He bent down and felt under it. "Prudence," he yelled again. He could feel an opening so he crawled into the narrow opening, he couldn't see his own hand because it was so dark. Once below, it felt like he was inside a pitch-black cave. He flicked the lighter only to see black more clearly. He trudged through dry brush and rocks. He could have been in a lion's den for all he knew. It was his last resort. "Prudence, Prudence." He screamed in vain. He decided to call 911 because she was gone. Malone sobbed as he climbed from underneath the rock and felt his way back onto the path, devastated. As he grabbed hold of some rocks to climb back up to the top, he heard movement and crackling as something moved closer. He bellowed out again louder, "Prudence."

"It's me." She sounded disoriented. They felt around until they found each other. Malone grabbed her hand.

"You scared the shit outta me. Where were you?"

"When I fell I must have hit my head on something, I just came to."

"You were lying on this path unconscious and I couldn't even find you. Thank God for this little landing or you would have been over that cliff " He hugged her. They climbed to the top where it was visible. They repositioned their blankets much further back, and resumed their positions next too each other.

The sapphire sky, full moon, and clusters of stars shined with radiance she had never noticed before. If wishing on a star worked, she would have wished that this moment could have lasted forever. Their entwined bodies were as warm and tightly woven as a knit sweater. Malone fell asleep. Prudence moved away to get something to drink from the basket. As soon as she returned to him, he pulled her close and they cuddled.

"She felt like talking. Thoughts kept blooming in her mind from nowhere, like flowers sprouting in a garden reaching to the sun after a rainy day in spring.

As she reflected on the evening's events, she stroked his face and watched him sleep. "My heart won't stop pounding," she whispered.

"Nor your mouth running." Malone jested.

"This is one of the most incredible nights of my life. Thank you so much Malone. I have never had anybody do anything that grand for me."

"You think this is incredible wait until you meet my old road dogs at the fundraiser tomorrow night. "

"That is gonna be fun, I can't wait." Malone touched her face as he admired her beauty. "You laugh a lot, I like that," he clenched both of her hands in his, "I really love you Prue, and I'm really gonna try not ever to do anything to jeopardize what we have. I hope like hell you don't either. Aunt Dodie used to always say you better watch what you do to people because everything isn't forgivable." A good woman is as hard to find as a good man." He smiled, "I know, I've gotten it wrong so many times. I want us to build a home together, travel, work out, have babies, then grandbabies, great grandbabies, God willing. I want us to trust, respect and be faithful to each other and build our foundation on God's integrity. I wanna be your man and your husband." There was a comfortable silence. When the chill from the wind arrived they wrapped up in the blankets and each other more securely.

They explored, licked, ate, drank, listened to music, laughed, talked, hugged and made love under the moonlight until the moon disappeared and the sun, ever so slightly, peaked its glowing, yellow presence over the horizon.

Chapter 40

Malone, Clive and the Trio was sponsoring a fundraiser for StatCar and P.A.W. charity organizations. The black tie affair was being held in Los Angeles at one of the cities finest hotel venues. It was a dinner, dance and fashion show. Five hundred guests were slated to attend. This was the first event they had given of this kind and that was because of their very special guest list. The event was primarily for old friends, family and associates who Malone, Clive and The Trio had grown up with. Many of them, well-respected businessmen in their own right. Their lucrative businesses however, were mostly of a *street persuasion.*

Malone and Prudence were the self appointed greeters for the event and both were stunning in black. Malone had on a timeless black suit and a fedora. Prudence wore a black formal gown with a wrap train. It was sheer with appliques positioned over her private parts covered and accentuated her flawless curves.

The crystal room was fabulous, decorated in rich colors of bronze and gold, huge chandeliers and a private bar. There was a fifty table capacity that was set with a ten place setting on each and breathtaking flower arrangements with gold tags inscribed, 'Blossoms.'

The gold leaf ornate doors opened electronically for the guest. A flamboyant OG (old gangster) and his two scantily dressed female companions were the first guests who arrived on the red carpet. They looked like a "household of three" throwbacks from the sixties. The garishly dressed male character wore a high beam yellow suit, matching patent leather shoes, a large, print bow tie and a wide, yellow, brimmed fedora with a black band around it. The entire ensemble was trimmed in white.   Accentuating his jaw-dropping attire was a floor length, white, heavily shedding, rabbit coat. He flossed his two ostentatious, diamond pinky rings as he strutted with his wooden cane that was inscribed 'BB.' Both initials were encrusted with diamonds that could be seen from a helicopter in flight. The two women wore fishnets and bell-bottom jumpsuits, which revealed a G-string, their breast, and belly buttons. Black, sequence, wraps were draped over their shoulders to conceal their nipples. Prudence motioned to collect their tickets to no avail as Malone greeted his elite crew with heartfelt salutations.

Most of the people scheduled to attend Malone hadn't seen in years.

"Malone, Malone, Malone, what's goin' on player?" The two men shook hands and hugged warmly. Despite his effort,

Malone couldn't conceal how mesmerized he was by their appearance.

"My brotha, Black Bishop. Man it's been a while. I been tryin' to hold it down man. BB, this is the love of my life man, Prudence. Baby, this is the renowned, Black Bishop." Malone winked at her.

"Oh no. Love don't mix with pimpin' man, what the hell are you talkin' about?" Bishop said as he gave her a spin and sized her up. Prudence played along. "Hey Blue, she'd do real good on the line man. With a body like this, a little direction, she would be a ho of perfection." Malone cackled.

"No man, I'm straight on that. How's business?"

"Hey man, business is great. I'm still turnin' tramps into champs. You know, ain't no bidness like ho bidness." They both slapped hands and grinned.

"Hey Black, you do know this is a black tie, not a straight outta the circus bow tie affair." Black Bishop's expression turned deadly quicker than he blinked his eye. He didn't find any humor in the insult. Malone instantly observed that his comment caused Black Bishop's disposition to take a dark turn so he put a spin on the situation by laughing out loud. Malone hugged him around the neck with one arm and said jokingly, "Man, come on, you know I was fuckin' with you. Yo' ass couldn't take a joke in grammar school and you can't take one now." After Black Bishop paused momentarily to regroup, he found himself engaged in laugher along with Malone. With all seriousness he could muster, he looked Malone square in the eyes and said, "Man, it pisses me off the way you have always been jealous of my eye for fashion and exceptional sense of style."

Malone tried to control his gag reflex, which hindered him from taking the conversation any further.

"So Bishop, I need your tickets man, then you all can go on in." Bishop's eyes were locked on Prudence. "Here's my ticket, they ain't got no tickets they're with me, man. I can pay you for her in cash, man," he remarked about Prudence. "I'm the pimp and she can be my ho, I can be the quarterback and she can pass me big doe. Blue, I been all over the world man, I ain't never seen no bitch with a body like this."

"She is sexy, isn't she? " Malone said proudly and flashed a smile at Prudence. "Each of you needs a separate ticket to get in man."

"Well, that wasn't my motha fuckin' understanding man. I thought the ticket was for me and my wife in-laws at five hundred dollars a pop, Blue." He tilted his headed from side to side as he spoke, "Let me get this shit straight. I'm payiin' five hundred dollars for a dry chicken leg, baked potato and some iceberg lettuce soaked in French dressing and you are telling me they can't come in with me."

"So see, we are on the same page. Man, this is for charity and the dinner is going to be off the hook." At that moment, the live soul band took their place on stage and began playing. Bishop Black was distracted by the oldies playing inside the ballroom. "Damn, that's my jam. Guess you two will have to sit your asses in the lobby and drum up some business while you wait." He stepped, old school style, inside, as his two companions proceeded to take seats in the lounge.

"Hey Black, your girls can sit out here man but they can not do any soliciting, we'll get shut down." Bishop Black didn't break his dance stride. Malone shrugged a shoulder, and planted a kiss on Prudence's lips and was amused as he said, "Baby, BB is ready to turn you out on the ho stroll."

"He says I can make big money, hello." She was flattered. "What made you give a fundraiser like this anyway?"

"Me, Stanton and the Trio grew up with these people, like family, and hung out with them for years. They are always on our collective backs because we never invite them to any of our affairs. King Michael, a notorious, drug dealer who grew up with Stanton, told him he thought he was better than everybody now. Him saying that hurt Stanton to his core because that's his boy. This group walks in different paths other than we do but they are crazy rich in their on right. So, we decided to have one in their honor.

        "Why can't they just come to the regular events that you host?"

"Baby, my folks will start clownin' at the drop of a dime. Then, when they get full on that alcohol, trust me, it wouldn't be a good fit. Can you imagine Noah and Levi's crowd with Bishop and King. "

"As a matter of fact, I can. I bet they'd have a ball. Come on, most men are hos and the ones in business suits are just well dressed hos. Hos love to party with their own kind. Most of the men on the money circuit do party girls. I know they could hang as long as the stuff that happened stayed where they played. And please, don't act like you ain't never partied with no hos." Malone avoided eye contact and suppressed smiling. Huh, you might have a point. But they'll never meet on my introduction. You've been around Vanessa too long you're starting to sound like her. He was glad to see Holiday, December and Farren enter on the arms of their three dates. "Well, don't the three of you look like you just stepped out of a European Vogue. Hey, how are all of you this evening?" Malone asked as he shook the men's hands.

"My God, I have never seen the three of you look this stunningly beautiful. I am shocked." Prudence's commented as her jaw dropped and her eyes scanned The Trio from head to toe.

"We clean up pretty good, huh?" Farren teased.

"Honey, you must be shocked about Farren and December 'cause I look good all the time," Holiday boasted with the utmost sincerity.

The Trio's indescribable gorgeous designer gowns were Valentino and Elle Saab and all three were equally as breathtaking. Their dates were handsome, buffed and impeccably dressed. After the introductions to Prudence, the six of them made their way into the crystal room.

"I've never seen any of those guys before," Prudence remarked as her eyes trailed them to the door. "They are gorgeous. Are they rented?" Malone laughed. "Holiday has been dating him for a while. December and Farren go out with them off and on."

"Wow, they looked amazing, "Prudence reiterated.

"Oh baby, make no mistake they know how to get sharp." Malone took a seat, "Hey Jr. and Tucker? Glad you could come Nicole and Taylor," he said as they gave him their tickets entered.

Then, Joseph and his wife Patricia entered. "Wow, I haven't seen you two in a long time, how's married life?" Malone came from behind the counter to hug them. Neither of them returned the gesture. Malone walked back to his seat.

"No, you haven't seen us because Joseph's ass got busted for dealing drugs again. This time, he was dealing outta some young bitches house that he's goin' with.

"Here you go. I told you a thousand fuckin' times I was not fuckin' with that bitch and she is eighteen years old." Joseph yelled back.

"Yeah, now maybe. That girl was under age, she was helping yo' ass sell drugs, you were giving her money and you all were fuckin.'" Patricia yelled louder, enraged. "When did she turn eighteen, Joseph? I am going to check and see. If she was, I'm gonna see to it that yo' ass is gets buried under the jail for child molestation." Malone stepped between them.

"You two need to calm down or take it outside. Patricia, you want me to see if your uncle Stanton has arrived yet?" They continued arguing around and through Malone like he was invisible.

"Bitch!!!! Don't front me off in public and in front of your uncle's friends. You need to stay out of my damn business anyway," Joseph shifted Malone to the side then he got in her face.

"Bitch, you got me fucked up. You must think you talkin' to your ghetto ass mammy!" As Patricia rolled her head and pointed her finger in his face, he leaped on her, causing them both to fall to the floor as he punched her. "Oh Lord," Prudence yelped.
Malone and Prudence ran to break up the scuffle. Malone positioned Joseph in a chokehold to restrain him. "You are getting your ass outta here Joseph until you calm down. Patricia, please, just go on inside. Prue baby, stay here and greet the guest. I'll handle this shit." As Malone wrestled him to the door Patricia said, "Oh, so you like hitting females huh?' She tagged him in the eye with a mean right hook, BAMM!!!

"Would you please go sit down," Malone yelled at Patricia.

"Fuck that. I'm kicking this mother fuckas ass. Going with some young girl huh," She connected a combination punch in his face. Another right hook in the other eye, *CRACK*, then a left punch in his mouth, *WOOSH*. The guests entering the venue were all unfazed by the commotion. One man as casually approached the three of them, "Hey, you all need some help?"

"It's cool Marco just go enjoy yourself man, good to see you," Malone huffed as sweat streamed down his face as he struggled to contain Joseph as he, in turn, made every effort to free himself.

"Oh, hey Blue, I didn't recognize you. You good man?" Marco stared at Patricia like a foreign object. "Damn," the man cheered, "I ain't never seen no woman hit like that." Patricia didn't acknowledge the man's comment. She tapped her fist together and shuffled around like a boxer staying loose.

"All good man," Malone answered flatly trying to discourage him from staying.

By the time Malone threw Joseph outside one of his eyes had blown up, the other was swollen shut and his lip was busted and gushing blood. As soon as he hit the ground, Joseph jumped back up and charged towards Patricia and Malone, almost running into Vanessa and Grey as they approached the entrance. Just as Grey moved to block him, Vanessa effortlessly, flipped and dropped him. Malone, Grey and Patricia were impressed. "What are you bionic? You took him down like you have been trained in law enforcement of some kind or something." Malone stared at Vanessa suspiciously for a moment. Vanessa acted like she didn't hear him.

"I can't move, I can't move. It feels like my back is broken," Joseph screeched in agony as he crawled away with a turtle's stride. "I got the keys to my car so don't even think you are leaving in it you degenerate pond scum," Patricia yelled as she followed everyone inside. When they reached the reception area, Prudence announced, "The auction and dinner just started why don't you all go right in?"

Grey and Vanessa were dressed in all black, stunning and classic, suits. Vanessa had a foxtail draped boa slug over one shoulder.

"Yeah, let's do that Grey. I don't want to miss a morsel of a five hundred dollar a plate dinner." Grey nodded in accordance. "Let me talk to Malone for a second then I'll be ready,"

Vanessa's second–take resulted in a 'take my breath away moment' when she noticed Prudence in her dress. In all the years they had been friends it wasn't until that moment that Vanessa realized that Prudence's figure could stop time. Vanessa never noticed because Prudence always kept her self modestly covered. The outfit she had on had Malone written all over it.

Vanessa stood to the side, alone and faded out in her thoughts watching Grey. She reflected on how unconditional their love had grown for one another during their on again-off again relationship. Their last breakup was the dagger through the heart. Her decision to terminate the relationship came after she realized how strong the possibilities of him going to prison were   Also, then just like now his drug usage was out of control. Communicating by collect, three-way calls, letters, monthly visits and putting money on books made the line easier to draw. If they had stayed together, she could have been named as an accessory to Grey's elicit activities. A blemished record would've ruined her chances of getting into the F.B.I. Her conscience bothered her about accepting gifts, money and trips, and so on if she wasn't willing to be there for him when his luck changed. After she had broken off the relationship, for more than a year he had been relentless in trying to contact her. Finally, his efforts ceased. What never ceased was the hope that maybe one day he would come back a rehabilitated man.

"Hello, hello," Grey snapped his fingers. Vanessa faded in and said, "I'm here."

"If you are here, you just got here, 'cause I've been calling you for a couple of minutes. You ready to go to the Crystal room?"

"Absolutely," The two of them walked inside with Patricia at their side babbling a mile a minute.

"Why don't' you go in with them baby and enjoy the dinner and the auction. I'll stay out here for the stragglers," Malone suggested tenderly.

"I'd rather stay out here with you. I didn't know the plates were that much. "

"Hey, they are all ballers it won't hurt them to help others for a change. Plus, we aren't serving no regular hotel food, I brought in some serious chef's who are preparing meals that can evoke culinary orgasms. With the dinner alone, we have collected $250,000 dollars. I had all of the designer clothes, handbags and shoes brought here to auction off from my company. Our company may use them one time and that's it. Every stitch of those clothes cost a fortune. They should bring in at least another $20,000 to $30,000 dollars for our charities." Stanton entered from a side door and inquired, "How's it been going, or should *I* ask? Did King Michael show up?"

"Just like you foretold it man. Well, at least now our ole homeboys won't be able to say we don't give anything and don't invite them. Yep King Michael is in there. Patricia and Joseph were here and that turned out to be a fiasco. Patricia hit him like I have never seen a woman throw a punch."

"Oh, she used to be a professional boxer. She throws a punch like a man. Her career could have gone far except she likes those high rolling dealers like Joe. The ballers give her everything she wants, and that makes her lazy. She drops one and gets another one. Well, I'm going to make a quick appearance and I am out of here. Hello Prudence, may I say that you take my breath away in that dress," he kissed her hand. Malone and Clive shook hands and

Clive exited out of the back door. Ice Chocolate and his twenty-
man entourage, all wearing dark shades, bandanas and jeans
meandered down the red carpet.

Ice and Malone had grown up together on the south side of
Chicago. He had about a half dozen number one hits and a string of
songs that hit the top forty and then just laid there. He lived far
larger than the money he had received from his royalties. Malone
was excited when he saw him and immediately walked over to greet
him,

"My main man. What's up? Glad you could make it."

"Yo, man, what's up? I brought my posse to yo' event to
give you some support." He addressed his entourage, "This is Blue
one of my oldest homies." Some gave an unconcerned nod and
most didn't acknowledge Malone at all.

"Lemme holla at you playa." Malone pulled Ice Chocolate to
the side, "Man, you know you only brought two tickets. So you and
one other person is all that can go inside. All the seating is
assigned."

"What the fuck you talkin' about Blue. I spent a thousand
dollars and you tellin' me my boys can't go up in there. What are
they supposed to do?"

"Do they have any money?"

"Yeah, why?"

" They can pay to get in or they can get with Black's hoes and hold up at a hotel. They have been looking for customers since they arrived. It would be nice to get them out of the lobby."

"Oh snap, Bishop Black is in tha house?" Ice expanded his chest and added some base to his voice. "Look man, this is yo' fuckin' event. You better figure out how my boys is gettin' in 'cause they ain't payin', they don't want them hos and they ain't sittin' in no damn lobby after I dropped a thousand dollars. Shiiit you the big baller, just give me my money back."

"Better? Look Herbert, do you honestly think twenty people are going inside on two tickets man? It's printed on the tickets, one person per ticket. I mean, you do know how to read, right?"
The rapper scoped the room to see if anyone in his crew had heard Malone.

"Ice Chocolate man. Don't call me that, I've changed my name, " he demanded sternly.

"Oh, sorry, Ice Chocolate," Malone cackled.

"Oh, so now you think it's funny. Blue, fuck this man, you gonna either let us up in there or we gonna set some shit off up in dis bitch. Don't even try me." Malone instantly got in his face,

"Herbert, are you threatening me man? We go back so far that I know, you know better. Don't make me embarrass you in front of your little friends, Herby." Malone gritted his teeth and said mafia style, as he pulled back his jacket to reveal a Beretta 9mm semi-automatic, "Whenever you and your boys are ready to set some shit off up in this bitch man, I'm ready." The famous entertainer jumped back, stunned and laughed, "Damn Blue, it ain't that serious man, shit, we like brothas. You need to calm the fuck down. I was just fuckin' with you man." Malone looked heavenward, and decided to humor him.

"So, you was just talkin' shit? Man, I knew that. I was just fuckin' with you too brotha." The two of them hugged and shook hands. As Malone walked back to the reception area, Ice Chocolate headed in the direction of his crew. Malone paused and inquired as an afterthought, "You and yo' boys do know this is a black tie affair right?"

"We ain't stupid man. Why do you think we all have on black jeans?" Malone stared at him as if he was in a trance for a long moment then shook his head in disbelief. Malone just sat down. He noticed Chocolate was calming down his yes men who had riled themselves up to assist him in *the two ticket- for twenty boys battle.* Finally, twelve of them exited the venue and two positioned themselves next to Bishop Black's hoes. As the rapper and one of his partners entered the ballroom, Prudence whispered in Malone's ear like a star struck, groupie, "Oh honey, I love Ice Chocolate's music can you get me his autograph, please!!!" As Malone flashed her a *you have got to be kidding me look* he noticed one of the hos jumping out of her seat in a rage. She hollered loud enough for everyone on the entire first floor of the classy establishment to hear clearly, "This is a bidness. Pussy ain't free. We gotta make our money jus' like you two motha fuckas."

Malone let out a long–suffering sign, "Oh boy, this is going to be a long ass night."

Chapter 41

Early the next day Vanessa sat perched on a small wooden footstool in the back of her closet. She rested her head on her knees, torn between decisions. Tears flooded her eyes as she stared at Patrick. Frustration had finally taken an emotional toll.

"Either way I go, I'm fucked," She sobbed to him while wiping her nose. "They'll get the short end of the stick. Everything they worked for in addition to what Malone had given them would all be confiscated. How can I be responsible for the thousands and thousands of people Malone has helped being thrown out of their homes, hospitals, senior care facilities, day care centers, universities and on and on and on and on and on and on," she bellowed in frustration. "This time it would be even worse for them. To have seen the light and then have to go backwards would make them abandon hope. If I arrest Malone, the Trio, and bust that organization, those people who have worked so hard to overcome their circumstances will be back to square one." She laid her head in her lap in an attempt to compose herself . As she slowly regained her composure, she locked her eyes on the man of her dreams seriously and asked earnestly, "Help me out here Patrick. What the hell would you do if you were in my place? How can I bust him under the circumstances?" Vanessa moaned in frustration.

At that moment, a hint of a shadow appeared on the mural. Startled, Vanessa turned, aimed her gun and gasped. Prudence roamed into the closet unfazed by the gun. "Put that thing away before you hurt someone."

"Damn Prue, when did you get home? Do you ever knock? I guess you won't be satisfied until you either give me a heart attack or I shoot you. I could have been in here masturbating for all you know. Plus, I thought you moved out." Prudence sat on the floor next to her. Vanessa stared at Patrick and Prudence joined in her gaze. "So what brings you home? How is Malone?"

"A change of clothes and he is wonderful," Prudence replied starry-eyed.

"You mean you still have some here?"

"A few."

Moments of silence passed. Prudence could tell her sister was visibly shaken so she switched the conversation to Vanessa's favorite topic. She knew it would take Vanessa's nerves from sixty to zero in two point five seconds or less.

"So, what about your guy there? You know Vanessa, for the first time, I believe that in some strange way you really do love

Patrick, you seriously do. What do you see in him, 'cause I want to see it too," Prudence pointed to the mural as she asked.

"You mean aside from the most obvious reasons? I love that he is soft-spoken and not at all flashy. He is a phenomenal actor, classy, sexy, and has an exciting screen presence. Galen is intelligent, witty and down to earth and a class act, I just know it. I can feel it. He looks great in Versace, loves to drive sports cars, bike riding and he even set up the Patrick Dempsey Center for Cancer Hope and Healing. That's a man who gives of himself. He started it because his mother had cancer. A man can never fully love a woman if he doesn't love his mother. To me he looks like a rich, creamy vanilla ice cream cone and I would love to lick his face. Mr. Dempsey is the only charming man I have ever seen. Prue, I really wish I could meet and get to know him."

"Galen?"

"His middle name."

"You mean you really wish you could meet and get to know him, his wife and their three children or just him?"

"Just him." Vanessa responded with a scrum size of irritability. "No relationship is ever perfect."

"I worry about you, Vanessa. Really, you are much too heavily invested in this fantasy. You are a wife's worst nightmare. I know his wife would pity you though."

"Why the hell would she pity me? She's got Patrick. They have been married for over nine years. I don't know her name it's J something. All I have is a fuckin' mural on the wall."

"J something? Like hell you don't know. You are a lot better off that way.   He could never live up to your insane fantasies." Vanessa smacked her lips, "Prue, he is the most gorgeous man I've ever seen in my entire life. He was truly hand sculpted by the lord, herself."

"Wait a minute, did I misunderstand you. Did you say the Lord *herself*?" Prudence eyes widened.

"That's exactly what I said."

"So, now you're telling me that you think God is a female," Prudence sighed.

"No, but let's explore the possibilities."

Prudence and Vanessa began the discussion just for the sake of discussing the way they did every Sunday, when they were kids, roller-skating in the park.

"I know I should absolutely leave this one alone and I know I'm going to be sorry I asked, but by all means, please, tell me how and why you came to that conclusion."

"Certainly not a conclusion, just a probability. Well, for one, if God created man in his own image and only God can procreate then he would have had to be a she because we are the only ones who can produce life."

"God doesn't procreate, he creates, and there's a difference." Prudence corrected her.

"If men were created first, then how come all babies are

conceived as females, then either remain as one or develop into a male? Take the word woman, for example, 'wo,' is the prefix, 'man' is the suffix. If woman were created from the rib of a man, how come we aren't a manwo instead of a woman?" Prudence gave her the usual hopeless stare, but toiled on through.

"Well, if God were a woman, how come she didn't give birth to her own son? Why did she have the Virgin Mary give birth to Jesus Christ?" Prudence asked.

"The Virgin Mary conceived Jesus through the Holy Spirit. I don't understand how these men could remotely be created in the image of such a wonderful, loving and forgiving God. The Ten Commandments had to be inspired by God. Man couldn't conceive of anything that beautiful and unbiased. Man isn't capable of giving love unconditionally. They are physical creatures whose emotions respond to sensation. I'm talking about them all," Vanessa asserted.

"So Vanessa, for the sake of argument, if God is a female and females were made in her image, why are there so many backsliding women out there? No getting around it, women can be as scandalous and cheat just as much as men." Prudence countered.

"Besides girl, if men wrote the Bible, it had to be inspired by God because a man's ego does not allow him to be that noble and humble. Interesting theory, though," Vanessa grinned egging her on.

"I say since we really don't know, until we do, everything is worth exploring. Even at our worst, as a whole, women are a lot more nurturing, capable of giving love, and at least try to have morals and a conscience if only on rare occasions. I can honestly say I don't know any men who are loyal in their commitments. Do you?"

"Honestly, yes, I know one now."

"Who?"

"Malone, of course. He is loyal." Prudence said giddily.

"Don't make me puke. The only thing he's loyal to is reducing figures in other people's bank accounts. If you say that's loyalty, noble and created in God's image, okay," Vanessa refuted.

Within an instant Prudence's mood and tone had transitioned from lightheartedness to seriousness.

"What in the hell do you mean by that?" she paused, "You don't understand him."

"I bet I'm not the only one who doesn't understand Malone's ass. I'm willing to bet those people whose bank accounts are a lot emptier because of him wouldn't understand him either," Vanessa sneered. Prudence's eyes flinched.

"What are you talking about and who in the world were you talking about when I came in your room? Who were you talking about when you asked how should you bust him. Malone?" Prudence quizzed.

Vanessa tried not to look away. Already out of sorts, she tried to appear as if she didn't have the slightest inkling about what Prudence was talking about.

"Girl, if the nature of my business hasn't taught you anything else, I know you know, I can't and don't and won't have you meddling in my cases. That's totally confidential."

With a straight-faced stare, Prudence stood up and paced the length of the closet area.

"I heard you ask Patrick, how could you bust him."

"And?"

"And who are you talking about and what did you mean when you said Malone is taking money out of people's accounts?"

"Don't act like you don't know," Vanessa sneered.

"I want to know why all a sudden you're such an emotional wreck over that case you have been working on? You've never been like this before."

"How would you know that? Maybe you didn't barge into my room at the right time to see me upset," Vanessa clamored.

"You didn't answer my question," Prudence insisted.

"As much as I appreciate your concern, Prudence, save it for the next victim you choose to eavesdrop on. See, this is the very reason I think it's so rude of you to storm in my room without knocking. Now you're jumping to conclusions about something you think you heard and don't know a damn thing about. Get the hell out of here with that bullshit!" Vanessa yelled.

The faster Prudence paced the more provoked she became. Vanessa trailed Prudence's movements with her eyes. Prudence looked directly at Vanessa but responded as if she hadn't heard a word she had said, "You know what I think?" Prudence asked.

"I can't imagine, " Vanessa snarled crossly.

Prudence stopped abruptly, stood directly in front of her belligerently pointing her finger in Vanessa's face. "It was you all the time," she growled. Vanessa forcefully pushed her hand away from her face. "How did you creatively come up with these incredible lies about Malone?" taunted Prudence.

"Don't play with me, Prudence!" Vanessa retorted. "You know what the fuck I'm talking about and who I'm talkin' about. Don't insult my intelligence by defending your felonious new man to me. I know you can't be that naïve. What do you think he is a shoe salesman?"

"I haven't the faintest idea what you're talking about, Vanessa. Look, don't let your shitty attitude get your snitchin' cop ass kicked up in here," Prudence threatened.   Vanessa sat up at attention with her eyes fixated on Prudence. She pressed her lip tightly and her face wrinkled in astonishment.

"By whom?"

"Whom do you see standing here?" Prudence snapped.

"I honestly don't know who I'm seeing right now." She stood up, barely hunched over, and placed one hand on her hip.

"Girl, you must be on drugs?"

"Well, we must go to the same dealer then. Anyone who could squeal on their own family must have the pipe talkin' to their ass."

"So what do you call yourself, standing by a scandalous man?"

Vanessa challenged.

"I knew the minute I heard you say you hated to arrest those people who you were talking about."

"You don't know a damn thing and if you do, then why are you asking? Girl, you know what? Why don't you tell me what's on your mind? I'm not in the mood to play these guessing games right now."

Prudence's voice trembled, "It was you all the time. I couldn't put it together or I didn't want to believe it."

"Believe what!!!"

"You are investigating Malone and Grey. I knew it. At first I thought it was too much of a coincidence. I couldn't imagine that out of all the cases in the world, you would get assigned to theirs. When you insisted that I not tell them what you did for a living, I knew that was the reason." Prudence looked at her with disdain.

"Nothing I've done in the line of duty has ever bothered you before. You have always felt it was the right thing for me to do." Vanessa answered.

"So, you admit it?" Prudence felt deflated.

"So, you don't admit that you know what Malone does?" Vanessa contradicted. "He has you teaching at his University. You are just his full fledged partner in crime now, huh?" Vanessa loved her sister. Watching the pain mount in Prudence was really more than she could stand.

"Well, this is different, Vanessa."

"Different! Prue! He defrauds people out of millions of dollars.

You say it's different for him. I know you don't honestly believe that bullshit. If you do, you are in some serious denial, honey. You been around street people a long time, I know you know better."

"I don't think he defrauded those people at all. Malone dedicates his life to helping others."

Vanessa tried to refrain from further confrontation.

"Love's got you lookin' real crazy right now, Prue." Tears formed in Prudence's eyes as she sat on the floor. Her voice was defeated.

"Vanessa, please, I've never asked you for anything before. Please don't," Prudence pleaded.

Vanessa interrupted, her expressive face couldn't conceal the pain. "Please Prue, please don't ask me what I think you're getting ready to ask me." She bent down to hold Prudence in her arms.

"Vanessa, I love him so much. I've never loved anyone the way I do him. He's your cousin, Vanessa, for God's sake. You know him, and you know he loves me too." They sat in a squatting position facing one another.

"I hadn't had a chance to tell you my good news because I've been with Malone so much I haven't seen you."

"I've seen Malone a lot during the day and you haven't been with him. He always tells me he doesn't know where you are," Vanessa challenged.

"Cause I told him not to tell you. I didn't want you to know

I've been teaching Culinary Arts at his trade school," Prudence confessed, her eyes welling. Vanessa acted shocked as if she didn't know.

"So now you've joined the organization?" accused Vanessa.

"He only does it to help people, Vanessa. Look, the point that I'm trying to make is, well, we were going to surprise everyone, but we're getting married," Prudence said happily.

"You're what? See, you are in a mubble." Vanessa paused,

"For God's sake, Prue, you've only known him four months. Have you lost your mind?"

"That's right, married. We're getting married," Prudence repeated starry-eyed.

"You have got to be fucking kidding me, right?" Vanessa was exasperated. "When did all this shit happen? Or when is it supposed to happen? After a two year engagement, I hope."

"Well, it'll have to be sooner than that." Prudence's face glowed through the tears, "Because guess what else?" Vanessa gulped. "You're pregnant!!"

"How did you know? Isn't it wonderful, Vanessa?" Prudence was ecstatic.

"No bullshit, Prue, you're pregnant?" Vanessa lit a cigarette and paced like she pushed in for patrol duty.

"Are you serious?" She gave Prudence a once over and said in an wearily,

"Have you lost your rabbit ass mind, Prue?" Vanessa sat down and buried her face in her hands.

"I haven't lost the rabbit, it died. For real, I'm having a baby. I wouldn't play about a thing like that, I'm telling the truth. I thought you'd be happy for me," Prudence responded disappointed by what seemed to be apathy on Vanessa's part. Vanessa's sentiments inwardly fluctuated. One second she felt like smiling; the next she felt like bursting into tears.

"And guess what else? Vanessa, you're really going to love this."

"Please tell me, more love is just what I need." Vanessa said displaying no emotion.

"I'm having twins." Prudence beamed. Vanessa gasped for air.

"You are going to be an Auntie."

Vanessa's covered her mouth with one hand.

"Isn't that amazing? Twins! Are you bragging or complaining Prue?" Vanessa fanned herself with one hand and continued, "Now wait, let me get this shit straight, you're having two babies?"

"Yep. Twins." Vanessa reached over to embrace Prudence. They held each other tightly and rocked in each other's arms.

"Prue, you're having twins, I don't believe it." She wiped her forehead with the sleeve of her shirt.

"Who is the father?" she asked dubiously, in a soft tone of voice, knowing who he is, but somehow hoping she was wrong. Maybe there was hope. Prudence never addressed the father question and whether that was done intentionally or not, Prudence kept right on talking.

"You're the first to know, besides Malone, of course. He's so excited, Vanessa. He wanted to tell you himself, but I told him you were the one person I had to tell." Prudence stared at her with a childlike innocence and said, "So, what do you think Vanessa, honestly, tell me what you think?"

Vanessa's voice faltered as she mumbled, "Prue, why in the world didn't you and Malone use a condom?" Prudence jumped up from the floor insulted.

"Don't ruin the happiest time of my life for me!" Prudence stomped out of the closet and Vanessa caught up to her and gently held her arm. Prudence snatched it away.

"You usually apply way more rationality to a situation before you jump into it to this degree," Vanessa tried diplomacy.

"You aren't excited because you're sending him to jail." wailed Prudence.

"Did you and he conjure up this little stunt on purpose, so I wouldn't do it?" Vanessa asked suspiciously.

"He still doesn't know any of your involvement, and unlike you, I'm more loyal than to snitch on my friends and family," she was fuming as she drew her arm back with a tightly clenched fist and released it toward Vanessa's face. Vanessa blocked her hand as she dipped to avoid the punch.

"What's your problem? You act like you've forgotten what my job entails. You want me to change what I do 'cause you've suddenly fallen in love?" Vanessa retaliated.

"Vanessa, Malone is your cousin and Grey is the man you loved all these years." Prudence recapped.

"Well, in all this conversation, you haven't mentioned what you have planned for me as a way to make money once I throw away my career for you and your Mr. Wannabe save the world hero," Vanessa affirmed. "If you knew what was happening from the beginning or even had the slightest inkling that I was on this case, then why would you do some dumb ass shit like this? Cause even if you aren't a hundred percent sure about it, I know damn well you know what kind of operation Malone and Grey are running. Didn't you think he would ever get busted? If it isn't me, it's going to be someone else." Prudence stared at Vanessa.

"My agency has been on their trails for a long time, in case you didn't know. Malone knows it. Obviously that's a point he forgot to share with you and I understand why. You two have been busy. Suppose Malone has to spend the next fifteen years of his life in jail, Prue? Did you think about the effect that would have on a child, children, before you brought somebody else into this mess?" Vanessa scolded.

"No, I didn't and it's too late now. Can't you bend your damn rules for once in your life?"

"Is that going to change anything?" challenged Vanessa.

Prudence charged through the door and ran down stairs. When she reached the bottom landing, she yanked her head around to look back up at Vanessa.

"Well, for someone who believes in the idiotic theory that God is a female, I hope you don't think you could ever qualify as one of her disciples. I'm going to Malone's house right now to tell him what kind of scum he has in his family. We'll move out of the country so fast you'll never find us," Prudence threatened.

"Prue, you need to slow down and calm down." Vanessa collected her thoughts.

"Don't be ridiculous, Prue. If you tell Malone or leave the country with him you know you would be an accompl...." Prudence interrupted throwing up a stop sign with her hand.

"I know he's helped a lot of people get an education, food, clothing and careers. My fiancé has fulfilled peoples' dreams of owning a home of their own which is five things more than you have ever done. And what? You say what!" her eyes welled and her voice shivered.

"That is your cousin for God sake. You wouldn't risk getting your good girl, gold star, pat on the back for your own family, then fuck you, Vanessa. FUCK YOU." Prudence said as she sprinted down the stairs and out the door. She slammed it so hard that the resounding bang vibrated to the second floor. Vanessa tried to convince herself that Prudence's comments had no affect on her. She leaned over the railing and yelled, "I hope you do leave, and make sure you all take that threesome of bitches with you, if not, I'm bustin' their asses too. Now run and tell him that." She continued screaming, at the top of her lungs, as if Prudence could hear her. "Whatever you do, please, for my sake, do it as soon as possible. Leave tonight, right now would be even better." She massaged her forehead as she walked back to her room. "Being around that mother fucka sure has given you a foul ass mouth." She looked at Patrick and addressed him, "See, she don' pist me the fuck off. In fact, I'm at the height of my pistivity. Lord have mercy, Jesus, that would be too much like right for them to make my life that easy by leaving Patrick. I wish the fuck they would disappear," she shrieked with a piercing cry. "Don' made me start cussin' up in here shit."

After taking several deep breathes to calm down she grabbed her purse and phone. As she reached the door, she turned back to Patrick and gazed at him lovingly. With one hand on her hip, she reassured him, "My life has taken a drastic change in the last four months. You don't have to feel insecure about anything though, 'cause one thing that will never change is the way I feel about you." She blew him a kiss, flashed a sexy smile, flipped off the closet light and bounced.

Chapter 42

Vanessa arrived at her mother's serene colonial style home in Santa Barbara, California looking and feeling like a dying duck in a thunderstorm. As she made her way up the white cobblestone walkway, Venice Hudson, Vanessa's six-year-old son, spotted her through the stained-glass picture window, leaped to the front door and bodily jumped in her arms, nearly knocking her off her feet.

"Mommy, Mommy," he oozed with excitement. "I'll be so happy to come home for the summer."

"Not anywhere near as happy as Mommy," she replied.

"Are you spending the night?"

" No honey. I'm only staying for a couple of hours. I have to go to work in a few."

They hugged, wrestled, and then snuggled affectionately. Tenderly, she forked through his hair with her fingers. He jumped on her back, kicked her sides with his feet, and yanked her shirt, singing, "Off we go!" Vanessa ran like a racehorse around the house.

Venice was the only good thing that resulted from Vanessa's year-and-a-half marriage to her ex-husband, Howard Hudson. Howard was at one time a handsome and successful New York attorney. He was stricken with the HIV virus during one of his gay liaisons or from a dirty needle. Selling sex was primarily the way he supported his heroine addiction after he lost everything.

Venice had inherited Howard's jet-black curly hair, which perfectly framed his round face, milk-chocolate complexion, hazel eyes like his mother and thin frame. Vanessa had found out about Howard's drug habit and devastating condition of his health two years after their divorce had been finalized. Once Vanessa digested the shock of Howard's diagnosis, it became motivation for her to finally join the bureau. She had felt the excitement of at last being able to fulfill a lifelong dream of becoming a Special Agent for the Federal Bureau of Investigation. Getting accepted served to ease the lingering shock and pain she harbored for Howard. Dodie had insisted that her only grandson move in with her since she was due to retire from the phone company the same week Vanessa entered the F.B.I. Academy in Quantico, Virginia.

After visiting with Venice in his nautically designed bedroom, Vanessa went to scout the whereabouts of her mother. Dodie was sitting in her flower-scented room with many flowers about her. Subtle, warm colors provided a serene atmosphere in her sitting room. The glass-covered greenhouse was the focal point of the room. Crammed inside were a variety of beautiful, well manicured, lush, green plants and flowers. Dodie looked as fresh as her garden when she entered. Dodie's medium brown complexion was as soft, clear and youthful as any women ten years her junior. Her silver gray, pixie cut hairdo and petite facial features cast an aura of sex appeal surrounding her 5'3" frame. Vanessa sat in a chair next to her mother with both feet crossed and propped on a footstool.

"You know Ma," she said, "I don't know what to do, Ma, about this cross fire situation I'm trapped in."

Vanessa tapped her fingers on the table one by one, repeatedly, producing the cadence of a marching band. Dodie finally snapped, "Vanessa, please! Stop that noise before I knock you out of that damn chair."

Uncontrollable tears streamed from Vanessa's eyes. The harder she tried to hold them back, the more readily they flowed. Her nose ran and the tears formed a continual streaming path that settled into her mouth. The warhorse had finally broken down. Her voice cracked from hopelessness, she felt defeated.

"Nessy, what's wrong? What is going on with you?"

"Oh Ma, things have suddenly become so confusing. I can't see how I ever had a clear take on anything."

"When things like this happen, it's probably just time for your perception to change."

"Ma, how do you know when you really love someone?" Vanessa ventured.

"When you act stupid over them like you do and always have over that damn Grey," Dodie turned away to tend to her plants.

"I do love him, Ma. I love Grey so much and I just can't help how my heart feels. I have withheld a large portion of the information I've acquired because I'm so confused. Now, the Bureau is on my back. If I don't make a move and quick, they're gonna come and arrest *me* soon."

"Why in heaven's name would you do some shit like that?" Dodie questioned.

"I should have taken myself off the case like you told me. I knew it was a conflict of interest. The shit is so deep, Malone and his Trio of partners are Philanthropists who run a multi–million dollar fraudulent organization that robs from the rich and gives to the poor."

"Vanessa, what in the world are you talking about?" Dodie was confused. Vanessa revealed her quandary.

"Malone works with three women called "The Trio", Holiday, Farren and December. They have funneled untold millions of dollars into charity. They have built universities, trade schools and housing from coast to coast. They fund orphanages, hot lunch, after school and art programs for inner city schools. They donated untold thousands to AIDS research. He's very humble and doesn't accept any special accolades for what he deems his calling."

"Well now, slow down now.   He doesn't want any public praise because his ass is wanted by the law. Let's keep it real."

Vanessa and Dodie were seated in Dodie's garden.

"So, what if they find out how the money was spent? It's gone now." Dodie picked dead leaves off the plants.

"The biggest problem I'm having with this case is that if I bust Malone, Holiday, December, and Farren, all the things they have set up for these hundreds of thousands of people will be confiscated, and that's a given.   It's called Forfeiture and Seizure." Vanessa explained wearily.

"What's that now, baby? Who are Holiday, December and Farren?" Dodie took notice of the worried stress consumed in Vanessa's face.

"If I turn them in, all the people they have helped over the years, everything they own will be taken away, literally.   All confiscated.   If I don't and the F.B.I. finds out I withheld information, my career is over forever and I'm getting jail time. The women Malone calls The Trio, they are his business partners and confidants. All three of them are smart as hell too."

"If you bust anybody in the organization, that is gonna happen anyways. Someone is gonna sing."

"Malone has skillfully managed to keep his involvement with his organization, The Red Rose, completely separate from his charity empire. None of his employees who work for him or The

Trio know who they are. The employees only deal with Grey."

"I know damn well that selfish ass Grey ain't giving no damn money to charity." Vanessa was taken aback by her mother's comment.

"Grey knows Malone's involvement but you're right, he has nothing to do with that leg of it. Why do you say that about him Mama? He really wants to do better."

"Girl please. Grey was born a scorpion and that's all he knows how to be. Everyone who knows him understands that about him but you. You are the only one silly enough to have hope that he'll change. Honey, you'll do better sticking with your little Patrick in the closet. So, if the four of them get busted, how do you know they'll confess how they spent the money?" Vanessa's mind was now preoccupied by Dodie's statement.

"All my people need is a bust. They want to see his legendary face and it's over. Plus, I have obtained all the evidence the bureau needs. I have a paper trail that leads right to P.A.W., Malone's non-profit organization and his silent partner, Stanton. I have more than enough to convict them all.

"So, what in the hell are you going to do now?" Vanessa was flabbergasted. "I don't know. I'm in a no-win situation here."

Dodie embraced Vanessa with both arms, "Can you get in trouble for not reporting your conflict of interest to the agency?"

"I wouldn't be in violation of any policy, but I would be in violation of poor judgment." Vanessa lit a cigarette and began a nervous tread. Vanessa massaged her forehead with her fingertips in a repetitive motion to relieve the pain devouring her head.

"Mama, you don't understand." Her words poured out, "These people have been given human dignity and self-worth, which is something you never think about until you lose it. I've never seen anything to this magnitude before. You, in fact, would have to see this to believe it. Who dedicates their life and risks their freedom, solely for the benefit of others? What greater gift can you give a person than this kind of hope? How do you or can you crucify someone who does?" Dodie interjected, honey, this would be a hard decision for anyone to make in your situation."

"That College for Life University is like receiving an Ivy League education. Malone is the founder and primary investor."

"What!" Dodie exclaimed, "You gotta be kidding me! Malone? There's no way. I've heard rave reviews on TV and everywhere about those colleges." Dodie put one hand over her mouth and the other on her hip.

Vanessa sat on the floor in front of her mother and rested her head in her mother's lap.

"And the children," Vanessa whimpered.

"What children?"

"All the children he has and does help." Her heavy crying caused her short repeated breaths as she struggled to continue.

"There was a thirteen-year-old girl who got her own room for the first time. I interviewed the girl's mother on a return trip I took to the site when Malone wasn't there. She told me that her daughter didn't come out of her room for a week because she was frightened someone would take it away. During Christmas, Malone and The Trio dresses like Santa and his helpers, they visit orphanages, hospitals and homeless shelters to deliver toys, food, clothes, money, and medicine all over the state of California. He has built hundreds of thousands of beautiful homes. The people living in them would be homeless if I arrested them." She looked up to Dodie, "Ma, all these wonderful things were created with stolen money and it's my job to take it all away."

"I had no idea my Malone had all that going on. He was always exceptionally smart. Vanessa, I got an idea baby," She blurted out with excitement. Vanessa stood.

"What Ma, what is it?"

"Shit, do you think Malone can get a couple of houses for a few of our needy relatives before you blow the whistle on all that?"

As much as Vanessa tried to resist she couldn't help but laugh. "Mother please, be serious!"

"Oh no, don't think for one moment that I'm not serious, honey."

Dodie was bewildered. She knew Vanessa wanted an answer. Vanessa had always crawled home to her mother whether she was backed up tightly in a corner or plagued by a nagging hangnail.

"This is the first time I've ever heard of anything like this in my whole life. This is unreal."

"Exactly."

"They are angels with dirty halos. I must say, I'm not surprised that Malone started in a life of crime. Shit, what choice did he have? He graduated from Princeton with straight A's and couldn't get a job anywhere. I blame that on the system though. Once you pay your debt to society, you should be able to start with a clean record, at least the first time around. It really turned him around when he could no longer pursue a career in government because he had a record after he did time for helping that woman he loved. I'm not shocked that he gives it all away though. Our family has always been among the givers. What do you think he should have done?"

"And the takers." Vanessa chimed. Malone didn't stop there. Please, try to guess what he gave Prue."

"I'm clueless," Dodie said not wanting to expend the energy of a guessing game.

"Twins and a wedding date."

Dodie smiled pleasantly. "They will be good for each other. I know you don't think I'm shocked though after hearing this other news. Plus, I always knew if they ever met it would be love at first sight. Malone and Prudence were made for each other. Twins. I know Stephanie is excited, I have to call her." They both sat in the parlor looking dumbfounded and smoking cigarettes. Dodie closed her eyes to collect her thoughts.

"No one deserves a pat on the back for being good to others. We're expected to do that. Give as much as you can for as long as you can to who ever you can, and goodness will always come back to you." Dodie chanted.

Vanessa interrupted her, "Ma please, what should I do?"

"I don't know how to answer that for you. I can't imagine what I would do myself. On one hand, I don't endorse Malone stealing money, but what can I say? He utilized it to help others. I can't for the life of me understand what made you want to be an F.B.I. agent especially with a background of our family." Dodie said, shaking her head, baffled.

"Ma, I'm giving up smoking for New Years." Vanessa mentioned as an afterthought. Dodie stared at her mulling over her situation, "Honey, listen to me." Vanessa gave her undivided attention. "Like I can't breathe or die for you nor can I look in the mirror for you in the morning when all this is over. I can tell you this though, whatever your decision, make it solely based on what's right for you and your conscience. You have to be able to face you in the mirror and live with your decision when it's over. You have always seen things in black and white and never had any tolerance for special sets of circumstances. Unfortunately, now it has hit home. These are the gray areas, Vanessa." Dodie smiled and continued benevolently as Vanessa fought to contain the tears .

"When people put you in a position of authority, Vanessa,

they do it for a reason. The F.B.I. trusts you. They know, that you know, that your number one responsibility is to be able to ensure them that these criminal's illegal actions are put to a halt. In this case, you may not choose the same orthodox method of doing it the way they expect, but the outcome will be the same. They know you will do what's in the best interest of your job first and abide by the guidelines of the law."

"So you're saying the bureau would understand if I don't involve the four of them?" Vanessa asked innocently.

"Don't be ridiculous; you sound like a damn fool. I'm saying the law is open to interpretation." As Dodie rose to leave the greenhouse she continued, "Vanessa, you said your heart told you to stay on this case, even though there was a conflict of interest. I know for a fact that your heart had nothing to do with it. You didn't request to be transferred because you wanted to prove to yourself and the men you work with and for that you are man enough to handle anything they can. Now, what you need to do is man up, go do what you have to do for you, and stop whining. I hate people who make gangster decisions and then when the shit gets twisted they start crying like a little bitch. Either you're a G or you aren't. If you are then this ain't nothing but a step for a stepper. If you aren't, then go be a Liberian in the boonies some damn place shit. You have moxie, do what is right as you use it. Remember, there is a God who sits high and sees low." Dodie's facial expression and body movements exuded finality. Vanessa stared at her mother until she was out of sight. She nervously bit her lip and twirled her hair around her fingers as she processed the discourse. She rubbed her forehead with the palms of her hands, in a failed attempt to relieve the hammering in her head. As she leaned back to rest her eyes, Venice plowed in. He cuddled on her lap, placed his head on her shoulder and closed his eyes also. Her arms gently engulfed his slender body lovingly.

Vanessa finally understood gray areas.

Chapter 43

The bank in Westwood was packed with a late afternoon crowd when Grey arrived wearing a black Hugo Boss suit, a fedora and a long cashmere overcoat. He shuffled from side to side as he waited in line for the next merchant teller to summons him to one of the windows. Finally, a green arrow flashed. He removed his Louis Vuitton checkbook from his matching attaché case, signed the first business check from the unused book, and handed the check to the teller.

The teller had ordered money and was prepared for the large withdrawal, since the branch manager had informed all the tellers on duty in the merchant area to be prepared for Mr. Carson's arrival. The transaction had already been authorized and verified earlier that day when Grey had phoned the advanced notification for the pre-order.

"All I need is your driver's license, Mr. Carson," the teller said with a flirtatious smile. "Thank you, Mr. Carson. Did you know that Malone is by far the most regal name I've ever heard?" She blushed and batted her eyelashes as she gathered his id along with his check.

Grey shot her an empty response. Once Grey made it clear that her invitation had been ignored, she instantly resumed a business decorum. The woman lowered her head to avoid further eye contact as she studied the check. The embarrassed teller slammed her drawer and headed to the back vault dejected. She returned with an officer-approved check and a CTR form. Grey, being familiar with the form, forged the signature of *Malone Carson* to a dead- on match.

"Your withdrawal is for such a large amount of money, I need to know how would you like it?" the teller requested in a bland tone.

Grey pondered momentarily.

"I'll take $150,000.00 in cash, hundred dollar bills only and the rest in cashier's checks." He requested politely in a soft-spoken tone. She laid the strapped hundreds and the cashier's checks across the counter as she counted the bundles. After everything was securely tucked away in his attaché case, the teller said without a smile, "Have a nice day sir."

He responded, "I'll do better than that, I'm not going to have nothing but nice days from here on out." He gave a meaningless wink and never broke stride as he headed out the exit door.

The moment Grey returned to his hotel room, he disposed of the prosthetics and promptly called Vanessa's house with ripping-at-the-seams excitement. He left a message then phoned her cell.

Vanessa had surrendered all the final information she had planned to relinquish to headquarters. Special Agents Johnson and Wilcox had used various reasons, factual documents, and concrete evidence beyond a reasonable doubt that supported their request for certified authorization for a wire intercept. Information was also submitted to obtain approval for Probable Cause affidavit, which was signed by a judge. When the search warrants were in place, they set up the arrest of all the criminals, pinpointed the location of the headquarters and offices, and at long last were in position to put the entire case to rest. Vanessa's findings were strong enough to prosecute everyone involved in the long awaited bust of the nation's largest, multi-million dollar, fraudulent organizations that robbed from the rich and gave to the poor. Agent Robert and Agent Vanessa had requested the assistance from the white-collar crime agents in the Chicago and New York offices. Simultaneously, agents had been dispersed to apprehend the staff, and the informants who provided information from the DMV, banks and credit card companies. The agents also confiscated the contents of the three offices. The Agents seized it all: iPads, file cabinets, cameras, thousands of potential profiles, profiles in progress, and a number of personal phone books. They also took fake identification cards, background checks on marks that included their net worth, and tons of print outs with driver's licenses, social security numbers, mother's maiden names and dates of birth that had been sent directly from the DMV's and Social Security offices through the mail. Everything from Toi's offices were seized as well.

Michael was in the New York office when the F.B.I. arrived. The moment he saw the agents in the security cameras he attempted to escape out of a hidden door in the back of the building. He was apprehended. Vincent was in the center of the street in route to the office when he witnessed the infiltration. He immediately called the emergency line and when December answered, he reported, "The New York office is being raided." Then he sprinted out of sight faster than a pick- pocket can clip you in Time Square.

Vincent was never apprehended.

Vanessa called him from another phone so everything Grey said wouldn't be heard and recorded to a monitoring station that was being overseen by one of the agents.

"Hello."

"Hey baby, I'm at the Marina Hotel. I withdrew half a million dollars from the bank and got the tickets for Europe. I made plans for us to be married in Paris since you loved it so much. Everything is in place and ready for us to make our move, so meet me here at midnight. Our flight leaves promptly at 2:45 a.m. I love you, Vanessa. I want you to know that I've decided to stop doing drugs so I can be a good husband to you and a good father for

Venice. Also, I'm giving that street shit up. Whatever I have to do for us to make it this time, I'm doing it. I promise. Oh, and I sent my mother some money." Silence.

" Hello, baby are you there?"

"I'm here," she said.

"Well, we'll talk when you get here. Don't be late. Someone is knocking on the door, I gotta go."

"Good-bye Grey," her voice trembled. Grey hung up the phone and answered the door. Vanessa watched Special Agent Robert and Peter cart Grey into custody through a pair of binoculars from the third floor of a hotel across the street.

She wept.

Chapter 44

Malone's street was pitch black. Either the lights were out of order or they had not come on yet. Vanessa got out of her car and looked around. She assumed Malone wasn't home since the modest house was pitch black.

'*Ohhh, good, he's gone.*' She mumbled under her breath. '*I'll finish my report, turn it in, boom, it's over.*' *If only it were that easy.*' she thought. As she reached for the handle on the car door, she heard Malone's faint voice echo from an upstairs window in a warm and welcoming spirit, "Are you by any chance looking for me, my dear cousin? What are you doing here this late?" He cackled.

Vanessa kicked the tire and slammed her hand on the hood. She turned and scanned the windows until she spotted him. Vanessa walked to the door as if it were a final march to the electric chair. As Malone opened the door to the stucco bungalow, she assumed an air of coolness. Once inside, she stopped to gather her bearings. Her eyes widened as she scrutinized the cramped living quarters.

"So, you're still here, huh?"

"Was I supposed to be goin' somewhere?"

"Nope."

"What the hell's wrong with you, Vanessa? You look like something has you spooked." Malone gestured for her to have a seat in the living room.

"You didn't see Elvis out there, did you?" He turned the light on.

"Let me start out by saying things aren't always what they appear to be cuz, you know?"

He looked at her as though the comment flew right over his head. He puckered to answer but decided to let whatever she said remain in flight.

The choice of the warm colors throughout was reminiscent of an elderly couple's homey esthetic. An array of photos lined the small mantle on the wood-burning fireplace. Lace doilies and slipcovers veiled the obviously worn furniture. The room presented no traceable evidence of his lifestyle.

"Have you seen Prue?" Vanessa quizzed.

"She's was here since early this morning and just left about fifteen minutes ago." Malone responded nonchalantly.

"And?"

"And, what?" he shrugged.

"And how long have you been living here?"

His broad smile and enthusiastic voice clarified how proud he was of his home.

"Eight years."

"Eight years?" Vanessa responded with skepticism.

"That's right. Me and the girls own it."

"How come I never knew about this place?"

"You wouldn't know about it now if it weren't for the fact that you are so damn nosey. There's a lot of things I do that you don't know about."

"I wouldn't bet on that," she mumbled.

"What?"

"Nothing. It's amazing you've been here all these years."

"Yep, I love this house. It's so me," he said in a show off sort of way like a peacock fanning his feathers.

"*I love this house, it's so me*," Vanessa mimicked. "What's this, some kind of decoy bullshit, Blue?"

"How rude to insult a man's abode. You know if the bottom ever falls out of your writing career you would be great as a lawyer. You certainly ask enough questions."

"I wouldn't think that placing people in the job market would be your area of expertise, since you've never had one," Vanessa returned the sarcasm.

"Now, I don't work a nine to five conventional job, but I do have one. Providing jobs for others is exactly my area of expertise," Malone asserted.

"Why would I need a decoy?" He backtracked to her comment.

"You call stealing from people providing sound employment?"

Vanessa rebutted, steering the topic.

"What do you mean stealing from people?" Malone was instantly guarded.

"Stop trippin,' Grey told me you all were still doing the credit card thing. Much larger scale though. The prosthetics, genius."

"He did, well, then you should know that in this current jobless market, it's been much more than sound. It's been lucrative, steady, and a source of help to thousands of people who would have been otherwise destitute," Malone defended.

"How fortuitous we stumbled onto this subject. Since that's precisely why I'm here."

"I thought you were here to challenge me in playing the dozens.

"I would only play something you would have a chance at winning," Vanessa responded seriously.

"Would you like a drink?" Malone offered.

"Herbal tea would be nice, thanks."

"I meant something from the bar. I don't feel like making no damn tea," he contended.

"Tea or nothing for me."

While Malone fumbled around the kitchen, Vanessa browsed around the living room. All the photos were of Malone, Holiday, December and Farren. All were taken in various places like the Caribbean, Hawaii, Paris, Aspen, Japan, Australia and a lot of places Vanessa didn't recognize. The years of memories they had compiled were endless. Vanessa glanced out of the back window and discovered three bungalows on the lot.

"Who lives in those little bitty houses?"

"Holiday, December and Farren."

Malone said as he leisurely walked out the kitchen carrying a silver tray. On it were cloth napkins with P.A.W. monogrammed on them in gold an assortment of tea bags, dunking cookies, mints, and fresh cut fruit.

Vanessa's thoughts swirled. '*How he could be so congenial and cool if he knew his organization had been seized. No one could have contacted him, yet? How could that be possible? She couldn't believe Prudence had remained loyal to their friendship by keeping her identity a secret from him after everything that had happened.*

As she examined the tray she voiced her compliments right away in anticipation that her visit may be brief. "I love that about you, Malone. You are the ultimate perfectionist. Your knack and appreciation for detail is what every girl dreams of in a straight man." As he walked back in the kitchen he asked, "Have I forgotten anything, baby?"

"Fresh flowers." He came out with a small arrangement.

"Huh." Vanessa sat on the couch behind the coffee table. He sat on a chaise lounge across from her. He poured water, selected a tea bag, and snuggled back on the lounger.

"So, what can I attribute to this wonderful visit?"

She followed suit. As Malone sipped, she announced, "Malone, I am here in an official capacity." She flashed her badge. "I am an undercover Special Agent assignment investigator for the F.B.I." He gagged as tea detoured down the wrong pipe. The coughing became so severe his face became flushed and he couldn't catch his breath. When it didn't stop, Vanessa forcefully hit his back until the choking almost subsided. Through the slight persistent coughs that remained, he asked, "What the fuck did you say? You know I don't like cop, sheriff, FBI, none of those kinda jokes, Vanessa."

"I am not joking."

Malone sat and tried to absorb the lethal blow. Suddenly, he hurled the cup and saucer to the floor then lunged to his feet.

"Have you lost your fuckin mind, bitch?" He paced the length of the living room, lit a cigarette and blew out a horrendous cloud of smoke. His body shivered and his hands trembled as his anger boiled.

As Vanessa picked a selection from the tray, he reached over and violently pitched the tray across the room. It soared through the air and crashed into other objects, breaking everything on impact. Vanessa yelped in agony frantically trying to wipe the splattered boiling water off her legs. After they cooled down, she sat back on the couch.

"Why don't you calm down, Blue and let's discuss this."

"Calm down, my ass, you no good, low down, scum bag bitch." He hit the palm of his hand on his forehead as if the light suddenly came on. He was breathing hard. "You're the one. You're the one who's had the spotlight on us all this time. You had my fuckin' office busted in New York!" He paused to catch his breath, so angry he felt as if he was hyperventilating. "My own cousin, ain't that a bitch! You dirty, motha fuckin,' black ass, snitchin,' woe ass bitch you."

Suddenly, he grabbed her by the collar and slung her all the way to the door, then viciously slammed her against it so hard the walls reverberated. Vanessa made no attempt to stop him.

"Get outta my fuckin' house you dirty, no good, son of a bitch, before I kick your fuckin' ass!" His jaws tightened and expanded. He snatched her up again, bodily lifted her off the floor and threw her into a wooden end table that exploded in pieces on her impact. She sighed in pain." Malone. If I hadn't done it, somebody else would have." He grabbed her by her collar tight around her neck, drew his arm back and aimed his fisted hand at her face.

"Oooohh, I have never wanted to kill anybody the way I want to kill your ass right now."

"Do it, if it'll make you feel better. By adding murder to that long list of charges I have on you, it won't make a damn bit of difference cause you ain't never gettin' out of jail anyway," she said in a strained voice as she gasped for air.

He snatched her face to face with him, stared into hers eyes and then threw her on the floor and just stepped over her. She staggered to get up, stood akimbo and said, "It gets worse, Blue. Not only did I bust your office in New York, I busted the Red Rose, your office in Chicago, all of your employees in all three cities, fifteen of your in the pocket people from the DVM, social security office and credit card centers. I'm sad to say, I'm going to have to bust you and the Trio too."

Another surge of rage turned his face a beet red and bluish veins protruded from his forehead. "Fuck you!" Malone roared.
Vanessa crawled to the couch. She didn't lift a hand to stop him. She understood how he felt. If the situation had been reversed, she would have felt the same way and done the same thing.

"Well, I guess it would be safe to assume that tea time is officially over, huh? I know, it's kind of funny, right? Imagine me an F.B.I. agent. Lets talk, maybe we can work a deal." Malone was exasperated.

"I am not amused, Vanessa. This is surreal. I just can't wrap my mind around this."

"I never thought I would have to do this to my own family. I had no idea you were involved in anything of this magnitude." She walked across the room to get out of the range of fire. He listened.

"In spite of the miraculous things you've done, I have accumulated enough evidence in the past four months to put you and your girlfriends away forever. The indictment contains charges of over 100 counts of conspiracy, that's one for every person in the organization and at least 45 counts each for Grand Theft, Grand Larceny, Identity Theft, Embezzlement, Interstate Transportation of Stolen Property, Mail and Wire Fraud and since this is white collar crime involving financial institutions, that holds charges as violations of R.I.C.O. which bears a maximum $1,000,000 fine and 30 years per count. That's only in L.A., mind you. In New York, how about enterprise corruption under the cities organization crime control act and Chicago, I won't even start. On top of all that, it would be just too overwhelming to think about the tons of cities you have been busy as a bee in spreading your stolen honey. In short, you'd be incarcerated for so many years that by the time you saw daylight again, outside of prison walls that is, which will be never, credit cards would be out of style."

"Sounds like you gonna give us all day on this thang. I'll take all the time, spend the rest of my life in prison, I will roll over on everyone in my pocket for Holiday, Farren and December to walk."

"Roll over? Wow, on everyone in your pocket. A snitch. Then you would be doing what you just jumped on me for doing. Huh, so it's okay when it's for your cause- only wrong for any cause other than yours."

She faced him, "Malone, this society is structured on a foundation that has rules that you must follow regardless of your good intentions or personal vendetta against the system."

"RULES!" His voice escalated. " You mean the rules set forth by our great politicians? The people who make up the rules, alter

the meaning of the rules, change the rules, enforce the rules, but
don't play by the rules? Minimum wage, eight dollars an hour, for
real? That's not enough to buy peanuts? Which one of those rule
makers or his kids do you think lives off that bullshit? Elderly.
Thousands, starving in the richest country in the world, after
working and paying taxes all their lives. A married couple, both
retired, on social security, husband dies, the wife will now only get
one check, the higher of their two. Why shouldn't a woman be able
to get her husband's hard earned money. Why should the state get
it? Now instead of living on two-fixed income that wasn't enough
she only has one. Public Education. Half these damn kids are
growing up illiterate. Who took prayer out of the schools? Why? I
bet the same person who took out books, art, music, computers, sex
education, and don't pay teachers shit!" he said caustically. Equal
opportunity employment, no matter what race, creed, religion or
color! If that worked why are there so many minority programs and
job quotas. Why is it an issue about gays in the military? The only
thing that should matter is love, how we treat people and the value
of human life; that's our assignment on earth." Malone enumerated,
"our job is not to stand in judgment of others. That's solely the job
of God. We need to straighten out our own sin-infested shit houses
first. We have a hard enough time doing what we're supposed to do,
like respecting and honoring each other's right to a fair life." If a
woman wants to have an abortion, that's her choice. Who should
have the right to make a ruling on what a person does with their own

body?"

"So, you agree with abortions?" Vanessa asked, wide-eyed.

"No, I don't, but I do think it's a woman's personal choice. The woman is the one who has to answer for that on judgment day, not the politicians who are making the rules. Everyone should have the right to do what the hell he or she wants with his or her body. How can you say abortions are wrong and then allow capital punishment? The hypocrite rule makers who sit around governing what's best for others are the main ones with the six figure salaries, mistresses, private jets, lavish vacations, fabulous offices, company cars, and let's not talk about expense accounts, perks and pay the least amount of taxes." Malone ranted on.

"That sounds exactly like your lifestyle.

"I don't have a mistress." He said dryly and continued his tirade. "A Democracy. Only people with money and plenty of it are free, and even then the skin color matters. If you're a failure in America, it's your own fault right?" Malone asked with staunch conviction.

"Vanessa, all people are not created equal or with the same set of opportunities, period. We are responsible for each other. The more that is given to you, the more that is expected of you. Who exactly do these rules work for? Face it Vanessa, we are a society of misplaced priorities." He threw himself in the chair and lit a cigarette. Malone smirked smugly. "So, you're the one they sent to enforce the rules on me. Make sure to give the feds my best regards. They really outdid themselves this time."

All the rebuttals she had rehearsed didn't fit because his double standards and selective blindness only occurred when he looked at himself. Malone was notorious for crediting himself on having the last profound word. He stared, she stared and silence lingered. She knew he wouldn't say another word until the ball was volleyed back into his court. She popped the knuckles on her fingers, rubbed her temples and volleyed back, "While I am moved by your gestures of kindness one must not forget it's done with stolen money and at the expense of others. You combined goodness with transgression and have proven to me that you are a man of your word. However, we live in a democracy, there are ample opportunities available for people to make changes and choices in their lives and do it within the guidelines of the law. Whether we like it or not, we have to follow the rules. Although you feel it is the duty of the wealthy to help those who aren't as fortunate, it is not your right to make that decision for them. How can you fault this country for stealing but justify your own?"

Malone retorted, "You have to be able to afford to make changes. Most people are products of their environment. Vanessa," he stressed, "people can change only when they are given choices. It is the responsibility of our country to provide alternatives. It is the duty of each person to change his own situation when the possibilities are presented. POVERTY ISN'T A PREFERENCE,

Vanessa. Anyone can be on the bottom or hit bottom."

"The welfare system was designed to help people," she said.

"Welfare is an on going problem. It makes people lazy and dependent. It wasn't designed for that purpose but that is what happened. That little money certainly won't solve any problems. Most people are on welfare because they have no other choice. Women have more babies to get more money. The problem is a lack of good education and job skills. Welfare should only be given predicated on continued education. You should have to be in college or a trade school. If you don't graduate in four years or two from the college or trade welfare is cut off. The only permanent solution in helping people is teaching them to help themselves."

"True." Vanessa meekly agreed.

"That's why our system isn't working. No solutions. Just additions to the problems."

"Being a common larcenist isn't a solution."

Malone smirked, "Ain't a damn thing common about what I do. I don't do what the system does. I don't steal people's money. I recycle it, for the good of others. I'm not running a Ponzi scheme or defrauding people of their life savings. They all get reimbursed. Banks are highly insured for those kinds of expenditures and losses," Malone defended.

"So, taking someone else's money is okay as long as they are insured and can be reimbursed. I'd call that stealing from the insurance companies. Also not a solution." Vanessa rebutted as she yawned and glanced at her watch. She knew he was going to talk forever. She wanted to shut him up but felt that she owed him at least the courtesy of letting him vent and vent and vent.

"I just don't know what would make you choose a career like this." Malone said in disarray."

"This is all you need to know. I'm offering you a take it or leave it deal." Vanessa said authoritatively. Malone cut her off,

"How are you in any position to offer me a deal? I didn't know F.B.I. agents had the authority to leverage a proposition."

"I'm bestowing the authority upon myself. I know you can understand. I have in my possession, all the trump cards containing every detail of information needed to make your long awaited conviction stick."

Malone listened intently.

"As of right now, shop is closed. Permanently. I want your word on behalf of your female posse and yourself that this is over the moment we consummate this deal." Vanessa demanded.

"So, what the hell would we do?" Malone meditated.

"I don't give a flying fuck, Blue! I didn't include Camouflage or Blossoms in my report, so you may want to start there." Vanessa said impatiently.

"I get your word or all of you go to jail."

"You know what," he pointed his finger, "to be honest, secretly I've often wondered what the experience of owning a restaurant would be like. Prudence and me have been exploring the possibilities. The Trio is ready to quit and build a legal empire. So, I guess things happen for a reason." Malone stood and stretched his shoulders and back.

Vanessa's shoes crunched across the broken glass on the carpet, as she moved toward the window and glanced outside. When finished, she swung around to face Malone.

"Do I have your word or not?"

Malone said sincerely, "Vanessa, you have my word, on God and all that's holy to me, that as of this moment, I will no longer engage in any illegal activities or disobey any laws."

"And The Trio?"

"Who do you think will be ordering the food, purchasing flowers and buying clothes for our businesses? Malone conceded.

"Now, that I have yours, I'm giving you my mine. If I ever hear of you or The Trio doing anything that doesn't conform to the rules of the law, I'll bust your asses faster than the speed of light. You have my word on God and all that's holy to me. Anytime you think I'm bluffing, Blue, call it. Busting you would mean incriminating myself and I don't give a damn. We'll all go down together, hand in fucking hand."

"So, why?"

"So, why what?"

"So, why in the world would you jeopardize your reputation and career by letting the four of us go?"

"I'm not letting you go. I'm giving you back the chance the system took away from you."

"But why?" Malone inquired again confused.

"Does it really matter why?" Vanessa held back.

"Well, considering how headstrong and obstinate you are, not to mention that you leveled my entire operation, from coast to coast, it does matter. If you're gonna let the four main people who pushed all the buttons walk, I'd like to know why." Malone pressed.

"I don't give a damn about you getting married, the Trio, twins, Prue, you being my cousin, Grey or Mama thinking I shouldn't go after you." She softened a bit. "Well, I do give a damn about Prue and the twins and that's all though. What you did is wrong, but you did it for all the right reasons. The money was insured and is being returned to the owners so, no harm was done. You did some exceptional things for a massive amount of people who otherwise may have never had a chance. It would be difficult as hell for me to live with myself knowing that all those people would lose everything they own. So, there it is." she said soberly as she walked to the front door, Malone trailing her.

"What about Grey?"

"What about him?" I wouldn't feel too bad if I were you. When we arrested him he had forged your name for $400.000.00 out of your account."

"Oh, that ain't nothing,' he does that shit all the time." Malone wasn't fazed.

"How could you do that to Grey? That's my brother and my best friend. I thought you loved him." Malone was choked.

"Blue," she belted sharply, "I can still do that to you, too. And, I do love him, but I couldn't factor that into my decision. He is taking the fall as the sole head of the organization and none of your people who got busted can say anything different because no one can identify you or the Trio.

"You set that up? Nice."

"Don't be ridiculous we didn't set him up. I could have hired someone. Grey insisted on that position." Vanessa stopped him, "If you feel that bad for your brother and best friend, don't let him take the fall for you and your comrades. Go turn your asses in and tell the authorities what's really going on. Yes?"

"And why would I do that, Vanessa? He's the one who told your ass every motha fuckin' thing. I told him to shut the fuck up. One of my strictest rules is to never take friends and family to The Red Rose and he took your ass any damn way."

"Wait, how did you know that?" Vanessa was taken off guard.

"I had cameras installed in the escape route."

"So, you saw everything?"

"Yep."

"Wow," all she could do was smile. "So, the answer is no, I take it. I thought so. Since you aren't going to surrender, all I can say is keep some money on his books." Vanessa unlocked her door.

"Does Grey know about you yet?"

"Nope. I have a feeling he'd understand. Oh, by the way," she said as she headed down the walkway.

"Twins, huh?"

"Wha'-cha have to say about that?" He beamed proudly.

"You should have used a condom." Vanessa answered dryly. He slammed the door then heard her yell from inside her car.

"Malone, Malone, by the way."

"What, damn?" He peeped out the door. As she pulled off, she yelled, "Congratulations and Happy New year."

Malone closed the door then collapsed against it and slid to the floor, defeated. His bloodshot eyes were weary and he mumbled in a crushed voice, "And it all falls down.'" The message hurt him so deeply he felt as if he had been stabbed multiple times in the spine bone and heart.

The messenger was the noose.

Chapter 45

A limousine was parked in front of Malone and the Trio's home. The uniformed Chauffeur loaded numerous pieces of luggage and trunks in the back of the limo, all Louis Vuitton. The Chauffeur opened the car door when he saw Holiday, Farren, December, Prudence and Malone exit from the house. He stood at the door until they had retreated into the back of the limo. They were all dressed in their own styles of black designer pantsuits, long cashmere coats, large quilted handbags, fedoras and sported red sole shoes.

"Gray Butte Air field, sir and may we speak in private, please."

"Right away, sir." The automatic window went up. Malone turned his attention to Prudence and the Trio.

"I don't want any of you to worry. Everything is going to be fine. If any worrisome situation arises, immediately turn it over to me. I am going to handle all of this, and we are going to be fine."

The Trio and Prudence gave Malone their undivided attention as he spoke.

"We got a few dollars and I have mapped out an entirely new plan of action for this New Year. We are going to breath some new energy into Camouflage and Blossom's, possibly expand, and or open multiple stores. I want us to put our heads together and brainstorm some businesses that we can start as a family and possibly franchise. We are going to scout for the perfect location to open a fine dining restaurant for Prudence. I have been thinking about marketing that barbeque sauce of yours, Farren. We'll start by promoting it in Prudence's restaurant. From now on we are going to start investing in more conservative stocks and long-term assets. After the wedding, which will take place in the Hamptons, we are gonna lay low in CPW for a couple of months to regroup."

"CPW?" Prudence blurted, stumped.

"That is where the four of us have resided in New York for the last five years," Holiday intervened, then noticed the figurative question mark still dangling over Prudence's head.

"Central Park West," December spoke vacuously." The question mark vanished. Malone continued, "Last, and most importantly, I have talked to Stanton and we are keeping all the charities afloat and moving right along with our global plans. "I'll find a way to ensure they continue to grow."

"We will find a way to ensure they grow like bean stalks in a fairy tale," Prudence reassured her husband as she locked eyes with each of them waiting for either one of them to cosign her expressions. Loving guises confirmed each of their support. They understood she hadn't melded yet simply by her need to voice what was inevitable. There was an unspoken bond between The Trio and Malone that, *'no matter how high they climbed, how low they fell, or where they'd go, love, loyalty and integrity would always be the foundation of their show.'*

Malone winked at his fiancé and continued. "I have hired a dream team of attorneys to collaborate on building a case for Grey. Unfortunately, it looks like he is going to be stuck for a minute. We have new additions coming to our family in September. I don't ever remember being this excited about anything Malone cackled. They will have their daddy, mommy and three aunties. How about that?" The Trio and Prudence smiled and relaxed in accordance.

After they arrived at the airport and emerged from the limo, The Trio and Prudence strutted to the jet like super models walking down a runway with Malone trailing on his cell and carrying an attaché case. After their luggage was secured on the plane and all seat belts were fastened, John circled the airfield, soared down the runway and ascended into the dark and cloudy winter sky.

Chapter 46

Vanessa came to a screeching halt in front of the Federal Bureau of Investigation building at 9 a.m. driving the red, convertible Porsche Carrera. She entered then waited for a routine clearance. When the two men on duty approached the door, she unbuttoned the front of her double-breasted suit jacket. They frisked past her service weapon that rested inside her shoulder holster. One of the men admiring her said, "Agent Saffore, you look gorgeous today, as usual."

"Thank you, as usual Deuce, for the nice compliment." When her clearance was completed, she buttoned her blazer and stepped through the large, steel double doors. A loud buzzer permeated the small inspection area and released another set of steel doors instantaneously. Vanessa passed several offices before she reached the door labeled Donald Dayton, Supervisor. Once inside she nodded slightly and said, "per your request." Donald raked back sparse hair that remained on his receding hairline. He stood at attention to greet her. A delightful smile captivated his face as he hurriedly walked around his cluttered desk to give her a firm handshake.

"Congratulations and Happy New Year. I'm so glad you had time to stop by before your flight leaves."
Vanessa returned his eye contact projecting no display of emotion. She really wasn't interested in listening to a thing he had to say. She intently watched his lips so he would assume she was.

"I personally wanted to congratulate you on the successful outcome of your case and the professional manner in which you executed it. I guess the department had it all wrong. I thought for sure, I mean all this time we figured, that it was two men who ran that organization, Malone Carson and Grey Young. I find it hard to believe that Mr. Young is the head of that organization and that Mr. Carson and those three women had no involvement at all." He looked at her questioningly. "Any thoughts?" he probed. Vanessa's poker face offered no answer. He scratched his bald spot again as he shook his head in confusion.

"Hard to fathom, I mean, we can't believe that Carson, Benton, McCormick and Lockhart had absolutely nothing at all to do with this fraudulent, ID scamming organization." He scratched his head as if in disbelief and said, "Although, all the employees that we interrogated so far have attested that they have never seen any of them before. They can only identify Young. We questioned him and he isn't singing a note, not yet anyway. When we start handing out those life-long stretches of time and plea-bargains, he might change his mind. Although, I'm interested to see the out come of this case because I must say, in all my years of service, I have never, ever seen an entourage of lawyers like he has. He has hired fifteen of the most expensive, high profile, powerful attorneys on the planet."

"Well, there you go. The employees have stated that they have never seen them or know who they are and still you don't believe? Well, that's on you, my job is done."

"No involvement what-so–ever huh? The three of them are just old friends of Mr. Young and know nothing of his involvement with the organization or the people in it. Go figure." Soberly she remained in direct eye contact, still no comment. Her chin rested on the fists of her woven fingers. He paused, his poker face continued to reflect that he was still holding out for an answer. Vanessa felt no need to give him one but thought it was her duty to humor him.

"That is what my final report will say, Captain." Moments later, she asked as if struck by an afterthought, "Is there a problem?"

He belted out the heartiest laugh he could conjure. "Oh no, no, no, no, absolutely not, no problem, no sir, not one, not even one. We were just a little surprised because, as you know, we've been trailing these guys for a long time." Vanessa's face was expressionless.

"Well Dayton, this is how I see it. If your team of so-called professionals had known what was going on, I'm sure you would have been successful bringing down this organization long before

now.   But since you had to call me back from a wonderful
vacation, that in itself lets me know you were clueless."

He took a stab at trying to lighten things up with the release of
another forced, fake laugh. Vanessa smirked and spoke in a barely
audible tone.

"You and your supervisors are not going to worry me, okay?"

"After the success of your last four cases and now this one,
why hell, you've made my department reach gold star status in a
manner of speaking." He didn't want to come out and say what he
had been informed, because he knew where it would lead.   He
didn't want to be liable and involved in a lawsuit because the suits at
the top were suspicious about her findings. He respected her a great
deal, and even more than that, he knew Vanessa was nobody to play
with on a hunch. He had to be careful how he selected his words.
He hoped she might somehow incriminate herself. Knowing how
ingenious and perceptive she was, he quickly abandoned that notion.
Vanessa leaned back coolly in the chair and crossed her arms. She
said, displaying little emotion, "If you have something to say
Captain, come on out and say it. We're not just co-workers, we're
old friends."

He could tell she was setting traps of her own. Vanessa was
waiting for him to open his mouth and insert his foot. He realized
the only way to get the information he needed would be to simply
ask. He laid it to rest. His soft chuckle grew louder until it escalated
to a full laugh. She knew he was not satisfied with the outcome of

her reports either.

"Besides, the organization has been busted, I guess that's all that really matters, right?"

His expression still showed distinct signs of apprehension. He sounded as if he were trying to convince himself. He had no choice but to let it go for now. His eyes dove in the direction of the desk as he spoke. "Vanessa this isn't over. I am sorry to inform you that the department of justice is going to conduct a priority investigation into the findings of your case." The news didn't make Vanessa blink an eye. He switched the subject before she could offer any response.

"I know you are probably thinking in four years we didn't come up with shit and you busted one hundred and fifteen people in four months and we still aren't satisfied." She was mentally soaking in fatigue, as she usually was after finishing a case and didn't want it misconstrued as guilt. Her remedy was to muster all the energy she could to offer an enthusiastic rebuttal to his remark.

"I am not surprised. That's how men are-never satisfied no matter what you do for them," she said with disgust. Her expression remained deadpan. Donald's options shifted.

"Vanessa, I really do want to apologize for this action on behalf of the department and assure you that I had nothing to do with this decision. Your record is flawless and under no circumstances warrants scrutiny to this degree. You did a great job. As far as I am concerned, this case is over."

"Did you say that to them, Captain?"

"If the suits want any answers, they'll have to ask these questions themselves. Vanessa, I am satisfied with your findings and I've got your back."

"From this point on, you mean?" Vanessa could sense his remorse for not standing on her behalf. "It 's all in a day's work. I don't know why you feel so violated by the action. I presumed this would happen and I thoroughly understand. You and the department prematurely concluded guilt before the investigation of the alleged evidence on those four people was completed. I didn't arrest who the department had pre-determined were the ringleaders. It's difficult for them to swallow this because of the abundance of painstaking evidence they had accumulated and believed was irrefutable. Of course they are forlorn, they feel like they dropped their ballots with the wrong decision into a locked, keyless box." Vanessa gave a wave of her hand that gestured her indifference.

"No matter though, it will only add credibility to my profile when I prevail in the investigations."

Dayton's expression perked up after she had offered him a bag of old-fashioned homemade chocolate chip cookies. It was apparent by the size of his gut that he appreciated the gesture. "Well then, I can expect you will be a participant in some of our future endeavors?"

She shrugged her shoulders, baffled by his question, "Did you think for one moment that I wouldn't? Thought I might resign?"

"No, no, not at all, not at all. So, you requested your lost vacation time off. Where are you going?" he quizzed.

"To a wedding with my mother and son. I'll only be gone a week."

"Do you need that extra time I said you could have?"

"If I do, I'll call you."

"When you get back, I'll have a hum dinger of a case waiting for you." She reflected for a moment, '*no matter what kind of case it is, nothing could ever top this one.*'

"Well Captain, it's been a slice."

He offered an official smile and routine handshake in accordance. She returned the smile and reached out to firmly shake his outstretched hand. He said, "You are one of our best. Thank you."

As Vanessa paced down the long, dimly lit hallway. The only sound that could be heard was the echoing of her high-heels clunking across the floor. She reminisced about the things Dodie had instilled in the family, including Malone, '*to give all you can, and as much as you can, for as long as you can, to whomever you can, and goodness will always come back to you. If your word ain't shit, you ain't shit. The value you place on your morals, principles, and depth of your faith can only be judged by how much you are willing to risk to remain true to them.*' If the number of her mother's mottos had come in the form of stars there would have been a galaxy. In all the years Vanessa had listened to her mother reiterate adages, it was all rhetorical until today. All she could do now was wait to see if there really was *honor amongst thieves.*

Hopefully, there was, not for her, Malone or The Trio, but for the sake of those untold hundreds of thousands of people whose lives had been restored by Malone's misguided generosity. That, and all they had worked hard to earn on their own would not be confiscated. She knew they would be far more devastated by their losses than she would. If it came to a point where she must surrender everything because of her decision, which was a strong possibility, this was a choice she was willing to roll the dice on, with no regrets.

Vanessa slid on her shades and strolled to the car with a confident swagger that revealed self-approval for a well-made decision. She got in, glanced in the rear view mirror to adjust a few strands of hair and freshen up her red lips; careful to stay within the lines of her cupid's bow. Once her hands were secured in her driving gloves, she rotated the ignition, shifted into first gear, then second, and cruised down the sunny, desolate street, her mind a million miles away. After shifting into third, she rummaged through her purse and pulled out a smokeless cigarette, quickly taking notice of the bangle on her wrist, bearing a hint of its remembrance of Grey. She whispered softly, "I do what I have to do and I have to do what's right for me. And you, of all people, should be able to understand that. If not," she shrugged her shoulders with an outstretched palm and let out a sigh, *"Oh well."* She cranked the cd to a full blast, revved the engine into fourth and jetted down the street like the checkered flag at the Indy 500 had dropped.

"Besides, there's always Patrick," she said and laughed out loud.

Diane Collins was born and raised on the south side of Chicago. She has worked in the film industry, as a Script Supervisor, for twelve years. Five of those years were spent doing second unit on the set of Grey's Anatomy. This is her first novel and she is currently writing a second one. If interested in learning more about her film industry work history visit www.imdb.com